About the Authors

Cat Schield lives in Minnesota with her daughter, their opiniated Burmese cats and a silly Doberman puppy. Winner of the Romance Writers of America 2010 Golden Heart® for series contemporary romance, when she's not writing sexy, romantic stories for Mills & Boon, she can be found sailing with friends on the St. Croix River or in more exotic locales like the Caribbean and Europe. You can find out more about her books at www.catschield.net

When Canadian Dani Collins found romance novels in high school she wondered how one trained for such an awesome job. She wrote for over two decades without publishing, but remained inspired by the romance message that if you hang in there you'll find a happy ending. In May of 2012, Mills & Boon bought her manuscript in a two-book deal. She's since published more than forty books with Mills & Boon and is definitely living happily ever after.

Lynne Graham lives in Northern Ireland and has been a keen romance reader since her teens. Happily married, Lynne has five children. Her eldest is her only natural child. Her other children, who are every bit as dear to her heart, are adopted. The family has a variety of pets, and Lynne loves gardening, cooking, collecting allsorts and is crazy about every aspect of Christmas.

D0674795

Royal Scandals

Royal Scandals: Royal Intrigue

CAT SCHIELD

DANI COLLINS

LYNNE GRAHAM

MILLS & BOON

First Published in Great Britain 2022
By Mills & Boon, an imprint of HarperCollins*Publishers,* Ltd
1 London Bridge Street, London, SE1 9GF

www.harpercollins.co.uk

HarperCollins*Publishers*
1st Floor, Watermarque Building,
Ringsend Road, Dublin 4, Ireland

ROYAL SCANDALS: ROYAL INTRIGUE © 2022 Harlequin Enterprises ULC.

Secret Child, Royal Scandal © 2016 Catherine Schield
Prince's Son of Scandal © 2017 Dani Collins
Indian Prince's Hidden Son © 2020 Lynne Graham

ISBN: 978-0-263-30472-5

SECRET CHILD, ROYAL SCANDAL

CAT SCHIELD

To Renee and Mary K.
Thanks for all the happy hours and the
conversations that have kept me sane.

One

Prince Christian Alessandro, third in line to the Sherdana throne, stood behind the current and future kings of Sherdana and glowered into the camera. No doubt he was ruining Nic and Brooke's fairy-tale wedding photos, but he didn't care. His last hope to remain a carefree bachelor for the rest of his life had been reduced to ashes the second his brother had gazed deep into his bride's starry eyes and pledged to love and honor her until the day he died.

Christian growled.

"Smiles everyone," the photographer cried, casting an anxious glance Christian's way. "This is our last photo of the complete wedding party. Let's make it count."

Despite his black mood, Christian shifted his features into less grim lines. He wasn't about to smile, but he could at least give his brother one decent photo. No matter how badly this marriage had disrupted his life, in the days to come he really would make an effort to be happy for Nic and Brooke. For today he'd simply don a mask.

"Let's set up over there." The photographer pointed to a small stone bridge that crossed a decorative creek.

The path beyond meandered toward the stables. Christian preferred his horsepower under the hood of a fast car, but he'd gladly take his twin nieces to visit their ponies just to get away. Bethany and Karina were old hands at being flower girls, this being their second royal wedding in four months, but being two-year-olds, they had a short attention span and were growing impatient with having to stand still for photos. Christian sympathized with them.

Since his accident five years earlier, he'd avoided cameras as much as possible. The burn scars that covered his right side—shoulder, neck and half of his cheek—had made him the least attractive Alessandro triplet. Not that it mattered much how he looked. His title, wealth and confirmed bachelor status made him a magnet for women.

Most women.

His gaze roamed over the multitude of assistants and palace staff required to keep the bridal party looking flawless and the photo shoot moving forward. Trailing the bride was a petite, slender woman with mink-brown hair and dual-toned brown eyes. Internationally renowned wedding dress designer Noelle Dubone had designed Brooke's dress as well as the one worn by Christian's sister-in-law, Princess Olivia Alessandro.

Born in Sherdana, Noelle had moved to Paris at twenty-two to follow her dream of becoming a fashion designer. She'd done moderately well until three years ago when she'd designed the wedding gown for the bride of Italian prince Paolo Gizzi. There'd been so much media coverage surrounding the nuptials that Noelle became an overnight success. Movie stars, European nobility and the very wealthy became eager for a Noelle Dubone original.

"Imagining your own wedding?" taunted a female voice from behind him.

Christian turned and shot his sister a sour look. Ariana was looking too smugly amused for Christian's taste.

"No." But the slim figure in blue-gray caught his eye again.

Noelle Dubone. The one woman in the world who'd come closest to taming the wildest Alessandro prince. He hadn't been worthy of her. She hadn't deserved to be treated badly by him. That he'd done it for her own good was what let him sleep at night.

"You should be," Ariana countered, looking stylish and carefree in a knee-length, full-skirted dress with puffy long sleeves. A fashion trendsetter, her wedding attire shimmered with gold embroidery and straddled the line between daring and demure with strategically placed sheer panels that showed off her delicate shoulders and hinted at more thigh than the formal occasion called for. "The future of the kingdom rests in your hands."

Christian grimaced. "Father's health has never been better and I don't see Gabriel dropping dead any time soon, so I suspect I will have time to choose a wife and get her pregnant."

Just the thought of it made him long for a drink. But as his mother had pointed out numerous times in the months since Nic had abdicated his responsibility to Sherdana by choosing to marry an American, Christian was no longer free to overindulge in liquor and women. The idea that he had to start walking the straight and narrow path after being the party prince all his life was daunting. He'd misstepped all his life. As youngest in the birth order, it was what he did.

Gabriel, as eldest, was the responsible one. The future king.

Nic, as middle son, was the forgotten one. He'd gone

off to America in his early twenties to become a rocket scientist.

Christian was the indulged youngest son. His antics had provided the paparazzi tabloid fodder since he was fourteen and got caught with one of the maids.

At twenty he'd been raising hell in London. He'd thrown the best parties. Drank too much. Spent money like it was being printed by elves, and when his parents cut off his funds, he'd started buying and flipping failing businesses. He didn't care about success. He just wanted to have fun.

At twenty-five several of his less prudent actions had blown up in his face, leaving him scarred and his heart shredded.

Now at thirty he was expected to give up his freedom for the crown.

"You only think you have time," Ariana countered. "Mother showed me the list of potential candidates. It's two-feet long."

"I do not need her help or anyone else's to find a wife."

"Neither did Gabriel and Nic and look how that turned out."

Gabriel had eloped five months earlier in a grand, romantic gesture that had rendered him blissfully happy, but by marrying a woman who could never have children, he'd left his two brothers holding short straws.

As the last born of the triplets, Christian had made it clear to Nic that it was his duty to step up next. In order for the Alessandro family to stay in power, one of the three princes needed to produce a son. But before Nic could begin looking for a potential bride from among Europe's noble houses or Sherdana's female citizenry, the beautiful American, Brooke Davis, had stolen his heart.

And with their wedding today, it all came down to Christian.

"I can find my own bride without Mother's help."

Ariana made a noise unfit for a princess. "You've already been through half the suitable single women in Europe.

"Hardly half."

"Surely there was one woman among *all* those you've spent time with who appeals to you."

"Appeals, yes." Christian resisted the urge to search for Noelle again. "But not one I want to spend the rest of my life with."

"Well, you'd better find one."

Christian ground his teeth together and didn't answer. He knew Ariana was right. The price one paid as a royal was to not always get to do as one liked. Gabriel had been lucky to choose Olivia to marry before he understood that he was in love with her. But right up until he and Olivia eloped, Gabriel had grappled with his duty to Sherdana versus following his heart's desire.

Nic had the same issue with Brooke. He'd known he needed to put her aside and marry a woman whose children could one day be king.

But in the end both men had chosen love over duty.

Which left Christian to choose duty.

One of the photographer's assistants came to fetch them for more pictures, putting an end to the conversation for the moment. Christian endured another tedious hour of being posed with his brothers, his sister, the king and queen, and various members of the wedding party. By the time the session was finished, he was ready to get drunker than he'd been in the five years since the accident that left him with a disfigured body to match his tarnished soul.

What stopped him from making a beeline for the bar was Noelle.

It seemed perfectly right to walk up behind her and slip

his arm around her waist. Christian dropped a kiss on her cheek the way he had a hundred times, a habit from the old days that used to speak to his strong affection for her. For a microsecond Noelle relaxed against him, accepting his touch as if no time or hurt had passed between them. Then she tensed.

"You look beautiful," he murmured in her ear.

She didn't quite jerk away from him, but she lacked her usual grace in her quick sideways step. "Thank you, Your Royal Highness."

"Walk with me." It was more a command than an invitation.

"I really shouldn't leave the party." She glanced toward the bride and groom as if hoping to spot someone who needed her.

"The photos are done. The bride has no further need for her designer. I'd like to catch up with you. It's been a long time."

"As you wish, Your Highness." To his annoyance, she curtsied, gaze averted.

The gardens behind the palace were extensive and scrupulously maintained under the queen's watchful eye. The plantings closest to the I-shaped structure that housed Sherdana's royal family were arranged in terms of design and color that changed with the seasons. This was the most photographed section of the garden, with its formal walkways and dramatic fountains.

Toward the back of the extensive acreage that surrounded the palace, the garden gave way to a wooded area. Christian guided her to a small grove of trees that offered plenty of shade. There would be more privacy there.

"You've done very well for yourself as a designer."

Christian hated small talk, and it seemed idiotic to attempt any with Noelle. But how did you begin a cordial conversation with an ex-lover who you'd once deliberately hurt even as you told yourself it was for her own good?

"I've been fortunate." Her polite demeanor contrasted with the impatience running through her tone. "Luck and timing."

"You neglected to mention talent. I always knew you'd be successful."

"That's very kind."

"I've missed you." The words came out of nowhere and shocked him. He'd intended to ply her with flirtatious compliments and make her smile at him the way she used to, not pour his heart out.

For the first time she met his gaze directly. His heart gave a familiar bump as he took in the striking uniqueness of her eyes. From a distance they merely looked hazel, but up close the greenish-brown around the edges gave way to a bright chestnut near the pupil. In the past, he'd spent long hours studying those colors and reveling in the soft affection in her gaze as they lingered over dinner or spent a morning in bed.

She gave her head a shake. "I'm sure that's not true."

"I might not have been the man for you, but that doesn't mean I didn't care," he told her, fingertips itching to touch her warm skin.

"Don't try to flatter me." The words held no heat. "I was a convenient bed for you to fall into after you were done partying. You came to me when you grew tired of your superficial crowd and their thoughtless behavior. And in the end, you pushed me out of your life as if two years together meant nothing."

For your own good.

"And look how you thrived. You moved to Paris and became an internationally famous designer." He sounded defensive, and that wasn't the tone he wanted to take with her.

"Is that what you think I wanted?" Her breath huffed out in a short burst that he might have taken for laughter if she hadn't been frowning. "Fame and fortune?"

No, it's what he'd wanted for her. "Talent like yours shouldn't go to waste."

"Do you want me to thank you?" she asked, her voice dripping with sarcasm.

During the time they were together, he'd been more honest with her than anyone else before or since. Not even his brothers had known of the demons that drove him. Maybe he trusted Noelle because they'd been friends before they became lovers. Her openness and gentle spirit had offered him a safe place to unload all his fears and doubts. And because of that, she'd gotten the full weight of his darkness.

"No."

"Then why are we having this conversation after five years of silence?"

Because once again he needed her solace and support. The pressure of fathering the future heir to Sherdana's throne was dredging up his worst qualities. She'd talked him through bouts of melancholy in the past.

"I need you."

Her expression reflected dismay. "I'm no longer that girl." Her tone heated as she continued. "And even if I was, I have other things in my life that will always take priority over a..." As if realizing what she'd been about to say to her prince, Noelle sucked in a giant breath and pulled her lips between her teeth. Her next words were polite, her tone tempered. "I am no longer in a position to be your *friend*."

She twisted the word *friend* into something ugly. Christian read her message loud and clear. She wanted nothing more to do with him. Not as his confidante, his champion or as his lover.

Before he could argue, she dropped another one of

those annoying curtsies. "Excuse me, Your Highness, but I should get back to the party."

Christian watched her vanish back along the path and marveled at how thoroughly he'd mucked up his most important act of selflessness. She was right to shut him down. He'd repeatedly demonstrated that he was nothing but trouble for her.

But after talking to her, he knew if he was going to get through the next few months of finding a wife and settling down to the job of producing the next heir to the throne, he was going to need a friend in his corner. And once upon a time, Noelle had been the only one he talked to about his problems.

He desperately wanted her support. And although she might not be on board with the idea at the moment, he was going to persuade her to give it.

The evening air accompanied Noelle into the small, functional kitchen of her comfortable rural cottage, bringing the earthy scents of fall with her. As much as she'd enjoyed her years in Paris, she'd missed the slower pace and wide-open spaces of the countryside. And an energetic boy like her son needed room to run.

She placed the tomatoes she'd picked on the counter. Her garden was reaching the end of its growing season, and soon she would collect the last of the squash, tomatoes and herbs. Autumn was her favorite season. The rich burgundy, gold and vivid greens of the hills around her cottage inspired her most unique designs. One downside to her success as a wedding-dress designer was that her color palate was limited to shades of white and cream with an occasional pastel thrown in.

"Mama!"

Before Noelle could brace herself, her dark-haired

son barreled into her legs. Laughing, she bent down and wrapped her arms around his squirmy little body. Like most four-years-olds he was a bundle of energy, and Noelle got her hug in fast.

"Did you have a good afternoon with Nana?" Noelle's mother lived with them and watched Marc after school while Noelle worked. She glanced at her mother without waiting for her son's response.

"He was a good boy," Mara Dubone said, her tone emphatic.

Noelle hoped that was true. In the past six months, Marc had grown more rambunctious and wasn't good at listening to his grandmother. Mara loved her grandson very much and defended him always, but it worried Noelle that her son was getting to be too much for her mother to handle.

"I was good." Marc's bronze-gold eyes glowed with sincerity and Noelle sighed.

She framed his face, surveyed the features boldly stamped by his father and gave him a big smile. "I'm so glad."

He had his father's knack for mischief as well as his charm. The thought caused Noelle a small pang of anxiety. Her encounter with Christian this afternoon had been unsettling. After almost five years of no contact, he'd finally reached out to her. That it was five years too late hadn't stopped her heart from thumping wildly in her chest.

"Why don't you go upstairs and brush your teeth," Mara said. "Your mama will come read to you, but she can't do that until you're in your pajamas and in bed."

"Yeah." With typical enthusiasm, Marc raced upstairs, his stocking feet pounding on the wood steps that led to the second floor.

"Was he really okay today?" Noelle asked as soon as she was alone with her mother.

Mara sighed. "He is a wonderful boy, but he has a lot of energy and needs a firm hand." Noelle's mother gave her daughter a sly grin. "What he needs is a man in his life who can channel some of that energy into masculine pursuits."

It wasn't the first time her mother had made this observation. Noelle nodded the way she always did. "Marc's friends are going fishing with their fathers next week. Phillip's dad offered to take Marc, as well. Perhaps I should take him up on his offer."

"That's not what I meant and you know it." Noelle's mother set her hands on her hips and shook her head. "You are not getting any younger. It's time you stopped pining for that prince of yours. It's been almost five years. You need to move on."

"I am not pining for Christian. And I have moved on. I have a thriving business that takes up most of my energy and a small boy who deserves his mother's full attention."

With a disgusted snort, Noelle's mother headed for the stairs. From above their heads came a series of loud thumps as Marc worked off his energy before bedtime.

Noelle walked back into the kitchen to turn off the light and then repeated the process in the dining room and living room before heading up to the bedrooms. For a moment she paused at the bottom of the stairs and listened to the sounds of her family. Her mother's low voice, patient and firm. Her son's clear tones, happy and dynamic.

A firm knock on her front door snapped Noelle out of her musing. She glanced at the clock over the mantel. Eight forty-five. Who could be visiting her at this hour?

Although her farmhouse sat on an acre of land, Noelle had never worried about her isolation. She had neighbors on all sides and they kept an eye on her and her family. Perhaps one of her goats had escaped again. She'd been having problems with the fence on the east side of their pasture.

Flipping on the light in the foyer, Noelle pulled the door open. Her smile died as she spotted the man standing outside her front door.

"Christian?"

Determination lit his gold eyes. While at his brother's wedding, she'd found it easy to discourage the arrogant prince who'd put his arm around her waist and boldly kissed her cheek.

"Good evening, Noelle."

Anxiety gripped her. She'd worked hard to keep her personal life private. Having Prince Christian Alessandro show up like this threatened that.

"What are you doing here?"

"We didn't get a chance to finish our conversation earlier."

Why was she surprised that after five years of no contact he would think she'd welcome his popping around with no warning the way he used to when they were together?

"It's almost nine o'clock."

"I brought some wine." He held up a bottle of her favorite red. *Damn the man for remembering.* He gave her a coaxing half grin. His eyes softened with the seductive glow she'd never successfully resisted. "How about letting me in."

She crossed her arms over her chest, refusing his peace offering. "I already told you. I'm not the same girl I was when we were together." She had said the exact same thing earlier that afternoon, but obviously he hadn't been listening. "You can't just show up here unannounced and think that I'm going to let you in." To warm her bed for a few hours.

"You're mad because I haven't called."

He was apologizing for not contacting her? "It's been five years." Half a decade of living had happened to her.

It took all her willpower not to shove him off her stoop and slam the door in his face.

"I know how long it's been. And I wasn't kidding earlier when I said I missed you. I'd like to come in and find out what your life is like now."

"I've been back in Carone for two years. Why now?"

"Talking with you today brought up a lot of great memories. We had something."

"The operative word being 'had.'" A tremor went through her as she remembered the feel of his fingers against her skin, working magic unlike anything she'd known before or since. "My life is wonderful. I'm happy and complete. There's no room for you or your drama."

"I'm not the same man I used to be, either."

From what she'd read about him over the years, she believed he'd changed, but it wasn't enough to invite him in. "What we did or didn't have in the past needs to stay there." She knew immediately that her words had been a mistake.

"Did or didn't have?" The light of challenge flared in his eyes. "You mean to stand there and deny that we were friends?"

Friends?

Is that how he'd thought of her as he made love to her for hours? When he'd told her he didn't like her going out after close with the guys from the café where she worked part-time and demanded that she stop? Friends? When he'd treated her more like his embarrassing secret?

Noelle realized her hands had clenched into fists at his declaration and tried to focus on relaxing. He was no less infuriating than on the day he'd told her they had no future and she should go to Paris and take the job at Matteo Pizzaro Designs.

"What do you want, Christian?" She asked the question in a flat, unfriendly tone that was intended to annoy him. It didn't.

"I never could get anything past you." He straightened, putting aside all attempt to charm her. Determination radiated from him. "Can I come in? I really do want to talk to you."

"It's late." From the floor above came the pounding of feet. Marc had grown impatient and would be coming to look for her any second. "Perhaps later this week. We could meet for coffee."

"I'd rather have a private dinner. Just you and me like the old days. Perhaps you could come to my place in the city? I have some things I'd like to discuss with you and I don't want to do so in public."

Bitterness gripped her. He'd never wanted to be seen out and about with her. She scrutinized his expression. He'd obviously come to her with an agenda. But she sensed what he had to say wasn't about her son. So far, her secret remained safe. If he'd known about Marc, he would have led with that. So, what was he up to?

"I'm afraid my evenings are booked." Spending time with her son was her greatest joy, and he was growing up so fast. She cherished her evenings with him and resented any intrusion. "Perhaps I could come to your office?"

There was thumping on the stairs as Marc jumped down each step, one by one. Noelle's heart hammered in time. She had to conclude the conversation with Christian before her son appeared.

"Call me. We can discuss this next week. Right now, I need to go." She started to shut the door, but Christian put out his hand and stopped it. Marc's feet thundered across the wood floor; he was coming closer. "Fine. I'll have dinner with you."

"Mama, where are you?"

Christian's eyes widened at the sound of Marc's voice. "You have a child?"

She could not let this happen. Noelle shifted to put her full weight against the door and get it closed.

"You have to leave."

"Marc, where are you?" She heard her mother coming down the stairs now and prayed that Mara could get to Marc before he came to investigate. "I told you your mother wouldn't read you a story unless you were in bed."

"I had no idea," Christian mused, his expression strangely melancholy.

"And now you see why my evenings are busy. So if you don't mind, I need to get my son to bed."

"Can I meet him?" The prince stared past Noelle into the home's interior.

"No." Hearing the snap in her voice, she moderated her tone. "It's his bedtime, and meeting someone new will stir him up. It's already difficult to settle him down enough to sleep."

"He sounds like me."

It was a remark anyone might have made. Noelle knew there was no subtext beneath Christian's comment, but she was hyper-secretive regarding the paternity of her son.

"Not at all."

"Don't you remember how much trouble you had getting me to sleep on the nights I stayed over?"

She ignored the jump in her pulse brought on by his wicked smile. What she remembered were long, delicious hours of lovemaking that left her physically drained and emotionally invigorated.

"This is a conversation for another time."

"Mama, who are you talking to?" Marc plastered himself against her hip and peered up at Christian.

Too late. She'd let Christian distract her with bittersweet

memories, and now he was about to discover what she'd zealously kept hidden from him all these years.

"This is Prince Christian," she told her son, heart breaking. "Your Highness, this is my son, Marc."

"*Your* son?" The prince regarded the four-year-old boy in silence for several seconds, his mouth set in a hard line. At last his cold eyes lifted to Noelle. "Don't you mean *our* son?"

Two

Christian wanted to shove the door open and turn on the lights in the front entry so he could get a clearer look at the boy, but instinct told him it wouldn't change anything. This was his son.

"I don't have a father. Do I, Mama?" Marc glanced up at his mother, eyes worried as he took in her stricken expression.

"Of course you have a father," Noelle stated. "Everyone does. But not everyone's father is part of their life." She soothed a trembling hand over her son's dark head.

"And whose fault is that?" Christian's shock was fading, replaced with annoyance and grudging respect as he surveyed the boy—Noelle had called him Marc.

Tall for his age, which couldn't have been more than four and a half, he possessed the distinctive gold Alessandro eyes and wavy brown hair. Undaunted by Christian's keen scrutiny, the boy stared back, showing no apprehension, just unflinching hostility. And maybe a little curiosity, as well. Christian inclined his head in approval. A child of his would possess an inquisitive mind.

"We are not talking about this right now." Noelle glared at him. Motherhood had given her voice a sharp inflection that demanded immediate obedience. Almost immediately, however, her eyes widened as if she recalled that the man standing on her doorstep was a member of the royal family. Noelle modulated her tone. "Prince Christian, this is not a good time."

"I'm not leaving until I know what's going on."

"I'll make him go." Marc pushed past his mother and took up a fighter's stance, one foot back, fists up and ready to punch.

Christian didn't like how the situation was escalating, but he couldn't bring himself to back off. Too many questions bombarded him. Instead, he stared, belligerent and stubborn, into Noelle's lovely, troubled eyes until she sighed.

"Marc, please go upstairs with Nana." Noelle set her hands on the boy's shoulders and turned him until he faced her. When he looked up and met her gaze, she gave him a reassuring smile. "I need to speak with this man."

This man. This *man*? Christian fumed. He was the boy's *father*.

"Are you sure, Mama?" Marc demanded, not backing down for a second.

"Absolutely." Noelle ruffled her son's dark hair, doing an excellent job of disguising her tension. "Please go upstairs. I'll come talk to you in a few minutes."

With a guard dog's sullen disapproval, the boy leveled a fierce glare at Christian before turning away. Despite the outrage battering him, pride rose in Christian. His son was brave and protective. Good traits for a future king.

Noelle waited until her son was shepherded upstairs by a woman in her midfifties before she stepped out of the house and pulled the door shut behind her. Noelle's eyes blazed, the heat of her annoyance radiating from her in the cool night air. "How dare you come here and say something like that in front of my son. *My* son."

"You've kept a pretty big secret from me all these years."

She shook her head at him. "You need to go."

"You're mistaken. I need answers."

"You will not get them tonight." With her mouth set in a determined line and her hands set on her hips, she let her gaze drill into him.

"Noelle, I'm sorry for what happened between us in the past." He let his voice settle into the cajoling tone that always made women give in. "I know you think what I did to you was insensitive, but I deserve to know my son."

"Deserve?" Her chest heaved with each agitated breath she took. "Deserve? Do you remember telling me five years ago that I should move on with my life and forget I ever met you?"

His heart twisted as he recalled that gut wrenching speech. "At the time I was right."

"I loved you."

"It wasn't going to work between us."

"It still isn't." She glared at him.

Her anger told him she still resented the way he'd dismissed her five years ago, but she'd come back to Sherdana to live her life. A life he'd told her he wanted no part of. And she'd been doing great without him.

Better than he'd done without her.

"Don't you see," he began, regret a heavy weight on his shoulders. "For everyone's sake, we're going to have to make peace. I intend to be a part of Marc's life."

"I'll not have you put my son through the same heartache I endured."

Her words were meant to wound, but Christian barely felt their sting. He was completely distracted by the vibrant beauty of the woman standing up to him. Never before had Noelle's temper flared like this. He regarded her in mesmerized fascination. When they'd been together before, she'd been so agreeable, so accommodating. The sex between them had always been explosive, but outside the bedroom she'd never demonstrated a hint of rebellion.

Now, she was a mother protecting her child. Her fierceness enthralled him. Abruptly the idea of reigniting their friendship seemed far too bland a proposition. He wanted her back in his bed. That she'd produced a potential heir to the throne made the whole situation clear-cut. He intended to marry her, and one day his son would be Sherdana's king.

"He's not just your son, Noelle. He's an Alessandro. Sherdanian royalty." Christian let the statement hang in the air between them for several beats. "Are you planning on keeping that from him?"

"Yes." But despite her forceful declaration, her expression told him she'd asked herself the same question. "No." Noelle stalked over to where his car sat in her driveway. "Damn you, Christian. He was never supposed to know."

"Then why did you bring him back here?" He followed her, repressing the urge to snatch her into his arms and see if she'd yield beneath his kisses the way she used to. "You could have very easily lived the rest of your life in France or gone to the United States." Had she come back to be close to him?

"My stepfather died two-and a-half years ago, leaving my mother alone. I came back to be near her."

His heart twisted at her explanation. Noelle's mother

had remarried when Noelle was six. "I'm sorry to hear that. I know you two were very close. You must miss him very much."

"I do." Sorrow tempered her irritation. "It's been a hard time for all of us. Marc loved his papi."

Regret assaulted Christian. Marc had another papi that he'd never know if Noelle got her way. That wasn't fair to any of them.

"Why didn't you lie and deny that he's mine."

She regarded him in bemusement. "Even if he didn't have the Alessandro features, why would I do that? Have I ever been untruthful with you?"

No. He'd been the one who'd held tight to secrets. "You kept my son from me for over four years."

"And if you'd made an attempt to contact me, I would have told you he existed."

"What about tonight? You weren't particularly forth-coming. If Marc hadn't come to the door, you'd never have admitted he existed."

"You aren't interested in being a father."

"That's not true." But in reality, he hadn't thought much about fatherhood other than as a duty demanded of him by his position.

"The whole country is buzzing about Sherdana's need for an heir, and they look to you as the country's last hope to produce one." Her somber tone matched his own dour meditations on the subject. She was no more convinced of his worthiness for the task than he was. "And now here's my son. Your heir. A simple solution to your problems."

A solution perhaps, but not necessarily a simple one. He had a duty to the throne and his country. It was up to him to secure the line of succession with a son. His bur-den had grown lighter with the revelation that he had a son, but his troubles were far from over.

"He can't be my heir," Christian said, his heart hammering as he regarded Noelle, curious to see if she'd connect the dots.

She'd always had a knack for discerning the true intent behind his actions. Except for the last time they'd been together five years earlier. He'd hidden his heart too well when he'd broken off their relationship.

When she remained silent, he continued. "Unless I marry his mother."

"Marry?" Her voice hitched.

He should try to convince her that that's why he'd come by tonight. Suddenly he knew this was the exact right thing to do. Marrying her would solve all his problems. Now that he'd seen her again, he realized there was no other woman in the world he could imagine being married to. Five years earlier they'd built a relationship on friendship and passion. He'd been a spoiled prince, and she'd been a naïve commoner who adored him. Instead of appreciating the gift of her love, he'd taken her for granted. He'd never understood why her generous spirit had brought out the worst in him. She'd loved him, flaws and all, and he'd been self-destructive and stupid. It made no sense, but he couldn't stop punishing her for loving him too much.

"You'd make a terrific princess," he said, and meant it. "The country already loves you."

"I made two wedding dresses. That's not enough to make me *worthy* of anyone's love." She shook her head. "You have aristocratic women from all over Europe eager to become your wife."

"But I don't want anyone else."

"Are you saying you want me?" She shook her head and laughed bitterly. "You want Marc." A pause. "You can't have him."

Christian could see there would be no convincing her

tonight, and he needed some time to assimilate all that he'd learned. He had a son. The impact had only begun to register.

"We will talk tomorrow," he said. "I will pick you up at noon. Clear your schedule for a few hours."

"I could clear my schedule for a few months and you'd get the same answer. I'm not going to give you my son."

"I don't want to take him from you." He hated that this was her perception of him, but he'd made her believe he was a villain so what else could he expect? "But I intend to be in his life."

Noelle stared at Christian, the urge to shriek building in her. She pressed her lips together as her mind raced. The cat was out of the bag. No way it was going back in. Christian knew he had a son.

I don't want to take him from you.

She pondered his words, hearing the warning. He wasn't foolish enough to tell her outright that he planned to take Marc away, but what Sherdanian court would let her keep her son if Prince Christian fought her for custody? For a second Noelle had a hard time breathing. Then she remembered an illegitimate son was no use to him. Christian needed her help to legitimize Marc's claim to the crown.

Her son a king.

Her knees bumped together at the thought. Marc was only four. It wasn't fair to upend his life in this way. She'd seen what being a royal had done to Christian. He'd grown up resentful and reckless. The third heir, he'd had all the privileges and none of the responsibility. She'd lost count of how many times he'd complained that he wished everyone would just leave him alone.

But with Crown Prince Gabriel and Princess Olivia unable to have children, and second-in-line Prince Nicolas married to an American, Marc wouldn't be a spare heir. He'd be in direct line to the throne.

"Noelle." Christian reclaimed her attention by touching her arm. "Don't make this hard on everyone."

Even through her thin sweater his warmth seeped into her skin. She jerked free before the heat invaded her muscles, rendering her susceptible to his persuasion. Her heart quickened as she backed out of range. It was humiliating how quickly her body betrayed her. A poignant reminder to keep her distance lest physical desire influence her decisions.

Five years ago she hadn't any reason to guard herself against him. She'd belonged to him heart, mind and soul. That was before he'd demonstrated how little she meant to him. It still hurt how easily he'd cast her aside.

Fierce determination heated her blood. Her cheeks grew hot. She'd do everything in her power to make sure he didn't do the same thing to Marc.

"You mean don't make it hard on you." Her tone bitter, she noted the way his eyes flickered, betraying his surprise.

Through all his past selfish behavior, she'd reminded herself that as a commoner of passing prettiness and limited sophistication she was lucky he'd sought her out at all. Pliable as a willow tree, she'd demonstrated patience and understanding. But having her heart broken had given her a spine, and five years of training in the cutthroat world of fashion design had forged that spine into tempered steel. If he continued to push her, he would discover what she was made of.

"But you're right," she added, deciding that arguing would only make him more determined to get his way. In addition, while she might no longer be a doormat, she hadn't lost touch with what was fair. "You are Marc's father and deserve a chance to get to know him. Call me at my office tomorrow at ten. I will check my schedule, and we can figure out a time to meet and discuss a visitation schedule." Seeing Christian's dissatisfaction, Noelle added, "You will do this my way, or I will take Marc beyond your reach."

Christian was used to getting his way in all things. The way his eyebrows came together told Noelle she'd pushed too far. But she held her gaze steady, letting him see her stubbornness. In the end he nodded. From the glint in his eyes, she doubted his acquiescence would last long. In business he was known as a clever negotiator. She would have to watch for his tricks.

Glancing up at the house, she spied a small figure silhouetted in an upstairs window. Marc's bedroom overlooked the front yard. He wasn't going to go to bed without some sort of explanation from her. Sometimes he could be wiser than a child twice his years. It was partially her fault. She routinely gave him responsibilities, and Marc knew there would be consequences if he didn't keep his toys picked up, the garden watered and help shuffle his clothes to and from the laundry.

"I have to get my son to bed," Noelle said. "I'll speak with you tomorrow."

"Noelle." Christian spoke her name softly, halting her. "I meant what I said earlier. I really do miss you. I'd like for us to be friends again."

If he'd tried to cajole her regarding Marc, she might have softened toward him. Christian had a right to his son, whether she liked it or not, and his determination to have a relationship with Marc would eventually soothe her ferocious mama bear instincts. But the instant he tried to appeal to what had once been between them, all sympathy for him fled.

"I have a life filled with family, friends and purpose that I love. There's no room for you in it." She resumed walking toward the house without a backward glance. "Good night, Christian."

She didn't collapse after shutting the front door behind her, although she leaned back against the wood panel and breathed heavily for a few minutes until her heartbeat slowed. Had she really just faced down Christian and gotten the last word in? If her stomach wasn't pitching and rolling in reaction, she might have thrown a fist into the air.

Instead, Noelle headed upstairs. With each slow, deliberate step she regained the poise she'd learned in the stressful world of high fashion. The last thing she wanted was to upset her son and give him a reason to distrust Christian. Despite her measured pace, when she got to Marc's room, she still hadn't figured out a good way to explain the unexpected arrival of his father, a man she'd never talked about.

No surprise that Marc was jumping on his bed. On a regular day his small body contained enough energy to power a small village. After tonight's drama, he was a supernova.

"Mama. Mama. Mama."

"You know better than to jump on the bed," she scolded, stifling a heartfelt sigh. At least her mother had been able to get Marc into his pajamas. "Did you brush your teeth?" When her son showed no indication of answering her question, she glanced at her mother, who nodded. With deliberate firmness Noelle urged her son beneath the covers.

"Did you make the bad man go away?"

Time to correct her first mistake of the evening: letting Marc become aware of the tension between her and Christian.

"That wasn't a bad man, Marc. He was your prince."

Aversion twisted her son's features, amusing Noelle as she imagined the hit to Christian's ego at being so disparaged by one of his subjects.

"Don't like him."

Noelle wasn't feeling all that charitable toward Christian at the moment, either. She scooted her son into the middle of the double bed and seated herself beside him. Drawing in a breath, she braced herself to tell Marc that Christian was his father and then hesitated.

She couldn't bring herself to drop this bomb on her son until she figured out if having Christian in his life would benefit him. "Prince Christian would like to be your friend."

His little face screwed up in suspicion. "Does he like dinosaurs?"

"I don't know."

"Can he play football?"

"I'm not sure." Noelle suspected Marc had a list of activities he wanted to know about and smoothly redirected the conversation. "You'll have to ask him what he likes to do when you see him next."

"Will he get me a Komodo dragon?"

In addition to being obsessed with dinosaurs, Marc had a fascination with lizards and had received a twenty-gallon tank and a seven-inch leopard gecko from her dear friend Geoff for his fourth birthday. Since then, Marc had been lobbying for a bearded dragon, which would be twice the size of his current pet and require double the space.

"You know very well that a Komodo dragon is not a pet. They are seven feet long."

"But he could keep it at the palace, and I could visit it."

As wild a notion as this was, Noelle wouldn't put it past Christian to buy his son's love with a new pet. She would have to warn Christian against such a purchase.

The last thing she needed was a houseful of tanks containing lizards.

"That's not going to happen." She steered the conversation back on track. "Prince Christian might come to visit in the near future and if you have anything you want to know about that, I want you to ask me." She brushed a lock of hair off Marc's forehead and stared into his gold eyes. "Okay?"

The way her son was looking at her, Noelle suspected she'd bungled the conversation, but to her surprise she wasn't barraged by questions.

"Okay."

"Good. What do you want me to read tonight?"

Unsurprisingly he picked up a book on dinosaurs. Marc enjoyed looking at the pictures as she read the descriptions. Noelle knew he had the entire volume memorized. The cover was worn, and a few of the pages had minor tears. Her active son was hard on most things, and this book was one of his favorites.

It took half an hour to get through the book. Marc had forgotten all about Christian's visit by the time Noelle reached the last page. To her relief he settled down without a fight, his head on the pillow. A glance at the clock told her it was not long past his normal bedtime, and she congratulated herself on her minor victory.

Downstairs, her mother had opened a bottle of her favorite Gavi, a crisp Italian white with delicate notes of apples and honey. She handed Noelle a glass without asking if she wanted any.

"I thought you might be in the mood to celebrate," Mara said, eyeing her daughter over the rim of her glass.

Resentment burned at her mother's passive-aggressive remark. "Because Christian discovered I've been hiding his son all these years?" She snorted. "For the thousandth time, I'm not in love with him."

Mara didn't argue. "What are his intentions toward Marc?"

"He wants to get to know him."

"And that's all?"

"Of course. What else could there be?" Noelle had gone outside and shut the door before her conversation with Christian had gone too far, and knew her mother hadn't overheard anything. Still, she experienced a flash of despair as she recalled how Christian had raised the notion of legitimizing Marc by marrying her.

"The kingdom needs an heir. Now that both Prince Gabriel and Prince Nicolas are married, the media are obsessively speculating who your Prince Christian will choose to marry. The pressure is all on him to produce a son."

"He's not my Prince Christian," Noelle muttered, letting her irritation show.

"And now he knows he has a son."

"An illegitimate son." Noelle wanted to take back the reminder as soon as her mother's eyes lit with malicious delight.

"And here you are single and Sherdanian. Not to mention still harboring unrequited feelings for him."

"Don't be ridiculous. I'm not going to marry Christian so that he can claim Marc as his heir."

Her mother didn't look convinced. "Wouldn't it be your dream come true?"

"You were living in Italy when I met Christian, so you don't know what it was like between us. He's not husband material, and I'm not going to marry him because he needs an heir." Noelle heard heartbreak beneath the fervor in her voice. Five years had passed, but she hadn't fully recovered from the hurt dealt to her when Christian pushed her out of his life.

It wasn't something she intended to forgive or forget.

The café table on his cramped, third-floor balcony was big enough for a cup of coffee and a small pot of hot pink petunias. Christian sat on one of the two chairs, ignoring the laptop balanced on his knee while he stared down the narrow street whose details were lost to shadow at this early hour. Thoughts on the encounter with Noelle the night before, he watched the light seep into this old section of Sherdana's capital city of Carone.

Although Christian had rooms in the palace for his use, he rarely stayed there, preferring the privacy of his own space. He'd lost track of how many homes he owned. He did business all over Europe and had apartments in the major cities where he spent the most time. He owned two homes in Sherdana: this cozy two-bedroom apartment in the center of the capital where he could walk to bakeries, cafés and restaurants, and a castle on a premier vineyard two hours north of Carone.

After discovering he was a father, Christian had lain in bed, staring at the ceiling while his thoughts churned. Eventually he'd decided to give up on sleep and catch up on his emails. Nic and Brooke had gotten married on a Wednesday, which meant Christian had lost an entire day of work. He usually worked from home until late morning. His active social life kept him out late most evenings, and if he saw the sun come up, it was more likely that he was coming home after a long night rather than getting an early start on the day.

Despite his good intentions, he couldn't concentrate on the reports that had been compiled by his CFO regarding his purchase of a small Italian company that was developing intelligent robot technology. The columns of numbers blurred and ran together as his mind refused to focus.

Noelle had borne him a son and hidden the truth for five years, a pretty amazing feat in this age of social media. Last night, as he'd driven back to the apartment, he'd been furious with her. It shouldn't have mattered that he'd let her believe he wanted their relationship to end. She'd been pregnant with his child. She should have told him. And then what? He'd thought letting her go to pursue her dream of being a designer in Paris had been the best thing for her. What would he have done if he'd known she was pregnant? Marry her?

Christian shook his head.

It wouldn't have crossed his mind. She'd known him well. Better than he'd known himself. As the third son, he'd had little responsibility to the monarchy and could do what he wanted. So he'd partied to excess, made a name for himself as a playboy, indulged his every desire and thought no further than the moment.

The accident had changed all that. Changed him. He'd risked his life to save someone and had been permanently scarred in the process. But the fire that had ravaged his right side had wrought other changes. His selfless actions had impaired his hedonistic proclivities. Made him aware of others' needs. Before the accident he'd enjoyed being selfish and irresponsible. Losing the ability to act without recognizing the consequences to others had been almost as painful as the slow mending of his burns.

Thus, when he arranged for Noelle to train in Paris, he'd known that letting her think he no longer wanted her in his life would break her heart. Hurting her had pained him more than sending her away, but he'd known that if she stayed with him, he risked doing her far greater harm.

And now, thanks to his discovery of their son, she was back in his life. He ached with joy and dread.

Showing up on her doorstep last night had been a return to old patterns. When they'd been together before, he'd often popped by unannounced late at night after the clubs closed.

He'd met her at the café near his apartment where she waitressed. Unlike most of the women he flirted with, she hadn't been intrigued by his title or swayed by his charm. She'd treated him with such determined professionalism that he'd been compelled to pursue her relentlessly until she agreed to see him outside of work.

They didn't date. Not in a traditional sense. She was too serious to enjoy his frivolous lifestyle and too sensible to fit in with his superficial friends. But she was exactly what he needed. Her apartment became his refuge. When they finally became lovers, after being friends for six months, she was more familiar to him than any woman he'd ever known.

Not that this had stopped him from taking her for granted, first as a friend and confidante, and then as the woman who came alive in his arms.

Christian closed his eyes and settled his head back against the brick facade of his apartment. The breath he blew out didn't ease the tightness in his chest or relax the clenched muscles of his abdomen.

Last night he'd suggested that they should marry. The ease with which the words had slipped off his tongue betrayed the fact that his subconscious was already plotting. Speaking with her at the party had obviously started something brewing. Why not marry Noelle? The notion made sense even before he'd found out about Marc.

Years before they'd been good together. Or at least she'd been good for him. Sexually they'd been more than compatible. She'd been a drug in his system. One he'd tried numerous times to purge with no luck.

Discovering they'd created a child together, a much-needed potential heir to the throne, pretty much cemented his decision to make her his princess. He didn't need to scour Europe trying to find his future wife. She was right under his nose.

He should have felt as if an enormous weight had been lifted from his shoulders, but long ago he'd developed a conscience where Noelle was concerned. After the way he'd broken things off five years ago, she didn't want him anywhere near her. Persuading her to marry him would take time, and once the media got wind of his interest, they would interfere at every turn.

He'd have to work fast. She'd loved him once. A few intimate dinners to remind her of their crazy-hot chemistry and she'd be putty in his hands. Christian shoved aside a twinge of guilt. Being cavalier about seducing Noelle was not in keeping with the man he'd become these past few years. Scheming was something he reserved for business dealings.

Christian headed inside to shower and get dressed. For his country and his family, he had to convince Noelle to marry him. If it benefited him in the process, so much the better.

Three

An extravagant arrangement of two dozen long-stemmed red roses awaited Noelle in her office at the back of her small dress shop in Sherdana's historic city center. Coffee in hand, she stopped dead just inside the door and sucked in the rich, sweet scent of the enormous blossoms. She plucked a small white envelope from the bouquet, but didn't need to read the card to know the sender. The scarlet blooms signaled Christian's intent to stir up her quiet, perfectly ordered world.

Knowing she would get nothing accomplished with the roses dominating her efficient gold-and-cream space, Noelle called her assistant.

"Please get these out of here." Noelle waved her hand dismissively. When curiosity lit Jeanne's eyes, Noelle realized she'd let her irritation show.

Jeanne scooped the vase off the low coffee table. "Should I put them in the reception room?"

Noelle wanted to tell Jeanne to drop them into the trash out back. "Why don't you put them in the workroom? That way the seamstresses could enjoy the flowers."

"Are you sure you don't want me to leave them here? They're so beautiful."

Noelle's temper flared, sharp and acidic. Lack of sleep and frayed nerves were to blame for her reaction. She shook her head and strove to keep her voice calm as she tried to put a positive spin on her request. "Everyone has been working so hard. The flowers are for all of us," she lied, feeling only the mildest twinge of guilt at deceiving her employee.

Once the flowers were gone, Noelle opened her office window to the beautiful morning and let in the fresh air, but after an hour she could swear the scent of the roses remained. Restless and edgy, Noelle slid her sketchbook into her briefcase. She would go to her favorite café and work on the designs for next winter's collection.

The bell on the front door jangled, announcing a visitor. Because of her location among the quaint shops in the historic district, occasionally someone passing by would pop in, stirred by curiosity. Noelle's shop carried no ready to wear wedding dresses, but because her wealthy clientele could often be difficult to please, she had several bridal gowns on hand that had been rejected for one reason or another.

Jeanne's greeting carried down the hall as she approached whoever had entered the shop. Noelle gathered several pencils and froze in the act of dropping them into her briefcase. A deep voice rumbled in response to her assistant's inquiring tone. The pencils clattered as they fell from Noelle's nerveless fingers. Strong footsteps rang on the wood floor of the narrow hallway leading to her office.

Feeling much like a cornered cat, Noelle glanced up and saw Christian's imposing shoulders filling the doorway.

Cross that he'd followed up the flower delivery with a personal appearance, she spoke with unusual bluntness. "You were supposed to call me at ten not show up unannounced."

"I came to see if you liked the roses." He took in her pristine office and frowned. "Didn't you receive them?"

"Yes. I put them in the workroom for my employees to enjoy."

Not one muscle twitched in his face to betray his reaction, but she could tell her answer displeased him. She hated the way guilt rushed through her.

"I sent them to you."

All the time they'd been together, he'd never once given her flowers. She'd understood her role in his life. First as a sounding board for all his frustrations and woes. Eventually, she'd become his lover, a convenient one that he could drop in on whenever he was feeling lonely or in need of comfort. She'd made no demands, expected nothing, and he'd given her mind-blowing sex in return. To be fair, while they'd been physically intimate she'd also enjoyed a great deal of emotional intimacy, as well. But out of bed, Christian donned the charming persona he maintained to keep people at bay.

The roses had reminded her how susceptible she'd once been to his charm. What if nothing had changed in the past five years? She needed to determine if she could trust her head to guide her. He mustn't be allowed to think he could sway her with romantic gestures. For gestures were all they were.

"You're not going to make this easy for me, are you?" He crossed the threshold, crowding her office with his powerful presence.

"Why should I?" Noelle liked having her elegant desk as a buffer between them, but didn't want her entire staff hearing this conversation. Stepping out from behind the desk, she gestured Christian away from the door and closed it, trapping them together in the small space. "Five years ago you wanted nothing more to do with me. Now, you're desperate for an heir and you want my son."

"You forget that I came to see you last night knowing nothing about Marc," he grumbled in his deep, beguiling voice. His intent was clear. He intended to throw every trick in his abundant arsenal at her. "I saw you at the wedding and knew I'd made a mistake letting you go all those years ago."

His claim was so ridiculous she should have laughed in his face. But the words made her chest ache. How many nights had she lain awake, praying for his knock on her apartment door in Paris? Dreaming that he'd burst in, sweep her off her feet and declare he'd been a fool to let her go and that he couldn't live without her. Too many. In fact, she hadn't given up all hope until Marc's first birthday.

"I don't believe you."

"If you give me a chance, I'll prove it to you." His dark gold eyes glittered with sensual intent.

A hysterical laugh bubbled up in her chest. She clamped her teeth together and fought to appear unflustered. No easy task when the masculine scent of the man awakened buried memories. A tingle began between her thighs as she relived the joy of his hands on her body, his lips on hers.

Last night she'd stood up to him, an alarmed mama bear protecting her cub. Today she was a woman confronting a man who intended to persuade and seduce. Heat bloomed in her cheeks. She scowled, angry with herself and taking it out on him.

"If you want me to take your interest in Marc seriously,

you'd be better off demonstrating that you have what it takes to be a father."

"I agree." He nodded. "Which is why I sent a gift to Marc, as well."

Noelle bit back a groan. "What sort of gift?"

"A small thing."

"How small?"

"A child-sized electric car. My assistant said her son loves to drive his cousin's. He is about Marc's age."

She hissed out a breath. "You can't just do that."

"Of course I can."

Once upon a time she'd have teased him about his arrogance. Once upon a time she'd been madly in love with him.

"An electric car is an expensive toy. I want Marc to value art and stories and music. Not things."

"He's a four-year-old boy," Christian scoffed. "They want to get muddy and have adventures."

Noelle knew it was ridiculous, but she could feel Marc slipping away from her with each word Christian spoke. Her son would love this thrill-seeking prince and want to go live in a palace, and never once miss his mother. "And you're an expert on four-year-old boys?"

"I was one once. And he's a prince. He should always get the best."

Panic rose. Her voice dropped to a whisper. "That's not how I'm raising him."

"We need to be together for Marc's sake." Christian caught her hand and gave it a gentle squeeze. "He shouldn't have to grow up without a father."

Christian seemed sincere enough, but Noelle couldn't ignore that he needed an heir and knew just how stubborn Christian could be when he wanted something. She tugged her hand free and squared her shoulders.

"I can't possibly be with you," she said. "I'm involved with someone and we're quite serious."

Christian absorbed Noelle's statement with a slow eye-blink, his thoughts reeling. He'd come in too confident, certain that he could win over Noelle with a few roses and a bit of persuasion. She'd always been there any time he needed her. It had never once occurred to him that she might be in love with someone else. Acid burned in his gut at the thought of her with anyone besides him.

"You didn't mention anyone last night."

Her expression, once so transparent and open, betrayed none of her thoughts. "All I thought about was Marc and the effect your sudden appearance in his life would have on him."

"Who is this man you're seeing?" The question sounded more like an interrogation than a friendly inquiry.

"Someone I met shortly after I moved to Paris."

Five years. Had she run into his arms after Christian had sent her away? A knot formed in his chest.

"I'd love to meet him. Does he live in Sherdana?"

"Ah." Suddenly she looked very uncertain. "No. He splits his time between Paris and London."

Christian was liking this more and more. "Long distance affairs are so difficult," he purred. "As I'm sure you're finding out."

"Geoff loves Marc."

Christian saw resolve blazing in the depths of her chestnut-colored eyes.

"And Marc loves Geoff. They have a great time together. *We* are good together."

He wondered at her vehemence. Was she trying to convince him that this Geoff character was father material or convince herself that he was husband material? Either way,

Christian saw a foothold that would allow him to breach her defenses.

"When does he plan to come to Sherdana next?" A long unused oubliette beneath the castle on Christian's vineyard might be the perfect place to stash Geoff until Noelle came to her senses.

"Why?" Noelle regarded him with narrowed eyes.

"I'd like to meet him. Does he visit regularly?"

"Of course." But she didn't sound all that sure of her answer. "That is, when his cases permit. He's the managing partner of a very successful law firm specializing in human rights law and extradition." Pride softened her lips into a fond smile. "And of course, Marc and I travel to London and Paris quite often to visit him."

"How serious are you?" The more Christian heard, the less concerned he became that Geoff was going to prove a hindrance. If something of a permanent nature was going to happen between Noelle and her absent suitor, it should have occurred in the past five years. "Do you plan on marrying?"

She glanced down at her clasped hands. "We've discussed the possibility, but haven't made anything official."

What sort of man waited five years to claim a woman like Noelle? A very stupid one. And that was just fine with him. Christian had no qualms about stealing Noelle out from beneath the man's nose.

"Have dinner with me tonight."

Her eyes widened at his abrupt invitation, but she shook her head. "I can't. Geoff—"

"Isn't here and from the sound of things isn't likely to visit any time soon." A half step brought him close enough to hear her sharp intake of breath and feel the way her muscles tensed as he traced his knuckles along her jawline. The old, familiar chemistry sparked between them.

"You deserve a man who will appreciate you every minute of every day, not whenever his business dealings permit."

Noelle batted his hand away. "What would you know about how I deserve to be appreciated? When we were together, the only time you concerned yourself about my needs was when we were in bed."

"You make it sound like that's a bad thing." He spoke lightly, hiding his regret that he'd hurt her. He'd been a selfish bastard when they were together and hadn't grasped her worth. How ironic that finally understanding her value had compelled him to send her away.

Yet was he behaving any less selfishly now? After ignoring her for five years, he'd suddenly decided to drag her back into his life because he needed her once again. Was it fair to disrupt the tranquil, comfortable world she'd made for herself? Probably not, but now that he'd begun, Christian couldn't bring himself to stop. They'd made a child together. He had a son. That wasn't something he intended to walk away from.

"Christian, you weren't good for me five years ago, and you're not going to be good for me now. I was so madly in love with you I was happy with whatever scraps of your life you were willing to share with me. That's not enough for me anymore. I have a son who deserves to be loved and nurtured. He is my primary focus. Every decision I make is with his best interests foremost in my mind."

Christian's temper flared. "And you don't think his mother being married to his father is the best thing for him?"

"Not if the only reason his parents marry is so the Alessandro line continues to rule Sherdana."

Christian wasn't accustomed to cynicism coming from Noelle. She'd been sweet, innocent and as trusting as a kitten. His opposite in every way. It was why he hadn't been able to give her up even when he started to see shadows darken her eyes and her smiles become forced.

"Making Marc my heir is not the only reason I want to marry you." Although it was an important one to be sure. "I can't forget how good we were together."

Noelle shook her head. "I'm not sure you were good for me."

"I'm no longer the man I was." In so many ways that was true. He'd lost the ability to be frivolous and irresponsible. "The accident saw to that."

She flinched. "And I'm not the woman you once knew. Who's to say it would even work between us anymore?"

"Who's to say it wouldn't be better?"

As if to demonstrate his point, Christian slid his fingers around the back of her neck and drew her toward him. Without giving her a second to process his action, he lowered his lips to her and drank in her sweetness. A groan gathered in his chest at the way her mouth yielded to him. She gasped softly as her lips parted. He remembered all the times he'd held her in his arms and indulged his need for her with long, drugging kisses.

With other women he'd been quick to get to his pleasure. He liked his lovemaking hot and frenzied. Being with Noelle had brought out a different side of his personality. He'd never been in a rush with her. Her warm, silken skin and the gentle rise and fall of her slender curves had been worth appreciating in great detail. He'd adored her every gasp and shiver as he learned what pleased her. After a month he knew her body better than any woman he'd ever been with and yet she continued to surprise him.

Desire buzzed in his veins, the intensity rising as Noelle leaned into him. He freed her lips before longing made the kiss spiral out of control. Heart thumping madly, he inhaled her light floral perfume. The fragrance was more sophisticated than what she used to wear, reminding him that time and distance had made them strangers. His lids felt heavy as he lifted his lashes and regarded her flushed cheeks.

"You didn't stop me from kissing you," he murmured in satisfaction, wondering if it could really be this easy.

"I was curious how it would feel after five long years." Her neutral tone dampened his optimism.

"And?"

"Your technique hasn't diminished."

Christian stepped back and gave her a lopsided smile. "Nor has my desire for you."

"Yes…well." She didn't sound as if she believed him. "I'm sure you can find any number of women eager to distract you."

"It's not like that anymore."

"The tabloids say otherwise."

"The tabloids exaggerate. Any drama attributed to my love life is concocted to sell newspapers."

"So how do you explain the twin models from Milan photographed topless on your hotel balcony in Cannes?"

"They needed a place to crash and I spent the night on the phone to Hong Kong."

Noelle's lips thinned as she nodded. "And the Spanish heiress who ran away from her wedding with you?"

"It was an arranged marriage and she was in love with an architect from Brussels who happened to be doing some work on my apartment in London."

"You're asking me to believe you're in the habit of rescuing women these days?"

He understood her skepticism. Five years earlier his playboy reputation had been well earned. But the day he'd arranged for Noelle to study in Paris was the day he'd begun to change. She'd been the first woman he'd saved. And the only one who'd needed to be rescued from him.

"There's a long list of women I've helped. I could put you in touch with some of them if it would help improve your perception of me." She wasn't going to take his pursuit seriously if she thought he hadn't changed.

"I'm sure there are scads of women who would line up to sing your praises."

"Have dinner with me." He repeated his earlier invitation, determined to convince her this wasn't a ploy or a scam. "We have a great deal to talk about."

She shook her head. "The only thing that concerns me is your intentions for my son. We can talk about ground rules here or at your office. There's no reason for us to become more than civil acquaintances."

"That's where you're wrong. I can name several very good reasons why we should take our relationship to a close, personal level. Starting with the fact that I make you nervous." He caught her chin and turned her face so he could snare her gaze. "I think that means you still have feelings for me. I know I have feelings for you. We belong together."

"I'm with Geoff. Nothing you can say or do will change that."

Christian slid his thumb across her lower lip and watched her pupils dilate. No doubt she was counting on her words and actions to effectively put him off, but there was no hiding her body's reaction.

With a slow smile, his hand fell away. "We'll see."

Four

With her pulse hammering in her ears, Noelle spent a full minute staring at the empty hallway after Christian had gone. What had just happened? Knees shaking, she retreated to her desk and dropped into her comfortable chair with a hearty exhalation. To her dismay, her fingers trembled as she dialed a familiar number. When Geoff answered the phone, his deep voice acted like a sturdy net she could fall into and be safe.

"Geoff, thank goodness."

"Noelle, are you okay? You sound upset."

"I've just done a terrible, cowardly thing." Such drama wasn't like her, and she noticed that several beats passed while Geoff adjusted to her tumultuous state.

"I'm sure it's not as bad as all that."

She closed her eyes, and his steady tone calmed her. She'd met Geoff shortly after moving to Paris. He'd been at a party her boss was throwing and they'd hit it off immediately. Both had been grieving losses. Noelle was fresh from her breakup with Christian and Geoff had lost his wife of fifteen years to cancer six months earlier.

"It's really bad. I made up a serious relationship between you and me."

Amusement filled his voice as he asked, "Couldn't you just have told the guy you weren't interested? That's worked for you up to this point."

Normally Noelle blamed her lack of interest in men on the demands of her skyrocketing career and being focused on her son. The truth was she didn't find anyone as interesting or attractive as Christian. In the darkest hours of the night when she couldn't sleep and got up to sketch or visit her workshop, she suspected that the love she'd thought had died when Christian cast her aside was really only buried beneath a thick layer of pain and disappointment.

"It's not just a guy." In her agitation, she snapped one of her drawing pencils in two. "It's Christian, and he figured out Marc is his son."

"Ah." Geoff had been a shoulder to cry on when she'd first discovered she was pregnant. Seventeen years her senior, he'd been a combination of close friend and elder brother.

"I told you about the delicate political situation surrounding the Sherdanian throne. Yesterday Nicolas Alessandro married an American girl, leaving Christian the only brother capable of producing a future king. Last night he came to the house and met Marc. Now he's got it in his head that we should get married so Marc can be his legitimate heir."

"And he won't take no for an answer?"

"He's determined to win me over." Noelle trembled as her mind replayed the kiss. She hadn't forgotten the chemistry between them, but five years had dulled her memory of how susceptible she was to his touch. "I can't let that happen."

"So you told him we were dating?"

"I panicked. Which was stupid because he doesn't believe me. I need to show him that you exist and that we're very happy. Can you come spend the weekend with me? I'll call and invite him to have dinner with us." Silence greeted her announcement. "Geoff? I'm sorry, I know I'm putting you on the spot."

"Noelle, darling, you know I'm happy to help you any way I can, but are you sure this is the best tactic? I don't live in Sherdana. Even if I appear once and we give a great performance of being madly in love, he's not going to be dissuaded by an absent lover."

She thought back to Christian's remark about long distance relationships. "You're right. Call Jean-Pierre and ask him if I can borrow an engagement ring. A big one." The jeweler owed her several favors for sending business his way.

"Our relationship is moving awfully fast," Geoff teased, but concern shaded his lighthearted tone.

"I know and I'm sorry. I'm taking terrible advantage of our friendship, but I'm feeling rather desperate at the moment."

"There's no one I'd be happier to be fake-engaged to than you, but have you thought this through? Are you planning on staying engaged forever? What happens when we don't actually get married?"

"Hopefully he will be under enough pressure to marry someone suitable that he'll realize he can't wait around to change my mind."

"This plan of yours is full of holes."

Christian had a knack for shredding her customarily

sensible behavior. "We can talk about that when you get here."

"Very well. I'll see you Friday evening."

Noelle disconnected the call feeling marginally less anxious. Pretending to be engaged to Geoff was a ridiculous ploy, but hopefully one that would buy her enough space to get her emotions back under control. Christian had been on the offensive since Brooke and Nic's wedding. Every step he'd taken had backed Noelle into a corner. It was time she came out swinging.

Christian sat at his favorite table in Seillan's, one of Carone's finest restaurants featuring French cuisine. It was owned by a long-time friend of his, world-renowned chef Michel Seillan.

"Hello, P.C. Are you dining alone?" Michel gripped Christian's shoulder in an affectionate vise. The two men had gone to school together since they were seven years old and had spent a great deal of time tearing up the clubs of London and Paris in their early twenties. The nickname P.C. had evolved when Michel had complained that addressing Christian as Prince Christian took too long.

"No, I'm expecting a couple of friends."

"Female? And are you needing some help to entertain them?"

"Only one is a woman, and when have I ever needed help keeping women entertained?"

"Years ago, I might have agreed with you, but lately you've slowed down." Michel smirked.

"These days I'm more interested in quality than quantity."

With a laugh and another thump on Christian's shoulder, Michel departed. Minutes later a waiter appeared with a dry vodka martini. Christian resisted the urge to down the drink. For some reason, he wasn't feeling calm as the top of the hour approached.

Noelle might not be in love with the British barrister she was bringing to dinner, but that didn't mean the reverse was true. During the years when Christian and Noelle had been together, he'd never worried that another man might steal her away. She'd been devoted to him first as a friend and then as a lover. But that was before he'd sent her away. Before she'd had to raise their child on her own for four years.

Christian had never been one for settling down. No doubt Noelle continued to view him that way. The fact that he had to marry in order to produce an heir for the kingdom didn't exactly recommend his willingness or ability to be a good husband.

What if Noelle was ready to build a life with someone steady? To have more children? She'd want a man with a constant heart who'd devote unwavering attention to her needs.

The sip of the martini he'd taken stuck in Christian's suddenly tight throat. He coughed and coughed again as the liquor burned. Through watering eyes, he spotted Noelle entering the restaurant.

She was eye-catching in a fifties-inspired black dress with a bodice embroidered in gold flowers that hugged her torso and bared her arms. A wide band of black fabric made her waist look incredibly tiny, and the full skirt skimmed her knees. She wove between the tables with effortless grace, and Christian's heart twisted. The lively smile curving her full red lips was for the man who trailed after her. She'd always been pretty, but confidence and happiness had transformed her into a vivacious beauty. Desire stirred in Christian. But it wasn't his hormones that came to life. He wanted her, not just as a sexual part-

ner, but as a supportive companion who lightened his bad
moods and made his troubles fade away.

He'd forgotten how easily she aroused his emotions.
How she made him ache for her laughter and long for the
soothing caress of her fingers through his hair.

Christian stood as Noelle and her escort approached
the table. The man was considerably older than Christian
expected. Tall and lean, with blond hair and laugh lines
around his gray eyes, he had close to two decades on Noelle. Seeing the level of fondness in her eyes, Christian
was prepared to dislike the man intensely.

"Good evening, Noelle," Christian said, keeping his
roiling emotions out of his tone.

"Good evening, Your Royal Highness. I would like to
introduce you to Geoff Coomb. Geoff, this is Prince Christian Alessandro."

Noelle's companion had a firm handshake and returned Christian's assessing gaze with confidence that
made Christian despise him even more. "It was kind of
you to join us for dinner."

"Not at all."

Us.

The word on the man's lips bothered Christian more
than he liked. It spoke of a familiarity that he no longer
enjoyed with Noelle. He'd underestimated the threat her
relationship with Coomb represented. While Christian had
fully intended to convince Noelle to marry him through
whatever means necessary, he'd presumed his methods
would involve seduction and winning his son's love. He
hadn't considered she might be perfectly happy with the
affection and emotional support she received from Coomb.

Resisting the desire to scowl at the lawyer, Christian
fixed a pleasant expression on his face and stepped forward to hold Noelle's chair out for her. To his annoyance,

Geoff was there a beat faster, and she flashed him another of her enchanting smiles as she sat. Christian waited until Coomb settled and then fell into the role of perfect host, all the while digging into the history between the two so he could figure out the best way to win Noelle back.

"Noelle told me you two met years ago in Paris."

"At a party," Geoff said, regarding Noelle with an intimate smile. "She was the most beautiful woman in the room."

Christian had little doubt of that. "And you've been together all these years?"

"We were friends awhile before we began to date," Noelle said, favoring Coomb with another of her glowing smiles. "Neither one of us was ready to jump into anything right away."

"I'd lost my wife a few months earlier to cancer." Geoff covered Noelle's right hand with his. "Noelle was a good friend to me. We grew very close."

Close was what Noelle and Christian had been until he'd ruined everything.

"Geoff kept me from quitting during that first year in Paris. Without his encouragement I would have run home at least once a week."

Despite the jealousy raging through him, Christian was glad Noelle had had someone to support her when he couldn't. He'd been too self-absorbed to appreciate what he had until it was too late. And then too stubborn to reach out and fix what he'd broken. After the accident, he'd reasoned Noelle had been better off without him. And he'd been right. She'd sacrificed too much to be with him.

But that was then. The noble part of him that had let her go five years earlier was no longer in charge of his actions. He was older and wiser these days. They had a son. She and Marc belonged with him.

The waiter brought Noelle a glass of red wine and a scotch for Coomb. As Noelle lifted her left hand to pick up her drink, the light from the chandelier overhead caught in the enormous diamond adorning her ring finger. Noelle noticed Christian's riveted attention, and her expression grew positively radiant.

"We're engaged."

"That's rather sudden." And convenient. The engagement had moved her beyond his grasp. Suspicious, Christian eyed the older man, hoping for some sign of subterfuge, but saw only fondness as the lawyer gazed at Noelle.

"Not sudden at all," Coomb replied. "We've been heading this way for years."

"You seemed content with the relationship as it was," Christian pointed out to Noelle. Had she been surprised by this turn of events, or was she guilty of deliberately misleading him? The Noelle he'd known had been free of guile. He didn't like to think she'd changed so much.

"I am content with our relationship in all its forms." Noelle gave Coomb a sweet smile. "I feel so very lucky to have such a wonderful man in my life."

Christian's gut ached as if he'd been kicked. Something ugly and dark formed inside him as he watched Noelle bask in Coomb's affection. Curses reverberated in Christian's thoughts. Being the uncomfortable third wheel wasn't how he'd expected the evening to go.

"But," she continued, fixing bright eyes on Christian. "I'm thrilled that we are going to be a family."

Was there a touch too much defiance in her delivery? Christian assessed her for a long moment before extending his arm to signal the attentive waiter. "We're celebrating," he told Antonio. "A bottle of champagne to toast the newly betrothed."

Inwardly seething, Christian waited while crystal flutes

were placed upon the table and filled, and then gave the newly engaged couple his most political smile. "May you enjoy a lifetime of happiness." She would assume that he meant her and Coomb.

Christian set the glass to his lips and drank the excellent vintage with little pleasure. While a part of him clamored to be the one she chose, more than anything he hoped she would be happy. *Idiot.* Why couldn't he stop doing the right thing where she was concerned? In all other aspects of his life he was a selfish bastard, but when it came to Noelle, he wanted what was best for her.

Of course, the solution was simple. He just needed to believe that the best thing for Noelle was for her to marry him.

In the days since he'd spoken to her at the latest royal wedding and discovered he was a father, Christian had lost numerous hours in daydreaming about his future with Noelle and Marc. Imagining long passion-filled nights in bed with her left him grinning in anticipation.

In contrast the thought of being a father distressed him. Nothing he'd done in his life had prepared him for such a daunting task. What part of buying troubled companies to tear apart and restructure gave him the skills to win the trust and affection of a four-year-old boy?

As a prince, he'd never had to work at making people like him. Those who didn't enjoy his company respected him because of his position. Foolish or ambitious women, who appreciated his money and position, vied for his attention. Sensible ones and those unsuitable for romancing he charmed without effort, but invested little of himself in the exchanges. His days and nights were consistently filled with an endless supply of business associates, social acquaintances or potential lovers. He cared little about any of them and his encounters blurred together in an indistinct gabble of memories.

Nothing about this shallow, drifting existence had bothered him until Noelle entered his life. She was a magnifying glass that sharpened his perceptions, making him see things as they were instead of as fuzzy renderings on the edges of his awareness. She'd provoked him to question why with all the money he made he wasn't using some of it to make a positive social impact. But when he'd donated to charities, he'd picked ones that would eventually provide a benefit to him and hadn't enjoyed the accolades heaped upon him.

Without meaning to she'd pushed him to do better. Be better. She'd never criticized his actions or made suggestions of things he should do, but as he discovered what was important to her, he'd begun to change. All his life he'd barely taken responsibility for himself, much less taken on the burden of anyone else's welfare. Suddenly he had this insignificant woman in his head all the time. In the morning he'd woken and wondered if she'd missed him in her bed. Throughout his day he noted things he wanted to share with her. She took up space in his narcissistic reality, and he resented her intrusion.

Realizing her effect on him had set off a chain reaction of bad behavior. She'd always forgive and forget, but that hadn't been the end of it for him.

He'd felt guilty.

And hated it.

Which had naturally led to even worse behavior and eventually the accident. Five years after the fact, that awful night continued to haunt him. He relived the pain and terror every time he caught a glimpse of his reflection or touched the puckered scars that marred his right arm and the right side of his chest, neck and face. The skin tingled in phantom pain. He could have undergone reconstructive surgery for the damage, but preferred to leave the scars as a reminder of his supreme failure.

Christian shook himself out of his dark thoughts and caught Noelle watching him. Worry, longing and regret raced across her face in rapid succession before she looked away. Christian stared at her as she laughed at something Coomb said to her. Was it possible that she still cared and was fighting desperately not to? Something inside Christian clicked into place like the resetting of a dislocated bone. He hadn't realized how out of whack his psyche had been until the pain vanished. In the peaceful aftermath, he began to plot.

Noelle might be engaged, but she wasn't married. The ring she wore represented a promise to wed, and he was notorious for making even the most stubborn, committed individuals change their minds.

Heart thumping in wild abandonment, Noelle gulped down the beginnings of panic. Despite the heartache and the half decade of separation, Christian continued to fascinate and disturb her like no other man. He'd been back in her life for three days, and her judgment was already lousy. She'd invented a fake fiancé and convinced Geoff to play along. All the while she fought against the longing to rake her fingers through Christian's thick, wavy hair and pull his mouth to hers.

Nothing good would come of getting caught up in the reckless desire that had hampered her innate common sense during the two years she'd loved him. He'd driven her to the highest peaks of ecstasy one day and left her wallowing in uncertainty and disappointment the next. Even accepting that she was responsible for her own happiness,

Noelle hadn't once barred her door or her heart against him. And in the end, he'd been the one to walk away.

Which was why she needed to be so careful now. There was more at stake than her foolish heart. She couldn't risk that Christian might hurt her son.

His son.

Noelle lifted her fork and held it suspended over the plate the waiter had placed before her. Her thoughts were too complex to sort out the ingredients of the elegantly plated meal. She saw her dinner as a mass of color: shades of brown from caramel to espresso, a range of greens and a golden sauce.

"Something wrong?" Christian prompted, his deep voice silky and sensual.

She made the mistake of meeting his burnished gold eyes. He looked as if he wanted to devour her right then and there. "It's too beautiful to eat."

His slow smile curled her toes. "I assure you it will taste even better."

Breathless in reaction to his dizzying charisma, Noelle jerked her attention back to the meal and admonished herself for letting him get to her. The cuisine that should have dazzled her palate tasted like sawdust in her dry mouth. When would Christian stop dominating her senses? She would have thought five years apart had dulled her body's reaction to him.

At least she maintained some control over her mind.

It probably helped that she had very little trouble resisting *Prince* Christian. Arrogant and confident, the royal persona represented everything that had broken her heart five years earlier. Especially when he'd shown up unannounced at her farmhouse after Nic and Brooke's wedding and presumed she'd marry him to legitimize Marc.

She gave her head a barely perceptible shake. Of course

he'd take the easy way out. Why go to the trouble to win a bride and get her pregnant when his former lover had already produced a potential heir. And then there were the two dozen red roses he'd had sent to her office. While grandly romantic, the gesture had barely aroused a twinge of temptation.

It was the vulnerability she'd infrequently glimpsed in him that destroyed all her self-preservation and led to repeated disappointments. During those moments, when his shoulders hunched and the cocky playboy vanished, her defenses crumbled. Whether or not he could accept it, Christian yearned for someone to believe in him, and until he pushed her out of his life, Noelle had naively thought that someone was her.

And now he was back. And making demands on her once more. Concern that Christian had appeared suspicious of her hasty engagement swept over her. Half acting the part of smitten fiancée, half because she needed reassurance, Noelle reached for Geoff's hand. He responded with a tender smile that would have made her heart flutter if she was actually in love with him.

Christian observed their exchange through half-lidded eyes and Noelle was convinced she and Geoff were successfully selling the fabrication. But when the stilted meal at long last concluded, it was Christian's hand, warm and too familiar, at the small of her back as they made their way from the restaurant. Geoff had deferred to Christian's rank, and she was now far too aware that her willpower wasn't as strong as she'd hoped. As she wove between the tables, a slowly expanding coil of heat threatened her peace of mind.

Christian's car and driver awaited him at the curb, but instead of bidding them good-night, he lingered while the valet brought Geoff's car around. They made an awkward trio.

When Geoff would have opened the car door and handed Noelle into the passenger seat, Christian used his height and broad shoulders as a not so subtle barrier to keep Geoff from reaching her.

"I've got this." Christian set his hand on the car door and lifted the corners of his lips, shooting Geoff a perfunctory smile that was quickly gone. When he shifted his gaze to Noelle, his eyes glowed with possessive intent.

"Thank you for a lovely evening," she said as Christian handed her into the passenger seat.

"I enjoyed meeting your fiancé, but we didn't get the chance to talk about Marc or our future. I'll call you tomorrow and we can discuss the best time for the three of us to get together."

Before Noelle could protest, Christian shut the door and with a brief, wicked grin at getting in the last word, backed away from the car.

Geoff glanced at her before pulling away from the curb. "Are you okay?"

"Sure," she lied, tearing her gaze away from Christian with effort. "Why wouldn't I be?"

"He's still watching us go."

Noelle's nerves were frayed by the tension. "How do you expect me to respond to that?" she snapped, her tone harsh. As soon as the words were out she hunched her shoulders. "I'm sorry. The man gets to me."

"From the way he was looking at you tonight, you get to him, as well."

Geoff probably meant for his words to reassure her. Instead, she just barely resisted the urge to drop her face into her hands and moan in misery. The last thing she needed was to speculate whether Christian's interest in marrying her was motivated by anything other than expediency.

"You're supposed to be the sensible voice that tells me

not to get involved with Christian." Noelle sighed, predicting a long sleepless night ahead. "I need to keep my head clear and my emotions on ice until he gives up on the idea of marrying me."

"You don't think he bought that we're madly in love and destined to live happily-ever-after?" Geoff's wry inflection had serious undertones. Earlier that day he'd tried to talk her out of her gambit, but she'd been too panicky to listen.

"Maybe at first."

"I thought I played the part of your ardent suitor very well."

"You did." The flaw in the plan lay solely at her doorstep. How could she pretend to be in love with Geoff if her heart still fluttered when Christian was near? With a woeful sigh she surrendered to the inevitable.

Noelle grasped the enormous diamond and slid the ring from her finger. It was a relief to take the clumsy thing off. She might have handled the weight better if she didn't feel so much regret about dragging Geoff into her schemes.

With one corner of his mouth lifted in a half smile, Geoff took the ring and popped it into his breast pocket. "And just like that I'm a single man again."

"It was my fault he saw through us. I shouldn't have attempted to trick him. He's far too astute for that. He's probably already had you checked out and knows we're not together."

Geoff's expression turned serious. "Your openness and honesty are what everyone loves about you. Don't let Christian turn you into someone you're not. Be honest with him about your fears for Marc."

At the moment Noelle wasn't feeling remotely honest or lovable. She was an anxious mother ready to defend her child through whatever devious or dirty means necessary.

"Are you sure the prince isn't sincere about wanting a relationship with Marc?"

"I don't know." Her heart had a different opinion, but Noelle couldn't trust the poor, misguided thing. "I'd feel better about it if he wasn't under pressure to produce an heir."

For five long years, a tiny, hopeful part of her had been waiting for Christian to appear on her doorstep the way he used to when they were together. Each year her optimism had dimmed until only a minute speck of it remained. Now he wanted back in her life. Not because he missed her or realized she was his soul mate, but because she'd given birth to his son, and Marc was a quick fix for his current predicament.

"You seem to have forgotten that you and Marc are a package deal." Geoff took his eyes off the road and shot her a somber glance. "The only way Marc becomes his heir is if he's legitimate. Which means Christian needs to marry you."

To her shame the thought sent a wanton burst of anticipation ripping through her. The way her stomach clenched was both familiar and unwelcome. She hated her body's involuntary reaction because that meant she was susceptible to the abundant tools in Christian's sexual arsenal.

She extended her hand, palm up. "You're right. Please return my ring. The engagement is back on."

Geoff shook his head, making no move to oblige her. "I'll not be jilted by you twice. You're going to have to sort out your issues with Christian without resorting to any more ill-advised schemes."

Five

Christian paced before the French doors that led from the green drawing room to the extensive garden at the back of the palace. He tugged his left sleeve down over his watch. During the past fifteen minutes, the movement had become a nervous tick as he'd checked the time every twenty seconds or so. Noelle and Marc were late to the meeting she'd finally agreed to. The waiting was eating away the last of Christian's calm.

He decided to take his agitation out on Gabriel. "I still can't believe you've known that I had a son and didn't tell me."

From his spot on the emerald-colored sofa in the center of the room, the crown prince of Sherdana glanced up from his smartphone, unruffled by his brother's aggressive tone. "Olivia and I suspected. We didn't know for sure. And until the DNA tests come back, you don't, either."

Christian snorted in reply as he continued his path

back and forth across the eighteenth-century carpet. The aimless movement wasn't improving his situation, so he stopped before his brother and scowled at him.

"He's my son. He has the Alessandro eyes and looks the way we did at four." Although the triplets weren't identical, as children they'd been enough alike in appearance to confuse strangers.

"So now you know." Gabriel's lips curved into a challenging smile. "What happens next?"

"I get to know my son."

From the speed with which his brother's attention returned to his phone, Gabriel hadn't approved of Christian's offhanded response. Irritation spread from his chest to his gut.

"What?" he demanded.

"You've always played it just a little too safe where relationships were concerned."

"And you haven't?"

It wasn't a fair criticism. Gabriel had fallen hard for Marissa Somme, the deceased mother of his twin two-year-old daughters. But unlike Christian, Gabriel was first in line to the Sherdanian throne and put duty above all else. From the moment he'd begun the affair with the half-French, half-American model, Gabriel had known it must end. Sherdana's constitution decreed that in order for his son to rule the country one day, the child's mother had to be either a European aristocrat or a Sherdanian citizen.

Marissa had been neither, and Gabriel had ended the relationship. At the time he hadn't known he was going to be a father. That bomb had been dropped on him weeks before he was to marry Lady Olivia Darcy. Her British ancestry made her an exceptional candidate for princess. Or that's the way it had appeared until her fertility issues had made her unsuitable to be Gabriel's wife.

When Gabriel didn't respond to his brother's ineffectual gibe, Christian continued. "What do you want from me?"

"An heir would be nice."

"Nice." Christian practically spit the word. *Nice* didn't describe the pressure his family had put upon him once Gabriel married a woman who could never bear children and Nic had announced his intention to make an American his wife. "You think I should marry Noelle."

That he'd already intended to do just that didn't lessen Christian's annoyance. He was sick of everyone telling him what to do.

"It's about time you put the needs of this family and this country above your own."

"What about Nic? He's been in America for ten years trying to build his damned rocket ship. Why does he get to keep doing what he wants?" Christian immediately regretted his petulant tone, but the resentment he'd kept bottled up for the past three months had a mind of its own.

"If you hadn't played the third-in-line-to-the-throne card like you always do, expecting me or Nic to be the responsible ones, you might have been able to marry the woman of your dreams, suitable or not. Then Nic would be the one ranting and raving about the unfairness of doing his *duty* to Sherdana."

Duty.

Christian was getting awfully sick of that word. Until four months ago, the only feeling Christian had about matrimony was utter relief that he'd never be forced down the aisle because the country required it. Producing an heir was Gabriel's obligation as firstborn. Christian enjoyed all the perks of a princely title without any of the demands. And he wasn't beleaguered by guilt over his freedom. If it was selfish of him, so be it.

"We all know I'm not marriage material," Christian

grumbled, casting a glance toward the doorway for the hundredth time. "I wonder what's keeping them."

He was eager to start bonding with his son. And convincing the child's mother that her life would be so much better as his princess. Princess Noelle had a nice ring to it. She might be resistant to the idea of marrying Christian the man, but once she saw how fast doors opened for her as his royal consort, she would realize that Christian the prince was a magnificent catch.

"They'll be here shortly," Gabriel said.

"Do you have some sort of tracking app on your phone that notifies you when guests arrive?" Christian's words were meant to irritate his brother, but the grim, uptight Gabriel of a year ago had been replaced by a relaxed, charming prince of the realm who was impossible to rile.

"No." Gabriel's lips curved in a private smile. "I'm texting with Olivia. She said Marc has finished his third cookie and Mother's ten-thirty appointment has arrived."

Adrenaline zinged through Christian. "Noelle and Marc are already here? How long?"

"About twenty minutes."

"Is that why you're in here with me? To keep me occupied while Olivia introduced Marc to our mother? Did it ever occur to you that I wanted to get to know my son a little before I sprang him on the family?"

"If that's the case, you shouldn't have arranged for him to come here today."

"Noelle suggested it. She didn't want me showing up at her home and bringing media attention with me, and I certainly couldn't spend time with them in public. The palace made sense, since she's been here several times." Christian massaged the back of his neck to ease the stiffness brought on by the stress of his brother's interference. "I thought we could have a quiet couple hours…"

Dammit.

He liked keeping his personal life as far from the palace as possible. While he didn't mind his romantic escapades making a splash in tabloids all over Europe, he'd never once gone out of his way to introduce any of the jet-setters to his family. His friends liked to party. So did he. End of story. Not one of them could have captured the heart of a nation the way Olivia and Brooke had. His women were flashy, spoiled and selfish. Not one wanted a deeper connection. That suited him just fine.

Noelle was the complete opposite. A timeless beauty, her meteoric rise in the world of bridal fashion had captured the media's attention. Every single article Christian had read about her in the past week had praised her vision and talent. They loved how she'd started as an assistant designer at Matteo Pizarro Designs and been mentored by the great man himself. Of course, Christian wasn't surprised by her success. He'd known five years ago that her gift for design would take her a long way. It was her lack of confidence that had held her back.

And her love for him.

"Did Olivia say anything about how the meeting with Mother went?"

With two royal weddings taking place within a couple months of each other, Christian had made himself scarce around the palace, but he was certain Noelle had met the queen during one of her dress fittings with Gabriel's twin girls who'd acted as flower girls for both Olivia and Brooke. Of course, on those occasions she'd been the talented fashion designer who'd crafted the fairy-tale wedding gowns worn by his brothers' brides. As the mother of what might just be the future monarch of Sherdana, she would undergo a vastly different scrutiny. What if the

queen decided Noelle wasn't suitable to become a member
of the royal family?

And what had the queen thought of her grandson?
Would the child pass muster? Christian couldn't rein in
his concern. "Did mother like Marc?"

From the way Gabriel's keen gaze rested on him, Christian had failed to sound casual.

"I'm sure Noelle will tell you all about it when she ar-
rives. Olivia is bringing them now."

Christian would have preferred a briefing from an
impartial third party like his brother's clever wife, but
clamped down on his agitation. Instead, he focused on
what he could recall of the boy. Their brief encounter had
left him with little more than a series of impressions. Fierce
Alessandro eyes. Protective stance. Disapproval of the man
his mother had introduced as Prince Christian.

Had Noelle already explained to Marc who Christian
truly was? Or did she plan to do so today with Christian at
her side? It was a question he probably should have asked
his former flame days ago, but Christian hadn't been thinking about how the news might rock the four-year-old's
world. He'd been too caught up in how the discovery had
impacted him.

"Do you and Olivia plan to stick around for a bit?"

Gabriel eyed him, his expression thoughtful. "We hadn't
planned to."

"Would you?" Christian suspected the strain would be
muted if he, Noelle and Marc weren't left alone right away.
"Just for a bit. Marc might be a bit overwhelmed."

"Yes," Gabriel drawled. "I'm sure it's Marc that we
need to worry about."

"If you're implying that I'm anxious…"

It wasn't like Christian to let anyone see him sweat, but
maybe just this once it would be okay. If anyone would un-

derstand how he felt, it would be Gabriel. Several months ago, Sherdana's crown prince had been surprised in the same way when twin toddlers, Karina and Bethany, had arrived on his doorstep after their mother died. Christian had been impressed how well his brother had adapted to fatherhood. Of course, the girls were two years younger than Marc and probably hadn't yet missed having a father. But a boy was different. He needed a male influence in his life. Someone to look up to.

"I have a four-year-old son I've barely met," Christian murmured, overwhelmed with awe and dismay.

"It's terrifying." Gabriel clapped him on the back, the solid blow knocking Christian away from the brink of panic. "Can't wait to meet him."

As if on cue, a dark-haired boy streaked through the doorway and dodged around several carefully arranged chairs, making a beeline for the enormous fireplace at the opposite end of the room.

"Look, I can fit in this one, too." Dressed in navy pants and a pale blue shirt, Marc stood framed in the white marble surround, arms outstretched and wearing a precocious grin.

The boy's compelling enthusiasm drew and held every adult eye in the room. Christian was the first to look away. Noelle had entered on Olivia's heels, and he stole a moment to drink in her quiet beauty.

In manner and appearance, Noelle was more like Gabriel's graceful, elegant wife than Nic's bohemian spitfire. Today Noelle wore a textured brown sheath with black side panels that accentuated her slender curves. A two-inch ruffled flounce at the hemline boosted the design from simple to striking.

"Marc, come out of there," Noelle scolded with a quick

apologetic glance to where Gabriel stood with his arm wrapped around Olivia's waist.

After four months Christian still wasn't accustomed to his brother's easy affection with his new wife. Even as a child Gabriel had been somber and formal most of the time, as if his future crown already weighed heavily on his head. Christian marveled to see him now, relaxed and smiling as he kissed Olivia on the cheek and whispered something in her ear that brought rosy delight to her cheeks.

Christian tore his gaze from the happy couple in time to catch the wistfulness that softened Noelle's expression as she too regarded the royal pair. A realization tore at him: he wanted the same intimate connection with Noelle that Gabriel had with Olivia. A partnership that sizzled in the bedroom and worked everywhere else.

Pity he'd already betrayed the trust that would permit him to have, either.

Noelle couldn't think straight with Christian and her son in the same room. Given Marc's adverse reaction to Christian the night he'd shown up unannounced, she was worried that her son wouldn't want to have anything to do with his father.

And that was the least of her problems.

Having a meeting with Christian's mother sprung on her had been bad enough, but to then watch her transform from imperious queen to adoring grandmother in the space of ten minutes had made Noelle question her decision to keep Marc's paternity a secret. Now that the truth was out, she expected the pressure to legitimize Marc by marrying Christian would increase tenfold.

Nor did it appear as if she would have a single supporter in the palace if she decided against marriage. Olivia had already said the twins would be so excited when Marc came to live in the palace, and Gabriel was obviously enjoying his nephew's antics. The suspicion Noelle expected to encounter had been nonexistent. Everyone seemed to accept that Marc was Christian's son.

Which meant whatever Noelle chose for her son's future, she had no one to blame but herself for the consequences.

Her eyes hurt with the effort of keeping her gaze from devouring Christian. Whenever he was near, she had to fight to maintain a neutral demeanor. After a five-year drought, spending so much time with him was starting to eat into her willpower. It wasn't fair how easily she regressed into familiar patterns. Back when they were lovers, she used to spend hours beside him in bed, content to work on her designs or lapse into frivolous romanticism and doodle their names, connecting the letters with intricate loops and flourishes. Looking back on it now, Noelle couldn't believe she'd been that foolish.

"Marc," she called, putting aside her memories of past imprudence, "come meet Prince Gabriel."

The little boy gave a green sofa and several chairs a wide berth to avoid Christian before coming to stand at Noelle's side and fixing solemn, unblinking eyes on the handsome, regal man beside Olivia.

Prince Gabriel put his hand out. "Nice to meet you, Marc."

Most four-year-olds wouldn't have known to be awed by the man who would one day rule the country, but Marc had his father's confidence as well as his mercurial temperament.

"Nice to meet you, Prince Gabriel."

Noelle was torn between relief and pride at her son's exhibition of good manners, but she held her breath as he continued to speak.

"I like your palace. It's very large. Do you ever play hide and seek?"

Prince Gabriel's lips twitched at Marc's earnest question, but he gave him a grave reply. "Not for many years. But my daughters are big fans of the game. Perhaps one day you can play with them."

Marc didn't look to Noelle for confirmation before nodding. "I'd like that."

"Would you like to see the garden?" Olivia asked.

Christian stepped up beside his brother. "He might be interested in the stables, as well."

"Are there pumpkins in the garden?" Marc asked, acting as if he hadn't heard Christian. "We have three pumpkins at home, and they're this big." He demonstrated their size with his hands, adding about two feet to the actual diameter.

"No pumpkins, I'm afraid," Olivia said, glancing from Christian to Noelle. "But we have a pond with goldfish."

Noticing Christian's taut expression, Noelle said, "Marc, why don't you let Princess Olivia show you the pond and I'll be out in a little bit."

With an excited roar, Marc raced toward the French doors, Olivia and Gabriel trailing behind. As the trio exited the room, Noelle's tension ratcheted upward. A muscle bunched in Christian's jaw as he tracked Marc's rambunctious dash across the lush, verdant lawn until he was out of sight. At last his hard gaze swung to Noelle.

"What have you said to my son to make him hate me?"

She wasn't surprised by Christian's question. "I haven't told him anything at all about you."

"Not even that I'm his father?"

Noelle sighed. "No, not yet. I've always said that I never told his father about him because I liked our family just as it was."

"And he was satisfied with that?" Christian sounded skeptical.

"He's four. For the moment it's enough." Noelle knew her son's innate curiosity wouldn't allow him to let the matter drop indefinitely. "He doesn't hate you," she added.

"Then why is it he gives me a wide berth?"

"You weren't exactly charming when you showed up unannounced at my home."

"I was upset to discover you'd been hiding a son from me all these years."

"I wasn't hiding him." Noelle blinked in surprise as she took in Christian's bitterness. "You would have known about him if you'd ever bothered to contact me in the months following our breakup." She fumbled over the last word.

His dismissal of her hadn't felt like a true breakup. He hadn't said he was unhappy with their relationship or that he wanted to see other people. He'd just told her to take the job she'd been offered at Matteo Pizarro Designs in Paris. After she'd given him her heart and two years of her life, he'd not been the least bit regretful that she'd be moving so far away nor had he offered to keep in touch.

"See, you are still angry with me," he said, pointing a taunting finger at her. "And you're inferring I didn't want to be a part of his life."

Yes, she'd been hurt by his rejection, but that was five years ago. Granted, it still rankled her, but had she turned her son against his father without meaning to? Uncertainty put her on the defensive.

"You don't know me at all if you think that." The man was an insufferable egotist. "And may I point out that simply by your absence you've become alienated from Marc."

"Did you ever try to contact me?" Christian persisted. "To let me know you were pregnant?"

"To what end? You made it pretty clear you were finished with me." She shook her head, throat contracting in remembered pain. "And if I had, what would you have done? When would you have found time between work and play to be a father?" She was warming to her argument now. "Marc deserves someone who will be there for him all the time not when it fits into his schedule."

"Someone like Coomb?" Christian grabbed her bare right hand and held it up. "Where's your engagement ring, Noelle?"

His strong touch sent a burst of heat through her. She hesitated too long before attempting to tug free. "Geoff and I talked. Given the circumstances, he thinks it would be less confusing for Marc if he stepped out of the picture and gave you and Marc a chance to bond." Chest heaving, she stopped trying to make Christian let her go and stood glaring at him.

"It wasn't much of an engagement if he gave you up so easily." Soft and measured, Christian's remark cut her deep.

"He's concerned for Marc." Geoff had been right about her scheme being a bad idea. It had backfired mightily, and once again Christian perceived her as mundane and unable to inspire a man's passion. "My son loves Geoff. You should appreciate that he was willing to step aside and not complicate an already tricky situation."

Terrified that Christian would see the tears scalding her eyes, she spun away from him and took several steps toward the French doors and the safety of the garden. But she wasn't fast enough and he caught her before she could slip outside.

"I was ready to battle him for you," he murmured, fingers grazing the wet streak on her cheek. "To demonstrate how committed I am to being your ardent husband and a zealous father to Marc."

Such beautiful words from such a challenging and unpredictable man. Noelle couldn't decide whether to laugh or cry. She was still debating when Christian cupped her face in his hands and brought his lips to hers.

The delicious pressure of his kiss held her immobile with shock. She was transported back in time to their first kiss. It had started very differently than this one, in merriment not bitterness. They'd been laughing at something silly, a bit of urban slang she'd used wrong.

In the beginning of their unlikely friendship, Christian had come to her apartment when he was feeling low and out of sorts. He claimed she had a knack for chasing away his shadows, and she was flattered that a charismatic prince, one whose favor was sought by everyone, saw *her* as special.

Noelle tunneled impatient fingers into Christian's hair and pushed her greedy body hard against his. She was starving for physical affection. Being hugged by her son was wonderful, but sometimes she just craved a man's hands on her. To feel a little helpless as he tore off her clothes and had his way with her. And Christian had a knack for this sort of thing. His firm, masterful touch reduced her to quivering need.

His fingers bit into her hip as she rocked against him, the ache between her thighs building. She rubbed her breasts against his chest to ease her yearning, but the friction only caused her to burn hotter.

Men's voices, coming from the direction of the garden, awoke Noelle to the insanity of what she was doing. She broke off the kiss, but hadn't the strength to escape Christian's embrace. Had she lost all sense? Any second they could be discovered by the palace's staff, Christian's family. Her son.

Christian took advantage of her unsteadiness and buried his face in her neck. His lips glided over her skin, leaving a tingling sensation in his wake. "I knew you'd come around."

An icy chill swept through her at his words. Noelle clenched her teeth and cursed her impulsiveness. She tensed and twisted away.

"I haven't come around to anything."

"Ten seconds ago you were melted butter in my arms." He crossed said arms across his formidable chest and lobbed a wolfish grin in her direction. "I'd say that's a pretty good indication that you agree it's better for all of us if we marry."

With her heart pumping gallons of hot, sexually charged blood through her veins, it was a little hard to pretend she was unaffected by their steamy kiss. "Sex was always great between us," she admitted, "but it's not a reason to get married."

"Not the only reason obviously, but wouldn't you be happier with a man who can drive you wild in bed? I do that for you. Why are you fighting this?"

His arrogance left her momentarily speechless. She spent a silent few seconds studying his face. What she saw gave her reason to believe his confidence was at least partially contrived.

"I'm not fighting anything. I'm trying to make a sensible decision based on what's best for Marc and me." Her cheeks heated a little at the skeptical look in Christian's eyes. Okay, plastering herself all over him hadn't been sensible, but to be fair, he had a gift for jazzing her hormones and muddling her judgment. "And being kissed by you isn't making that any easier."

He stretched out his hand and cupped her cheek in his palm. Her wobbly knees hadn't let her move beyond his grasp, and she found herself held in place while he closed the narrow gap and dropped his lips to hers once again. Hard and brief, the kiss affirmed that he respected her admission and wasn't about to back off.

She sighed as his hand slid away. "I really need to go see what Marc is up to."

"Let's go."

Christian refrained from touching her as they exited the room and headed across the lawn in the direction of the koi pond. Longing knotted Noelle's muscles. Already she was too aware of the exact distance from his hand to hers. The expressive nuances of his gold eyes as he darted a glance her way. The heat pooling in her belly as she relived their kiss.

Marc was lying on one of the flat rocks surrounding the pool, his nose inches from the surface of the water as Noelle and Christian approached. Her son's enthusiastic chatter wasn't distracting enough for Noelle to miss the curiosity in Olivia's gaze as it bounced between her and Christian. Unable to stop the rush of heat that suffused her cheeks, Noelle wasn't sure whether she liked the princess's obvious approval. With so many people counting on Christian to produce an heir and Marc waiting in the wings to be legitimized, the pressure on Noelle was mounting.

Would anyone understand if she turned Christian down? Was she wrong to want her son to grow up without the responsibility of ruling a country looming over his head? And was it selfish to take her own feelings into consideration? Christian might be the sort of lover every woman dreamed of, but was he husband and father material? No, based on her past experience with him. But five years had changed her. Could the same be said for him? And how involved was she going to let herself get before she knew for sure?

Six

Christian stopped on the opposite side of the fishpond from his son and drank in the sights and sounds of the energetic boy from behind a polite mask. His heart continued to drive against his ribs following the encounter with Noelle in the green drawing room. An odd lightness had invaded his head as if he wasn't getting the proper amount of oxygen. Which was ridiculous because he was gathering huge lungsful of air laden with the scents of fresh-cut grass, newly turned earth and Noelle's light floral perfume. He suspected her scent was affecting his equilibrium.

Marc laughed as one of the big orange koi flipped its tail and sent water splashing onto his cheek. "Mama, did you see that? The fish waved at me."

"I saw. Why don't we take a walk to the barn?"

"It should be about time for Bethany and Karina's riding lesson," Gabriel added. "Maybe you'd like to see their ponies?"

"Sure." Marc got to his feet and went to slide his hand into Olivia's. "Will you take me?"

She exchanged a brief, poignant look with her husband and then shook her head. "I'm afraid Prince Gabriel and I have someplace we need to be, but Prince Christian knows the stables inside and out. He can take you."

Olivia and Gabriel said their goodbyes and headed for the palace. Marc watched them go before turning to his mother.

"Can't I just stay here with the fish? I don't care about ponies."

"A second ago you were ready to visit the barn," Noelle pointed out, the skin between her sable eyebrows puckering as she frowned. "And since when don't you like ponies?"

"I'll go if he doesn't come with us."

"That's impolite." Thunderclouds formed in her eyes. "Prince Christian is a very busy man. He is taking time away from his business to spend it with us."

"Can't he just go back to work?"

Noelle's lips firmed into a tight line, and she cast a mortified look Christian's way. Despite being frustrated that he was his son's least favorite person, Christian liked that she was concerned about his feelings.

"First the stables," Christian said, his tone shutting down further argument. "Then I'm going to take you and your mother to lunch at a really wonderful restaurant down by the river." Neither lunch nor being seen together in a public place had been a part of their original plan for the day, but Christian was feeling a little desperate at the moment.

"I'm not hungry." The boy had become sullen.

Christian was not going to give up. "That's too bad because this is a new American-style restaurant that has the best hamburgers and milkshakes in Sherdana." It didn't occur to him that Noelle might not want her son eating the less than healthy food until he noticed she was regarding the slim gold watch on her wrist. "It's okay if we go there, right?" he belatedly asked, giving her a winning grin.

"I wasn't planning on taking time for lunch. I have an appointment in an hour."

"Marc and I could go by ourselves." He smiled at the boy. "And I could drop him off after."

"I suppose that would work. How does that sound to you, Marc?"

The four-year-old dug the toe of his brown loafer into the ground and stared down. "I don't feel good."

Christian recognized a losing battle when he saw one. How was he supposed to get to know his son when the boy didn't want to have anything to do with him? "Perhaps another time then."

"Can we go home, Mama?"

"Of course." Noelle ruffled her son's dark wavy hair and mouthed an apology to Christian. "And straight into bed. That's where sick boys belong."

"But I was supposed to play with Dino this afternoon."

"I'm not sure you'll be feeling better that fast."

Marc aimed a surly glare in Christian's direction, obviously blaming him for the canceled play date, before taking the hand his mother put out to him.

"It was nice seeing you again, Marc." Christian sounded more like a prince and not at all like a father.

The boy said nothing. So, Christian tried a smile, but the muscles around his mouth didn't want to cooperate. His awkwardness around his son made him come off stilted and unfriendly. It wasn't at all like him. Gabriel's two girls adored Uncle Christian. He snuck them sweets and helped them play tricks on their nanny and the maids charged with caring for them. That he wasn't developing the same rapport with his son frustrated him.

"Please say goodbye to the prince," Noelle said.

Her firm prompting produced a grumbled response from Marc. Looking exasperated, Noelle tugged him in the direction of the palace. Christian watched their progress and waited until they'd reentered the building before heading back himself.

He was met halfway by his mother's private secretary. Gwen had been with the queen since the triplets had been born. Despite her sensible two-inch heels, her head barely came as high as Christian's shoulder. Her diminutive size sometimes caused her to be underestimated. No one made that mistake twice.

"The queen would like you to come to her office."

The summons wasn't unexpected. After meeting Marc, she was sure to have questions for Christian. "Right now?" His mother only sent her secretary when she expected immediate results, and the question would irritate Gwen, but he needed to release some steam.

Gwen's eyebrows arched. "You have somewhere more important to be?" So much for riling Gwen.

Christian shook his head. "Lead the way."

"I have things that require my attention. I'm sure you can find your way on your own."

Despite his foul mood, Christian grinned. Perhaps he'd gotten to her after all.

As much as he'd have liked to drag his feet on the way to his mother's first-floor office overlooking the meticulous gardens that were her passion, Christian figured the sooner she spoke her piece, the faster he could get back to the challenge of persuading Noelle and Marc that they should be a family.

"Good morning, Mother," he said as he entered her office and took a seat across from her. "Your gardens look lovely as always. I don't know how you do it."

The queen was not to be distracted by his flattery. "I'm surprised you noticed. It seemed as if your attention was focused on Noelle Dubone and that son of hers." The queen paused and tilted her head, prompting him to answer the unasked question. When Christian remained mum, she continued. "Or should I say that son of yours. You're planning to marry her, I presume. We simply cannot have any more illegitimate royal children running around Sherdana."

"I'm working on that."

"Good. I'd like you to have a ring on her finger before the media gets hold of this. We've had enough scandalous romance at the palace in the past year to last several generations of Alessandro rule. There aren't any other of your progeny running around Europe, are there?"

"Not that I know of." He didn't add that he hadn't known about Marc either, but if he was honest with himself, he hadn't always been as careful with Noelle as he'd been with other women.

His answer did not please his mother one bit. "Christian!"

"No. There aren't."

"How can you be sure?"

"I've been careful."

The queen's expression grew even more severe. "Not careful enough."

"Noelle was different." It was almost a relief to let himself think about her all the time. He'd spent five years pushing her out of his mind. When a bit of music reminded him of slow dancing in her apartment, her body languid against his as his palms coasted along her curves. Or when he'd catch a whiff of the perfume he'd bought her and remembered introducing her to several new places to wear the scent.

"Christian?" His mother's sharp voice jerked him back from those heady intoxicating days.

"Yes?"

"We need an heir for the throne." She didn't need to add that he was their last chance to make that happen.

He gave her a short nod. "I'll do whatever it takes to convince Noelle to marry me." He was more determined than ever because if Noelle refused him, he wasn't sure he could marry anyone else.

Noelle's shop was sized to cater to exclusive clients. Generally the brides arrived with a single assistant or an entourage of no more than six. Today's appointment was taxing the salon space. There were twenty opinionated family members and one browbeaten bride. The youngest daughter of a billionaire Greek shipping magnate, Daria was the last of her four sisters to marry, and they all had advice for their baby sister. Additional guidance was being provided by two grandmothers, the girl's mother, soon-to-be mother-in-law and several current and future sisters-in-law.

In advance of this appointment, Noelle had provided a dozen sketches in three rounds of correspondence over a period of two months. The bride or—as was looking more likely—the bride's family had chosen five of the twelve. Knowing she wasn't the only designer the bride was looking at, Noelle had pulled out all the stops. The gowns were elegant, fantasy creations perfect for a twenty-year-old bride. She looked gorgeous in each and every one.

While her family squabbled over every look, Noelle could see her designs had not yet resonated with Daria. The bride's bland expression grew more distant with each gown. She answered Noelle's questions in an unhelpful monotone. Rather than worrying that a two hundred thousand euro commission was slipping through her fingers, Noelle pondered what would make the young woman happy.

Noelle stood beside the door in the large dressing room while her assistant designer and head of alterations worked together to free her dissatisfied client from the latest frothy wedding dress.

"I have one last dress for you to try," Noelle stated, hoping the startled confusion on her assistant's face hadn't been noticed by the client.

"But I've already tried on the five gowns."

"I decided to make up an additional dress from the sketches I sent you." The gown was the first designed by Noelle based on a get-acquainted interview she'd had with the bride shortly after the engagement was announced. She'd been surprised that the design had been rejected during the first round and couldn't get it out of her head that the style was perfect for Daria. "Are you interested in seeing it?"

"Of course."

To Noelle's delight, a flicker of curiosity sparkled in the girl's dark doe-like eyes. "Wonderful. Calantha, could you please get Woodland Snow." Since each wedding dress had a personality all its own, Noelle named all her gowns.

"That sounds so pretty."

Noelle's spirits lifted at Daria's comment. It was the most animated the girl had been all day.

"I know it's not one of the designs you initially chose," Noelle said, taking over Calantha's role and helping Daria step out of the rejected gown. Handing the dress to the head of alterations, she made a surreptitious shooing gesture. The woman understood. Noelle wanted the bride's attention to be 100 percent on the new design. "But I think you'll find that the dress is much more striking in person than on paper."

The door opened, and Calantha entered with Woodland Snow. Daria's breath caught as she glimpsed the gown and her brown eyes brightened. This was the reaction Noelle had been hoping for.

"It's beautiful," Daria murmured, reaching out to finger one of the organza flowers sewn onto the sheer white overlay. "I remember this dress. It was my favorite."

Noelle bit the inside of her lip to keep from asking the girl why she hadn't fought for the design. She already knew the answer. Reports stated her father was spending upward of eleven million euro on the wedding. Daria was marrying the son of a very wealthy Italian count, and the event promised to make a huge media splash. The wedding dress Daria wore would have to be over-the-top to start tongues wagging, and this gown's beauty was in the details.

Working quickly, Noelle and Calantha slipped the gown over Daria's head and settled it into place. The young bride stood with her back to the three-way mirror to allow for the perfect reveal. First impressions were the strongest, and Noelle wanted the young woman to fall in love all at once.

"Okay, you may turn around."

Daria stared at her reflection. Tears filled her eyes. "It's perfect."

The gown was a single layer of white chiffon sewn with fluttering organza flowers and a scattering of pearls that mimicked clustered berries over a strapless nude liner. The simple boat neckline and capped sleeves drew the eye to Daria's striking bone structure and beautiful brown eyes. The other dresses had overpowered her, emphasizing her youth and inexperience. But as Noelle watched her consider her appearance, Daria's expression took on a look of proud determination.

"Do you want to show your family?"

Daria shook her head. "There is no reason. This is my wedding and I want this dress. They can see it on my wedding day."

Noelle nodded. "I'll send Yvonne in to see what alterations are needed. I'm thrilled we were able to find you the perfect wedding dress."

She excused herself and headed into the room that held Daria's family. With a smile that balanced diplomacy and firmness, Noelle announced that Daria had chosen a dress and was looking forward to surprising everyone with her choice on her wedding day. There was a mixture of surprise and annoyance on the women's faces.

An hour later, the exhausting group was gone, and Noelle dropped into a chair in her now-empty salon. To her delight, the young heiress had paid for the dress herself, declaring that by doing so the only opinion that mattered was her own. Noelle's staff joyously broke out the bottles of champagne reserved for occasions like these and joined their employer in celebrating.

Noelle was halfway through her third glass when the tinkle of a bell announced someone had entered the shop's reception room. Waving her staff back to their seats, she went to speak to their visitor. Two-and-a-half glasses of champagne consumed over an hour and a half were not enough to make Noelle tipsy, but the sight of Christian's imposing presence for the second time in one day made her head spin.

"Christian? What are you doing here?"

"I want you and Marc to join me at my vineyard this weekend."

She frowned as her body reacted positively to his invitation. "That's moving much too quick."

"I'm sorry, but I don't want to spend months and months tiptoeing around. I want to marry you and be Marc's father. He needs to know who I am and that you and I are serious about becoming a family."

Thanks to her nerve-racking encounter with the queen and the Greek bride's chaotic family, Noelle's diplomatic skills were in short supply. "But what if I'm not serious?"

"Come to the vineyard this weekend and let's talk."

"Just talk?" She suspected Christian would love nothing more than to get her horizontal to plead his case. "I'm not the susceptible girl I once was. You won't be able to seduce me into agreeing with you."

"How about if I just seduce you for the fun of it."

She was far more open to this suggestion but couldn't let him know it. "You should concentrate on your son. He is the one you need to win over."

"Are you saying if Marc comes around you'll marry me?"

Noelle shook her head. "It's just not that easy, Christian. I think you deserve a chance to be in your son's life, but I'm not convinced that what's best for him is to have his life turned upside down as the royal heir."

"What if we'd gotten married before Marc was conceived? Would you still feel the same way?"

He hadn't meant for his words to sting, but Noelle had once been very conscious that they came from vastly different worlds, and Christian was less than enthusiastic about inviting her into his.

"Since that was obviously never going to happen, the issue never crossed my mind." Her voice was stiff. Muscles rigid.

Five years ago, being his secret plaything had bothered her more and more the longer they were together. Then the tabloids began publishing pictures of him with the beautiful daughter of a Dutch viscount and speculation gathered momentum that they were on the brink of an engagement. She'd convinced herself to break things off. Christian had disputed the rumors and made love to her with such passion that she forgot all about the outside world for a while longer.

"Noelle." His deep growl of frustration sent a shiver through her. "I was young and foolish when we were together five years ago. I had no idea what I was losing when I let you walk out of my life."

"Let me walk?" Outrage flooded her with adrenaline. "You shoved me out."

Christian snorted. "Hardly. I told you to take a fantastic career opportunity."

"I wanted to stay with you." There, she'd admitted what had been in her heart five years ago. Spoken the words she'd been too afraid to declare the last time she'd seen him.

"You don't think I knew that? But I'd already taken too much from you, and you deserved better." His statement rang with conviction. "I cared about you more than I was willing to admit. Even to myself."

"I can't believe you." If she did, it would undo all the anger and resentment she'd built up over the years and leave her heart open to being hurt again. "You didn't want me around anymore."

"I know it's easy to blame me for the way things ended between us, but you can't truly tell me you were happy near the end."

Noelle shook her head. "No. I wanted what I couldn't have. To be the woman on your arm as well as the one in your bed."

"We tried that and it didn't work out very well, remember?" He was referring to the night of the accident, and the fact that her foolishness had almost gotten him killed.

"I remember. So, what makes you think it will be any better this time?"

"You'll just have to trust me that it will."

Seven

The luxurious town car slowed as it passed through the quaint village of Paderna, eight rolling miles from Christian's vineyard. Beside him, Noelle stared past her sleeping son at the shops lining the main street visible through the rear passenger window. With each mile they'd traveled, she'd relaxed a little more. And Christian's tension had grown.

"Just a little bit farther now," he murmured, his voice husky from disuse. They'd spoken little during the two-hour ride. After their contentious discussion three days ago, he was loath to bring up anything that might charge the atmosphere in the car and cause further damage to his relationship with either Noelle or their son.

"I forgot how beautiful the wine country is. And so close to Carone."

"Don't you have cousins up near Gallard that you visit?"

"Not in years, I'm afraid. Work keeps me too busy to

travel for fun." She probably wasn't aware of how wistful she sounded.

"Then I'm doubly glad you agreed to join me this weekend. Some time away will do you good."

She patted her briefcase. "This time is for you and Marc to get to know each other. I have several clients to prepare sketches for."

"You'll at least take an hour or so to tour the winery. I'm very proud of it." Although he made millions buying, fixing and selling corporations, his true passion was crafting the finest vintages in all the country.

He'd acquired Bracci Castle and surrounding vineyards six years earlier from Paulo Veneto, a Sherdanian count who had gambled his way deep into debt. As soon as the hospital had released Christian after the accident, he'd come here to hide and recover. At first the plodding country pace had pained him as much as his scorched flesh. Between his many business dealings and his numerous social engagements, he was used to operating at frenetic speed. Needing something to keep his thoughts occupied and off both the pain in his right side and the agony in his heart, he started learning what it took to produce wine.

At the time, the winery was barely breaking even and the wines were abysmal. Christian figured out that the general manager and winemaker were selling the grapes produced by the vineyard and buying inferior ones at half the cost, pocketing the difference. Within a week Christian had fired and replaced them with two men he'd wooed away from the competition. After sinking a ridiculous amount of money into desperately needed new equipment, he'd held his breath and hoped the grapes were as good as promised. The first harvest had gone well, and the wine produced that year won the winery its first award.

"These are all my fields," Christian said, indicating the rows of well-maintained grapevines.

"I remember when you mentioned buying the vineyard. You don't usually hold on to anything for long. Why keep it?"

"The place makes the finest wines in all Sherdana. Why would I want to give that up?"

"So it's a prestige thing." Her tone revealed that his answer had disappointed her. She wanted him to speak the truth not give her flippant responses.

"I have grown fond of the place."

She nodded. "I can't wait to see it."

And he couldn't wait to show it to her. The seven-hundred-year-old castle had a quirky charm so unlike his sleek, sophisticated apartments at the center of activity in Paris and London. His circle of friends thought he was mad to spend any time here. They couldn't figure out how he kept himself entertained without clubs or expensive restaurants. The isolation that had first bothered him was now like a balm to his soul. One he enjoyed too infrequently thanks to his business commitments.

The car rolled through the arch and beneath the portcullis that was the only way into the castle's outer courtyard. Where in medieval times this large area would have been cobbled, Christian had turned the space into a grassy lawn with paths. The car followed the circular driveway and stopped outside the keep's arched double doors. As the driver got out and opened Christian's door, several staff flowed out of the imposing stone building and headed toward the car. Christian hesitated before sliding out and turned to Noelle. Marc was starting to stir in his car seat.

"Why don't you let me carry him into the house," Christian offered, hoping the child would be less likely to protest since he was drowsy.

"Of course." Noelle exited the car behind him and stood looking up at the towering stone structure in front of her. "This really is a castle, isn't it?"

"What were you expecting?"

She wrinkled her nose. "Something more fairy-tale-like."

Christian chuckled. "It is a hulking brute of a thing, isn't it? Don't worry. You'll like what I've done to the inside. It has running water and electricity."

"No heated buckets of water hauled up from the kitchen and winding stairwells lit by torches?"

"You sound disappointed." It was good to banter with her. The repartee erased the years of separation and recalled why they'd once enjoyed each other's company so much.

"There's a part of me that is."

With his mood growing lighter by the second, Christian unbuckled his son from the car seat and lifted the boy in his arms. The weight of Marc's sleepy head on his shoulder filled Christian with blazing joy. Holding his child was such a simple thing. How many fathers didn't give it a second thought? For Christian the moment was precious, and he closed his eyes to imprint the memory, after which he followed Noelle inside.

The entry hall was a wide room that ran for twenty feet on either side of the front door with a fireplace on each wall. Here they were met by a handsome woman in her midfifties wearing a simple navy dress and a tasteful silver brooch in the shape of a lily.

"Noelle, this is Mrs. Francas, my housekeeper. Whatever you need, you may ask her."

The brunette smiled in welcome. "Ms. Dubone, how lovely to have you and your son staying with us. I will have your bags sent to your rooms. As Prince Christian stated, anything you need, please let me know. We look forward to making your stay extra special in the hopes you'll return."

When Noelle's eyes widened in surprise, Christian cocked his head at Francas's not-so-subtle hint. She'd been Christian's favorite nursemaid when he, Gabriel and Nic were growing up, and as such he gave her a little more latitude when she voiced her opinions than he might have with someone else.

"Thank you," Noelle murmured with a friendly smile.

They entered the great hall. In its heyday everyone in the castle would gather there for meals. The lower section of the thirty-foot walls was lined with dark wainscoting, and enormous paintings depicting hunt scenes were hung above.

"I feel a little bit like I've been transported back to the fourteenth century."

"When I bought the castle, it was in pretty bad shape. Veneto hated the country and rarely spent time at his estate. The stone floors were chipped and uneven. Plaster was crumbling everywhere. I decided to take some of the walls back to the original stone. Where the paneling was in better shape, it was restored."

"Oh!" she exclaimed, pointing at several suits of armor that stood at attention on one end of the room. "Marc is going to love those."

Hearing his name seemed to rouse him. Marc lifted his head from Christian's shoulder and blinked blearily. "Mama?"

"We're at Prince Christian's castle. Look at how big this room is."

Marc's eyes went wide as he gazed around. "Wow." He squirmed a little as he swiveled to check out the space in every direction, but made no attempt to get away from Christian.

Deciding to give up while he was ahead, Christian set down his son. "Go check out that armor over there." He pointed at a set with intricate gold filigree that looked too ornate to have ever been worn into battle.

"Is it yours?" For a couple seconds hero worship blazed in Marc's burnished gold eyes, and Christian reveled in his son's admiration. "Have you ever worn it?"

"No. It was made specially for one of my ancestors and only fit him," Christian explained.

"Did he wear it in battle with trolls?"

"Ah, no." He shot a questioning glance toward Noelle.

"One of his friends has an older brother who is into fantasy novels and likes to tell his brother and Marc all about them."

Christian nodded his understanding. "My great-great-great-great grandfather wore it to defend Sherdana's borders." He had no idea if that was true, but he suspected one of his ancestors had worn the armor, and the story had captured his son's interest.

"Neat."

To Christian's delight Marc was demonstrating none of his usual displeasure when his father was around. While the boy raced from the armor to the display of swords and battle-axes, Christian set his hand in the small of Noelle's back and guided her toward the salon. Here, carpet stretched the length of the stone floor, and paneling covered the rustic walls. Long windows, framed in royal blue velvet, overlooked the castle's inner courtyard. Late-afternoon sunshine fell upon the last of the summer roses. There was a cozy sitting area with wing chairs and a plush sofa before the large fireplace.

"This is where I spend most of my time when I'm here. The stairs—" he gestured to his right "—lead to the first floor and several guest rooms. I can have my housekeeper show you to your rooms now or..."

He hadn't thought much past getting Noelle and Marc here.

"Or?" Noelle prompted, fixing him with a curious stare.

Christian laughed. "I have no idea. How do you feel about exploring outside? There are some terrific views of the countryside from atop the walls."

"I think Marc would love that."

With their son racing ahead of them, Christian and Noelle strolled side by side through the courtyard and up a set of stairs that led to the battlements. The autumn sunshine heightened the greens and golds of the fields surrounding the castle. A light breeze blew Noelle's silky dark hair around her face and tugged at the floral scarf knotted about her slim neck. Christian stroked a strand of hair off her cheek and noticed the way her lashes fluttered at his touch.

Gripped by the desire to take her in his arms and kiss her soft, full lips, Christian trailed his fingertips down her neck and around to her nape. Her faint sigh was nearly his undoing. Only awareness of Marc running back and forth across the battlements, chattering about the height of the walls and pretending he was shooting arrows at the enemy below, kept Christian from acting on the impulses driving through his body. But it didn't keep him from talking about it.

"I think I'm going to go crazy waiting to taste you," he murmured close to her ear, near enough to feel the way her body started at the hot brush of his breath against her skin.

"I can't make any promises until I see how Marc settles down tonight." She peered at Christian from beneath long, sable lashes. "But I very much want to get my hands on you, as well."

His body reacted predictably to her bold remark. Heat poured into his groin while his muscles tightened in delicious anticipation. She left him breathless and off his game. He slid his fingers around her waist and drew her against his side while his lips grazed her temple.

"No one has ever gotten to me the way that you do." Before hunger overrode his willpower, he set her free and raked both hands through his hair. "What changed your mind?"

"I haven't."

"But you just said…" He regarded her, his brain blurry with confusion, wondering what to make of her secretive smile.

"That I've given up trying to fight the chemistry between us. I want to make love with you. It's all I thought about the entire trip here, but I long ago discovered, sex with you does not necessarily mean we have a future."

Noelle hadn't meant the remark to be cruel, but he had to understand where she was coming from. "I'm sorry if that sounded harsh."

"Don't be sorry. I had that coming. You're right. When we were together before, I had no intention of giving up my freedom. I lived in the moment and enjoyed being irresponsible and egocentric."

His words rang with regret, but Noelle wasn't sure he'd changed all that much. "And yet without the actions of your brothers putting you in the difficult position of being the only one who can produce an heir for the throne, you wouldn't be here with Marc and me this weekend."

The truth weighed heavy on her heart. But it didn't stop her from wishing he wanted her and Marc in his life simply because he cared about them. When she tried a smile, the corners of her mouth quivered with the effort of appearing poised and understanding.

"I'm not as bad as you think I am."

"You misunderstand me. I don't think you're bad. I just don't want you to think it's unreasonable for me to doubt your sincerity."

"What does that mean?"

"Be truthful. You want to have sex with me and hope that I will fall back in love with you so we can marry and you can fulfill your obligation to Sherdana."

"You make me sound like a coldhearted bastard." He glared down at her. "Yes, I want us to have sex. Making love to you remains the most inspiring, mind-blowing pleasure I've ever had with any woman. Was I a fool to push you out of my life and give that up? Of course. But I was stupid and afraid, and at the time it seemed like the best thing to do."

Noelle's breath lodged in her chest at his passionate declaration. She could believe that he valued their physical intimacy as much as she had. Although she'd been relatively inexperienced where men and sex were concerned, Christian had been as susceptible to her touch as she'd been to his.

"This is all so complicated," she murmured, her gaze trailing after Marc as she tried to remind herself where her priorities lay.

"It doesn't have to be."

Christian took her hand and squeezed with firm tenderness. Then he lifted it to his face and grazed the inside of her wrist with his lips. Noelle's full attention returned to Christian. Inside she shivered half in terror, half in delight. But when he gave her a smile of heartbreaking gravity, her heart skipped a beat.

Was he right? Should she just forget past disappointments and focus on the future? Once upon a time she would have given anything to marry Christian. Would she have cared if he only wanted her for the child she carried?

No.

She would have wanted her son to know his father and claim his birthright. Being afraid of getting hurt again was not a valid reason to keep Christian and Marc apart.

Noelle gathered a deep breath. "After dinner we should tell Marc you're his father. If we let this drag out much longer, he's going to be very confused that we didn't tell him sooner."

"I'd like that."

They completed the circuit of the battlements and headed back inside the castle to clean up before dinner. Marc was covered in dirt, but Noelle judged him too wound up to attempt a bath. Instead, she washed his hands and face and urged him into clean clothes before leaving him occupied with a game on her tablet so she could freshen up and change for dinner.

Noelle pulled out of her suitcase a simple black V-neck sheath made of rayon, with enough spandex to allow the material to mold to her modest curves. Diagonally placed black piping created interest on what could have been a forgettable dress. Over it she slipped a sheer black short-sleeve cropped jacket ornamented with clusters of downy black feathers. Peep-toe pumps completed the outfit. Noelle felt confident and sexy. Ready to match wits with Christian.

With her son racing down the corridor ahead of her, Noelle made her way back to the ground floor. Christian met her at the bottom of the stairs, looking dashing in a dark gray suit and a crisp white shirt. In a nod to country informality, he'd gone without a tie and left the top button of his shirt undone to expose the strong column of his throat.

Although she'd thought herself calm and sophisticated enough to take Christian to bed without succumbing to feverish, emotional drama, the man was so damned charismatic her heart fluttered wildly the instant their eyes met. Parts of her came to glorious life at his slow, deliberate grin. He would not let her withdraw her admission that she wanted them to make love. A heavy ache began low in her belly. She craved his hands on her. Judging from the heat blazing in his eyes, before the night was out he intended to make that happen.

But first, they had to get through a difficult conversation after dinner. Noelle knew by telling Marc the truth she was setting them on a path neither might be ready for. Never before had a meal dragged on the way dinner with Christian and Marc did. If Noelle's thoughts hadn't been in such turmoil, she might have been able to enjoy the excellent lamb chops and the decadent chocolate dessert. As it was, the food barely registered. She listened with half her attention to Christian's attempts to draw out Marc. He had regressed from his earlier friendliness on the battlements back to wariness.

After dinner Noelle guided her son into the salon where one of the maids had placed a pot of coffee. Christian's face showed none of the anxiety Noelle was feeling as she sat her son on the sofa before joining him on the soft cushions.

"Marc, I have something important to tell you about Prince Christian."

Her son squirmed as if fidgeting could somehow let him escape the sudden tension in the room. Noelle set her hand on his knees to stop him from kicking his feet against the sofa frame.

"What?" He slid down so his back was flat against the seat cushions and he was staring up at the coffered ceiling.

Noelle could tell she was losing her son and spoke

quickly. "I wanted to wait until you were old enough to understand."

As if paying no attention to her words, Marc let his body go limp and slid onto the floor. "Did you see that, Mama?"

"I did. Now please come sit on the sofa and listen to what I'm telling you." Her temper rarely flared with Marc, but the past ten days had left her emotions raw and her nerves frayed. She waited until Marc had flopped back into his original seat before setting her hands on his forearms and compelling him to look at her. "Prince Christian is your father."

"No." Marc shook his head hard enough to dislodge the controlled waves his mother had combed his hair into before dinner. "I don't have a father."

"You do. And he's Prince Christian."

Marc got to his knees and leaned close to whisper in her ear. "But I don't like him."

"Of course you do." She aimed a glance at Christian to see how he was reacting.

As if taking this as an invitation, he hunkered down beside his son and offered an engaging smile. Noelle's insides melted at his earnest warmth, but Marc wasn't swayed.

"I don't like him. I like Geoff."

"Just because you like Geoff doesn't mean you can't like your father, too."

"He's not my father. I don't know him."

"I'd like to change that," Christian said. "You and your mom can come stay at the palace, and we'll all get to know each other."

"I don't want to stay at the palace. I want to stay in my house." Marc's face grew red as his frustration grew. "Please, Mama. Can't we stay at our house?"

Noelle hated seeing her son upset and shook her head

at Christian. "It's a lot for him to absorb all at once. Why don't I take him up to bed? We can talk more tomorrow."

Christian ran his large hand over his son's dark hair, looking unsurprised but bleak when the boy flinched and pressed his face against his mother's chest.

"Of course." Christian got to his feet. "Given how we were doing earlier, I had hoped that would have gone better."

"As did I." Noelle dropped a kiss on Marc's head and stood. "Good night, Christian."

Heart heavy, she led her son upstairs to his bedroom where she urged him into his pajamas and found where the maid had put his favorite dragon when she'd unpacked his suitcase.

"Mama, you're not going to let Prince Christian make us live at the palace, are you?" Marc's plea carried less defiance than he'd shown downstairs.

"Not if you don't want to." She lifted the covers, indicated he should get into bed, and then fussed with the sheets and comforter while she sought for some way to convince her son it was all going to be okay. "But I think you might like the palace. You have grandparents, and an uncle and aunt and two cousins who will love spending time with you."

"I only want you and Nana."

What was really going on with Marc? He was usually excited to experience new things. He'd rushed into his first day of school without once glancing back at his mother. An extrovert like his father, he made friends easily.

"You know that Nana and I aren't going anywhere, right?"

Marc sat up and hugged his mother, his arms showing a desperate sort of strength. "Don't make me live with him."

"You don't like the prince?"

"He's okay." Marc sat back down and toyed with his dragon. "Do you like him?"

"Yes, of course." Noelle sensed there were more questions to come and wondered where her son's thoughts were taking him.

"Are you going to marry him?"

With all the time she and Geoff had spent together, Marc had not once asked her that question. Why did he think things were different between her and Christian? Had he overheard them talking, or was it just a logical progression because Christian was his father and in Marc's mind, parents were married?

"I don't know."

"Do you want to?"

Noelle chose her words carefully. "Not if you don't want me to."

Marc took a long time to think about his answer. At last he gave her a solemn nod. "I'll sleep on it." It's what his grandmother often said to him when he asked for something out of the ordinary.

Hiding a smile, Noelle leaned down and kissed her son on his brow. "I'll await your answer in the morning."

After reminding her son that she was right next door, Noelle departed Marc's room. She left the door cracked so the light from the hallway could flow across the soft carpet. They were in a strange place and occasionally he didn't sleep straight through until morning. She didn't want him to wake up to total darkness and get upset.

In her own room, she changed into her favorite ice-blue nightgown and picked up her sketchbook. Finding time to be creative these days was harder and harder as the practical needs of her growing business occupied her more every month. She had employees to supervise and financial data to keep track of. Fabric came in wrong or late. Equipment broke. Clients changed their minds. A hundred details demanded her attention every day.

With a weary sigh, she sat on the window seat that overlooked the inner courtyard and flipped to a blank sheet. For a long moment she stared at the empty page, her mind playing over the conversation she'd just had with her son.

Did she want to marry Christian? If she spoke with her heart, then the answer was a resounding yes. But she'd grown jaded in the past five years and more often chose to follow her head. It kept her from making mistakes and being hurt.

So if she was thinking and not feeling where Christian was concerned, why had she admitted to wanting to make love with him tonight? Heat flooded her core. She shifted on the comfortable cushion, but there was no escaping the pressure between her thighs. Her nightgown's cool silk caressed her flushed skin. Breath quickening, Noelle closed her eyes and let her thoughts drift from one erotic image to another.

A while later, Noelle glanced at the clock, surprised to see an hour had passed. She always lost track of time when Christian occupied her thoughts.

Noelle set aside her sketchbook. She pinned up her hair before slipping into the robe that matched her nightgown. She knew the way to Christian's room. He'd made certain of that when showing her which rooms she and Marc would use during the weekend. Feeling like the heroine in a gothic novel, Noelle moved swiftly along the forbidding stone corridors of the keep. Her light footsteps made little sound on the carpet, but to her sensitive ears, she could have been an entire marching band. By the time she reached Christian's door, her thudding heart and rapid breathing betrayed both nerves and excitement. She took a second to compose herself before knocking.

Wearing pajama bottoms and a scowl, Christian threw open the door as if he intended to shout at whoever had interrupted him. In an instant his annoyance vanished. "Noelle?"

"I'm sorry how Marc took the news that you're his father."

Christian's gaze flicked over her precarious updo, silk robe and bare feet. "You came here dressed like that to talk about Marc?"

"No." She put her hand on his bare chest, savoring the warmth and power of him for a split second before pushing forward. "I just thought it sounded like a more civilized opening than *I want you naked and inside of me before either of us knows what hit us.*"

Taking two steps backward, he gave way before her determined advance. Then his long fingers snagged in the belt that held her robe closed and he tugged her hard against him. She reveled in his passion, anticipation searing along her nerve endings. But as his lips neared hers, she turned her head aside. His breath stroked along her cheek.

"First we need a few ground rules," she murmured, fighting to keep her voice even as his fingers slipped her belt free and parted the robe.

"Ground rules?"

His hot breath against her ear made her shiver.

"This is about sex and nothing more. It doesn't mean I've changed my mind about doing what's best for my son, and it's not a promise that anything will happen between us in the future."

"You're pretty bossy for a half-naked woman."

Her robe fell to the ground, and Noelle gulped as his palms grazed over her silk-clad hips and up her spine. "Just sex," she repeated, her voice a hoarse rasp.

"So this is okay?" He cupped her breast, fingers playing over her rapidly hardening nipple while he watched her expression from beneath thick black lashes.

"Yes."

"And this?" His free hand dislodged the pins in her hair. He sank his fingers into the thick mass that fell around her shoulders and tugged to drag her head back and expose her throat.

Noelle forgot to breathe as he placed his mouth over the pulse in her neck and sucked. Her heartbeat shifted into an erratic rhythm. "Sure."

"So this isn't off-limits?" Moving with slow tormenting precision, his hand left her breast and glided down over her belly to cup her, the heel of his hand applying the perfect pressure to weaken her knees.

"Yes." She barely got the single syllable out before he began pulling his hand away. Frantic, she grasped his wrist and held him in place.

"But you said…"

"I meant no."

"Ah." The word sighed out of him. "I'm going to take you to bed now."

"Lovely."

She was off her feet an instant later.

Eight

Christian lowered Noelle onto the bed and stepped back to regard her. He'd seen her naked before. Made love to her too many times to count. But for some reason, every time held a special fascination for him. Bracing his hand on the mattress beside her, he trailed his fingers along her skin at the edge of the nightgown. When he reached one of the thin straps that held the gown up, he nudged it off her shoulder.

There was curiosity, not wariness, in Noelle's eyes as she watched him. Uneasiness tangled with desire in his gut. Did she have any idea how the glimpse of one pink nipple peeking above the neckline of her nightgown made him crazy? Her power over him was complete. He would do whatever she asked, give himself over to her pleasure and wait to take his own until she was thoroughly spent.

His erection pulsed as she slid the straps down her arms, taking the bodice with it. As if understanding his weakness, she shimmied the blue silk over her hips and kicked it off. Naked, she lay before him, her gaze confident and direct as she waited for his next move.

"Gorgeous." He ran shaking hands through his hair, savoring the moment. He'd waited five long years to make love to her again, and he'd be damned if he'd rush. "I've missed you."

She sat up and hooked her fingers in the waistband of his pajamas. "Then what's taking you so long to get started?"

The cool air against his naked flesh did little to reduce the heat pulsing through him. He stepped out of his pajama bottoms and caught Noelle's wrists before her fingers could close around him. Putting her hands around his neck where they'd be safely out of the way, he leaned down to take her lips in an explosive kiss.

Together they fell to the mattress. He lay on his back with her draped over him. His hands were free to roam her body at will. Skin like the smoothest satin slipped against his fingertips. Her body was perfect, not because she didn't have flaws but because he never viewed her with a critical eye. Long lean lines of sleek muscle balanced with graceful curves and small, round breasts. Too short to walk a runway, she was his ideal height. In heels, her forehead reached no higher than his lips.

He was kissing her when the need to have her beneath him struck. She gripped his hair as they rolled, laughing until he nipped at her exposed throat. Her back arched as he moved lower and pulled one hard nipple into his mouth.

"Christian." She panted his name as his fingers began their slow descent to the heat between her thighs.

"Yes, Noelle?"

Blood rushed to his groin as he found her wet and ready. Trembling at the effort of keeping his pace easy and unhurried, he slipped a finger around the knot of nerves and felt her shudder.

"Torture," she murmured, but the smile playing at the corners of her mouth told him she didn't mind.

He kissed his way toward her second breast, determined to give it equal and fair treatment. "You sound agitated. Do you wish me to stop?"

"No." She shook her head and lifted her hips as he trailed his fingers down the inside of her thigh to her knee. "I want more."

"More of this?" He swirled his tongue around her nipple and felt her fingers tighten in his hair. "Or…?"

Her head thrashed from side to side as he traced the seam between her thighs. Delighted to see he had her full attention, he slipped one, then two fingers inside her, touching the sensitive spot the way he knew she loved and watching her muscles tense with pleasure. Within seconds she came apart beneath his hands. He savored her every cry and quake, and was a little shocked at the speed and intensity of her orgasm.

As she lay with her eyes closed, her chest heaving with each uneven breath, he reached into his nightstand and pulled out a condom. When he turned back to her, he found her up on one elbow, watching him with glowing eyes. Her pale skin wore the rosy flush of climax, and she looked ready and eager for round two.

Happy to oblige her, Christian slid on the condom and leaned down to snag her gaze with his. "This time we'll come together," he promised and at her nod, positioned himself between her thighs.

Still not fully recovered from one orgasm, but eager to have Christian inside her, Noelle opened for him and felt him nudge against her. Anticipation tightened her nerves to bowstrings, and she told herself to let go. Instead, her body tensed still more. Panic grew as a myriad of half-hysterical what ifs bombarded her mind.

"Easy." Christian's soothing tone lessened her anxiety. "There's no rush."

That's where he was wrong. She needed the rush of passion to keep her brain disengaged. Thinking about what she was doing led to her questioning the wisdom of coming here tonight.

"I'm sorry. It's just…"

While Christian hadn't been her first lover, he'd been her last. For five years she'd concentrated on her son and her career, putting her personal life on ice.

Christian backed off and peered down at her. "Relax. It's fine." He caressed her disheveled hair back from her cheeks with gentle strokes of his fingers. "Talk to me."

"It's been awhile." The flush in her cheeks stopped being about passion and became embarrassment.

Wonder softened the aristocratic planes of his face. He cupped her face with his hands and forced her to meet his gaze. "Then we'll take it very slow."

His lips trailed over her cheek and found a corner of her mouth. She tipped her head to kiss him, but he'd already moved to nuzzle against the sensitive skin beneath her jawline. She closed her eyes and shifted position to offer him better access, shivering as the faintest brush of his lips tickled her skin.

"Touch me," he murmured. "You know what I like."

His words made her smile. She did indeed. She'd clutched his biceps when he'd moved between her thighs, but now, with his encouragement, she let her hands roam. Down his sides, across his tight abs. Her fingertips rode the ridges and valleys of his superb muscles. So much leashed power all hers.

He kissed her then, his lips moving over hers with mastery and controlled passion. He was letting her set the pace. Granting her the time to adjust to being loved by his hands and mouth. Almost immediately her body quickened. Uncertainty fell away. She wrapped her arms around his shoulders and tilted her hips to find his erection waiting for her.

"You know what I need," she whispered, rocking against him, feeling him slide through her slick folds and probe her entrance.

"Are you sure you're okay?"

"Never better."

He rocked forward, easing his way into her with smooth, gradually deepening thrusts. While her mind had blocked all awareness of her arousal, her body had its own agenda. She expanded to welcome Christian's possession and cried out in pleasure as he seated himself fully inside her. With barely a pause, he withdrew, and together they found a familiar rhythm.

How had she forgotten how perfectly they fit together? Bodies attuned, hands knowing exactly how and where to touch—their movements were so perfectly choreographed they could've made love the night before.

Christian's steady thrusts intensified the pleasure building in her body in the same way his rough, unsteady breathing and whispered words of encouragement and praise made her heart sing. Once again Noelle's climax claimed her fast and hard. As aware of her body's reactions as he was of his own, Christian timed his own orgasm so perfectly that they came at nearly the same moment.

In the aftermath, Noelle lay panting and dazed beneath Christian's weight, glad she'd been rational enough to be able to forget this bliss these past five years. Only by focusing on what had been bad about their relationship rather than recalling the good had she learned to live without him. And now he was back. And so were her memories of how amazing his lovemaking had been.

As soon as Christian shifted to lie beside her, Noelle scooted off the bed and made a beeline for her nightgown and robe. She was almost to the door before Christian spoke.

"You're leaving?" He'd levered himself onto his elbows and stared at her in blank shock.

"I think it's best."

"But we haven't talked." He frowned. "And you used to like to snuggle after we made love." He sounded so put out that she had a hard time repressing a smile.

She reached behind her for the door handle. "Yes, well, I don't want to give you the wrong impression."

That brought him to a sitting position. Looking adorable with his hair mussed and his strong, broad shoulders slumped, he asked, "What sort of wrong impression?"

"Sex with you I can handle," she explained, echoing what he'd once said to her. "But I can't do intimacy."

Then before he could rise from the bed to challenge her bold declaration, she slipped out of the room.

Shortly after dawn the next morning, Noelle woke facedown in her own bed, and her first emotion was relief. She stretched her arms and legs, luxuriating in the cool sheets and the unfettered peace of early morning. As amazing as the previous night with Christian had been, she wasn't prepared to dive back into the intimacy of sleeping in his arms and being roused by his morning erection and sensual kisses.

Her skin prickled at the thought, and she smiled in memory of his shocked and worried expression when she'd blithely slipped out of bed after what had been the best sex of her life. If he'd had any clue how shaky her legs had been, he might not have let her go without an encore. Instead, exhausted by her long and stress-filled work week and abundance of exercise both on the battlements yesterday afternoon and in Christian's bed last night, she'd enjoyed a blissful six-and-a-half hours of deep, restful sleep.

She'd barely finished heaving a deep, contented sigh when her bedroom door opened and the slap of four-year-old feet sped across the tile floor. A second later a small body landed on the mattress beside her, and Noelle rolled over to scoop her son into a snug embrace.

"Morning, dumpling," she cooed in his ear, savoring the squeeze of his strong arms around her neck. "Did you sleep well?"

"I dreamed I was a dragon who ate everyone in this castle."

"Even me?" She prodded him in the ribs and tickled him.

Marc writhed and giggled. When she let him gather a breath, he said, "No, Mama. I wouldn't eat you." He gave her a smug grin. "But I ate Prince Christian."

"Your father," she corrected, forcing a light note into her voice. "I don't know that it's polite to eat one of your parents."

"It's okay, Mama. He didn't mind."

Noelle decided not to belabor the point. "Are you hungry? What do you think they'll have for breakfast?"

"Waffles?" Marc asked, his eyes round with hope.

"I don't think they'll have those."

"I can make a special request to the cook," said a deep voice from the direction of the hall. Christian stood framed in the open doorway Marc had come through only moments before. "I'm sure she would be happy to whip up a batch."

Christian looked so handsome in khaki pants and a crisp white shirt with sleeves rolled up to expose his strong forearms. His unexpected appearance when her defenses were down sent her emotions flipping end over end. Somehow she managed a friendly smile. If she'd thought sex with Christian would simplify her feelings for the man, she was a fool.

"We wouldn't want her to go to any trouble."

"I'm sure she wouldn't mind." Christian surveyed her disheveled hair and bare shoulders and she blushed.

"Waffles." Marc crowed the word happily and tried tugging her off the bed. "Get up, Mama. I'm hungry."

"I'll go and arrange it. How long will it take you and Marc to get ready?"

"Half an hour?"

"Are you sure that's enough time?" Christian gave her a slow, complex smile that would take her hours to unravel. "I don't want you to feel rushed."

"It's fine."

With Christian lingering half in and half out of her room, Noelle wasn't inclined to ditch the covers and let him drink his fill of her in the clingy silk nightgown. That he'd seen it last night and much more besides didn't mean she wanted to parade before him in the light of day.

"Marc, why don't you go to your room and get dressed?" she said. "I put out your clothes last night. Don't forget to brush your teeth."

Her son scampered to do as she asked, but although Christian stepped aside to let him past, he showed no interest in withdrawing. In fact, he took a single step into the room. Having a man in her bedroom wasn't something Noelle was used to. Back when she and Christian had been lovers, she'd grown comfortable with being nude around him. But since Marc had come along, she'd fallen into the habit of conservative modesty. The only time she left her bedroom wearing just her nightclothes was in the middle of the night when Marc was a baby or if he had an infrequent nightmare.

"Shouldn't you be getting up, too?" Christian asked.

Noelle bit back a tart retort and slid out of bed. As the cool morning air found her bare skin, she shivered and reached for the silk robe that matched her nightgown. She moved with more haste than grace as she slipped her arms into the sleeves. Last night's confident vixen had been an illusion of shadow and lamplight.

"Don't you need to check with your cook about Marc's waffles?" She wanted him to go and take his penetrating gaze with him. The longer he stared at her, the more her poise suffered.

"As soon as you come here and give me a kiss."

She wrinkled her nose at him. "I haven't brushed my teeth, and I'm far from presentable."

"Do you think I care?" His velvet voice bore a trace of steel. "Come here."

Her muscles moved of their own accord, setting her on a direct path into his waiting arms. As she crossed to him, the glow of his smile thawed her chilled limbs. A second later, his warm hands slipped around her waist and the ardent pressure of his fingers pulled her snug against his unyielding torso. Abruptly impatient, she lifted up on her toes to bring her lips into contact with his sooner.

The kiss was hot and fast. Electricity arched between them, the voltage off the scale. Noelle's body came to instant life, and she moaned beneath Christian's mouth.

Almost as fast as she'd ridden desire upward, she was crashing back to earth. She couldn't let Marc see her and Christian locked in a passionate embrace, so she broke off the kiss and pushed her palms against the unyielding granite of his shoulders.

"Marc mustn't…" She sucked in much-needed air to clear her head.

"Damn." Christian stepped back. Chest heaving, he blinked several times before he managed to focus his gaze on her. "Noelle…"

She had no idea what he intended to say. Nor apparently did he because he merely stared at her for a long, silent moment and then shook his head as if to clear it.

"You said something about checking on breakfast," she prompted, overjoyed to see that the kiss had rattled him. Before last night he'd always been the one in control. His masterful seduction had swept her along. Past comfort zones and pride, reducing her every defense to ashes while he kept his thoughts private. "Waffles?"

"Waffles." With a brief nod he turned away, but before he left he spoke over his shoulder. "Take your time. I'll send one of the maids to check on Marc." And then he was off, striding down the hallway.

Noelle leaned against the heavy wood door, taking stock of the graceless lethargy in her limbs and the fanciful fluttering of her heart. She touched the tip of her tongue to her lips, noting they were still tender from last night's fervent kisses.

She closed her bedroom door and headed for the bathroom, determined to enjoy a long hot shower. Catching sight of her reflection, she noticed the invigorating start to her morning had put a smile on her face. The urge to hum surprised her, and she pushed aside the rational side of her brain that wanted to squash all her reckless joy. Monday morning would be soon enough for her return to cold reality. Until then she intended to see where this new beginning with Christian would take them.

* * *

Christian was still cursing his lack of control around Noelle as he reached the ground floor. As if summoned by his thoughts, Mrs. Francas popped into his line of sight and he stopped short.

"Is it possible for waffles to be served for breakfast?"

"Cook has a new recipe she will be happy to show off."

"And could you send one of the maids to check on Marc? I told Noelle we would take care of him this morning."

"Of course. I will send Elise." Mrs. Francas bowed. "There's coffee and this week's paper waiting for you in the salon."

"Thank you."

After his sleepless night, Christian was ready to consume an entire pot of the strong black stuff his cook brewed. The local paper awaited him beside the silver coffee service. When he came to Bracci Castle, he enjoyed immersing himself in the country life and unplugging from the world at large. Some trips he was more successful than others. Multimillion-dollar business deals rarely went smoothly. This weekend, however, he'd warned his assistant not to bother him with anything short of total bankruptcy.

He needed his complete focus on winning over Marc and demonstrating to Noelle that he was ready to be a father and a husband. Yesterday had been an emotional roller coaster for him. For a while during the afternoon, when Marc had abandoned his antagonism, Christian thought his troubles were over. He should have known it wouldn't be so easy. The boy was an Alessandro, after all. Maybe not in name, but certainly in personality and stubbornness.

Christian was on the sofa with a cup of coffee at his elbow, deep into an article about a northern Tuscany mudslide that swept away a house, injuring several people, when he heard a pair of voices coming down the stairs toward the salon. His composure took a hit as excitement and anxiety built. This weekend was a significant step toward the rest of his life. What happened here not only determined the future of his country's stability, but also any hope that Christian might have for happiness.

He pushed aside the thought that he didn't deserve Noelle or the joy she brought to his life. He'd lost her once because of his selfish stupidity. Screwing up a second time was not an option.

Christian was on his feet and moving to the stairs as his energetic son brushed past him in a mad dash to get to the dining room and the promised waffles. Chuckling, Christian held his hand out to Noelle as she completed her descent. His pulse bucked as she placed her elegant fingers against his palm and he found his lips curving into a foolish grin.

"Good morning," he said, his voice low and intimate. "You look beautiful."

Today's dress was a half sleeve, French blue sheath, paired with a whimsical pendant necklace. She'd donned flats instead of her usual pumps, which reminded Christian of her petite stature and inspired his protective instincts. Not that she needed his help. Her brown eyes sparkled with confidence above her cheerful smile.

"Thank you." To his surprise, she linked her arm with his as they headed out of the salon. "It was nice of you to send Elise to watch Marc. I was able to shower and dress without any interruption."

She gave a heartfelt sigh that made him long to pull her into a quiet corner and sink his fingers into the dark, wavy hair cascading over her shoulders. The lingering aftermath of the morning's fiery kiss continued to pulse through his veins like a potent cocktail consumed too quickly.

"You're welcome." Despite three cups of strong coffee, he felt sluggish and tongue-tied with her body pressed along his side.

"Will we be going to your winery today? I'm looking forward to seeing where Sherdana's finest vintages are made."

"I've arranged a tour and lunch with pairings of our best wines. Bracci Vineyards and Winery employs a world-class chef, and he's promised to amaze us with his cuisine."

"That sounds wonderful, but what about Marc?"

"My winemaker has several children near Marc's age who are eager to meet him. I assure you he will not be bored."

"Sounds like you have it all figured out."

Christian smiled at her, wishing that was true. His heart and mind were on the same page. He wanted to marry Noelle and make Marc his legitimate son, but instinct told him what might happen for appearance's sake wouldn't bring him the fulfillment he craved. There were those in-between moments when she didn't notice his attention, her smile faded and the sparkle left her eyes. She was putting on a good show for both Marc and him, but Christian sensed she had doubts.

After breakfast Christian spent an hour throwing a ball with Marc in the outer courtyard while Noelle looked on. The boy was crazy about American baseball and had brought a ball and his mitt with him. Christian didn't spend a lot of time in the US, but had several business colleagues he spoke to regularly who had introduced him to the sport. Given his son's fascination with the game, Christian decided he'd better get up to speed quickly.

On the five-mile drive to the winery, Marc rattled on about fastballs and curveballs from the backseat of the blue convertible Maserati Christian kept at the castle. Since the autumn day was sunny and mild, he drove with the top down, his attention split between the empty country road and Noelle's flawless profile as she lifted her face to the sun.

"What a glorious day," she said, stretching her arm across the seat to rake her nails through his hair. "Did you plan this, too?"

Something about her tone made him think she was mocking him. "I ordered it specially for you." He dropped a kiss in her palm. "I only want the best for you."

She withdrew her hand and made a fist as if to capture his kiss. "It's nice to hear."

"You don't believe me." It wasn't a question, but an accusation.

From the backseat, Marc interjected his own question. "When we get there, will I get to stomp grapes?"

Christian's mood brightened at yet another chance to curry favor with his son. "Sure." Although the grape harvest wasn't set to happen for another week, there would likely be a way to pick a few grapes and let Marc and the other kids participate in the ritual.

"No." Noelle shook her head, adamantly opposed.

"Mama, please."

"I think your mother is worried that it will stain your feet purple."

"Will it? That's great."

He shot Noelle a triumphant look, not the least bit daunted by her scowl. Christian intended to do whatever it took to win his son's love. Even if it meant siding with him against his mother from time to time."

"Christian, I don't think that's a great idea."

"It'll be fun. Something he can show off at school and make the other kids jealous."

"Wine-colored feet?" She shook her head in a maternal show of disgust. "Okay, you can stomp grapes."

While Marc whooped in the backseat, Christian reached over and squeezed Noelle's hand in thanks. Her lips softened into a smile at the gesture, and she put her hand atop his.

The car rolled down a long driveway flanked by fields of grapevines and came to rest near the low building that housed the tasting room and an intimate space available for private parties and lunches such as the one Christian had planned today with Noelle.

Almost before Christian turned off the engine, Marc had unbuckled his seat belt and was keyed for the instant his mother opened the passenger door and tipped her seat forward. He wiggled through the door and was off across the lawn in a flash, heading for the tasting-room door. Noelle called after him, but Marc was too excited to slow down. By the time she and Christian reached the building, Marc had disappeared inside.

"I love his enthusiasm," Christian commented as he held the door open for Noelle. "Everything is an adventure. You've done a good job raising him."

"Thank you, but the job's not over yet." She paused in the doorway and touched Christian's arm. "I know I haven't done much to improve your relationship with Marc, but I want you to know that watching you with him this weekend has made me realize how important it is that you two bond." She paused. "No matter what happens between us, I want you and Marc to have as much time together as possible."

"I appreciate that." While he was grateful for her approval, he was less than pleased that she continued to doubt whether they had a future as a family.

"Mama, is this where I get to stomp grapes?" Marc tugged at her hand. "Can I do it now?"

Christian chuckled. "Let me talk to Louis and get it all set up," he told his impatient son. "Why don't you see if Daphne has some fresh grape juice for you to try." He indicated a pretty blonde girl behind the bar. While Marc raced toward the bar and climbed up onto the tall stool, Christian turned to Noelle. "Give me a couple minutes to get Marc settled. Then we can go on our tour."

Nine

Noelle waited until Christian disappeared through a door in the back of the tasting room before joining her son. Even without a single sip of wine, she was suffering the effects of intoxication. Not that she could be blamed for feeling giddy and light-headed when Christian turned on the charm. The man had convinced her to let her son stomp grapes. Noelle shook her head, contemplating the reactions of Marc's teachers and his classmates' parents after he broadcast his weekend's activities at school. No doubt she would have some explaining to do.

But to see her son so happy was worth it. Noelle sighed. Watching Marc's wariness toward his father fade made her question her decision to not tell Christian that she was pregnant. At the time she'd been afraid he'd reject her again. No. That wasn't the whole truth. She'd also been angry.

She was still angry.

Last night she hadn't gone to Christian's room motivated solely by desire. She'd had something to prove to herself and to him. She needed to prove that she could surrender her body to the passion he aroused without giving over her heart at the same time. Leaving as abruptly as she had was meant to demonstrate that this time around she wasn't going to lead with her heart but her head. The woman she was today never would have taken the little Christian had offered her five years earlier.

But she would never be truly happy keeping her emotions bottled up, either. There had to be a happy medium between giving too much and not giving enough.

At Marc's insistence, she sat beside him and tasted his grape juice, pronouncing it delicious. He gave her a huge grin and then went back to telling Daphne all about the armor he'd seen at Bracci Castle. Noelle ran her fingers through his thick, dark hair and considered how many times a day he reminded her of Christian.

As if summoned by her thoughts, he appeared at her side. "Ready for the tour? Louis's son is going to take Marc to where the other children are. They'll play for a while and have lunch. Afterward Louis is going to set up the grape-stomp contest to see who is the best stomper."

"Me!" Marc exclaimed, jumping down from his stool, fists in the air.

Noelle laughed at his enthusiasm. "Well, you certainly have the energy for it." She ruffled his hair and watched him run toward a tall boy who was gesturing for him to follow.

Half an hour later, she and Christian came to the end of the tour, and Noelle was eager to sample some of the wines she'd learned about. "I'll never take wine for granted ever again," she promised Christian before thanking their guide, Bracci Vineyard and Winery's exceptional wine-maker, Louis Beauchon.

"I'm glad to hear it." Louis was a handsome man in his early forties with prematurely gray hair and striking blue eyes. He had a ready smile and an abundance of hilarious stories about people he'd worked with during his twenty-five years of winemaking. "You'll have to let me know what you think of our wines after lunch."

"I'm afraid my palate is nowhere near as experienced as Prince Christian's, but I look forward to sharing my impressions."

"That's all I need. I'll see you later at the grape stomp."

Christian steered her along a curving path that wound through the garden at the back of the tasting room and through a set of French doors that led into an intimate dining room. At the center of the space was a single table set for two and covered with a white tablecloth and fine china. Two servers, dressed in black and white, stood to one side of the room, welcoming smiles on their faces.

Once Christian had assisted her into her seat and joined her at the table, the servers stepped forward and poured the first wine. Noelle lost herself in Christian's deep voice as he described the wine being served and commented on the meal to come. One course followed another, each being served with a different wine. Despite the small portions, Noelle was beginning to feel overcome by all the rich, flavorful dishes by the time dessert arrived.

"Chef Cheval is a genius, but I don't think I could eat another bite," she protested, as a delicate chocolate basket filled with white chocolate mousse and a single raspberry was placed before her. As with each course, the gorgeous plating made the food irresistible. How could she resist dessert? "Maybe just a bite."

Noelle didn't notice Christian's intense regard until

she'd scraped the plate clean and set her spoon aside. She cocked her head at him but had no opportunity to ask why he was staring. A short, round man in chef's whites entered the room, his toque set at a jaunty angle.

"Prince Christian!" the man exclaimed in a deep baritone. "How wonderful to have you back."

"Chef Cheval." Christian gestured in Noelle's direction. "This is Noelle Dubone."

"Chef, this was the most amazing meal I've ever had. Thank you."

The chef bowed to her. "I'm so glad you enjoyed it. Prince Christian said I must prepare only the best for you."

"He did?" She shot Christian a wry look, wondering how many other women had been given such royal treatment. "Well, you've both made my visit to Bracci memorable."

"You will come back? I appreciate a woman who likes to eat."

Noelle laughed. "Of course," she said, growing more and more accustomed to the idea of becoming a permanent fixture in Christian's life. "I appreciate a man who cooks with your flair."

"Well, good." The chef gave Christian an audacious wink before taking his leave.

The servers cleared the dessert plates and topped off both water and wineglasses before taking their leave. Noelle swirled her wine, soothed by the excellent food, the early fall scents and the distant sound of children at play. Relaxed to the point of sleepiness, she wondered if there might be time for a nap when they returned to Christian's castle.

"Did you mean what you said about coming back?" Christian's abrupt question cut through her lethargy.

"I did." She stumbled a little over the words, wondering why he'd grown so serious. "Why?"

"I didn't want to pressure you this weekend by talking about the future, but after last night, I think I have a right to ask about your intentions."

"My intentions?" Noelle wondered when the world had turned upside down. "Since when does a man ask a woman about her intentions regarding their relationship?"

"Since the man has stated his desire to marry the woman, and she comes to his room with seduction on her mind and leaves the man feeling as if he's been nothing more than her plaything."

Noelle pressed her lips together to hide a smile, but couldn't stop her eyes from dancing. Christian growled at her in mock severity.

She replied with an equally insincere apology. "I didn't mean to take you or your body for granted. As for my intentions, I plan to continue as I did last evening, exploring our mutual chemistry and seeing where things lead."

To her surprise Christian sat back and crossed his arms over his chest. "Not good enough."

"No?"

"I'm serious about you. This isn't going to be a casual affair where we play it by ear or take it one day at a time."

"Because your family is pressuring you to marry and produce an heir who can rule one day." Noelle tensed at the unwelcome reminder of why she and Marc were here this weekend. "I'm not going to decide the rest of my life or Marc's in a few short days no matter how wonderful they've been. I need time to decide what's right for him."

"And you're not yet sure I am?"

"It's not about you. It's the responsibility he'll face one day. You once told me how Gabriel changed when he realized he was destined to be king. I don't know if I want that for Marc."

Christian reached across the table and took her hand in his. "With my father in perfect health and Gabriel so young, Marc will be more than ready when the time comes for him to rule."

While Noelle appreciated Christian's logic, she wasn't ready to lose her baby to the country of Sherdana. "I just wish he was old enough to help me with this decision."

"Mama." Marc skidded through the doorway, flushed and disheveled. "We're going to stomp grapes. Come on." Without waiting for her, he ran back out of the room.

Laughing, she got to her feet. "You heard your son," she said, tugging on Christian's hand. "Let's go."

"He certainly has the imperious demeanor of a future monarch." Grinning, Christian threw his napkin onto the table and stood.

"Don't you mean tyrant?"

"He must get his bossy nature from his mother." Christian's arm snaked around her waist before she reached the French doors. "I find that an unexpected turn on."

He spun her into his arms and captured her lips in a sizzling kiss. Noelle sagged against him, admiring his knack for turning a lighthearted jab into a sincere compliment. Even knowing they could be caught at any second, Noelle darted out her tongue to taste the smooth chocolate and heady wine lingering on Christian's lips. His fingers tightened almost painfully against her ribs before he pushed her to arm's length.

"You are bad for my willpower," he told her, his voice a husky rasp. "First this morning and now..."

"Mama, are you coming?" Marc's plaintive wail came from across the yard.

Noelle gathered a shaky breath. "If we hold up the grape stomp much longer, my son will never forgive me."

Hand in hand they walked around the corner of the building where the bulk of the wine process happened and came upon a gathering of children and workers. Although the official start to the harvest was a week away, enough grapes had been gathered to fill three half wine barrels for the children to stomp.

In addition to Marc, Louis's youngest son and the vineyard manager's daughter were barefoot and ready to begin. The half casks had been set on a platform. Below each stomping container sat collecting jars for the juice. The children would pulverize the grapes with their feet, and the first one to produce the required amount of liquid would win. Seeing her son's grim determination, she knew Marc would give it his all.

"He has my competitive spirit," Christian murmured near her ear a second before Louis's wife signaled the start of the contest.

Noelle relaxed against the arm Christian slipped around her waist, enjoying his solidness against her back. "Yes. Some days that gets to be a problem."

Despite her words, she rooted for her son. Not that Marc needed the encouragement. Displaying the abundant energy that exhausted both Noelle and her mother on a daily basis, he ran in place, his concentration riveted on the grapes beneath his feet. Watching him, Noelle realized that while he was her baby and she wanted to protect him from harm, Marc was more resilient than she gave him credit for. He wouldn't suffer beneath the extreme media attention on the horizon. Nor would he be pushed into uncomfortable circumstances by Christian's family. There was too much of his father in him for him to take on the weight of rule until he was damn good and ready. And she hoped he had enough of her common sense to know when that moment was.

Beside her, Christian cheered as Marc was the first to accumulate the requisite amount of juice. After planting a firm, enthusiastic kiss on her cheek, Christian strode to the platform and swung his triumphant son out of the half cask. Noelle winced as vivid purple juice dripped from her son's feet and stained Christian's khaki pants. Heedless of the damage to his clothes, Christian set Marc on his hip and each threw a celebratory fist in the air.

Noelle felt the tiniest prick of sadness. Where once she'd been everything to Marc, she recognized that his father would soon be occupying more and more of his attention. Noelle couldn't help the panic that welled up. She'd built such a comfortable, safe life for herself and Marc, but so many changes were looming on the horizon.

Louis's wife came to her side. "Try lemon juice to get the grape stains off his feet."

"That works?"

The woman grinned. "It will help."

While Noelle chatted with Louis's wife, Christian cleaned off Marc's feet and wrangled him back into his socks and shoes. Hand in hand they then walked in her direction.

"Did you see how good I stomped, Mama?" Marc ran in place, demonstrating his winning technique. He gripped a bottle of sparkling grape juice, his prize for winning.

"I did." She noticed Marc hadn't released Christian's hand. Her chest tightened, but she offered her son a proud smile. "You are the best grape stomper in all Sherdana."

"He certainly is," Christian said, his gaze fond as it rested on Marc. "Are you ready to head back to the castle?"

"I think I've had enough excitement for one day. And someone needs a bath." She gazed pointedly at her son's feet.

"No, Mama. I want to show everyone at school that I stomped grapes."

"You can tell them about it," Noelle countered.

To her surprise, Marc didn't argue further. Instead, he waved goodbye to his new friends and trotted ahead of his parents to the lot where Christian's car waited.

On the way back to Bracci Castle, Marc's excited chatter gave way to silence.

Christian glanced over his shoulder. "He's out."

"Not surprising." Noelle felt a yawn coming on. The slow country pace combined with the delicious, filling lunch was making her sleepy. "I guess his bath will have to wait until later."

"I could use a nap myself," Christian said. "I didn't get a lot of sleep last night."

Noelle ignored the pointed look he shot her way. "That's odd. You were in bed by eleven."

"Yes, but I had a very eventful evening and couldn't figure out why it came to such an abrupt end."

"Perhaps because it wouldn't do for the eventfulness to become common knowledge."

"Why not when it's only a matter of time before we make our relationship official?"

"You seem very sure that's how things will go."

"I'm not so much confident as determined. Now that Marc is getting more accustomed to me, I expect to spend a lot more time with him. Which means you'll also be seeing more of me. You can't resist me forever."

Noelle sighed. Truth was, she couldn't resist him at all.

Christian slid into a charcoal-gray suit coat and straightened his blue-gray tie. The full-length mirror in his Carone apartment dressing room reflected back a somber aristocrat with chiseled features and wary eyes. It was not the face of a man about to propose to the mother of his son.

Since returning from the weekend at Bracci Castle five days ago, Christian had spent every evening with Noelle and Marc. They'd dined at her farmhouse, the palace and the restaurant that served American burgers. Tonight, however, he'd arranged for a private yacht to take Noelle and him on a romantic cruise down the river. During dinner, he planned to officially ask her to be his wife. On his nightstand sat the five-carat princess-cut diamond she would be wearing three hours from now.

As his driver wove through Carone's streets on the way out of the city, Christian reflected that he wasn't giving Noelle the time she'd asked for to decide if this was the right future for her and Marc. Last weekend it had been easy to promise her space. They'd reconnected both physically and emotionally. But these past five days had been hell.

He wanted to wake up with Noelle and have breakfast with Marc. To throw the ball with his son in the evenings and read him a bedtime story before taking Noelle in his arms and spending the night making love to her. A chaste good-night kiss at eight o'clock was completely unsatisfying.

When the car stopped in Noelle's driveway, Christian didn't wait for the driver to open his door. He was impatient to see Noelle and get their evening started. Before he could knock, Noelle's front door whipped open and Marc grinned at him from the foyer.

"Mama," he called, whirling on stocking feet and racing back into the house. "Prince Papa is here."

The blending of his two titles continued to amuse Christian. He suspected that the "prince" half would eventually go away. Until then, he was satisfied that his son had accepted Christian's role in his life.

"Marc, I'm right here," his mother admonished as she emerged from the main living room. "There's no reason to shout."

Christian stepped into the house and shut the door behind him. Word was out that he and Noelle had been spending time together, and he didn't want any telescopic lenses capturing the kiss he was about to give her.

Tonight's dress was a retro-style teal silk with a matching long-sleeve coat. The hemline was a bit shorter than usual and displayed a tantalizing amount of shapely leg. She wore her hair in an elegant topknot that he couldn't wait to dishevel. Simple pearls adorned her delicate earlobes, and a matching strand encircled her neck. She gave him a welcoming smile, and he stepped forward to draw her firmly into his embrace.

The warm feminine scent of her made his head spin as he claimed her mouth in a tender, poignant kiss. He kept a ruthless hold on his libido. This was not the time nor the place to show her how five days of abstinence had driven him mad with longing. They had all evening and much of the night for him to demonstrate how fully beneath her spell he'd fallen.

"Shall we go?" he purred beside her ear, feeling the shiver that passed through her muscles. "I have a full night planned."

She pulled back and regarded him with alarm. "I can't stay out all night. Marc gets up early and will expect me to be here."

"I will have you back before the roosters start to crow." For most people this would only be a saying, but in fact Noelle kept several chickens on her acre of land, and Marc had mentioned the rooster's predawn bugling several times.

"Thank you."

Christian held her hand as the town car wove through Carone to where the yacht was moored. Earlier that day, he'd prepared a speech. It ran through his mind like a hamster on a wheel and he found himself oddly tongue-tied. Thankfully, Noelle had never been bothered by silence between them, but tonight her tranquil acceptance offered him no solace.

After boarding the yacht, Christian led her to the salon. The September warm spell would enable them to enjoy a romantic dinner on deck where they could observe the lights of the city reflecting off the water as dusk became night. But that would come later. He had something he needed to get out of the way first.

A bottle of champagne was chilling in a silver bucket on the bar. Two tall flutes stood beside it, waiting to be filled. Christian had asked for privacy during this cruise except while dinner was being served. He wanted no audience this evening. Since the champagne had been opened, all Christian had to do was pour the sparkling liquid and hand Noelle a glass. He was happy to see that his hands didn't shake as he clinked his flute with hers.

"To us." He felt rather than heard his voice break awkwardly and swallowed far too much of the fizzy wine. The bubbles burned as they went down, and he coughed.

Noelle peered at him over her flute and cleared her own throat. "I think we should get married."

A racing speedboat passed recklessly close to the yacht, almost drowning out her words. Wondering if he'd heard her properly, Christian searched Noelle's expression.

"Did you say we should get married?" The noise of the speedboat was receding, but Christian continued to hear buzzing.

"Why do you sound so surprised? I thought that's what

you wanted." Anxiety flitted across her delicate features. "Have you changed your mind?"

"No." Explaining to her that he'd planned out the romantic evening with the sole intent of proposing seemed a little anticlimactic. "You've just caught me by surprise."

"I said I needed some time to think about it." Her gaze was fixed on the passing shore. "After watching you with Marc this week, I realized just how much he's missed not having his father in his life."

"So, this is about Marc and me." He'd been thinking in terms of finding the sort of marital bliss and perfect little family that Gabriel and Olivia enjoyed with the twins.

"Well, yes. Isn't that what you've wanted all along? To become Marc's father and to legitimize him as your heir?" Her obvious confusion proved she had no clue how his feelings for her had grown over the past couple of weeks.

And now he had no reason to tell her. She was happy with her decision to marry him. They would have a good partnership, and the sex between them was fantastic. Why muddy things with sentimental declarations of romantic love?

"It's exactly what I want," he told her, pulling the small jewelry box out of his pocket and opening the lid so she could see the ring. "And I've had this waiting for the moment you agreed."

Christian was happy to let her think he hadn't planned for anything out of the ordinary tonight. He lifted her left hand and slipped the ring onto her finger. As eager as he'd been all day to present this token of his commitment, the way the moment had played out left him with a hollow feeling in his gut.

"It's beautiful," she breathed, sounding more emotional than she had while suggesting they get married. She lifted onto her tiptoes and kissed him.

For once desire didn't consume him at the slightest brush of her lips. He tasted the champagne she'd sipped and inwardly grimaced at the bitterness of his disappointment. Calling himself every sort of fool, Christian plunged his tongue into her mouth and feasted on her surrender. She was his. That was all that mattered.

"We should tell my family tomorrow," he said, sweeping kisses across her forehead. He drew back and gave her his best smile.

"Marc first," she replied. "I don't want him hearing it from someone at school. Can you come by in the morning?"

"Of course."

They carried their champagne outside and sat at the beautifully set table. Around them white lights had been strung to provide a romantic atmosphere. Servers brought the first course and, by mutual agreement, Christian and Noelle spoke no more about their plans for the future until they could be safely alone again.

"The timing on this is quite good," Christian said. "Ariana returned from Paris yesterday, and Nic and Brooke aren't set to leave for Los Angeles until the end of the week. We can tell my whole family at once."

"That's wonderful news. Have you thought when you'd like the wedding to take place?"

"We could elope to Ithaca the way Gabriel and Olivia did."

Noelle shook her head. "I don't think your mother would approve. Perhaps we could have a Christmas wedding?"

He didn't like the idea of waiting three months to make her his wife, but having been on the sidelines for his brothers' weddings, he understood a great deal went into organizing a royal affair.

"Whatever you desire."

She gave him a funny little smile. "Just don't bother you with any of the details?"

"I'm sure between you, Olivia and my mother, any opinion I might have would be shot down in an instant."

The large diamond on her left hand winked at him as she lifted the champagne flute to her lips. "I promise you can have a voice in the arrangements if you tell me the one thing you always pictured having at your wedding."

"I never imagined getting married." Christian saw no reason to avoid the truth.

"No, I suppose you didn't."

Her smile wasn't as bright as some he'd seen, and he felt compelled to change that.

"It took the right woman to change my mind."

"The right circumstances."

Christian wanted to argue. To convince her that he had other reasons for marrying her besides legitimizing Marc and securing the throne for his family. Five years ago, knowing she'd never choose success over love, he'd manipulated the circumstances that swept her out of his life. She'd never believe he did it for her own good. Or that his actions had been noble even if on the surface they appeared selfish.

So, instead of creating conflict on the heels of a great victory, he did what any sane man would. He said to hell with dinner, took her in his arms and carried her to the master cabin.

Noelle rolled onto her side in the yacht's roomy master bedroom to watch the play of muscles in Christian's back and the delectable curve of his bare butt as he crossed the cabin to open a window and let in some cool evening air.

"The crew is going to wonder what happened to us,"

Noelle commented, her breath catching as Christian turned in her direction and shot her a wicked grin.

From his lustrous mahogany hair to his absurdly long toes and every magnificent line, dip and rise in between, he was hers. The jubilant thought lightened her heart and weighed on her mind.

"You don't think they heard us and know exactly what we're up to?"

Fresh air spilled across her overheated flesh and she broke out in goose bumps. She should feel embarrassed that her impassioned cries and his climactic shouts had penetrated the stateroom's thin walls. Instead, she found herself grinning.

"Too bad we didn't open the window beforehand. We could have given the entire riverbank something to talk about tomorrow."

Christian dropped onto the mattress and reached for her. "We could go for an encore."

Laughing, Noelle batted his hands away from her breast and thigh before snuggling against his left side and dropping her head onto his chest. His fingers traced soothing patterns on her hip as they lay together in silence.

It was hard to be this close to such a superb example of masculinity and not let herself go exploring. He sighed as she traced his collarbone and worked her way across his pectoral muscles. Glancing at his face, she noted his thick lashes lying against his cheeks. This gave her the chance to survey the right side of his upper body, where the worst of the scars were gathered. Moving with care, she grazed the tips of her fingers over the damaged flesh. Christian flinched.

She jerked her hand away. "Did I hurt you?"

"No." His chest expanded as he sucked in a ragged

breath. He stared at the ceiling, gold eyes dull. "The scars are ugly." His voice rang with self-disgust.

Noelle doubted many people saw this darker side of Christian. In public he exuded capability and confidence that she knew took a great deal of energy to maintain. Only with those he truly trusted could he let down his guard. Noelle had been happy to lend him what strength she could.

"You got them rescuing Talia after Andre lost control of his car," she reminded him. "They're your badge of courage."

"You know what happened?" His muscles tensed. "How? That was never public knowledge."

"You forget that I spent a great deal of time with Olivia in the days leading up to her wedding. For some reason she wanted to impress upon me what a brave, honorable man you were." Noelle suspected the princess had known Marc was Christian's son for some time. She kissed his damaged shoulder and felt a shudder rage through his body. "I don't understand why you kept the truth about the accident a secret. You were a hero."

He shook his head. "I blame myself for the crash. If I hadn't been chasing after Andre's car, he never would have driven so recklessly and lost control."

He'd raced into the night after Talia, his ex-lover, abandoning Noelle at a party to do so. Getting ready for the party that night, slipping on the bracelet Christian had given her for her birthday, she'd been giddy with anticipation of their first public appearance as a couple. But after that night, it was a long, long time before she was happy again.

Noelle wasn't sure why she'd picked the evening of her engagement to dredge up the past. Maybe her subconscious wanted to remind her that Christian held too much power over her happiness. Message received. This was going to be a marriage built on respect and passion. Friendship and sex. No reason she needed to yield her heart and risk being hurt again.

Christian's long fingers swept into her hair as he brought his lips to hers for a long, searing kiss. Noelle melted beneath his hot mouth and caressing hands. As her blood raced through her veins and pooled in her loins, she smiled. Her body she could give him without reservation.

She would be his wife, his princess and the mother of his children. Noelle hoped it would be enough.

Ten

Noelle sat on her office sofa, her bare feet tucked beneath her, and tapped her pencil against the sketchbook on her lap. The enormous diamond on her left hand felt awkward and strange. She caught herself staring at it a dozen times in the past hour as her mind struggled to assimilate the dramatic changes taking place. She was engaged to a prince. And not just any prince, but the prince of her dreams. It didn't seem possible.

Of course, it wasn't a fairy-tale engagement. Last night she'd been the one to suggest that they marry. She had merely formalized what Christian had already proposed, but it wasn't as if he'd dropped to one knee and pledged his undying love. At least he'd been ready with a ring.

She spun the diamond so it wasn't visible and turned her attention back to the sketchbook. To no avail. In two hours she and Christian would be breaking the news to his family. She'd already told her mother, but Marc didn't yet know. He'd woken before dawn with a stomachache and she'd kept him home from school. With him sick it hadn't seemed the best time to divulge that she and Christian were getting married, despite the fact that he and his father were getting along very well these days.

Her cell phone buzzed, and Noelle abandoned her work with a relieved sigh. The number on the screen caused a spike in her pulse. She sat up straight and slipped her shoes back on.

"Noelle Dubone," she said in a crisp voice, wondering if it was good or bad news to hear back so soon on a business venture.

"Noelle, it's Victor. I hope I'm reaching you at a good time."

"Yes. Fine." She sounded a trifle breathless and told herself to calm down. "How are you?"

"Good. Good. I'm calling to let you know that I just spoke with Jim Shae, and he is very interested in backing you with a ready-to-wear line of bridal fashions here in the States."

Victor Chamberlain was a friend of Geoff's who she'd met in London several years ago. An American businessman whose daughter had been looking for something fresh and unique in a wedding dress, he'd become Noelle's first big client. Last February during New York Fashion Week, he'd introduced her to several venture capitalists and suggested she should consider expanding into ready-to-wear.

Creating one-of-a kind wedding dresses was vastly different from mass-producing an entire collection, so she'd teamed up with Victor to create a business plan that he'd pitched to investors.

"That's wonderful news." With joy dancing across her nerve endings, it took a few seconds for reality to strike. What was she thinking? She was engaged to a Sherdanian prince and needed to start planning now in order to make a royal wedding happen by Christmas. Keeping up with her current clients would be stressful enough. She didn't have time to start a new business venture.

"Can you be in New York next week? Jim would like to meet with you and discuss details."

Next week? Noelle worried her lower lip as she went to check her schedule. "How many days would I need to be there?"

Victor hesitated before answering. "At least three. Besides Jim, I want to set up meetings with buyers from the top bridal shops and media interviews. You should start planning for New York Fashion Week in February. You'll need a terrific venue. I know someone who can help with that."

"Three days…" Noelle's mind worked furiously.

Perhaps she and Christian should postpone the announcement of their engagement until after her New York trip. With a start she realized there was no question in her mind that she intended to embark on this business venture. Was splitting her attention between Sherdana and New York a wise move at the beginning of her marriage? On the other hand, did Christian plan to stop all business travel? Not likely.

"Let me know as soon as possible when you'll be flying in," Victor continued.

"I'll make all my arrangements and be in touch later today."

First of all, she needed to tell Christian what had just happened. But as she scrolled through her contacts for his number, she faltered. How would he view her decision to jump into a major business venture without talking to him about it first? He should be happy for her. But would he question her priorities? Her commitment to this marriage?

Or was she the one questioning her commitment?

Noelle sank into her office chair and stared out the window overlooking the alley behind her salon. In two hours she would be announcing her intention to marry Christian. She spun the ring on her finger. Once word got out, she'd better be ready to go forward. Not only would a broken engagement create a scandal the country didn't need, but her actions would confuse Marc and set a bad example for him.

Conflict churned Noelle's insides. Christian deserved to be a full-time father to Marc, and that would be better accomplished if Noelle honored her engagement and married Christian. Marc benefited. Christian benefited. The country benefited. Three wins. Noelle didn't have to feel guilty about focusing on her business instead of playing the part of dutiful wife. Christian was getting the heir he wanted.

Despite arriving at a reasonable conclusion, Noelle wasn't convinced Christian would agree. She keyed his number and heard the call going through.

"Noelle." He purred in her ear. "I was just thinking about you."

Her toes curled in her pink, superfine Louboutin stilettos. With his warm brandy voice flowing from the phone's speaker, she was hard-pressed to summon all her earlier doubts. Of course, she wanted to marry Christian. No other man could make her come alive just by breathing her name.

"I've been thinking about you, as well." Was that her coming across all sexy and mysterious? She curved her body sideways in the chair, any trace of the capable businesswoman lost beneath a rush of feminine pleasure at hearing her lover's voice.

"I'm heading into a conference call in a moment. Is everything okay with Marc?"

Suddenly Noelle couldn't find the words to share her

confusion and doubts. "He's better. Turns out it wasn't the flu but an entire bag of cookies that caused his stomach-ache. I just wondered if you wanted to have dinner at my house tonight."

"Absolutely. If you think Marc will be well enough, we can tell him about our engagement."

"That's what I planned. The sooner the better." And she would also tell him about her new venture. Together they would figure out the best way forward.

"I have back-to-back meetings between now and when I'm supposed to pick you up for our meeting with my family, and I don't want to be late so I've arranged for a car to take you to the palace."

"That's not necessary. I've made my own way to the palace a dozen times. I'll be fine."

"It's what I want. You are no longer visiting as a de-signer or a guest."

Hearing his determination, Noelle conceded. "Very well. Just don't leave me facing your family alone."

"Never fear." Rich amusement filled his tone. "I'll see you at three."

Noelle disconnected the call and sat with the phone in her lap, preparing herself to do the right thing for all concerned.

Christian stared at the slow-moving traffic ahead of him, about to break the promise he'd made to Noelle two hours earlier. He had ten minutes to get to the palace and fifteen minutes of driving ahead of him. He should have anticipated that his meeting with Gaston would run late. The man was a savvy politician in the perfect position to block Christian from securing land he needed outside Carone to develop his next project. The negotiations had been difficult.

With Sherdana's economic troubles easing thanks to an influx of technology businesses, Christian had decided to focus more of his attention on investing close to home. This would mean less travel and more time spent with Noelle and Marc. It was important as a new husband and father to put his family first.

Drumming his thumbs against the steering wheel, Christian willed the cars in front of him to move. His impatience wasn't just about the traffic. He was eager to see Noelle again. Having to postpone telling Marc this morning had been disappointing, but sharing their news with his family was the next best thing.

When Christian arrived in the family's private living room, Noelle was already there with his parents, Nic, Brooke and Ariana. Standing at ease beside his sister, Noelle looked stunning in a richly embroidered pale pink coat over a simple ivory dress. Before making his way to Noelle's side, Christian swung by to greet his parents.

"You're late," the king scolded.

"Traffic," Christian explained. "Besides, Gabriel and Olivia aren't here yet."

The queen offered her cheek for his kiss. "You'd better have good news for us."

"The best." He smiled his most confident grin.

Obligations satisfied, he headed toward Noelle. As he took his place beside her, Gabriel and Olivia rushed hand-in-hand into the room. Their exuberant smiles drew everyone's attention. Christian experienced an uncomfortable stab of envy at the strength of their connection. They were surrounded by family and yet so in tune with each other. Would he and Noelle ever get to a point where they enjoyed that sort of intimacy?

"We have wonderful news," Gabriel began, his unrestrained delight making him seem far younger than thirty. "We are going to be parents."

For a moment the room was deathly quiet as Christian's family absorbed this impossible announcement. Olivia had undergone a hysterectomy four months earlier, rendering her incapable of having children.

The queen was the first to recover her voice. "How?"

"My eggs were viable for a month after my operations. The doctors were able to harvest several. We found a surrogate and just came from her first doctor's appointment. Everything looks good." Olivia turned a radiant smile on Gabriel.

He bent his head and gave her a quick kiss. Then he glanced around the room. "And we're having twins."

Ariana ran to Olivia and threw her arms around her sister-in-law. Nic and Brooke stepped up next. While a part of Christian was thrilled for his older brother, most of him was numb. He glanced at Noelle to gauge her reaction. She watched the happy couple through eyes that shone brightly with tears. Christian felt his throat lock up and could only stare, mind blank, as his parents stepped up for their turn to congratulate their son and daughter-in-law.

Noelle poked him in the ribs and whispered, "Go congratulate them. This is amazing news."

"What about our news?" He sounded like a grumpy old man. "It's pretty amazing, too."

"This is their moment. I don't want to ruin it." She placed the flat of her hand against his back and gave him a shove. While she didn't have the strength to move him, her recommendation was clear.

Was there some other reason why she didn't want to announce their engagement? Was she thinking of backing out now that Gabriel and Olivia had figured out a way to supply an heir for the throne?

Christian pushed aside concern and caught Noelle's hand in his. Together they joined the circle of well-wishers.

"You seem to have a knack for producing twins," Christian told his brother, smiling despite his heavy heart.

"At least these two won't be identical," Gabriel replied.

Several members of the staff brought the champagne that Christian had made sure was on ice to toast his engagement, and everyone except Brooke—who was pregnant—enjoyed a glass. No one seemed to recall that Christian had organized the family meeting or wonder what his announcement might have been.

The frustration he'd begun feeling the instant Noelle suggested they put off sharing the news of their engagement began to grow. He'd put all his energy into convincing Noelle that they belonged together as a family and now his brother had to come along at the absolute moment that Christian was the happiest he'd ever been and spoil everything.

Thirty minutes into the celebration, he pulled her aside. "I really think we should announce our engagement."

Noelle glanced at Gabriel and Olivia. "Now isn't a good time. And I need to get back to my shop."

His dismay expanded. "I thought we'd have the afternoon to celebrate making our engagement official."

"Something came up earlier that I need to take care of."

Considering that he'd arrived at the palace almost twenty minutes late because of his own meeting schedule, Christian forced down his irritation.

"What time should I come by tonight?"

She pressed her lips together and didn't meet his eyes. "About that. Why don't we wait a little while before we tell Marc."

"Why don't I take you back to your shop, and we can discuss that on the way there."

"Christian—"

"You owe me an explanation for your sudden turn-around."

She ducked her head and nodded. "I know."

Without drawing attention to themselves, they slipped out of the room and headed to the side entrance nearest the family quarters where Christian had left his car.

After assisting Noelle into the passenger seat, he slipped behind the wheel and started the powerful engine. Wasting no time on preliminaries, he stomped on the gas and, as the car shot forward, demanded, "What's going on?"

"Gabriel and Olivia are going to be parents. This changes everything."

It did, and he hated them for it. "It changes nothing. I'm still Marc's father. I deserve to be in his life."

"Of course you do, but now we don't need to rush into anything." Both her words and her tone betrayed her relief.

Christian ground his teeth together, using only half his attention to negotiate past slower-moving vehicles. "I didn't realize we were rushing."

"Didn't you? We were planning for a Christmas wedding." She was spinning her engagement ring around and around. "You wanted to make Marc your legal heir as soon as possible so that your family would continue to enjoy political stability."

"I want to be a family with you and Marc," he corrected.

"And we still can, but it's nothing that has to happen right away."

The problem with her argument was that each day Christian grew more impatient to live under the same roof as her and Marc. His bachelor lifestyle no longer interested him.

"My brother has already demonstrated that he only

knows how to produce girls," Christian argued. "What makes you think this time will be different?"

"In a month or so they'll be able to tell the sex of the babies. In the meantime…" Noelle slipped the ring from her finger and held it out to Christian.

"You're breaking off our engagement already." A statement, not a question.

His heartbeat slowed to a near standstill. This couldn't be happening to him.

"It isn't a real engagement." Clearly her perception of their relationship differed from his. "I mean, we aren't in love or anything, so it's just an arrangement."

She wasn't wrong. He'd used legitimizing their son as an excuse for marriage. As always, taking what appeared to be the easiest path had led him into a bramble hedge. Now he was stuck with the consequences.

"I care about you. I don't want to lose you."

She smiled. "And I care about you, but as you often used to remind me, you aren't cut out for marriage. You were marrying me out of duty. Now you don't have to."

"Keep the ring." He tightened his grip on the steering wheel. "We'll postpone announcing our engagement for a month."

Noelle closed her fist around the diamond and set both hands in her lap. "I don't feel right keeping it."

"It's yours. I bought it for you." He didn't want the damned thing back. "We'll proceed as we've been for a few weeks longer. You're right that we rushed. Circumstances pushed us too fast. Now we have all the time in the world."

When she didn't respond, he glanced over at her. His stomach twisted at her obvious discomfort.

"What?" he prompted.

"See, the thing is…" She hesitated, and stared out the passenger window for so long he thought she might have forgotten he was beside her. "I called you earlier today to tell you about something that just came up."

He did not like the sound of this. "What sort of something?"

"A business opportunity. I have a meeting with an investor next week. He's interested in backing a line of ready-to-wear bridal gowns."

"That's fantastic."

She smiled at his enthusiasm. "I'm very excited."

"You don't seem to be."

"It's just that the potential investor wants me to expand my business in the US, specifically New York City. That's where my meetings are next week."

He was starting to see why she was so subdued. "That's a long commute."

"I was worried about it."

"And now you're not?"

"I think Gabriel and Olivia's news might have allowed us to dodge a bullet."

"How so?"

"You didn't really want to get married, and now you don't have to. Marc is your son. As he gets a little older, we can figure out a visitation schedule that enables you to see as much of him as makes sense."

"And in the meantime?" Christian was having a hard time keeping his rising anger out of his tone. "Am I supposed to just let you take Marc to New York and not see my son?"

"No, of course not. I'll have to travel back and forth between New York and Europe. I have many clients on this side of the Atlantic whom I can't afford to neglect. But I'll be creating a collection to show at New York Fashion Week in February that will kick off my ready-to-wear line and

I'll probably be spending the bulk of my time in America leading up to it."

"Marc should stay here with me." It's not what Christian had intended to suggest. He couldn't imagine living without Noelle or his son, but once again he'd used Marc as a decoy to distract her from the full scope of his emotions.

"I can't leave him in Sherdana. I'm all he's known his whole life. He's too young to understand why his mother is leaving him."

"You don't take him with you every time you travel for business. We'll start small. How long are you going to be in New York next week?"

"A few days."

"That's perfect."

"No."

"You go to New York and meet with your investor while I stay here and take care of Marc. If we'd gotten married, it's what would have eventually happened. The only difference is the lack of a legal document."

She gave a soft gasp. "A custody agreement?"

"A marriage license." Christian stopped the car in front of Noelle's shop and put it in Park. Turning in his seat, he took her hand that held the ring and opened her fingers. "I'm not giving up on the idea of marrying you," he said, slipping the diamond onto her right hand. "Take this ring as a sign of my faith in us as a couple and as a family."

"I'll wear it until I return from New York. At that point we will sit down and discuss what's best for Marc and for you and me."

Which meant he had a little more than a week to convince her to go forward with their plans to get married. If he hoped to convince her they belonged together, he'd better pull out all the stops. He wasn't going to make the mistake of letting her go a second time.

* * *

The morning she was scheduled to leave for New York, Noelle woke with her stomach twisted into knots. She was about to embark on the most ambitious project of her career. To fail would mean she'd not only risked damaging her reputation as a designer and a businesswoman, but had created a rift between Christian and her for nothing.

She'd decided not to leave Marc at home with either his father or her mother. This wasn't a two-day hop to Paris or Milan. This was a ten-hour plane ride and an ocean between them. Her son didn't share her anxiety about their separation. Taking him with her meant Marc would be missing a field trip to the zoo. He'd protested vehemently, and reminding him that they'd visited less than a month ago had only made things worse.

"Marc, please go upstairs and brush your teeth. You must get dressed. The car will be here any moment to take us to the airport." She turned to her mother. "Why is he being like this?"

"He doesn't want to go. Why don't you leave him with me? He shouldn't be stuck in a hotel room in New York while you're working."

While a part of Noelle knew her mother was right, she couldn't quell her uneasiness at the thought of leaving him behind. She'd made arrangements for a nanny to stay with Marc while she conducted business, but didn't know if she was comfortable letting the woman roam around the city alone with him.

A knock sounded on the door. The car she'd arranged to take her and Marc to the airport had finally arrived.

"Marc, the car is here. There is no more time for games." She experienced an uncharacteristic longing to bury her face in her hands and cry. "Mama, can you get him upstairs to change?"

Still in his pajamas, Marc was running the circle from the kitchen, through the dining room, into the living room and back to the kitchen, arms held out, pretending he was an airplane. Noelle glanced at the clock. She wore no makeup, had thrown her hair into a damp updo because tussling with Marc had robbed her of the time to dry it, and her blouse was stained with syrup.

Noelle went to answer the door and discovered not a driver, but Christian standing on her steps. His eyes narrowed when he caught sight of her, and she realized he'd never seen her in such disarray.

She gestured him in. "Good morning, Christian. Please come in. There's coffee in the kitchen." Behind her came Marc's protesting wail and her mother's warning tone. "As you can tell, my household is in chaos and I'm running late. I thought you were the driver I hired to take us to the airport. He was supposed to be here twenty minutes ago."

Rather than walk past her, Christian backed her against the entry wall and cupped her face in gentle hands. Her muscles went limp as his lips covered hers. The kiss was tender and full of longing. She opened to him, sliding her hands into his hair to keep their mouths fused together.

A low groan built in her chest. It was the first time he'd touched her like this since she'd broken off their engagement, and she felt like a spring flower coming to life after a long, harsh winter.

"Prince Papa." Marc's slippered feet thudded down the hall toward them.

Christian broke off the kiss and surveyed Noelle with enigmatic eyes before turning to scoop his son off the floor and lift him high above his head.

While her son shrieked in delight, Noelle put a hand to her chest and snatched several seconds to recover. In the long years apart from him, she'd forgotten that being kissed by Christian was an excellent way to begin her day.

As Christian set Marc back on his feet, Noelle nudged her son toward Mara. "Marc, please go upstairs with Nana and get dressed so we can be ready to leave if the car ever gets here."

"Noooo." And before Noelle could stop him, he'd bolted out the still-open front door, his howl fading as he raced away.

She started for the door, but Christian caught her arm. "I'll get him. Why don't you take a couple minutes and have some of that coffee you mentioned earlier."

"We're already running late. If we don't get going now, we'll miss the plane." She thought of the appointments set up for later that day and bit her lower lip in frustration.

"I'll get you there."

She shook her head. "I have a car coming."

"I mean to New York."

Behind him, Marc flashed by on the front lawn. Noelle was so focused on her annoyance with Marc that it took a moment for Christian's words to penetrate.

"How are you going to do that?"

His slow smile sent goose bumps racing over Noelle's skin. "I have a very luxurious private plane gassed up and waiting for us at the airport."

"Us?" What was he saying?

"I've cleared my schedule for the next few days so I could accompany you and Marc to New York. I thought that while you worked, Marc and I could play."

Instantly Noelle knew her son would love that. Spending time with his father had become something he now looked forward to, and it would ease Noelle's mind knowing Marc wouldn't be cooped up in a hotel room with a stranger their entire stay.

"I can't ask you to do that."

"You didn't. I volunteered."

Her mind flashed to the kiss a moment earlier. "I hope you understand I'm going on business. What just happened..." She made a vague gesture toward the spot where he'd pinned her to the wall and kissed her senseless. "I hope you don't think..."

The glow in his eyes told her that's exactly what he was thinking, but he shook his head. "I'm going to spend time with Marc. You don't need to worry that I'll distract you from any of your plans."

Oh, he'd distract her, all right. The craving to make love with him purred in her body like a contented cat. It would only be a matter of time before it woke and dug in its sharp claws.

"I guess then I can send the driver on his way."

"Already done."

Before she could protest his high-handedness, Christian was out the door.

"You'd better put on some makeup and fix your hair," Mara said, rich amusement in her voice. "Not that Prince Christian will care one way or another. He seems to approve of you no matter what."

Cheeks burning at her mother's teasing, Noelle raced upstairs to change out of her stained blouse and finish packing. If a couple new pieces of lingerie found their way into her suitcase as well as a sexy black lace nightgown, that didn't mean she had changed her mind about staying focused on business.

Since Christian was dressed casually in jeans and a gray sweater over a white collared shirt, Noelle decided against her original choice of a tailored burgundy suit and slipped into black skinny pants, a denim shirt and her favorite pair of black flats.

To show her mother that she didn't intend to go all out for Christian, Noelle applied black liner on her upper lids and enhanced her lips with a brilliant red. By the time she emerged from her bedroom with her suitcase, Christian had Marc dressed, his hair combed and teeth brushed. Noelle didn't marvel at how he'd accomplished so much in such a short period of time. She merely sent him a grateful look and headed downstairs.

Christian's driver fetched their suitcases while she settled Marc in the backseat and slid in after him. A moment later Christian joined them, his body solid and reassuring at her side. The worry and doubts that had plagued her these past few days abruptly lost their power. As the car began rolling down her driveway, Noelle sighed and squeezed Christian's arm.

"Thank you for coming with us."

He covered her hand and smiled. "No thanks necessary. I'm happy to be with you and Marc."

It wasn't a calculated line to impress her, but the unadorned truth. Noelle's heart expanded. Suddenly her decision to break off their engagement appeared like the worst one she'd ever made. Christian loved Marc. And she loved Christian. The truth flashed in her mind like a neon sign. Of course she loved him. She'd never stopped. For five years she'd ignored the truth by focusing on maintaining a balance between her career and being the best mom she could.

But her realization came too late. She'd already agreed to marry him and then called it off, freeing Christian from any moral obligation he might have felt toward her and Marc.

Christian tugged on the dark green scarf she'd knotted around her neck. "Where'd you go? You're a long way off."

"Sorry."

"Marc and I were just discussing our plans for New York. He's very excited to go to his first baseball game."

"I packed my glove," the boy announced. "So I can catch a home-run ball."

"Actually, we'll be sitting behind home plate so you'll have to catch a foul ball instead."

"Foul balls!" Marc exclaimed, kicking his feet. "And the zoo."

"Bronx or Central Park?" Christian asked.

"Both."

Noelle laughed. "You're going to be busy."

"It'll be fun. I've never had much opportunity to sightsee in New York. Every time I've been there it's been for business."

"I think I'm a little envious of you two," Noelle said and meant it. Ever since finding out she had an investor for her ready-to-wear line, she'd been caught up in all the deal's details. Now, she wished someone else could take care of business while she hung out with her two favorite men.

"Mama has to work." Marc grinned past her toward his father, and the two shared a special moment that excluded Noelle.

"Mama has to work," she agreed, so glad her son had this wonderful man in his life to love him.

Eleven

When the pressure changed in the jet's cabin, Christian stretched his legs and glanced toward his son. Despite his excitement at visiting New York, Marc was a good traveler. Considering the boy's abundant energy, Christian had worried that Marc would be a restless terror. At the beginning of the flight, he'd settled right down with crayons and a coloring book. Later, Noelle and Christian had taken turns reading to him for an hour after which he'd had lunch, napped and was now quietly enjoying a Disney movie.

This had offered plenty of time for Noelle and Christian to talk. By mutual consent, they'd not strayed into any tricky personal topics while their son sat nearby. Instead, Noelle had laid out her business plan and asked Christian for feedback.

"Your third-year numbers seem a little conservative. Are you really convinced your business will grow at only seven percent?"

"Seven is a little above average and a safe estimate."

"You've never struck me as the sort who goes for safe." He hadn't imbued the comment with subtext, but Noelle's eyes narrowed.

"I have Marc to think about now. I can't jump into something if there seems to be some inherent risk involved." Although her tone was mild enough, tension formed little lines around her mouth.

"I understand." But Christian wasn't sure he did.

"Do you? Because doing what's best for him is my top priority."

Somehow they'd strayed from discussing business, and Christian had no idea what she was trying to tell him. "I understand." Repeating the words didn't have the effect he'd hoped.

Noelle grew even more agitated. "I know I've been hard on you. And I've been selfish."

Since it was obvious she had something to get off her chest, Christian kept his mouth shut and let her vent. She was beautiful, with her tantalizing lips painted bright red and the green of her scarf heightening the chestnut tones in her eyes. She'd kicked off her pointed black flats and sat with her feet tucked beneath her. The pen she'd been using to make notes was jabbed into her topknot for easy access. He wanted very badly to haul her onto his lap and kiss her silly.

"I want Marc to see you as a permanent fixture in his life."

All day she'd been swapping the engagement ring back and forth between her right and left hands. He doubted she was even aware that she was toying with the ring or that at the moment it rested on her left hand exactly where Christian wanted it.

"I thought that's what we've been doing with the dinners and outings."

"Yes." She kept her gaze trained on his shoulder. "But I think we should have something formal in place."

"A custody agreement?"

Her shoulders stiffened for a moment as if she were wincing from a blow. Christian could tell the offer wasn't easy for her. A second later she nodded.

"I think Marc will benefit from more time with his father."

"Not as much as his father will benefit." Christian kept his tone light to conceal his heavy heart. Always impatient, he wanted to claim both Noelle and Marc as his.

Noelle gave him a tremulous smile. "You always know just what to say."

"What sort of time did you have in mind for Marc to spend with me?"

"Obviously it will depend on your travel schedule. I thought maybe when we get back you could take him overnight and see how it goes."

"I didn't get a chance to tell you last week, but I've restructured some of my business dealings to keep me in Sherdana more. I'd like as much time with Marc as you're willing to give me." And with Noelle, but that didn't seem as likely now.

"That's wonderful. Seeing more of each other will only strengthen your relationship with Marc."

"And what are you planning to do with all your free time?"

Giving him partial custody would offer her a break from motherhood. An opportunity to date. Although he was convinced she wasn't in love with Geoff, he couldn't claim to know how the lawyer felt about Noelle. Suddenly Christian wasn't so sure he liked where things were heading.

She laughed. "I suspect for the next year or so, I'll be working around the clock to launch my ready-to-wear line and continue expanding my couture business. While he's with you, I won't have to worry that Marc is being neglected."

Christian considered what she'd said. It hadn't occurred to him that she'd feel guilty for working hard at her thriving business. "It will be good to have both of us there for him."

"You're right." She leaned forward, her expression earnest. "I didn't realize how much Marc needed a father until these past few weeks. I'm sorry I didn't tell you about him sooner."

Christian was touched by her apology but knew he couldn't let her take all the blame. "I never gave you any reason to think I would be there for Marc." He regretted missing Marc's first four years, but also for failing Noelle even as he thought he was trying to help her. "I wish I could take back the past five years."

Noelle shook her head. "I don't. If you hadn't broken things off I never would have gone to Paris and had a chance to learn under Matteo."

"And become an internationally famous wedding gown designer."

"You see. It all worked out perfectly in the end." But her smile wasn't as bright as her voice. "In the end you did me a huge favor."

Maybe he had, but Christian acknowledged that he'd also done himself a disservice by letting her go.

An exhausted Noelle returned to her suite at the Four Seasons after a grueling second day of meetings and interviews to find her son wearing a Yankees jersey and cap and carrying an autographed baseball in his mitt.

"And then he swung like this." Marc demonstrated a dramatic swing that spun him in a circle. "The ball went like…gone…gone…gone. Home run!" He threw his arms into the air and ran around the suite's living room as if running the bases.

"Goodness." Noelle looked to Christian, who stood with his hands in the back pockets of his jeans, watching his son with such fondness a lump formed in Noelle's throat. "Sounds like it was a fun game."

"It was grrreat." Marc charged toward Christian, who absorbed his son's enthusiastic hug with a grin. "And tomorrow we're going on a boat ride to the Statue of Liberty."

"You two are certainly taking advantage of all New York has to offer." Once again Noelle found herself regretting all the quality time she was missing with her son.

Christian picked up on the source of her melancholy as he swung Marc into his arms. "You could cancel your meetings and join us."

"Tempting." She smiled through her weariness. "But I only have tomorrow morning to get the last of the details hammered out."

"You're running yourself ragged."

"I know, but it will be worth it in the end." Satisfaction suffused her. As grinding as the pace had been since the jet's wheels had touched down on the New York runway, her ready-to-wear line was getting the right backing and garnering the perfect buzz.

"I'm really proud of you." While Noelle had been lost in thought, Christian had set down Marc and stepped close. "I want you to know that whatever you need I'll be here to help."

When his arm slid around her waist, drawing her against his body for a friendly hug, Noelle's pulse bucked. The man smelled like sunshine and soap. She longed to rest her cheek against the cotton stretched across his broad chest and let the world fade away. Her hunger for him flared. It had been a week since they'd made love, but with all that had happened in the meantime, it felt more like months.

Noelle leaned back and gazed up into Christian's molten gold eyes. Her knees weakened at the heat of his desire, and her lips parted as he lowered his head. A small body crashed against them, reminding Noelle that she and Christian weren't alone. She set her hand on Marc's head, frustration making the ache of longing that much more intense.

"What sort of plans do you have for dinner?" Christian asked, his arm sliding away from her body. He'd booked a suite at the Four Seasons in order to be close to his son. "Marc had a hot dog, popcorn and cotton candy at the ballpark, so I thought it would be a good idea to feed him a healthy dinner and we hoped you'd be able to join us."

As hard as it was to turn down the offer with two pairs of matching gold eyes trained on her, Noelle shook her head. "I'm having dinner with some designer friends of mine, and then there's a gala I'm attending afterward."

Marc showed less disappointment at this news than Christian. Their son was having far too much fun with his father to notice his mother's absence. As Marc dashed over to retrieve his mitt and autographed baseball from the coffee table, Christian's deep voice rumbled through her.

"I'm sorry you can't join us."

"So am I." And she meant it. "If it wasn't business…"

He nodded in understanding, his hands sliding into his pockets once more. "That's why you're here."

While part of Noelle appreciated his support, she couldn't stop wishing he'd ask her to cut her night short so she could tuck Marc into bed and maybe invite Christian to linger for some private time with her. Instead, he headed to his son, leaving her free to get ready for her evening out.

Three hours later, Noelle stood beside Victor, her mind far from business and the well-dressed crowd gathered to support a local food pantry. She was wondering if she could plead a headache and get back to the hotel in time to put her son to bed.

And the other thing...

All night long her heart and body had been wrestling with her mind regarding Christian. She longed to spend the night in his arms. To pretend she hadn't broken off their engagement in a foolish rush because she'd thought to beat him to the punch. But could she have married him thinking that he was merely following through on a contract he'd made with her? It had been one thing to marry him knowing he didn't love her when they were both taking steps to secure the future of the country.

"This has been a fantastic couple of days," Victor said, his enthusiasm dragging Noelle's attention back to the ballroom. "I think your line is going to be a huge success."

"Have I told you how much I appreciate all you've done?"

"I've just started things rolling."

"You've done more than that. You've created a tsunami of media interest and made sure that I'm meeting all the right people to make this line a success."

"I believe in you." Victor's shrewd brown eyes softened. "I wouldn't have partnered with you if I didn't. You're talented and business-savvy. It's been a pleasure working with you."

"It's been wonderful working with you, as well." Throat tight, she gave him a smile as she squeezed his hand. "Now, if you don't mind, I'm going to go back to the hotel and tuck my son into bed. I've neglected him terribly these past two days."

"I understand perfectly."

Noelle turned down Victor's offer of his car and left him to make her way out of the ballroom. It was nine-thirty, but she doubted Marc was in bed yet. She was in the process of sending Christian a text letting him know she was on her way back when someone behind her called her name. With a weary sigh, Noelle turned and spied a tall, bone-thin woman in her early thirties coming toward her, recognizing her as the *Charme* magazine editor who'd been overheard making disparaging remarks about her most recent fall couture collection. Not surprising, since she and Giselle had been rivals at Matteo Pizarro Designs and Giselle knew how to hold a grudge.

"Giselle, how lovely to see you." Noelle gave her former coworker a polite smile.

"I understand you and Prince Christian Alessandro are hot and heavy once more."

In the old days, before she'd realized what a snake Giselle could be, Noelle had told the seemingly sympathetic woman all about her two-year relationship with Christian. "We are friends." There was no way Noelle was going to tell the woman anything.

"Friendly enough that he accompanied you and your son to New York."

Although there had been speculation, the media hadn't yet discovered Christian's true relationship to Marc, and Noelle had no intention of sharing anything with Giselle.

"He's a friend," Noelle repeated, keeping her tone bland. "Now, if you'll excuse me, it's been a long couple of days." She turned to go, but Giselle's next words stopped her.

"I hear you're launching a ready-to-wear line."

Reminding herself that despite the animosity between

them, Giselle had an influential position in the industry, Noelle put on her interview face. "That's why I'm in New York. To meet with my backer and start making arrangements for manufacturing."

"Oh, Prince Christian isn't backing you?" Giselle's surprise didn't ring true. "I thought with you two being so close...and since he's helped you out before."

What was Giselle trying to get at?

"Prince Christian has never helped me."

When triumph flashed in Giselle's eyes, Noelle felt her uneasiness rise. Giselle had sabotaged her efforts several times when Noelle had first joined Matteo Pizarro Designs. Naively believing Giselle had been her friend had enabled the older woman to take credit for Noelle's ideas and ruin an entire week's worth of sketches before they were set to present their designs to Matteo as part of a special runway collection he was to exhibit at the Louvre. When, in the hour before they were to meet with Matteo, Noelle had crafted five sketches and Matteo had selected one of those, Giselle had been livid.

"You can tell the rest of the world such lies, but I know the truth."

"What truth?" Noelle knew better than to ask, but Giselle's absolute confidence had rattled her.

"That you never would have gotten the job with Matteo Pizarro without your prince's help."

"That's a lie."

"I heard Matteo speaking to Claudia about it. He said you were too inexperienced to hire, and he never would have considered you except that he was doing a favor for Prince Christian."

Noelle awakened to the truth as if she'd been slapped in the face. She'd been so shocked that she'd landed a position with such a prestigious designer. Her work was acceptable, but not outstanding. Only after she started working for Matteo Pizzaro and been inspired firsthand by the man's brilliance had she begun to gain confidence as a designer and take chances.

"It might be true," Noelle conceded, "but that's because Prince Christian believed in my talent before I did." And he'd see it as a great way to end their relationship.

But did that really make sense? Surely Christian had ended things with dozens of women without finding them a dream job that sent them five hundred miles away.

Giselle must have perceived Noelle's confusion as vulnerability because she stepped closer. "You'd be nothing if he hadn't used his influence to get Matteo to hire you."

"Maybe I wouldn't be a wedding gown designer to the wealthy and famous," Noelle agreed, no longer the naïve twenty-five-year-old girl Giselle had been able to take advantage of. "But I would still be the mother of an amazing little boy. And I'd be all the better for never having met you."

So much for playing nice with the media. Noelle turned on her heel and slipped from the ballroom, her heart racing after the ugly encounter. Her thoughts were a chaotic jumble as she slid into a cab for the two-mile trek back to the Four Seasons. She didn't doubt Giselle spoke the truth about Christian arranging for her to get the job with Matteo. What she couldn't sort out was how she felt about it.

Fifteen minutes later she let herself into her hotel suite, surprised to find Christian watching TV in her living room. There was no sign of Marc.

"You're back early," he said, using the remote to turn off the TV. He got to his feet as she crossed the room.

"I wanted to tuck Marc in, but it looks like I'm too late."

"He fell asleep on the couch around nine. The last two days have been pretty busy."

"You didn't have to stay. What happened to the nanny?"

"I sent her home. I have a couple things on my mind to talk to you about."

"I have something on my mind, as well."

Christian regarded her curiously as he gestured toward the sofa. When they were both seated, he said, "Do you want to begin?"

"I found out something tonight that I'd like you to confirm."

"Go ahead."

"Did you get me the job at Matteo Pizarro Designs?"

He looked startled, but whether by her question or the lack of accusation in her tone, Noelle couldn't guess.

"Yes."

"Why?"

"Because you were talented, and I knew you wanted it."

She shook her head. "And so you could break things off and not feel guilty?"

"I broke things off so you'd take the job."

Such altruism was not in keeping with his character, and Noelle wasn't sure she believed him. "You broke things off because you wanted to be with Talia."

He took Noelle's hand and lifted it to his right cheek. She touched the puckered skin of his scars. "How much do you remember about the night of my accident?"

Her first impulse was to pull away, but he held her fast. Christian wore his scars from that night on his skin. She wore hers inside. "We went to a party and I drank too much and got out of control because I thought you and Talia took off together."

"You didn't drink too much." Christian's expression hardened. "You were drugged."

"What?" The night had been unusually fuzzy, and she didn't remember more than one drink. But drugged? Why would he have kept something like this from her? "By whom?"

"Someone I thought was my friend." The anger in his voice was very real.

"Why?"

"You know how wild the crowd I ran with was. We treated the world like it was our playground, and we could do whatever we wanted without consequences. In contrast, you were sensible and worked hard at your career. The more involved I became with you, the less I saw them. They didn't like it very much, especially when I tried to bring you into our circle. They decided to go after you."

"By drugging me?" Noelle shivered as she realized just how vulnerable she'd been that night. She'd woken the next morning in her own bed with no idea how she'd gotten there. There'd been a video of her on the internet. She'd been dancing like a drunken fool. Because she couldn't remember any of it, she wasn't sure if she'd acted out because Christian had left with Talia or if he'd taken off because of how she'd been acting. "I thought you broke up with me because of how I behaved that night."

"I did. When I realized how much danger being with me had put you in." He shook his head. "They wanted you out of my life. It worked."

"But you left the party." She remembered being told that he was gone. Well, that wasn't quite true. Memories of the evening's events grew very indistinct after the first hour or so. The next morning the internet had lit up about the horrific car accident. There'd been no mention of a passenger, but she assumed the royal family simply covered that up.

"Because I thought you did. Talia used your phone to text me, saying that if I couldn't treat you any better then maybe one of your friends would. I chased after you and thought that you were leaving with Andre. At the time I didn't realize it was Talia. I followed them."

She couldn't grasp how his mind had been working that night. "You thought I left with Andre?" The skeptical laughter bubbling in her chest died beneath Christian's somber gaze. "How could you believe I would do that?"

"You'd been unhappy for a while. I thought perhaps you'd had enough."

"But to leave in the middle of a party after sending you a text? And with one of your friends?" It stung that he'd understood her so little. "You knew how I felt about you."

"Yes. But I let you think I wasn't exclusive even when I knew you weren't seeing anyone else."

His phrasing caught her attention. "You let me think? What does that mean? That you weren't seeing Talia and all the others you'd been photographed with?" Christian had never made excuses for his freewheeling lifestyle or said the sorts of things a girlfriend wanted to hear. Social media had buzzed with his exploits, and while that had hurt, Noelle had recognized that if she wanted him in her life, she had to share him.

"Not after the first few months. I didn't want to be with anyone but you." He rubbed his temples. "I hated that."

"Because I wasn't beautiful and exciting like all the other women you partied with?"

"You were both beautiful and exciting. But I didn't like having anyone relying on me for anything. And the way you looked at me…" He sighed. "Things were happening to me that I didn't like."

"Things?" she echoed, half afraid of what he might tell her. She'd mostly succeeded at never reading between the lines with Christian, knowing that way led to madness. But then he'd never been particularly vague. Voice light, she prompted, "What sort of things?"

A fissure formed in his granite expression. "Feelings."

"I can see why that upset you." She couldn't resist some faint mockery. It helped hide the pain his words caused.

Why had caring about her been something he'd been so unhappy about? At the time, she would have been thrilled beyond belief to think that she'd meant something more to him than just a tranquil pit stop in his eventful social life.

"I knew from the first that I wasn't good for you." He caressed her cheek with his knuckles. "Instead of taking your talent to Paris or London, you stayed in your tiny Carone flat, working for a man who claimed your designs as his own. Being with me kept you stuck. That's why I encouraged you to send off your résumé and portfolio."

"It wasn't your fault that I was afraid." Of taking a chance with her career and finding out she couldn't compete. Of losing the man she loved. "I just wasn't ready to leave Sherdana."

"But once you thought we'd broken up, you jumped at the chance to interview for a position at Matteo Pizarro."

"That's not fair. When I thought you'd chosen Talia, I knew I had to get away from Sherdana." It wasn't until she'd settled in Paris months later and discovered Christian and Talia weren't together that Noelle recognized her insecurities had worked against her.

"Exactly my point. Even after you got the job with Matteo Pizarro, you hesitated."

She'd paused in the middle of packing and visited him in the hospital, hoping he would ask her to stay. He'd been so cold. "You told me you'd moved on."

"Would you have left if I hadn't?"

She couldn't meet his eyes. "I wanted to be with you."

"And being with me caused you to be in danger. For your own good I sent you away."

"What would you have done if I'd told you I was pregnant?"

Christian shook his head. "I'd like to believe I would've done the right thing, but I honestly don't know."

"What would have been the right thing?"

"Marry you. Settle down. Become a good husband and father."

Noelle couldn't stop the wry smile that curved her lips. "Neither one of us was ready for that."

The way his eyebrows shot up said she'd surprised him. "You were."

"I was happy in Paris. I loved what I was doing. It was hard to manage my career and being a new mom, but I discovered such satisfaction in my ability to do both."

"See, breaking up with me was the best thing that could have happened to you."

"That's not true." But she couldn't deny that in many ways he'd done her a favor.

"So what happens now?"

"Now?"

"I'm no longer a young, irresponsible cad. You are thriving in your career and as a mother. We've demonstrated that the chemistry between us is hotter than ever. I have a son that I love, and want to be a full-time father. Marry me."

She saw what he was offering and spun the large diamond ring on her finger. He'd always been what she wanted. So, why couldn't she just say yes?

Twelve

Christian saw Noelle's hesitation and felt his heart tear.

"Victor convinced me to move to New York for the next six months so I can focus on the ready-to-wear line."

"Victor convinced you?" Christian probed her expression. "Or did you have this in mind before you left Sherdana?"

"A little of both," she admitted. "Thanks to you Marc loves it here, and I don't know how I'm supposed to take care of all the manufacturing issues and marketing details if I'm in Europe."

"You let me believe that I would have partial custody of Marc. Have you changed your mind?"

"No. We will figure something out about that."

"But you and I won't be together."

She stared at her hands and shook her head. "Being Marc's parents and having great sexual chemistry aren't strong enough reasons to get married. I don't want to get divorced in a few years because the only time we're compatible is in bed."

"I don't plan to divorce." Just the thought made his chest ache. "I intend to spend the rest of my life with you."

Again she didn't answer right away. If her goal was to convince him that she didn't share his commitment, he refused to let her succeed. Pushed to fight for the woman he wanted, Christian stood and scooped Noelle into his arms. He silenced her protests with a fierce glare and marched toward her bedroom. Setting her on her feet near the bed, he shut the door and stripped off his shirt before turning to face her.

"Christian, this isn't going to change my mind about staying in New York." So she said, but her gaze roamed his bare torso in hungry desperation.

"I have no intention of talking you out of moving to New York." He eliminated the distance between them with deliberate strides, letting passion incinerate his fear of losing her. "I only want what's best for you."

He hadn't meant for his words to upset her, but suddenly she looked stricken. Moving with slow tenderness, he slipped the dress from her body and worshipped her soft skin with his fingers and lips. The catch on her strapless bra popped free, no match for his expertise, and she sucked in a sharp breath as he took one breast in his hand.

With his desire spiraling in ever tightening circles, Christian dropped to his knees before Noelle and hooked his fingers in her white, lacy panties, pulling them down her thighs. The vibration in her muscles increased, threatening her stability. To keep her upright, he framed her slender hips with his hands. Her flat stomach quivered as he trailed kisses across it.

He'd missed the chance to watch her belly grow round with his son. He set his forehead against her, overwhelmed by how much more he stood to lose if he couldn't win her love. His sudden stillness prompted her to ride her palms across his bare shoulders and dragged her nails through his hair. He wrapped his arms around her and set his cheek against her abdomen.

"Christian?"

He'd never fully appreciated the power of her soothing touch. How her quiet voice and fervent embrace created a sanctuary that let his worries slip away.

"I wasn't completely truthful when I said I only wanted what was best for you. What I really want is what's best for me. And that's you."

"Make love to me."

Not needing to be asked twice, Christian lifted her off her feet and set her on the mattress. Together they stripped the comforter away, exposing the cool sheets. Noelle knelt on the bed and snagged the waistband of his trousers, drawing him toward her. Moving with confidence, she unfastened his belt and slid down his zipper until she'd freed him.

He had the package open and the condom ready, but when she began to slide it down his erection, the heaven of her strong fingers closed around him ripped a groan from his lips. Rolling her fingers over his sensitive tip, she gave a half smile as his hips bucked forward. Shuddering, too aroused to withstand her ministrations for long, Christian sucked in a sharp breath and freed himself from her grasp.

"You drive me crazy," he growled a second before claiming her lips in a hot, fiery kiss.

Tenderness vanished beneath the onslaught of her answering passion as she pushed her breasts against his chest and drove him crazy with the seductive sway of her hips. Filling his hands with her adorable butt, he shifted her off the mattress and coaxed her thighs around his waist. With his erection hardened to the point of pain, he laid her on the crisp sheets and moved between her thighs.

But he didn't enter her as she'd expected. Instead, his lips grazed over her mound, causing her head to lift off the bed and her gaze to sharpen. Enjoying the play of emotion on her face, he dipped his tongue into her sizzling heat and tasted her arousal. With a groan, her head fell back and her hips strained forward. Christian grinned as he began again, finding the rhythm that she liked and coaxing her toward climax.

She came against his mouth, her back arching, his name on her lips. In the aftermath, she lay with her eyes closed, her chest rising and falling with each unsteady breath. Smiling, Christian kissed his way back up her body. He settled between her thighs and kissed her with all the longing that filled his heart. Then, at her urging, he eased into her tight heat. She burrowed her fingers in his hair and set the soles of her feet on the mattress, tipping her hips to meet his slow, deep thrust.

Now it was his turn to cry out. Burying his face in her neck, he began to move. Pleasure swept over him in a stormy rush. He set his teeth against the glorious friction, fighting against the orgasm that threatened to claim him. By slowing his movements, he was able to regain some control, but the provocative sweep of Noelle's hands over his hot skin wasn't making things any easier.

"Faster," she murmured, her teeth catching at his earlobe. "I want you to come hard." Her throaty voice and the flick of her tongue over the tender spot where she'd nipped him caused him to shudder and almost lose control.

"Damn it, stop that," he growled, cupping one butt cheek and adjusting his angle just a bit to allow his pelvis to rub her just so.

With her eyes closed and her lips curled into a satisfied grin, she yielded to his pace. Content to watch her, Christian barely noticed the heat building in his groin until it threatened to engulf him.

"Come with me," Christian said. It was a plea rather than a command.

He thrust more powerfully. Her lashes lifted and her eyes met his. This is what they were good at. Connecting at this intimate level. Her vulnerability had taught him openness. Her strength had made it safe for him to let go. She'd never judged or demanded. Just given. It had made him want to give in return.

Fighting against his orgasm until she started to go over the edge, Christian felt something inside him struggling to get free. Noelle's beautiful eyes widened as the first spasms of her climax began. Wild with relief, Christian drove forward into his own release, the force of it ripping a harsh cry from him. Blackness snatched at him as stars exploded behind his eyes. Dimly he heard Noelle call his name.

For what felt like an eternity, wave after wave of pleasure pounded him. At last there was only peace and ragged breathing. Weak and shaky, Christian shifted his weight off Noelle and gathered her into his arms. She returned his hearty embrace with matching energy. They lay entwined for several minutes before Christian went to the bathroom and came back with a towel and her nightgown.

She'd never liked sleeping naked, which was fine with him because he enjoyed gliding his hands over her silk covered curves and stripping her bare each time they made love. Once her glorious breasts, tiny waist and slender hips were concealed beneath the pale green fabric, Christian set the alarm on his phone to wake them at 5:00 a.m. and pulled the covers up over them both.

This would be the first time they spent the night together since reconnecting, and Noelle's lack of protest made Christian wonder if she'd changed her mind about his proposal. If he could spend the rest of his life with Noelle, he would be happier than he deserved to be.

He stopped resisting the pull of exhaustion. Keeping up with Marc's boundless energy had taken its toll. Content in a way he hadn't been for a long time, Christian buried his nose in Noelle's fragrant hair and sighed.

"I love you," he murmured and drifted off to sleep.

Christian's words lanced through Noelle, shocking her to complete wakefulness. Before the echo of his voice faded, his deep breathing told her he was unconscious. Her first impulse was to shake him awake and force him to repeat the words. Had he meant them? Had he even realized what he said? Why was it the man couldn't speak his heart unless he was semiconscious?

Noelle lay awake for a long time, her cheek on Christian's bare chest, listening to the steady thump of his heart. She pondered the impact her expanding business was about to have on her son and her love life. Was it wrong to want it all? Success with her ready-to-wear line? The family she'd longed for with Christian? The thought of reaching out and grabbing nothing but air worried her, but she wouldn't see stars without overcoming a fear of the dark.

No solutions revealed themselves that night. She awoke to an empty bed and a brief note on hotel stationery from Christian, letting her know he had taken Marc to his suite so she could get ready in peace. The note was brisk and informative, lacking the romantic overtones left over from the previous night.

Heaving a sigh, Noelle got up and went to shower. Had all her what-ifs and how-tos from the previous night been a waste of time? Perhaps in the hazy aftermath of some spectacular lovemaking she'd only imagined what she longed to hear Christian say.

No. Noelle refused to believe that. She knew what she'd heard. Christian loved her. Based on how he'd protected her from his friends and pulled strings to get her on the path to a fabulous career, he'd loved her for a long time. That he had a hard time being vulnerable didn't surprise her.

Not only had he run with a condescending group of entitled troublemakers who tormented anyone who showed weakness, he'd also been the youngest of three princes, far from the throne with no expectations placed on him. Christian had once shared that he often felt like an afterthought. Noelle suspected this was what had led him to act out.

On the way to her first meeting, Noelle called her assistant back in Sherdana to check on her appointment for later in the week and was delighted to learn that the bride had postponed until the following month. This opened up the rest of the week, and more than anything Noelle wanted a quiet dinner with Christian and to spend a day roaming New York City with him and their son.

Knowing that Christian had cleared his entire schedule so he could be there for Marc, she sent him a text asking if they could postpone returning to Sherdana. He responded with a photo of him and Marc cheek to cheek, both giving a thumbs-up. Warmth spread through her, and she clutched the screen to her chest. Loosing a ragged sigh, she sent back a smiley face and spent the rest of the ride organizing a romantic dinner for two.

At a little after four in the afternoon, Christian carried his sleeping son across the Four Seasons lobby and into an elevator. Along the way he caught several women watching him, their expressions reading *isn't that sweet*. He resisted smiling until the elevator doors closed. He wasn't accustomed to women approving of his deeds and found he rather liked it.

Noelle was working at the desk in her suite when he let himself in. She started to rise, but he waved her back. In the past couple of days, he'd grown accustomed to caring for Marc and enjoyed it a great deal.

After taking his son's shoes off and tucking him beneath a light blanket with his favorite stuffed dinosaur, Christian returned to the living room. Noelle had put away her laptop and was standing near the wide windows staring out over the city. As Christian drew near, she smiled at him over her shoulder.

"Another hectic day?"

"I don't think there's a single question about the Statue of Liberty that Marc didn't ask."

"I'm sure." She leaned her head back against Christian's shoulder as he slipped his arms around her. He felt more than heard her sigh. "I love you."

Unsure if he'd heard her correctly, Christian held perfectly still, afraid to say anything and ruin the moment.

"But I think you already know that," she continued.

"I don't. I didn't." Chest aching, he turned her to face him. "I love you, too. You know that, right?"

She smiled at his earnest tone. "I didn't until you told me just before you fell asleep last night."

"I'm sorry it took me so long to say it. Those three words have played through my mind a hundred times over the past week. A thousand times since we first met. I guess I've avoided the truth for so long that it became a habit to hide it from you, as well."

"You're not the only one who has trouble breaking old patterns of behavior. I ended our engagement because I didn't believe you could possibly want me as something other than the mother of your son."

Cupping her face in his hands, heart racing to the point where he was light-headed, Christian searched her expression. "Does that mean you've changed your mind about wanting to marry me?" He sounded neither calm nor casual as he asked the question. To his relief she didn't leave him in suspense for long.

"I've always wanted to marry you," she teased. "Nothing could change that."

No longer capable of holding back his impatience, Christian put his hands on her shoulders and gave her a little shake. "Are you going to marry me?"

"Yes!" She threw her arms around his waist and lifted her lips to receive his kiss.

Christian wasted no time letting her know how delighted he was by her decision. One ravenous, joyful kiss followed another until a weight struck their legs. Setting Noelle's lips free, Christian glanced down at his son. Noelle's hand was already smoothing the sleep-tossed waves of Marc's dark brown hair.

"Mama, I'm hungry."

Snatching breath back into his lungs, Christian chuckled. "How is that possible after everything he's eaten today?"

"He has a lot of growing to do before he'll be as big as his father, and that takes fuel."

Christian bent and hoisted his son into his arms. Marc wrapped one arm around each of his parents as they stood close together.

"Your mother and I are getting married so the three of us can be a family," he said, catching a glimpse of Noelle's nod. "What do you think about that?" It was risky to ask a four-year-old such an important question when his stomach was empty, but Christian refused to wait another minute before making the engagement official. And telling Marc was as official as it got.

"Yeah. Will I get to live at the palace?" A couple weeks earlier it was the last place he'd wanted to visit, but now that he'd met his cousins and explored some of the rooms, he'd become much more interested in making it his home.

"Sometimes we can spend time there…" Noelle began, shooting Christian a quick frown.

Marc squirmed in Christian's grasp, his hunger once again snagging his attention. "May I have some cheese?"

Noelle made Marc a snack out of supplies stocked in the small refrigerator. When her son was content, she turned to Christian once more.

"Where are we going to live? The farmhouse is too small. Your apartment in Old Town has no outside space for Marc to play."

"I am in negotiations for an estate about twelve miles from the center of Carone. When I first learned about Marc, I decided he'd need more space than I currently have. If you approve of it, we can live there." He paused, wondering if she'd forgotten last night's decision to live in New York for six months. "As for the time you're planning to spend here, we can always rent an apartment near Central Park."

"We?" She looked hopeful.

"Before my brothers chose love over duty to the Sherdanian throne, I'd been considering expanding my ventures into the US. This seems like an excellent time to explore new territory."

Almost before he finished speaking, Noelle wrapped her arms tightly around his waist and pressed her cheek to his chest. "I'm so relieved to hear you say that. I didn't know how I was going to live apart from you these next six months."

Christian hugged her in return. "You didn't seriously think I was going to let you get away a second time, did you?"

She tipped back her head and gave him a wry smile. "Get away?"

"You have no idea what it cost me to let you go."

The torment in his voice made her shiver. She pulled him down for a kiss. Mindful of Marc's presence, they kept it affectionate and light. There would be plenty of time for passion later when they were alone.

As soon as Marc finished his snack, Christian lifted him into his arms and pulled out his cell phone. Earlier that day he'd realized that as many pictures as he'd taken with his son these past few days, not one of them had included Noelle. As the three of them clustered together in front of the window overlooking the New York skyline, Christian snapped their photo and sent it to his parents and brothers with the message that he and Noelle were engaged. Despite the time difference, he received immediate congratulations from everyone.

"It's official," he warned her. "There's no backing out now."

She regarded him with sparkling eyes. "You almost sound worried that I might."

"I learned the hard way never to take you for granted." He kissed her temple. "That will not happen again."

"We've both made mistakes and learned from them. I can see us making more."

"But as long as we don't let doubts come between us, we'll be just fine."

"Better than fine," she said, resting her head against his

shoulder and watching Marc put together a puzzle of the Statue of Liberty. "We're going to be gloriously happy."

Christian's arm tightened around Noelle. "That, my dazzling wife-to-be, sounds just about perfect."

* * * * *

*

PRINCE'S SON OF
SCANDAL

DANI COLLINS

Back in 2012 I received a call – The Call – from editor Megan Haslam, telling me she wanted to buy my book. It was my first sale and terribly exciting. I have since worked with some of the other fabulous editors in the London office, but with *Prince's Son Of Scandal* I came back to working with Megan. I'd gone so far down a rabbithole with Trella in the first three books of this quartet I really wasn't sure I could pull off her story. Megan offered just the right feedback to help me make it work. We're reunited and it feels so good!

I'd also like to dedicate this book to you, Dear Reader, for your wonderful letters and support for the Sauveterre Siblings. I'm so glad you love these characters as much as I do.

CHAPTER ONE

Six months ago...

WHEN THE GREETER at the ballroom entrance asked Trella Sauveterre for her name, she nearly gave an arrogant "you know who I am."

She bit it back. Her sister was never acerbic. Not with strangers, and definitely not with underlings. Her twin was perfectly capable of terse words and might even hurl some blue ones at Trella when she learned what she was doing right now, but Angelique's personality was one of sensitivity and empathy. Gentleness and kindness.

Trella? Not so much.

"Angelique Sauveterre," Trella lied, wearing her sister's polite yet reserved smile. She ought to feel more guilty. She ought to feel like an overused cliché from a children's movie, but she didn't.

She felt *alive*.

And apprehensive. Terror could overcome her if she let herself dig deep enough. This was like swimming toward the middle of a lake, where the bottom was too deep to imagine. Who knew what dangers lurked in those dark watery depths? Monsters. They existed. She had met them. Had nearly been consumed by them.

But she wouldn't think about that.

Nothing in her outward appearance revealed the way her heart bounced and jostled in her chest, fighting internal battles. She moved gracefully, even though her muscles felt stiff and petrified, twitching to run.

Because, along with the trickles of fear, a tumbling waterfall of joy rang through her. It was all she could do to keep tears from her eyes or laughter from escaping her throat.

I'm doing it! she wanted to call her family and cry. *Look. I'm in public. By myself. I'm not shriveling like a vampire in the sun.*

But they didn't know where she was and it was best to keep it that way. This was the sort of sneaking out a window she should have done years ago, when she'd been an adolescent. Instead, she'd been a grieving survivor with an eating disorder and more baggage than a passenger jet.

Still was, if these people only knew.

She quashed the negative self-talk and moved like a normal person through the crowd. Gazes lingered, noting Angelique Sauveterre had arrived. Her bodyguard kept anyone from approaching, though. Maybe that wasn't normal for everyone, but it was for the Sauveterre twins, even the eldest set of brothers.

With her sister's aloof nod, she returned a few greetings to people she imagined she was supposed to know.

In a few weeks, she would come out as Trella and have nothing left to hide behind. No more walls, literal or technical. No broad-shouldered brothers. No playing her sister to avoid being herself. She had determined, had sworn on the blood she had shed when she nicked her ear cutting her own hair before Christmas, that this was the year she would free herself from the prison she had created.

For now, she was still hiding behind Angelique. She had impersonated her sister a few times recently, with her sister's permission, escorted by their brother Henri to watch his twin, Ramon, race. They'd also taken in a fellow designer's latest collection during fashion week. It had been spectator stuff where they didn't interact with anyone and kept to places her sister had been seen with their brothers before.

Trella had never walked out in public alone. In her entire life, she had rarely done anything alone. As a child, Angelique—Gili to her family—had been the needy one and Trella, the protector. She had held Gili's hand so her sister wouldn't tremble and cry at the attention they had received. Their brothers had barely given them breathing space even before Trella's kidnapping at age nine, always ready to catch a tumble from a swing or to keep them from wandering too far from the group.

Then she'd been stolen and had *wished* that her captors had left her alone.

She swallowed and veered her mind away from those memories. They were guaranteed to bring on an attack and she was doing far too well. It was coming up to two years without one.

The attacks had manifested years after her rescue, when she should have been finding her feet and moving on with her life. Instead, she had become a horrible burden. Her siblings would never say so, but they had to be sick of being on call for her. She was certainly tired of being the weakest link. She *had* to change.

Tonight was another step toward that. The press would go mad when she finally came out of seclusion at a friend's wedding in a few weeks. She had to be ready, but she had to *know* she was ready.

So she was testing herself, if somewhat impulsively, because this charity dinner hadn't been on her agenda at all when she had arrived in Paris.

She had been beside herself with pride when she'd landed, high on travelling from the family home in

Spain—by private jet with trusted guards, always—but without her mother or siblings. It had taken her newfound independence to the next level.

So, when Gili tentatively had asked if she could run to London for a hot secret weekend with her new paramour, *of course* Trella had told her to go. Her sister had looked incandescent when she'd spoken about Prince Kasim. He was clearly something special.

Trella wanted her sister to be happy, wanted to quit holding her back. Spending a night alone at their tightly secured living space above their design house, Maison des Jumeaux, had seemed a perfect cherry on top of Trella's already sweet split from old fears.

As the evening stretched on, however, she had restlessly poked around the flat, picking up after her sister and teetering on feeling sorry for herself. Wistfulness had closed around her.

Would *she* ever have a romantic liaison? Her feelings about men were so ambivalent. At fourteen, she'd had the usual rush of hormonal interest, even shared an embrace with the gardener's son behind a rosebush. Then their father had died and the most terrifying predators had emerged online, threatening her in vile ways. Her fear of men, of *everything*, had compounded a hundredfold. As her panic attacks escalated, the deepest fear of all had crept into her very soul—that she was so damaged and broken, no one would ever want her.

For years, she had barely allowed men near her, interesting or otherwise. She slipped from one secured location to another through shielded walkways, accompanied by a mostly female guard detail. Occasionally, her brothers introduced her to a friend, but even if she had wanted any of those bankers or race-car drivers to make a pass, Ramon and Henri wouldn't have allowed it.

Their dearest family friend, Sadiq, was the only man she'd spent real time with and theirs had never been a romantic relationship. He was the shy, heart-of-gold computer nerd who had helped the police locate her, returning her to her family. She loved him, but as her savior, not as a man.

Which was why his engagement had shaken her out of her ivory tower. She would do anything for Sadiq. If he wanted her at his wedding, of course she would attend, even though it meant overcoming her demons and returning to the public eye.

It had been a struggle to come this far, but now, as she stood on the cusp of achieving something like a normal life, she found herself resetting the goalposts.

She wanted her sister's anticipation for a weekend with a man. She wanted to be the person she would have been if she hadn't been stolen and assaulted, stalked and bullied, but it would never happen if she kept living behind these damned walls!

A disgusted toss of the latest fashion magazines onto the coffee table had sent a pile of paperwork sliding to the floor, revealing an invitation to this ball.

The fundraiser benefited orphaned children, something that would go straight to Gili's tender heart. Even if Gili had sent regrets, the Sauveterre checkbook was always welcome.

Not letting herself overthink it, Trella had briefed a security team and slipped on one of her sister's creations.

Where Trella loved powerful touches like strong shoulders and A-lines, along with eye-catching beadwork and bold colors, her sister's style was gentler. The champagne gown had a waifish quality in the way the sleeves fell off her shoulders. The bodice and torso were fitted to her figure, but the ruched skirt across her hips created a sensual impression of gathered satin sheets around a nude form.

She added her sister's earrings and a locket with a panic button, but kept the look simple, arranging her hair into a fall of dark locks and painting her lips a soft pink.

Now she was here, breathless and petrified, yet filled with more optimism than she'd experienced in years. She moved to speak to the aloof Russian host and his much warmer British wife, Aleksy and Clair Dmitriev.

"I'm so glad you came," Clair said, drawing her aside in a confiding way that revealed Clair had no idea she was talking to Gili's twin. "You're not my only supporter who comes without a date, but you're the only one who won't be silly about my guest of honor. Don't even ask how I got him here. I was hideously shameless, interrupting their trade talks and putting him on the spot in front of everyone. I talked him into auctioning himself for the first dance."

Trella scanned for a glimpse of this exalted personality. Clair continued her confession as she wound them through the crowd.

"Aleksy said at least I use my power for good instead of evil, but I feel a little evil because the ravens surrounded him the minute he arrived. They'll back off if you're there, though. I know you'll put him at ease. Everyone loves you. Do you mind?"

Trella could see how Clair got what she wanted, sounding sincere in her flattery as she took agreement for granted. Still, she was curious enough to murmur, *"Bien sûr,"* in her sister's preferred French.

Clair beamed and gently pushed into the thicket of gowns.

The mystery man turned, revealing a red sash beneath his black tuxedo jacket. He was tall. Intimidatingly tall, with broad shoulders and an economy of movement, suggesting a huntsman's physique lurked beneath his sophisticated attire. The blond glints in his light brown hair looked natural, given the hint of gold in his eyebrows.

Those eyes. They were such a piercing blue they struck like slabs off a glacier, peeling away to fall and rock the world. The rest of his features were precisely carved in sweeps of long cheeks under sharp cheekbones, a jaw hammered square and a mouth of two perfectly symmetrical peaks over a full but uncompromising bottom lip.

He was so compelling a force, so beyond her experience, the room faded from her consciousness. They became trapped in a noiseless, airless bubble as they took each other in.

Had she really longed to be seen as a woman? Because it was happening. He skimmed his gaze down in unabashed assessment. She saw the flash of interest in his gaze as it came back and locked with hers. He liked what he saw.

He saw Gili, though. Sweet Gili who was used to being in public, where men routinely sized her up as a potential conquest.

The strangest reaction slithered through Trella. She ought to have prickled with threat, or acted like Gili and let his male interest drift past her as if she didn't notice or care.

Instead, she took issue with her sister being seen as a trophy. Protective instincts honed since birth pushed her confrontational personality to the forefront of the image she presented.

You'll have to go through me, she projected, tucking Gili safely behind her.

His stare intensified. *Burned.* He saw *her.* Whatever shields she had walked in here holding—including her sister's persona—were gone. She felt completely unprotected against his thorough exploration of her face, his gaze touching each curve and dip of her features.

It felt like a spill of magic, making her cheeks tingle. She had to disguise a rush of unprecedented sensual awareness. Men didn't affect her, but the spell he cast sent invisible sensations from her throat to her nipples and her pelvis, into her thighs and terminated in a paralysis that nailed her feet to the floor. All the while, delicious stirrings swirled upward through her, making her feel drawn toward him.

"Your Highness," she heard Clair say from what seemed like another universe. "Have you met Angelique Sauveterre?"

"Ms. Sauveterre, the Crown Prince of Elazar, Xavier Deunoro."

Xavier had known exactly what he was doing when Clair Dmitriev had cornered him into making an appearance at her charity event. He was buying a future favor from her powerful husband, a man who was notoriously difficult to influence.

He had also known it would be an evening rife with what he had before him: Women in daring gowns, swishing their hips in enticement, sweeping lashes in false shyness while they twisted their hair in invitation.

As Europe's most eligible bachelor, he was used to having his pick from such an array. He only needed to drop a claw and let it pick up one of the brightly colored toys before him. It didn't matter which one fell into his hands. They were all the same, providing brief entertainment and something soft to embrace for a night, before forgetting them in the hotel room when he left the next morning.

Given the news he had received this morning, tonight's plaything would be his last before his royal duty took precedence. It was another reason he had agreed to this ridiculousness. At least he had a decent selection for his final visit to the amusement park.

He was taking his time singling out his companion. They all had their charms. Was he in the mood for voluptuous or fair? Should he be practical and choose the one wearing enough gold not to covet his own? Or go with the one who promised some spark as she set her chin and glared at the rest?

Then his hostess presented a newcomer like a gift, one who made the rest of the women take sharp little breaths and step back.

She was taller than most, with divine features that matched her name. Her skin was soft and flushed, too warm to be called cream yet not dark enough to be olive. Golden as a sunrise glancing off a snowy peak.

A muse, clearly, since he felt poetic stirrings just by gazing at her. How could he not admire her? Her figure was goddess-perfect, her mouth sinful, her eyes fey and mysterious, colored somewhere between gray and green. If he pulled her from the cloud of perfume surrounding them, he bet she would smell like mossy forest and clean cold streams.

That was what she presented on the surface, at least. In a blink, she had shifted ever so slightly and it was as if she'd hit exactly the right angle to catch and reflect the sun. Something less tangible than external beauty seemed to concentrate and strike out in a sharp white light that pierced his eyes, like a star being born.

She was the diamond in a bowl of imitations, a woman of facets and contrasts, infinitely fascinating and priceless. If recognizing that caused him a stab of regret because he didn't have time to fully explore her depths and contradictions, he ignored it. Such was his life. He took what he could, when he could.

Tonight, he would take her, *grazie mille*.

"Good evening." He bowed over her hand, letting his breath warm her knuckles and feeling the tiny flex of her reaction. "It's an honor to meet you."

"A rare treat indeed." The tilt of her lips suggested an inside joke. "The honor is mine."

"I've seated you at the VIP table," Clair said. "Please find your way when you're ready. Has everyone seen the silent auction items?" Clair broke up the knot of disgruntled women, most of whom drifted off.

A few opportunists remained, one being the redhead with the determined chin. He sighed inwardly as the redhead flashed a too sweet smile before asking, "Angelique, how is your sister? Still keeping to herself?"

Ah yes. That's why the name had struck him as familiar. The family had a tragic history. One of the twin girls had been kidnapped as a child. She was rumored to be batty, so they kept her out of sight. As someone who had been reported as everything from born of an alien to outright dead, he put little store in such gossip, but did wonder how she would respond to such a blatant intrusion. It was clearly meant to disconcert.

She swung a scythe-sharp glance at the redhead, revealing the compressed carbon beneath her sparkle.

"She's excellent." Her tone struck him as ironic. "What's your name? I'll tell her you were asking about her."

"Oh." The redhead was startled, but flicked him a glance and decided to take a final stab at snaring his interest. "*Lady* Wanda Graves."

"I'll be sure you're added to our list." She smiled distantly and turned to him. "Shall we find our seats?"

She didn't see the redhead brighten briefly before a darker thought struck, one that tightened her mouth. The other women who'd been standing by widened their eyes then averted their gazes before they scurried off.

He offered his arm and dipped his mouth to her ear. "You have a blacklist?"

"Nosy people do not wear our label."

Catty, ruthless, or both? Either way, he was entertained.

And now he was reminded that the sisters had some kind of design house. Women's fashion was last on his list of interests, but he took a fresh assessment of her gown, appreciating the peek of thigh exposed by the slit and the gather of strapless satin that left an expanse of upper chest and breast swell to admire.

"This is one of your creations? It's pure artistry."

"I can tell when I'm being patronized," she warned.

"Then you'll know I'm sincere when I say the dress is lovely, but I see the woman inside it. Which is the point, is it not?"

"Do you?" She tilted a considering look up at him, something dancing in the elfin green of her eyes. He could have sworn they were gray a minute ago. Her gaze dropped to his chest, where the band of silk slashed across his heart. "I see the crown, not the man. Which is what this is meant to convey, isn't it?"

Astute, but a woman who made her living with clothing would understand such nuances.

The sash in question felt unaccountably restrictive this evening. Duty hovered in his periphery, set there by a brief news item passed along from his PA about Bonnafete, a small principality in the Mediterranean. The reigning prince's daughter, Patrizia, had called off her marriage to an American real estate mogul.

Patrizia was a longtime acquaintance. Xavier was not as sorry as he had implied when he had sent his condolences. He was in need of a titled wife. His grandmother wanted him married so she could step down. Patrizia was infinitely suitable.

He had asked that his grandmother be made aware of the broken engagement. It was an acknowledgement of his responsibility toward her, their bloodline and the crown.

Loath as he was to marry, he preferred to spearhead such actions himself, rather than wait for her to issue orders. She might be the one person on this earth with the power to govern his actions, but he didn't have to encourage it. He was confident she would approve and God knew she would let him know if she didn't.

"Is it heavy?" his final sown oat asked of his sash. The levelness in her tone told him she didn't mean physically, proving she was even more perceptive than he'd imagined.

Compassion was not something he looked for in anyone, though, least of all his temporary companions. There was no room for any weakness in his life. No one saw him flinch. No one was privy to his bitterness at the hand life had dealt him.

It was a wasted emotion to feel.

So he ignored the chance she might understand him in a way no one else ever had and held her chair. "Nothing could weigh me down while I'm in your beguiling company, *bella*."

She froze and looked over her shoulder. "Why did you call me that?"

"It's an endearment. Elazar's official language is an Italian dialect, though French and German are commonly spoken along with English." He adjusted her chair as she sank into it then leaned down to speak against her hair where it fell in loose waves against her nape. "Why? Don't you like it?"

Tiny bumps lifted on her skin in a shiver of reaction. Her nipples tightened into peaks against the silk that draped over them, making him smile. She liked it.

Awash in more sexual anticipation than he'd felt in a while, perhaps ever, he seated himself, pleased he would end his bachelorhood with such a terrific bang.

* * *

Trella was a natural extrovert. The chatter and color around her, the voices and music and attention, was like standing in the sunshine after years in an *oubliette*.

But to have this man glance at her with that admiring look on his face as he seated himself next to her was a deliciously sweet accompaniment. He was clearly an accomplished seducer, wearing charm and entitlement as comfortably as his sash, but she was excited to be singled out by him all the same. It was the flirtation she had yearned for.

"What brings you to Paris?" he asked.

Although, if she was going to do this, she wasn't settling for plain vanilla.

"Surely you can do better than asking what a nice girl like me is doing in a place like this?"

"Let me consult my app." He glanced at an imaginary phone. "How about... What sign are you?" He affected sincere interest.

Her mouth twitched. "Gemini. Twins. Obviously. You?"

"No idea. August sixth."

"Leo. The lion. King of the jungle."

"Obviously," he said, with a self-deprecating tilt of the corner of his mouth.

She bit back a smile, intrigued by his position, but only because she knew what it was to be in the spotlight. He'd glossed over her query about the weight of his crown, but surely he wearied of attention and responsibility.

"You take horoscopes seriously?" he asked, nodding at a server who offered them champagne.

"Not as a belief system, but I used it as inspiration for a collection a few years ago. *We* used it," she amended quickly, clearing her throat over the white lie and sliding her gaze to ensure the people searching for their seats hadn't overheard her. It was well known in fashion circles that *Trella* had designed that particular line.

"How?" He seemed genuinely curious. "The patterns in the fabric?"

"Not that literal. More how the nature of each sign is perceived. They fall into different qualities, like fixed or mutable, and elements, like air and fire. There's a lot to play with. I work better with deadlines so I approached one sign a month. It was an interesting exercise." She leaned closer, wrinkling her nose. "Also a terrific marketing hook."

The corners of his mouth deepened. "Beauty *and* brains. Always an irresistible combination."

This prince, causing her heart to thud-thud under a simple compliment, should have sent her running. She had learned healthy caution from her childhood, but even though most men put her on edge, this one filled her with a giddy *lack* of fear. It was like breaking out of a shell. Like discovering she had the ability to fly.

She definitely wanted more time with him before this evening ended.

On impulse, she motioned for her guard, who was actually one of Gili's, and quietly gave him an instruction about the silent auction. He melted away.

Was she being too forward? Reckless?

Their table filled up, forcing her to wait to find out. Dinner passed in a blur of neutral conversation. Someone asked the Prince about his country's foray into green energy. She vaguely recalled his mountain kingdom between Italy and Austria had been accused of providing a tax haven during the world wars. Elazar sounded very modern and self-sufficient now. He spoke about exporting hydropower, since rivers and streams were one of their few natural resources. There was also a decade of investing in education, attracting engineering and technology start-ups, solar and wind power.

Her inner businesswoman should have been taking mental notes, but she was mesmerized by his casual command over his audience and subtly seduced with how close his sleeve came to touching her arm. Beneath the table, she imagined she could feel the heat from his thigh mere inches from her own. All she could think about was dancing with him.

Dancing. Tears pressed the backs of her eyes. She ached for that simple pleasure.

This adolescent reaction was ridiculous, but she let it happen. Embraced it. This is what she should have been doing at twenty, not hand-sewing sequins on mini-dresses for other young women to wear to exclusive clubs, killing hours with concentrated work so she could get through one day, one more hour, without a breakdown or the drugs that were supposed to prevent them.

Then Prince Xavier turned his terrifically handsome face toward her, bathing her in the light of his regard. "You must travel a great deal for your work? What drew you to fashion?"

He had given each of the others a moment in his attentive sunlight. Now it was her turn. He must engage in small talk with a thousand people a day, at ribbon cuttings and children's hospitals, but she would have sworn on her life the tension around his eyes eased as he met her gaze. He'd been doing his duty, impatiently waiting to get back to her. She felt delirious even as she prevaricated her way through her reply.

"Both of us are quite creative." Gili more so. She was the artist who designed out of love and ran the business out of necessity. Trella was the ambitious one, determined to turn a healthy profit. Practicality, not passion, had driven her into making her own clothes, because she couldn't bear being judged by trolls for merely *buying* something, let alone how it looked on her.

"We had some start-up help from our brothers but surprised them and ourselves with our success." Another fib. She wouldn't have rested until they were making buckets of money. She was competitive and driven by an I'll-show-you desire for revenge against those who had thrown shade.

"It can't be an easy field. I'm sure your success is due to hard work as much as anything else."

He was trying to get her into bed. She knew that with the brains he'd said he admired, but his flattery *worked*. She was ridiculously affected by his compliment. She wanted to say "It was a ton of work. Thank you for noticing." Gili was the face of Maison des Jumeaux, which meant she received the bulk of the credit—not that she didn't deserve a lot, but Trella worked just as hard and was not a naturally humble person. Hearing his praise went into her like a transfusion, tipping her further under his spell.

Their hostess moved to the podium to make a short speech, thanked the guests for their donations then announced the winners for the auction items. Trella grew increasingly self-conscious as the moments ticked down, certain she had truly lost her mind this time. Maybe she should leave before—

"Finally, our most coveted prize, a dance with the Prince of Elazar, has been won by… Angelique Sauveterre!"

The applause was polite, the knives in her back proverbial, but she felt them. She privately smirked, then blushed as Xavier showed no surprise. Was he so sure of her?

"I'm flattered."

"You should be. I promised to double the next highest bid. You had better dance well enough to be worth it."

"I do," he assured her, rising to help with her chair, doing that erotic thing of speaking against her hair so tingles raced all over her skin. "For that sort of generosity, *bella*, I'll give you the whole night."

Oh, he was good. Lightheadedness accosted her every time he called her *bella*, the same nickname her family called her. Her pulse pounded so hard she thought it would bruise her throat, but it fed the thrilling excitement washing over her. He made her feel so alluring. *Sexy*.

He made her feel as though he wanted *her*.

That was beyond captivating. She had spent a lot of dark nights telling herself how flawed she was, how she didn't want men anyway, so she didn't care if they didn't want her. She did want, though. She wanted to feel normal and alive. Happy and desirable.

The touch of his hand on the small of her back had a terrific effect on her. The awareness that had been teasing her all evening became a suffusion of deeply sensual lethargy. Dear Lord, was she becoming *aroused*?

It was what she'd envied her sister for—which was when it struck her what was happening. She and Gili had a twin connection. They didn't read each other's thoughts or anything so intrusive, but they picked up hints of the other's emotions despite whatever physical distance might separate them. The preternatural sense was stronger on Gili's side. Trella had been so messed up for years, taking antidepressants to quash anxiety attacks, she hadn't been as receptive to her sister's moods.

Lately, however, she'd become more aware, particularly if Gili was restless or having an off day. Tonight, her sister was with a man who truly excited her. She was usually so careful, so rarely selfish, yet she was basking in something that made her incredibly happy.

Her sister's buoyant heart lightened Trella's. She was

happy for Gili, happy her sister wasn't weighed down by all the things Trella had put her through. It added another lift of carefree joy to her own evening.

"You dance well yourself," Xavier said as he spun her in a waltz.

She was too exhilarated to respond. The sparkling ballroom circled around her in a kaleidoscope of colors. His embrace was confident and reassuring, making her feel light as a fairy.

"I feel like Cinderella." It was too true. She was the smudged sister who had escaped from the attic, wearing borrowed clothing to dance with a prince.

"You look like something out of a fairy tale." The line of his brow twitched and the corner of his mouth deepened, like he both surprised and disparaged himself for saying. "You're very beautiful," he added gruffly.

Gili was the beautiful one. Trella had fought hard to get back to the same weight as her sister, wanting to feel as good as Gili looked. She had let her hair grow out to her sister's length so she could impersonate her for her dry runs going out in public, but she never thought of herself as beautiful. She too often thought of herself as broken.

Not tonight. She diverted herself away from any thoughts other than how *glorious* this was. Around and around they went. His thighs brushed hers, his fingers splayed as though trying to touch more of her. She let her fingers trail closer to his collar so she could rest the side of one finger on the hot skin of his neck. It was electrifying. The magnetic sensations grew as he kept her dancing into the second song, tugging her toward an unknown crescendo. When someone tried to cut in, Xavier shrugged him off.

"The privilege of position?" she teased.

"I've never seen anyone glow like you. I'm enthralled."

Again, misgiving seemed to flicker like a shadow across his face. He didn't like admitting to whatever he was feeling, but it added to her own exuberance.

"I feel like… I can't even describe it. Like it's Christmas. Like anything is possible." She brought her gaze down from the chandelier into the turquoise blue of his eyes.

She reminded herself that becoming over-excited could have a rebound effect. She didn't want to backslide. It would be a long fall from this height.

Then she forgot any sense of caution when he said, "I need to kiss you." The desire in his words was a sensual squeeze that stole her breath.

A very long time ago, she had been quick to agree to anything that sounded adventurous. A dungeon full of shackles and bars had kept her grounded since then, but somehow, with a few words, this man reached past all the darkness and invited her into the light. To be the impulsive, audacious person she was in her heart.

"Me, too," she said through sensitized lips. *It's only a kiss.*

His sharp gaze moved beyond her. The next thing she knew, he had her off the dance floor, through a small break in the crowd and into an alcove hidden by the giant fronds of a potted plant.

She wasn't given time to decide whether she'd been too quick to agree. His arm tightened across the small of her back, pulling her in, arching her against the layers of his tuxedo. He was steely beneath his civilized covering. He knew what he wanted. His hot mouth covered hers without hesitation.

For a second, she was terrified. Not of him, but of how she would react. Would she panic?

Then her senses took in the way his mouth fit against

hers, moving to part her lips, questing for her response. Something primitive moved in her, shaking her foundations, waking the woman she might have been if her life had been different, drawing her beyond old traumas into a place she barely understood.

Pleasure flooded her, making her stiffen, wary of such a strong reaction, but primal need quickly took over. Her brain might not be able to process what was going on, but her body knew how to respond.

Rather than put the brakes on, her hands went behind his neck. She found herself running her fingers into his short hair, shaping the back of his head as she drew herself up, parting her lips so he could plunder at will.

His arms tightened around her and she thought he made a growling noise. It should have scared her. Male aggression, especially the sexual kind, was something she'd taken pains to avoid.

Strangely, with excitement pulsing through her, she found herself thrilled by his response. She kissed him back with abandon, just as if she knew what she was doing.

Something flashed behind her closed eyes and he abruptly lifted his head.

"That was a camera," he muttered, fingers digging in near her tailbone as he pressed her close enough to feel the thick shape straining the front of his trousers. "Let's find some privacy."

Her analytical mind urged caution, but her old self, her true self, trusted her instincts. She released a breathy, "Let's."

CHAPTER TWO

HE DIPPED HIS head to lightly scrape his teeth against her neck, urging against her ear, "You leave first. I'll follow you upstairs."

She gasped, mind going blank before a million thoughts rushed in.

"You have a room here? In the hotel?" What had she thought when he had said *privacy*? Was the idea of being alone with him intriguing or alarming?

"The penthouse, yes."

"Is it safe?"

"Of course." Good gracious he was handsome, even when he frowned. His features weren't too refined. There was just enough toughness in the intensity of his gaze, just enough stubbornness in the square of his jaw to make him look stern and rugged.

As he read her hesitation, his hand cupped the side of her head while his gaze flicked with irritation at the noise around them. "I want you to myself."

Empathy panged within her. She knew the wear and tear that being in the spotlight took on a person. She instantly wanted to give him the break he needed. He was a sophisticated man. She had nothing to fear from him physically, but was compelled to say, "I have guards. For a reason."

She was using her sister's tonight, both to give her own

a much-deserved night off as well as to maintain the illusion she was her twin. *She should tell him who she was.*

"The room is completely secure. More secure than here," he added, mouth twisting in dismay at their having been photographed. He led her back to their table. "I won't keep you waiting long."

Voices of caution crowded into her head, but when would she have a free pass like this again? When would she meet a man who made her feel anything like this? It wasn't just physical, although that part was so heady she felt drunk, but there was a rarity, too. There were other men in the world who were a safe bet, men vetted by her brothers, but when would she feel this pull? This compulsion to know more about *this* man?

Before she talked herself out of it, she let her finger press *up* for the penthouse. It wasn't that she didn't have misgivings, or that she ignored them, she *overcame* them. It was different. It was another small triumph that had her stepping lightly off the elevator onto thickly carpeted floor.

It was easy to spot the Prince's room. Two guards were stationed outside the door. Her own accompanied her as she approached them.

"Mademoiselle Sauveterre," one greeted with a respectful nod. "We were notified to expect you." He stepped inside and invited her guard to sweep the rooms.

Both men behaved with the utmost professionalism, not betraying a hint of judgment about what they must know was a preliminary for seduction.

A smile touched her mouth as she thought about how her brothers would blow their tops if they knew where she was right now, even though they had both been on the Prince's side of this equation hundreds of times, the hypocrites.

Then she was left alone and she took in the elegant shades of ivory and sage green on the walls and the furnishings. A glass of watered-down Scotch had been abandoned on an end table, ice long melted. She sniffed, then dared a sip, thought about looking at the view, then decided to leave the drapes closed.

The double doors to the bedroom stood open. She stared at the bed, taking another quick sip of liquid courage just as the main door opened. His star power impacted her anew, making her heart skip.

"You made yourself comfortable. Good."

"This is yours." She tilted the glass, then set it aside, instantly wishing she'd kept it to keep her hands busy.

"I'll make you a fresh one. Or, how about champagne?" He moved to the bar. As he peeled the foil from a bottle, the crinkle seemed overly loud.

This was the moment she should have admitted she was Trella.

A very real fear sat within that admission—that he would develop his own misgivings. He would either want explanations she didn't care to give, or he might jump to conclusions that made him averse to being with her. In no scenario did she imagine this exciting, lighthearted atmosphere would continue.

"You're nervous," he noted as he popped the cork.

"You're observant," she said, compelled to at least confess, "I don't do this."

It was true no matter which twin she represented. Gili running away for a weekend with a prince was as out of character as her being here with this one.

"I already guessed that." He set two glasses as he poured, canting his head to eye her. "You're not a virgin, are you?"

She choked. "No."

True again for both twins, but she had to look away, mind skipping off the dark memory like a stone off the water's surface.

No, that was another reason she was here. Being alone with a man was another snapped link in the chain that bound her to the past. She was really, really proud of herself right now. Even though her proffered excuse of "I'm just out of my comfort zone" was the understatement of the year.

He brought the glasses across the room to her and offered her one. *"Saluti."*

"Salud."

They sipped, gazes locked, unspoken expectations hovering between them. Her throat grew abraded by the bubbles.

"What if I change my mind about being here?" she asked in a soft rasp.

"Then I will be disappointed." His intent expression didn't change.

"Angry?"

"Disappointed. Very disappointed, *bella*." His gaze acted like wildfire, igniting her blood as he swept it across her cheek and down her throat.

He turned away to set music playing. The notes were low and sultry, matching the thick feeling in her veins, the sensual throb of her pulse.

"Either way, I'm pleased to have you to myself." He came back to her, steps laconic, touch smooth and confident as he looped his arm around her. "Whether you want to talk or dance or…pass the time in other ways."

He swayed them into a dance that was really just the press of two bodies. Foreplay. They both still held their champagne flutes. Held gazes.

"I wasn't in the mood to fight other men for your attention."

"Was anyone else even trying? I hadn't noticed." She batted her lashes.

His mouth tilted. "I like that wit, *bella*. I find myself regretting we only have tonight."

She tucked her chin and gave him an admonishing look. "You're patronizing me again. I don't need the rules spelled out. I'm not *that* green."

"See? Such sharp intelligence is the sort of thing that holds my interest longer than a few hours."

"Is that how long your liaisons usually last?"

He stopped dancing, arm remaining across her back, but loosely. "That's probably not a good topic of conversation."

"I know." Bubbles tickled her nose as she sipped, trying to wash away a strange bitterness on her tongue. It shouldn't matter what his past looked like. Whatever man eventually attached himself to her wouldn't come to her pristine. She couldn't expect it when she had such a complicated history herself. "I think I'm looking for reasons not to like you so I won't feel so..."

She frowned. The hand she'd rested on his shoulder slid down to splay on his chest as if she had the right to touch him with such familiarity, but touching him felt very natural. Her fingertips dipped beneath the ribbon of red, sliding the tips of her polished nails beneath it as she ever so slightly lifted it off the crispness of his shirt.

"I'm not a pushover. I'm normally the most contrary person you could imagine. A fighter." Her family told her that all the time, so why was she letting this happen? Her usual streak of rebellion was absent.

Actually, she realized with a spark of insight, it was directed against the life she'd been leading, pushing her to break free of old restraints. No one was stopping her from spending a night with a man except her. All she had to do was *choose* to.

"I'm not trying to pressure you. I'm sincere that I wish we had more time to get to know one another, but my life has never allowed for long term relationships." His hand shifted to splay in a warm brand against her lower back, offering a soothing caress. "For what it's worth—" He bit the inside of his cheek, seeming to weigh what he was about to say. The shadow moved behind his eyes again, telling her that he was uncomfortable with how revealing his words were. "If you walked out of here right now, I wouldn't go looking for someone else. You're the only woman I want to be with tonight."

"Why?" It came out of her with a pang of disbelief. "Please don't say it's because you like the way I look." She didn't want him to want Gili. It would break her heart— it really would.

His breath came out in a soft snort of disbelief. "Because of the way we make each other feel."

He lowered his head to graze his damp lips along her jaw and down to her neck, making her shiver. Her nipples pulled tight so quickly they stung. He chuckled softly at the way she audibly caught her breath.

"We're positively volatile." His hot breath bathed her ear before his teeth lightly closed on her lobe, nearly causing her knees to buckle.

She pressed her hand more firmly to his chest.

"No?" He drew back, but held her close. Held her up, if she was honest.

"I'm trying to think," she gasped, nearly overwhelmed by sensations that were the furthest thing from fear.

"And you can't? Then we feel the same." His tight smile only made the edgy fist of need inside her clench harder. "Feel, *bella*. Feel how much you're exciting me." He moved her hand all the way under the sash, so the pound of his heart slammed into her palm. "This isn't anything I've ever experienced, either."

Her scalp tingled. She dropped her champagne glass,

ignoring the delicate break of crystal, wanting too badly to touch him with both hands. She slid her fingers to the back of his neck and raised her mouth, inviting him to kiss her. It was pure instinct and he didn't hesitate, covering her parted lips as though he'd been let off his leash after having been tempted for too long.

The world stopped then spun the other way, dizzying her. She made one whimpering noise, astonished by how thoroughly such a thing could devastate her, wilting all her muscles.

She distantly heard another delicate shatter, then he picked her up, lifting his head to reveal a fierce expression. Victory? Not quite, but there was something conquering there. Something exalted.

Yet his bright gaze asked a question.

She nodded, unable to speak, just gave herself up to it, to him. She knew when to fight her body and when to surrender. Perhaps it was the silver lining to all those years of having to accept that physiology trumped logic. This was bigger than anything she could make sense of.

He set her on the bed and she watched him throw off his jacket, shaken by the feelings that were carving a valley through her. He joined her and dragged her half under him, kissing her again. Thorough, drugging kisses that set her alight, yet she felt stiff and frozen.

"What's wrong?" He lifted his head, proving himself to be attuned to her in a way that was reassuring and disturbing all at once.

"I'm shy," she admitted, ducking her head as she said it because that wasn't her at *all*. Her eyes stung with emotive tears at how monumental this was. She was alone with a man, on a *bed*, and he had set the sun inside her. He made it radiate outward, filling her with such heat and joy she was going to burst. "I want to touch you, but I don't want to make a fool of myself. I don't know if I can contain myself."

"Don't even try." His voice brimmed with graveled warning, which might have made her chuckle, but she released her breath and let her hands move to greedily stake a claim.

He was firm everywhere, taut and strong. Hot. Her fingers discovered the textures of his clothes, then slid beneath his shirt as he yanked it free of his belted pants. He made an approving noise as she found satin skin and the tension of his abdomen, then the shape of his rib cage and the sleek muscles across his chest. The sharp beads of his nipples fascinated her.

She made her own appreciative noises, utterly rapt with the contrast of his body to her own, all flat planes and crisp hair and indomitable strength.

He released her zip and dragged down the loosened front of her dress. As he bared her breasts, something elemental gripped her. The spirit of womanhood. She melted onto her back and arched, emphasizing their differences, liking that he made a noise that sounded almost suffering, yet growly and ferocious. He opened his mouth and engulfed her in such a place of earthy pleasure, she released her own cry of agonized joy.

Volatile. Was that what this was? She hadn't known she could feel like this, frantic yet intoxicated. Impatient yet timeless. She wanted to stay like this forever, running their hands over each other, kissing, mouths needing to fuse and breathing be damned. But as his hands moved on her, shifting silk with a touch so hot it burned her through the fabric, she wanted more. So much more.

His fingertips grazed the slit in her gown and she found herself offering more of her leg then trembling in anticipation, waiting for the feel of his touch on her skin. The pet of his hand on the outside of her thigh made her shiver. She gloried in the way he kissed her harder, deeper, hand shaping her hip, exploring her belly, then tracking to her other thigh. He squeezed the taut muscle then moved with delicious confidence to cup the center of her.

Breath stalling, eyes opening, she waited for panic, but before she could entertain a grim memory, he firmed his touch and rocked his hand, sending a jolt of incredible pleasure through her pelvis. Her eyelids grew heavy again and she found herself lifting, spellbound by the lightning bolts of sensation that grew in strength as they kissed and he caressed her.

How could anything feel this good?

She wanted to touch him as intimately, but she could hardly think of anything but how he was making her feel. Just as she tried to shape him through his pants, his touch changed, exploring beneath silk with knowledge and intention.

She bucked in reaction. "I can't—My heart is going to explode."

She moved a reflexive hand to cover his, not quite stopping him, because the slide of his fingers against her was so mesmerizing, but so sensitizing she almost couldn't bear it. Her entire focus narrowed to that delicate circle and stroke.

"I want to be inside you, but I don't want to stop touching you. Like that?" He pushed a long finger into her.

She couldn't speak, could only hear a keening noise that came from her as he penetrated and circled where she was so sensitive and molten that she ached. She tightened, trying to savor, trying to hold back the build, but wanton mindlessness took over. Her hips danced against his hand, the pleasure growing too acute to bear, tension growing and growing until she couldn't stand it—

"*Oh!*" Her world exploded in a sudden release that had her shaking and shuddering, flesh pulsing and eyes tearing at the absolute beauty of it.

She pressed his hand still, trying to ease the sensation, trying to catch her breath.

He kissed her, tongue questing for hers, and continued to gently caress her, soothing and teasing so her level of arousal didn't fade, only edged into deeper desire.

With a groan, she rolled into him, strangely ravenous. She wanted the barriers between them gone. Wanted *all of him.* What was he *doing* to her?

He made a feral noise and they tugged at each other's clothing, stripping in seconds, then rolled back together, naked, gloriously naked. Now he was hers, all hers. She swept her hands over him, enamored with his broad shoulders but equally fascinated by his rock-hard biceps and the way his Adam's apple bobbed in a swallow.

When she cradled the fiercest part of him in her palm, she wasn't frightened at all. She felt powerful, especially when he looked agonized and closed his eyes and breathed, *"Bella."*

With a smile, she pressed her mouth to his throat and tried to roll him onto his back. He rolled her beneath him instead, pressing over her as he kissed her, letting her caress him as he used his tongue to mimic what he wanted to do until she couldn't take it and tore her mouth from his. "I need—"

She didn't know what she needed. She was restless and urgent, loins feeling achy and neglected. Empty.

He reached over to the night table then rose over her, knees sliding between hers and parting her legs with effortless strength.

She felt so many things in that moment. Vulnerable, yes, but strangely trusting. It didn't matter if she didn't particularly enjoy this part. She wanted to know she could take a man—

"Oh."

He paused, tip pressing for entry, the invasion startling enough that she tensed.

His head came up. His whole body was taut, his cheeks flushed, his eyes glittering, but there was a shred of man still governing the animal. "I might literally die if you've changed your mind."

Maybe that's what made her smile. Maybe it was the fact her body was so eager for his. Maybe it was simply the joy of this crazy, magical night.

With a little arch, she invited him to complete his thrust and he did with a shudder, sinking deep, gaze never leaving hers, but glowing hot as the center of a flame as their flesh melded.

To say she became a woman under his possession was silly, but she *felt* like a woman in that moment. Mature and whole and *sacred*. She was responding exactly as nature intended under the advances of a mate. *Her* mate. With this act, he gave her back her sexuality, her desire. Her *self*.

She closed her eyes against something too big to contemplate, but it only made the sensations intensify as he took a testing withdraw and return. She shivered as though velvet passed over her skin.

"Yes?"

"Yes," she moaned, savoring the deliciousness that lingered with anticipation for another stroke. "More."

Lucidity faded as he did it again. And again.

He began to thrust with more purpose. She found her hips rising to meet his, longing for the return of his. Needing it. The dance delivered such acute pleasure, she released a strangled groan of enjoyment.

He picked up the tempo and magnificent sensations ran through her. She wanted to tell him but couldn't speak, as she was too enraptured. Tension gripped her. A kind of tortured ecstasy—her body searching for an answering call in his.

She needed him to be as driven beyond himself as she was. To come with her to this place where nothing existed but this new being they had become with their joining. Scraping her nails down his back, she grasped at his buttocks and pulled him into her. Into the eye of the storm.

They struck the pinnacle together, the climax so intense, she opened her mouth in a soundless scream. Pleasure like she had never known flooded in, drowning her as he held himself magnificently deep inside her, throbbing in her jubilant grip as he released a ragged cry of exhilaration and shuddered with completion.

Xavier swore.

"What's wrong?" Trella murmured, hands moving with endless appetite over his damp shoulders.

He withdrew and rolled away. "The condom broke."

She was glad it was dark now. After the first time, they had turned out the lights and slid under the covers to fondle and caress for ages, barely speaking, just kissing and enjoying. Bonding, she might have been tempted to think, something in his silence, and the condoms in the night table, told her he had done this a lot.

She had suffered a hollow ache as she'd forced herself to accept that, despite his sweet words, she was merely the woman *du jour* for him. A lady of the night, really.

Whether he had sensed her withdrawal, or she was just that easy, he had grown more passionate. The second time had been even better than the first. Her inhibitions were gone and he held out, giving her two shattering orgasms before taking her on a third ride that nearly killed her, their shared climax being so powerful.

She was too sweaty and lethargic to be triumphant, but she was pretty darned smug at having taken a lover. She had distantly been hoping she had rocked his world as thoroughly as he had rocked hers, but reality struck like a brick through a window at his words.

"It's okay. I won't get pregnant." She swallowed, trying to clear the thickness that gathered in her throat.

"You're on the pill or something?"

Or something. "Yes."

"I have physicals all the time."

"I'm fine, too." Did people really have these conversations? It scraped the romance off a wonderful evening, leaving her thinking about the rest of reality. Guilt crawled in. She had kept secrets from him and—far worse—from her family. They'd be worried sick if they knew where she was.

As if on cue, her phone plinked with the harp notes of her sister's ringtone. Like some kind of empath, Angelique was picking up on her sudden discord.

"I have to get that," Trella murmured, then she groaned. Her muscles ached as though she'd run a marathon. She forced herself to rise and move naked across the shadowed room, finding her clutch where she'd dropped it in the lounge, then came back to the bedroom door.

She stayed there, slyly hoping he was looking at her, silhouetted by the lamplight. In a quick exchange of texts, she reassured her sister she was fine. Gili knew something was up, though. Tendrils of misgivings began working through Trella's system. It was time to call it a night. She needed to hole up at the flat where she knew she was completely safe and process all of this.

"I have to go." She clicked off her phone and sent him a smile of cheerful resignation.

"Is everything all right?" He rose to pull on his pants, not bothering with underwear, which pleased her for some reason, but he didn't invite her to stay, which depressed her as well.

"Just my sister. She needs me to get home." She texted her guard that she would be ready in fifteen minutes and stepped into her thong.

Xavier shook out her gown and brought it to her, then moved behind her as she stepped into it. Hurrying her? She pulled up the gown then lifted her hair while he zipped.

His hands lingered on her skin, not moving, not holding her in place, but his grave words pinned her motionless. "I remember her kidnapping."

She dropped her arms, letting her hair fall over his hands, as helpless and as terrified as she had ever been. Her breastbone turned to ice and her ears strained to hear what he would say next.

"I was fourteen. My father was renouncing the crown. My mother was already gone, exiled by my grandmother for their divorce. I was feeling very sorry for myself. Then I saw photos of this little girl, so pretty and happy, stolen. I stopped worrying what would happen to me. I was so relieved when she was recovered."

His fingertips stayed across her shoulders, not caressing, just resting in small hot prints. She thought she would bruise from the contact. Not in a painful way. It was the opposite of injury. Healing?

He drew in a sharp breath and pulled his touch from her skin. "I don't know why I said that. It was far too personal for both of us. You're clearly still worried about her if you're rushing off." He bent to retrieve her shoes. "I hope she's all right."

It was me. She should have said it, but her throat was too tight.

She knew there were people who had rooted for her family all the way along, but it was so wrapped up in their notoriety, she didn't differentiate the kindly meant from the intrusive or downright cruel. Her family hadn't asked to be famous for the odd trick of nature that had created two sets of identical twins. They were just people, perhaps better looking by certain standards, definitely richer than average, but regular humans.

Yet the world was insatiably curious about what brand of soap they used and held strong opinions on how they should conduct themselves.

To have this man, who was completely removed from it, reveal such a personal memory connected to her affected her, changing the careful constructs inside her. Defenses that held darkness at bay while keeping her open to the people who loved her shifted and angled to provide space for him to enter.

No. She couldn't let him in! Tie herself to a man? Lose herself behind someone else's goals and wishes and expectations when she had so many unreached aspirations of her own? She couldn't attach herself to someone whose life was bigger than hers. She was trying to escape all the restraints that had bound her for so long.

Shaken at how vulnerable she was to him, she jiggled her bodice against her breasts, then perched on a chair to strap on her shoes, hands trembling.

"Is she really as beautiful as you?" He watched her with his fists pushed into his pockets. His naked shoulders were relaxed and outlined in pale gold while the shadows in his face suggested a brooding expression. The dark patch of his chest hair narrowed to a suggestive line, arrowing to his navel, then lower.

He was the beautiful one. She memorized this last intimate glimpse of him.

"Exactly as beautiful." She smiled, amused with her own joke, then poignant gratitude accosted her. "Thank you for tonight. I—" She stopped herself from saying something truly gauche.

She wanted to ask if he'd meant it when he'd said it wasn't always like this for him. She wanted to tell him what he had given her. She wanted to get out of here before she revealed too much.

She glanced at the clock. If she didn't show her face promptly, her guard would knock and enter. They were paid very well to be diligent and investigate when she wasn't where she said she would be.

Xavier moved to offer a hand, helping her to her feet. "Thank *you*. This was lovely." The words came off light-hearted, punching into her as she imagined the legions of other women who had heard such offhand praise. Not even, *I won't forget you*. Just, *this was lovely*. A pleasant meal. Nothing life-changing.

He brought her hand to his mouth, exactly as he had when they'd met, except this time he turned her hand over and kissed her palm.

Trying to hide how deeply that affected her, she said, "Goodnight, sweet Prince."

He snorted. "I could have you beheaded for that."

With a lightning move, he pulled her close and wove his fingers into her hair, planting a real kiss, a final one, on her mouth. It was painfully sweet. Thorough, yet tender. Oddly heartbreaking.

For her.

And even though she was the one to draw back, her lips clung to his. Temptation to stay, to say more, gripped her, but he distracted her.

"You've lost an earring." His fingertip flicked at her lobe.

"No!" Both hands went to her ears, finding one empty. "Here? In the room? Did you notice if I had both while we were downstairs?"

"I'll buy you new ones," he offered with an offhand shrug.

"They're sentimental. A gift from my father." *To Gili.* She clicked on the lamp and flung back the bed covers, searching.

A polite knock tapped on the main door, her guard telling her the car was in position. They avoided waiting whenever possible. It drew a crowd.

"I'll find it and send it to you at the design house."

"Promise?" She looked from his muscled chest to the sheets to his eyes. Oh, he was spectacular in the golden light, emptying her brain all over again.

"I only make promises I can keep."

"Thank you." She didn't bother worrying about him addressing it to Angelique. She would intercept it or come clean if she had to. "I really did, um, enjoy this."

His eyes warmed with laughter. "My pleasure, *bella.*"

She was starting to sound like the neophyte she was. Definitely time to make her escape. She ducked her head and made for the coach before she turned into a pumpkin.

CHAPTER THREE

Present day...

COMMUNICATIONS FROM PRINCE XAVIER's grandmother fell into three categories. All were delivered by the palace's Private Secretary, Mario de Gaul.

"Your grandmother requests a meeting to discuss…" Fill in the blank. Those were routine and benign. She listened to her grandson's opinions and they worked together on a strategy for whatever event, negotiation or dignified visitor stood on the horizon. They were equals, more or less.

The second, more ominous type of appointment began with "Her Majesty invites you to join her at…" Fill in the meal. Those were more dictatorial instructions on how she wanted something handled. A parliamentarian or ambassador needed massaging. A high-level staff member needed firing. He was doing her dirty work.

Then there was—

"The Queen is in her receiving room. She expects you."

Mario entered with that missive on the heels of Xavier's Personal Assistant, who still stood before him, his speech bubble of grim news dissolving in the air above his pleading don't-shoot-the-messenger expression.

"Of course." Xavier rose from his desk. It was the appropriate response. One didn't refuse the Queen. One certainly didn't leave her waiting.

Still, his agile brain leapt to all the triage he needed to accomplish in the next few minutes, not least of which was to reassure his new fiancée, Patrizia, before she saw the headlines herself.

Switched Before Birth!
Future King an Expectant Father?
Trella Tricked Everyone—Including the Prince!

He should have said something a few weeks ago, of course, when the first bomb went off. Trella Sauveterre, lately returned to the public eye, had turned up pregnant. The reaction had been loud enough to shake the world off its axis, forcing him to reach out to her, again, much to his dismay. He didn't want anything to do with her after realizing how thoroughly she'd duped him.

Why had she done it?

The sting of chasing her to Berlin a week after Paris, like a fool with his first crush, came back hot and fresh under his skin. He'd had a very real duty to meet with Patrizia, but he had put it off, stealing an extra few days of bachelorhood, inventing excuses so he could…what? Have sex with a stranger once more?

Sex was sex. He'd had many lovers over the years and experienced varied degrees of pleasure. He put down the better experiences to chemistry, the less satisfying ones to inhibitions and incompatibility.

That night in Paris had seemed extraordinary while it was happening. She hadn't been a virgin, but she'd made sex feel new again. She'd been so responsive. So sensual. So *abandoned.* His stomach tightened just remembering it.

So what? He knew from his father's history that letting the brain below his belt do his thinking was disastrous.

Nevertheless, a day later, when he had read that *Angelique* would be in Berlin, he had reconfigured his entire schedule. Rather than courier her earring as promised, he had sought her out—only to find her with another man.

It had been the most lowering of moments, not because his ego was dented, but because he had revealed something of himself to her. Somehow, she had tricked him into believing they had a connection that went beyond the physical. What had possessed him to talk of those dark hours when his parents had been banished?

He didn't form intimate friendships. He was an only child raised by a grandmother whose life was too demanding to offer affection. Yet, for some reason, he had entrusted a one-night lover with his private thoughts.

He had trusted *her*. When she had said she didn't sleep around, he had believed her.

Judging by what he found in Berlin, however, she'd moved on very quickly. The innocent act was part of her routine, he had concluded, castigating himself for acting so callow as to follow her.

Nevertheless, when he had the chance to catch her alone, he approached, waiting for the catch of excitement she had kindled in him the week before.

Nothing. She was desirable the way all beautiful women were, but whatever he'd felt in Paris was gone. It had perplexed and annoyed him, made him doubly irritated with himself for thinking they'd had something special.

He's stood there searching for whatever it was that he'd found so enthralling and she had pretended she didn't even know him, staring blankly as though he had broken into her bedroom and stolen the diamond hoop earring he was returning.

In those seconds, he had felt as though she was even more of a stranger than she had been before they'd made love—which she was, he promptly learned. He hadn't slept with Angelique. He had slept with her twin, Trella.

The revelation had been welcome and infuriating. He didn't care for dishonest people, but his desire to see Trella had renewed itself. He had asked Angelique to pass along his contact details, wanting an explanation. Wanting something he refused to acknowledge, but…

Nothing.

Not one returned call, message or text.

What did it matter? He made himself get over her, focusing on more important things, primarily his duty to marry.

He had made a concerted effort to avoid all headlines containing the name Sauveterre, which wasn't easy. First, the mysterious, reclusive Trella had come out at a friend's wedding. That had kept the gossip industry booming through spring and summer, along with other news within the family, making it a challenge for him to change channels or flick screens fast enough to avoid catching sight of her.

Then, just as things seemed to have died down, she'd been caught climbing from her brother's car looking less svelte than in previous photos. *Pregnant*, the avid Sauveterre watchers speculated.

So what if she was? It didn't make a hill of beans difference to anyone's life, least of all his.

Still, Xavier had looked closely at the photos that emerged, one showing her in a stunning maternity gown at her brother's engagement party. She didn't look *very* pregnant. She had said she was on the pill. If she was carrying his child, she would have returned his calls. He didn't have anything to worry about, he assured himself.

This latest inflammatory sound bite was more of the same. Had to be. He had a walk-on part in the episodic drama that was the Sauveterre serial. He had slept with her *one night*. He resented being drawn into scandal for it. He was now engaged. That made besmirching his name unforgivable. Immediately after allaying his grandmother's concern, he would insist Trella clear him of involvement so he could reassure Patrizia their marriage plans could continue.

Damn it, he had completely forgotten about Patrizia. He paused to text.

I'll have this cleared up shortly.

Their match was perfect in every way. Not only would it strengthen both of their countries, but they liked each other. Neither had unrealistic notions like love and passion to muddy the waters. She was nursing a bruised heart and was keen for a stable, reliable situation. A civilized relationship, she kept calling it.

He was pleased to perform his duty in a way he could stand. Patrizia was intelligent, attractive, well-bred. She would have children for the same reason he would: They were expected to. They respected one another. They were on the same page.

He wanted this marriage.

Mario paused with him and knocked, then announced him.

His grandmother didn't rise as Xavier entered. She didn't even look up from whatever she was writing with her antique silver pen. The crackle in the fireplace became the only sound along with the scratch of her pen.

He took the bull by the horns. "I'll refute it and press charges against the source."

The pen went down and she peered at him over her glasses. She was a well-preserved seventy, her eyes were the same Deunoro blue as his own, her hair more iron than silver. She was overdue to start her morning audiences, which always made her salty.

"The Queen Mother of Zhamair is the source."

Xavier's PA had also pointed out that the story had stemmed from Angelique's soon-to-be mother-in-law. "I haven't had a chance to confirm that. If she made a statement, I'm sure it's in reaction to some online nonsense."

"She is reacting, I am informed, to remarks made about her son and his fiancée. She wanted to set the record straight that Angelique was not the woman kissing you in the photos that emerged some months ago from Paris. Angelique has always been faithful to King Kasim. Is that true?"

"I couldn't say whether she's been faithful, but I'm told I was with Trella."

"You were *told*?"

"They're twins." He shrugged, not bothering to feel awkward discussing his sex life with his grandmother. She had had "The Talk" with him herself when he was an adolescent, explaining in no uncertain terms that royalty did *not* produce bastards and had offered explicit tips on how to prevent such a thing.

"That particular twin is pregnant." She used her most imperious tone. "A source intimately connected to her family has stated you were with her at an appropriate time for conception. Did you take precautions?"

"Of course."

The condom broke. Are you on the pill?

Yes.

"She would have told me if there were consequences." Tension gathered in the pit of his gut. He didn't know which one of them he was trying to convince. "Any woman who sets out to trap a man does not hide it for six months. Even if it was an accident, there's no reason to keep it from me. She might be pregnant, but *it's not mine*."

Her brows went up in regal disdain. "Perhaps you should confirm that."

As if that hadn't occurred to him? "Of course," he said. Dutifully.

"Because it would be a shame if this were to cause any delay in our schedule." She intended to step down the minute he was married. To Patrizia.

"Understood."

It was hot in Innsbruck, despite the elevation and the calendar showing the last days of summer. But maybe the heat was caused by this extra human she was carrying.

Trella lifted her face into the gentle breeze, enjoying the sweet scent of it. She was six months along and felt it, even though she wasn't showing much. Her mother had possessed the same tall, model-slender figure and had barely shown with twins until the very end. This was only one and with the right clothes, she barely looked pregnant.

She needed that ambiguity. Prince Xavier's texts had devolved to the two-word kind.

Call me.

She had ignored the latest, received this morning, exactly as she'd ignored every other text and call she'd received from him, the first immediately after he'd met Angelique in Berlin, and most recently after she'd been exposed by her sister's soon-to-be mother-in-law as the twin in his arms at the ball in Paris.

She had her reasons. That's what she kept telling herself, even though it was pure emotion that drove her and that emotion was cowardice.

"They're blocked by a service vehicle," her guard, Benita, said of their car, lifting her gaze from her phone to continue her scan of the street. "Let's wait inside."

Benita was as tall as Trella and had a mannish demeanor when she was on the job. No nonsense, no makeup, hair scraped into a bun, communications terse.

Trella didn't mind. She wasn't the most cooperative principal. To her occasional chagrin, she was a high maintenance person in every way. Acknowledging that about herself didn't stop her from saying, "I'd rather stay out here."

The day was gorgeous and she would be on bed rest soon. She wanted to enjoy the outside world while she could.

"Killian said—"

"I know. Take extra precautions." She scoffed at a lot of things, but not security reports. "I spoke to Sadiq. He's the one who discovered the hack and restored all the firewalls. No one even knows I'm here."

Except the handful of people inside the building who had just taken selfies with her. They were no doubt posting those as she spoke. She was a celebrity, whether she liked it or not. It was only a matter of minutes before lookie-loos began pulling over, wanting their own photo with a Sauveterre, especially the elusive pregnant one.

"My gut doesn't like it."

"Because Killian trains you to be overprotective."

Benita had tried to cancel this trip as soon as the security bulletin had come through. Trella wasn't sure why she had insisted on making what amounted to a house call for a joint venture she wasn't sure she would pursue, but she had.

Ah, she knew why she had come. For starters, her sister

had been doing this kind of thing on her behalf for years. It was yet another burden she had placed on her twin and it was her turn to pay it back, now that Angelique was starting her life with Kasim.

Oh, her sister was in love. It was as majestic a sight to behold as the timeless sparkling peaks around them. Trella was deeply happy for her, but so very envious.

Her gaze tracked to the sharpest, highest peaks to the south. To Elazar.

Was he texting from inside that border, sitting in his palace office, cursing her for ignoring him?

A flutter in her midsection had her resisting the urge to press her hand across her belly. She didn't like to draw attention to her pregnancy when she was in public. Besides, it wasn't the baby that caused that stir in her middle. It was a complex mix of emotions.

She wanted to tell him she was grateful. She wanted to see him again, to discover if the magical connection she'd felt in Paris had been real or just a product of an exciting foray into independence. She wanted him to know they were expecting a baby.

She also wanted to hold their night in her memory as the ideal that it was. She didn't want the harsh fallout she would have to face once she acknowledged this baby as his. Most of all, she didn't want to be a burden on a man who had seemed too perfect to want anything to do with someone as flawed as she was.

Her expected black sedan with its darkened windows slid up to the curb.

"There. See?" Trella said, even as she noted a man approaching in her periphery.

"That's not—" Benita's voice cut off.

Perhaps Trella went deaf at that moment because noth-

ing penetrated beyond the fact that the back door opened
and the Prince of Elazar rose from the interior.

He was as remarkable as she remembered. Like a knight
of legend, his hair shot with glints of gold, his visage sharp
and stern, his air one of heroic power. He was so godlike,
she couldn't move. She was too mesmerized.

Then reality rushed in as a scuffling noise and a grunt
penetrated. She swung her gaze to see Benita in a fight.
A *fight*. With a *man*. He tried to twist Benita's arm behind her back as she bent forward, trying to use leverage
to flip him.

Training, the kind Trella had attended to daily until
pregnancy had sent her into yoga and water aerobics, jolted
her into action. As Benita's attacker pulled back his weight,
dragging Benita off her feet, Trella stepped in and nailed
him with a solid, knuckle-bruising punch, right in the nose.

The man grunted and Benita twisted, nearly escaping.

"What the *hell* are you doing?" That *accent*. Strong
hands grasped her upper arms and pulled her away from
the struggling pair.

Trella turned into him, stomach flip-flopping in response as she felt his solid abdomen against her bump.
Adrenaline coursed through her, but she only felt reassurance as he drew her protectively close. Her gaze stayed
over her shoulder, fixed on the fight, which seemed to be
more of a wrestle for dominance. A bloody nose wasn't
slowing down the man and Benita wasn't giving up, biting out in Spanish, "Run."

"Help her—Wait. What are *you* doing?" Trella cried as
she realized she was being shoved into the back of the car.

Xavier easily overpowered her, pushing her in and following without ceremony.

She was so shocked that it took her a moment to resist.

By then his big body had created a wall of shoulders and chest that were impossible to get past.

Before she could touch the door on her side, he pulled his own closed and the locks clicked. The car pulled away, leaving her guard scrapping on the sidewalk with a brute whose shirt was the same color as both men in the front of this car.

Far too late, she realized what was happening.

She was being kidnapped. *Again.*

CHAPTER FOUR

"Stop this car. *Now.*"

Xavier respected her ability to sound so authoritative, but he ignored her and opened the privacy window long enough to accept an ice pack from his physician, Gunter, then tapped the button to close it.

"Hello, Trella. Have I got that right?" He knew he had the right one. It was impossible to explain, but the minute he had seen her, he had known.

He pushed aside the ridiculous high that rocketed through him as he finally had her alone and held out his palm. He wiggled his fingers, urging her to release the pendant she was pinching and let him examine her hand.

"What were you thinking, getting involved in that?" The mix of rage and fear he'd experienced at seeing her step into the fight was reflected in his tone. Even if she wasn't pregnant, it would have been a foolhardy, dangerous thing to do.

But she was pregnant. There was no denying it. The narrow waist he'd held in the crook of his arm had thickened with an undeniable bump. Her breasts…

He dragged his gaze up, refusing to let fantasies sidetrack him, but her features were a distraction all on their own. Her face was rounder, her mouth lush and pouted. The urge to kiss her struck him with a fierce pull.

Damn it, what *was* it about her?

He met her glare with his own, thinking that he would have sworn her eyes were green, but they were steely. Bright as a cornered cat refusing to stay that way.

"I thought I was preventing myself from being kidnapped. Once again, I have trusted the wrong person." Her unpainted lips seemed bloodless, which gave him a moment of pause, but too much of his life had been set off balance by her. He wanted answers. Today.

"It's not a kidnapping." He set the ice pack near her thigh. "It's an improvised meeting to discuss mutual business, so drop your pendant. I know it's a tracking device. Your guard won't be harmed, only delayed. Your car can't chase us. It's still blocked."

"Which sounds a lot like a kidnapping." A harsh ringtone emanated from her purse. "That's for you." She pulled out her phone and used her thumbprint to accept the call then handed it to Xavier. Her hand might have trembled.

Desperate times called for desperate measures, he'd told himself when he'd concocted this intervention. As he picked up on Trella's shaken nerves, he wondered if he was using a sledgehammer to kill a fly. It hadn't occurred to him she might be anything but angry at having her timetable interrupted. He couldn't be happier if he inconvenienced the hell out of her. He was beyond incensed at the way she was impacting his life without any attempt to mitigate it.

Explaining that would have to wait. He'd been warned to expect this video call. He took the phone and met the formidable expression of a man who resembled Trella. Henri, Xavier suspected, since the other brother was in Brazil.

"Your demands?" Henri asked without greeting.

"A blood sample for a DNA test."

Trella made a strangled noise. "Like hell."

He glanced at her. "I would accept her word as to

whether she's carrying my heir, but she's lied to me more than once already."

Xavier willed her to lash out with denials of his paternity. With an explanation. An *apology*.

She hitched her chin and turned her face to the window.

"Return her to where you took her. I'll see what I can do about the blood test."

"You can't even get her to return a call. I can't wait any longer."

Trella's silence was gut-knottingly damning. Whatever lingering favor he had felt toward her went ashen and bitter. A jagged lump hardened in his throat. He swallowed it, but the acrimony only moved to burn as a hot knot behind his collarbone. Each minute that she failed to deny his paternity was a tiny, incremental progression toward accepting what he had been refusing to believe. What he still didn't want to believe.

"I have your coordinates," Henri said, dragging Xavier back from staring at the woman who was ruining his life. "A team has been dispatched. We don't need an incident. Return her to Innsbruck."

"If you're tracking us, you know we'll be in Elazar soon." Xavier leaned toward the window to see a helicopter chasing from the distance. "I'll close the borders if I have to, but she's perfectly safe, especially if that's our future monarch inside her. Stand down from trying to stop us."

"Unless my sister gives me her safe word, this escalates."

Xavier handed her the phone. "Your move, *bella*."

She flashed him a sharp glance then looked at her brother.

"We're coming," Henri said.

"I know." She nodded, pale and grave, then said, "Begonia."

"Vous êtes certain?"

"Sí."

"That's tomorrow's word," Xavier said.

She shot him a startled frown.

He shrugged. "I do my homework."

"Then you'll know I'm buying you twenty-four hours." She turned back to her phone, expression haughty. "I'm sure Killian knows by now who hacked him. Ask him to drop a virus into the Elazar palace networks, won't you?"

"Killian has Elazar's Minister of Foreign Affairs on the phone, along with a more aggressive team assembled."

Xavier suspected that remark was more for his benefit.

"Gracias. Tell him I'll handle it."

"Will you?"

A leaden silence followed where she only gave her brother a tight-lipped look.

Xavier wondered if others were also frustrated by the avoidance game she had been playing.

"Bien," Henri said. "If I don't hear from you every hour, your prince may expect a gun against his temple. *Je t'aime."*

"Te amo." She ended the call and slipped her phone back into her purse, then folded her hands into her lap. "Why did you say I lied to you more than once?"

Xavier admired the way she attempted to take control of the conversation, but he was not prepared to give her any concessions until he had what he wanted.

"Why did you speak Spanish and he, French? Was it code?"

"Habit."

She tried to leave it there, but he lifted a skeptical brow.

"It's true. Our father was French, Mama is Spanish. We grew up speaking both. I only told one lie."

"That you were on birth control."

"That I was Angelique. You asked if I was on the pill

or something. I said yes because that was true. At least, I thought it was." She bit the corner of her lip.

"Your *or something* failed?"

She flinched, making him realize his voice carried a thickness close to contempt or even hatred.

He grappled to hang onto his temper. "You assured me pregnancy wasn't possible. How have we arrived at having this conversation?"

Dumb question. They both knew how babies were made. They'd made love. She had come apart in his arms again and again. He'd been greedy as a starved beast certain he would die from the pleasure of being inside her when she shattered around him like that. Then, when he couldn't hold back any longer, he had joyously thrown himself into the small death of simultaneous orgasm.

In that post-climactic moment, when her breaths had still been jagged and his heart had pounded against her sweating breasts, he had felt…restored. Not just a release of tension but as though deeper needs had been met. Withdrawing had provoked a painful, abandoned sensation he had impatiently tried to forget.

"*Is that my child?*"

She jolted at the grate in his tone. "You said you wouldn't believe me no matter what I said."

"You'll submit to a blood test, then?"

Her eyes narrowed in mutiny.

"You can submit nicely or I can pin you down while my doctor takes it." He was clearly a sadist because something in him longed for her to push him into restraining her.

"Touch me and I'll break *your* nose." She started to lift a threatening fist and flinched, quickly cradling her right hand—which is what she'd been doing since her hands had gone into her lap, he realized.

He caught her wrist and held on when she tried to pull

away. The backs of her fingers were an angry red, her knuckles puffy.

His heart lurched.

"Did you break any bones? Can you move your fingers? That's what this is for." He picked up the ice pack, incensed all over again that she had waded into the fight.

"I know how to throw a punch." She took the ice and flexed her fingers against it, showing only a wince of discomfort so he presumed she hadn't fractured anything.

"What were you thinking? It's a damned good thing his reflexes didn't take over. You would have been on the ground."

"My bodyguard was being assaulted."

"No, *my* bodyguard was moving into position to cover *me*. *She* attacked *him*. Then you did. Do you understand what bodyguards are paid to do? There is no reason you should have involved yourself."

Her brows flicked in dismissal of his concern.

Was this really the mother of his heir? If he'd gone to a brothel and bought a *man*, he couldn't have picked someone less suitable.

"A simple blood test could prove I'm not the father. We could have it done before we cross the border." He pointed at the sign they passed that stated they were less than a mile away.

"I'm afraid of needles."

"Be afraid of *me, bella*."

Her flat smile died. Something vulnerable flashed in her expression.

His conscience pinched.

"Is that the problem?" His voice still sounded gruff and aggressive. His animosity hadn't evaporated just because he was finally getting answers. He didn't want to soften toward her at all. She was far too dangerous. But fear was an explanation he could understand.

"Have you been afraid of my reaction? I'm not happy." That was a gross understatement. A well-practiced aloof demeanor had always served him well, but it was impossible to find in the face of this life-altering situation. Still, he tried to reassure her. "Nothing bad will happen if the baby is mine. I'll recognize him or her as our future monarch. We will marry so it's legitimate. That's all. No stake burnings or feeding to dragons. Were you afraid I'd pressure you to terminate? Is that why you've kept it from me?"

Silence. She turned her attention out the side window again, so he couldn't read her expression.

"Do you not *know* who the father is? How many contenders are there?"

Her glare swung like a blade to slice through him.

"I don't *care* how many men you've slept with." Much. He was disturbed to realize he did, actually. It wasn't because of the paternity question, either. The passion between them had been unprecedented. He didn't like to think she reacted that way to every man she slept with. It would have made all of this even more intolerable.

"How pregnant are you? Let's see if that eliminates me, shall we?"

"Pregnant enough to need a pit stop. Can we stop here?"

"No." The border guard waved them through with only a very minor slowing of their speed, recognizing the plates. "We'll be at my chalet shortly."

The car sped along the pass that formed part of the border between Austria and Elazar. As they rounded a bend, the valley opened, allowing a glimpse of Lirona, the capital, once a modest fiefdom, now a thriving city of culture, intellect and wealth. It sat like a heart against the shore of

Lac Lirona, the arms of the mountains stretching out to embrace the blue water he loved with everything in him.

Over the centuries, his ancestors had fought to maintain their governance over this small kingdom many times. His great-grandmother had taken up with one of Hitler's top advisors to keep the Nazi invasion at occupation rather than annihilation.

That is where the bar is set when it comes to duty, his grandmother had extolled as a history lesson, explaining why Xavier's father was unfit to rule. *We are custodians. We do what we must. To put yourself before Elazar is treason.*

This, because his father had followed his libido into a high-profile affair with a topless waitress from Amsterdam then married the woman's aunt, owner of a drug café. His divorce from Xavier's mother had already been ugly and, even worse in his grandmother's eyes, *common.*

His grandmother was a hard woman—her father, King Ugo, hadn't forgiven his wife and Queen Julia had grown up in a harsh climate of blame and sacrifice. If her spare had survived, things might have been different. Instead, she had forced her only son to renounce the throne, disowning him and keeping her grandson as Elazar's future.

It was all on Xavier to perpetuate the monarchy into the next generation. He had planned to do so through an elegant association with Patrizia, a respected princess with a degree in social justice and a pedigree that couldn't be faulted.

Instead, he had behaved as impulsively as his father, tangling with a fashion designer whose life was stained with one scandal after another.

He was running out of hope that her child was not his. Whether his grandmother could find it in her to forgive him for this transgression didn't matter.

He would never forgive himself.

CHAPTER FIVE

As SOMEONE WHO had grown up in obscene wealth, Trella didn't bat an eye at the chalet that turned out to be a three-story modern fortress with a nod to its rustic ancestors in its gables and tiered verandas.

She was more interested in counting pairs of eyes—one at the gate, two at the door, the physician who followed them into the house, the chauffeur who took the car around to what she presumed was the garage, a butler who greeted them and a woman named Inga who was asked to prepare tea.

"Powder room?" Trella clung by her fingernails to control.

Ghosts—terrible, terrible ghosts—were creeping in at the edges of her consciousness, but something pressured to diamond brightness inside her kept her from becoming hysterical. *This time she would get away.*

As each of the Prince's attempts to draw her out had pulled at her laser-like focus, she had resentfully allowed that she was taking the rough road, not the high one. She could still call in a team to break her out if she wanted, but a furious, too often helpless, part of her demanded she prove she could rescue herself.

Over the last months, she had come close many times to calling him. The problem was, she wasn't as stupid as many would conclude from her behavior. She knew what would happen and he had confirmed it. He would marry her.

Which meant a profile in the public eye that was even higher than the one she already occupied. One from which she couldn't retreat at will.

Worse, it meant being honest with him. She would have to reveal exactly how crazy she was. She would have to explain these ghouls tickling across her skin, making her want to scratch herself all over. The nightmare could spring to life with a beat of her heart, the cold sweats and shaking, the profound helplessness...

She hadn't suffered an attack since well before their night in Paris, but one ticked like a bomb inside her. She could feel it. But *no*. She wouldn't succumb, even though fighting it made it worse. She knew that.

With a dry mouth, she locked herself into a bathroom that smelled of potpourri. The small space was pristine, with a porcelain sink in a cherry wood vanity. She glanced from the full bath and shower to the frosted window that, once carefully opened, looked out onto the woods at the back of the house.

No balcony below this window, but it was big enough to allow a woman with a modest six month swelling in her middle to crawl through, and close enough to the nearby balcony she could swing a leg that direction and clamber across.

Not a kidnapping? Damned right it wasn't.

"I'm sure she'll come around," Xavier told Gunter. He hadn't lied when he had threatened to hold her down, but he didn't want to. It wasn't his habit to manhandle any woman, pregnant or otherwise. "Did she look six months to you?"

Gunter shook his head. "It's difficult to say. Every woman carries differently. The fact she was able to hide it so long leads me to wonder, but…"

They needed a blood test.

"And this?" Xavier waved to where she had disappeared to use the toilet.

"Extremely common. Although…" He glanced at his watch.

That's what Xavier had thought. He hadn't taken his eyes from the closed door and she was still in there. He didn't want to be indelicate, but he moved to knock.

Silence.

Fainted? His heart swerved.

"Trella." He tried the handle, found it locked and rattled it. "She wouldn't have—" The window dropped about thirty-two feet to the ground. That's why he hadn't bothered assigning someone to watch that side of the chalet.

"I'll send someone to check." Gunter hurried away, moving through the kitchen as Inga appeared with keys and a concerned expression.

Xavier gave the key a hard twist and walked into an empty powder room. A fresh breeze came through the open window. He glanced out to see Gunter below, holding Trella's clutch, a grim expression on his face as he tracked the distance to the nearest balcony.

At least *she* wasn't lying in the dirt below. Tramping through the alps in trendy heels wasn't much better. Damn it, this woman was turning into a nightmare.

"Alert security," he told Inga, and he strode outside to join the search.

Crammed beneath the sink was a little too much like the horrid cellar she'd been locked in during her first kidnapping. The shelf had easily moved to the bottom of the vanity, making room for her to curl herself on top of it, but she'd had to cover herself with the towels and was overheating.

Panicking.

No. One minute at a time. *Uno naranjo, dos naranjos...* She counted the seconds, counted the oranges, a scent she always associated with family since they had a grove of them at Sus Brazos. She would get through this. It was another test of her ability to move on from her past.

She did her breathing exercises while she listened for footsteps. When she was confident everyone had moved outside, she carefully opened the cupboard door and groped her way out of the small space, thankful for her yoga practice.

Carrying her shoes, she paused at the door. There were security cameras. She had noted one in the foyer as they'd entered. Someone would be watching the screens. She had to move fast, but—*thank you, Killian*—she had what amounted to an SOS flare in her phone. It was supposed to be for signaling help, but she hoped it could have another use.

She took the device from her bra, turned on the blinding white light, and walked into the hall, aiming the beam directly at the first camera she came to. It sat like a brilliant spotlight on the dark orb. She prayed it blinded the lens as she hurried through the house to the garage.

There was no one in the kitchen and keys hung neatly on the hook beside the door. She tucked her phone back into her bra and took all the keys, deducing from a keychain which one belonged to the top-down cobalt blue Audi.

Outside the garage doors, she heard footsteps jogging across gravel.

Her entire body trembled, but she fought to keep a focused mind. She *wasn't* helpless. She *would* get away.

She set all the keys on the passenger seat and climbed behind the wheel of the Audi, then hit the button on the visor to open the garage door, ready to start the car as soon as the door climbed high enough.

There was a click, the hum of a motor and a rattle of effort, but the door didn't budge. She jabbed her finger onto the button again, glancing at the jumble of keys. Should she take a different car?

The door to the interior of the chalet opened and Xavier came into the shadowed garage.

Nooooo! She jabbed again and again at the stupid button, then started the car with a roar of its high-performance engine.

"The house is locked down. Don't try to drive through the door. It's reinforced. You'll hurt yourself. And my car." He moved past the other three vehicles with smooth steps, pausing beside her to lean in and turn off the engine, pocketing the key. "But that was a very good try. I'm impressed."

She gripped the steering wheel, staring straight ahead, concentrating on not revealing the tears gathering hotly behind her eyes.

"Come back into the house."

"No."

"We'll talk here then." He moved to flick a switch on the wall. A fan came to life with a low drone, quickly sucking away the lingering exhaust.

He came back to set an elbow on the top of the windscreen. She felt his eyes studying her, but kept her nose pointed forward.

"I'm trying to be patient, *bella*, I really am, but I don't understand why you're being so combative. This doesn't have to be a fight."

"I could drive this, you know. Probably better than you."

"Not without keys."

"You'd be surprised." She worked her hands on the steering wheel's soft leather, more than a little enamored with cars, thanks to Ramon. "I can hotwire and drive anything. I've been up to two hundred and twenty on a closed circuit in my brother's Pur Sang. The Gs nearly crack my ribs when I brake from that speed, but it's quite a rush. Have you ever driven this the way it was designed to drive?"

"No." His tone was one of forced patience.

"Ramon got into racing after taking evasive driving lessons. We all had to take them." Like Ramon, she had tried to outrun herself on the track more than once, but it was never a permanent solution. At some point, she had to park the car, take off the helmet and face reality. "Because of my kidnapping."

She sensed him grow very still, indicating she had his full attention.

Had he thought that wouldn't come up? She hated that it defined her, but it did. She worked around it as often as she could, but when she did have to face it, she did it head-on with her foot to the floor, even though it also had the power to crack her ribs and shatter everything inside her.

As the silence lengthened, she suspected he was reviewing what he had said in Paris—when he had thought he was talking about her but had been speaking *to* her.

"You think *you* were worried when I was stolen." Her voice trembled against her will. She soothed herself by running light fingers across the bumps in the bottom of the steering wheel, playing over them like keys on a piano, but her hands shook.

His voice was grave. "If I was triggering you today, you should have said."

"Really?" A smile touched lips that felt so dry they

might split. Her body vibrated with fight-or-flight. She was going to crash hard after this, but she couldn't think about that yet. "Because I did tell you to take me back and you ignored me. Which is exactly what happened the first time."

Her knuckles whitened where she grasped the wheel again, trying to keep a grip on herself. It was time for the head-on collision.

"I said *stop*, and *no*, and *please* so many times I lost count. I said it when they threw me in their van and I could see Ramon running after us. I said it when one of them pulled me onto his lap and shoved his hand under my skirt and *hurt* me. I said it when he slapped me because I was fighting him. I said it when he locked me in a cold, dark cellar and I said it a lot when he let me out three days later, only to put me on a filthy stinking mattress and call me lucky. *Lucky*. Because he was going to show me what men liked."

She knew it was an assault to throw that at him. It was one of the reasons she rarely spoke about it, but she wanted to hurt him. She wanted to *scar* him.

"I should check with my therapist, see if my experience of being assaulted might create a profound desire to control my own destiny. Gosh, what an enlightening moment of self-discovery you've provided, Xavier. Yes, I'm quite sure that's why I'm *combative*."

He couldn't move, wasn't even sure he was breathing, as he tried to un-hear what she'd said. Who would do such a thing? To a *child*?

He didn't have a particular affinity for children, not having had a childhood to speak of himself. Royal duties took him into contact with them, but children were just one more foreign culture with whom certain rituals were observed. He didn't live among them or desire to.

What he did understand was that they were vulnerable. Those who exploited the weak were beneath contempt. Only a true monster would hurt someone as helpless as a nine-year-old girl, especially sexually.

"I didn't think I could get pregnant." Trella's thin voice echoed off the concrete and steel of his garage, underpinned by the drone of the fan. Her profile was pale and still, grayed by the half-light beyond the row of windows in the doors. "The damage he did was that bad. Do you understand what I'm saying? Because I don't want to get any more specific."

A twisted, anguished feeling struck his middle, clenching talons around his chest and squeezing his throat, pushing fear and helplessness to such heights inside him, it became a pressure he could barely withstand. He knew his heart was beating because it throbbed with painful pounds that rang in his ears, but he couldn't move or speak.

There were no words, no reactions, that fit this situation. Only a primal scream that would have no effect whatsoever. It wouldn't reverse the past, wouldn't erase her dark memories. He was at a complete loss.

"When I realized I was pregnant, I had to give the baby a chance. Even though the odds were against it. I've been expecting a miscarriage every single day. What was the point in telling you if I was only going to lose it? Even now, I'm terrified of becoming too attached in case something happens."

It was his. The knowledge crashed over him like a wave, bringing a sharp sting of heightened awareness to his whole body. It changed everything. His entire life, every decision and action, filtered in a blur through this lens of a new life they had created.

The cogs in his brain finally began turning, but with a rustiness that scraped at his detachment.

"So this is…delicate?" What if she lost it? For some reason, neat as that solution might sound, the idea appalled him. "Are you all right?" He should have asked these questions the minute he'd had her alone. "Has this put you into labor? Are you in pain?"

"No." She skimmed her hair out of her eyes and let herself relax into the seat of the car, hands settling over her bump. Her complexion was pale, but she sounded calm. "We're both quite healthy, all things considered. But I see a specialist in London and she wants me on bed rest for the third trimester. She was an intern in Spain when I was a child and knows everything I've been through. I'll let your doctor take my blood, but I'm not giving some stranger my medical history. He touches my arm. That's *it*."

He nodded, still trying to put the pieces together.

"I know I should have told you sooner, but I also knew that if I carried this baby to a stage where it could survive birth, then I would have to marry you. I don't want to."

Her gaze finally came up, striking into him like a harsh winter wind. Bleak.

"I thought if I ever married, it would be for love." Despondency pulled her brows together and her thick lashes swept down to hide her eyes again. "That makes me sound like a romantic and I'm not. I just don't want to be something taken on in sufferance. My sister fell in love. I know it's possible."

Her elbow came up to rest on the door and she set her teeth on her thumbnail.

"Plus, my life is already high profile. Yours is worse." Her hand dropped away and she flashed him a look of blame. "Why can't you be a mechanic or something? Your life comes with even more restrictions than I imposed on myself. Why would I sign up for that? Of course I avoided telling you."

He certainly wouldn't live this life if he had a choice, but it struck him as odd that she disparaged his station. Every other woman aspired to be his queen.

"So, yes, I've handled this badly. God knows I've been informed of *that* more than once." She rolled her eyes. "I probably owe you an apology."

"Probably?" Did she have any idea the damage she had caused by avoiding him?

"I'm not sorry. I will never be sorry that I'm trying to have our baby." Her chin came up, defiant and fierce, but with deep vulnerability edging her unblinking eyes.

Something stirred in him. Gratitude? How? This baby was a disaster.

As if she read his mind, the corners of her mouth went down. "And I think we'll do enough damage to each other in the next while that if we start apologizing now, we'll be peaking way too early."

Never trust anyone who can't make or take a joke, his father had told him once. *Your grandmother, for instance*, had been the rest of the crack.

His grandmother. Yes, indeed, there would be hell to pay and many, many apologies to make.

Before he could fully grasp the scope of impact, a dull buzz emanated from the front of her shirt. "Goodness, an hour gone already?" She reached inside her collar to bring her phone from her bra, voice shaken but trying for light-hearted. "*Hola*, Henri. I'm fine. Just congratulating the father of my child. Does he look green to you?"

Trella could ignore the signs for only so long. The nausea churning in her belly, the heart palpitations, the hot and cold sweats. An attack was upon her. Of course it was. This was one of the most stressful days of her life and she was doing everything wrong, making it worse. Maybe she *did*

self-sabotage, the way her brother Ramon sometimes accused, but she would rather eat live worms than admit he
was right about anything.

She hated to admit any sort of weakness, because she
knew, deep down, that she *was* weak. There was no hiding it from her family, but few others knew exactly what a
basket case she was. That's why she'd spent so many years
sequestered in the family compound. It had provided the
security and stability she'd needed to overcome the worst
of her issues, but it had kept her pride intact, too.

Ridiculous pride that kept her from admitting she was
falling apart to Xavier and his doctor.

Gunter took her blood then her blood pressure, which he
noted was elevated. He frowned and began asking pointed
questions about her pregnancy.

She clammed up. The truth was, she wasn't combative
as a result of being kidnapped. She'd been born that way,
much to her family's eternal frustration. Her experience
only gave her an excuse for it.

At her silence, Xavier turned from the window where
he'd been standing in quiet contemplation. "Pass the read-
ings to her specialist. She can determine if further action is
necessary and advise a treatment plan. Request her doctor
come to Lirona as soon as possible and stay for the dura-
tion of the pregnancy."

"She has other patients," Trella pointed out.

"None so important as you," he stated with a humor-
less smile.

"Flatterer," she tried, but her own sense of humor was
buried beneath an onslaught of sensory overload ticking
toward detonation.

"Sir, I've performed many deliveries," the doctor argued. "There's no need—"

"Sweeten the deal however you must. Our women's

health initiative is due for an upgrade, I'm sure. Expenses won't be spared."

"Very generous, sir," the royal physician said more firmly. "I'm sure many Elazarians would benefit, but..." He cleared his throat. "Perhaps such an undertaking should wait until DNA results are received."

"The results are for the Queen. I'm confident this is my heir. But I do have to inform her. *Bella*, please advise your brother we'll be on the move again, but not for long. The palace isn't far."

That was when she should have said, *I can't.*

She knew what kind of self-care was needed. A quiet, dark room. A sibling holding her hand, talking her down from her mental ledge.

She didn't say anything. Her stupid, tender pride, knocked to the ground so many times, locked her teeth while the rest of her began a slow collapse.

Now she sat in the back of his sedan, gripping her elbows as the ghouls came for her. It was going to be a bad one. She could taste it. The sheer frustration of not being able to stave it off made her eyes sting. Her mind spun down ever more scary avenues. Dark, harmful thoughts crowded in, feeding the anxiety.

This is my life now.

There would be no escape from the attention. It would be worse. Harsher. More judgmental. All the things she had tried to avoid by keeping her pregnancy secret and withholding the father's name were going to come true now.

The pressure in her chest grew worse, suffocating her, and even though her specialist had assured her from the beginning that suffering an attack wouldn't hurt the baby, she was convinced it would, *knew it.* She was going to lose her baby because she couldn't control these awful spells.

While Xavier watched her lose *everything.* He would

reject her for being the disaster she was. Even if she managed to keep his baby and deliver it some weeks from now, he would take it from her. He might have her locked away.

She needed Gili. She took out her phone and gripped it so hard her hand ached. Where were Henri and Ramon? They wouldn't let anyone take her baby. They would always keep her safe.

No. She couldn't keep expecting them to turn up and save her from herself.

"Why are you breathing like that? Are you asthmatic?"

She shook her head and turned her face to the window, wanting to die because now he'd noticed she was off and was staring at her.

"I'll ask Gunter if he reached your doctor." He started to lean forward.

She grabbed his sleeve. "Don't."

"You're flushed." He touched the backs of his fingers to her cheek then her forehead, making her flinch. "Sweating."

"It's nothing," she lied in a strangled voice, and was both relieved and horrified that her phone began to ripple with the heavenly notes of a harp.

It took two tries to open the call. When her sister appeared, she wasn't in focus. Tears of homesickness and failure filled her eyes. "Gili."

"I know, *bella*," she sounded equally anxious. "I can feel it. Where are you? Still at the Prince's chalet?"

"I don't know." The realization that she was in a strange land had been stalking her. Admitting it made it real and added to her terror. Her heart was so tight, she feared it was going into arrest. She clutched at the front of her shirt. "We're driving. How will you find me if we're moving? I'm so scared, Gili."

"I know, *fillette*. Breathe. Count your oranges. I'm coming. See, I'm going through the door. Henri has been tracking you all day. We'll always find you, you know that. Are you still with the Prince?"

Trella looked up and saw Xavier staring at her like her hair was made of snakes.

It was the most humiliating moment of her life. She couldn't make it worse by having her sister come to her like she was a child. *Couldn't.*

"No." She turned back to her phone. "You're married now. You have to stay with Kasim."

"He understands. I've already sent someone to tell him and prepare the helicopter."

It sounded so outlandish. What other person had family flying in from all corners to save her from imaginary threats?

"No, Gili." She managed to sound firm, even though turning away her sister felt like plunging a knife into her own chest. "I don't want you to come. I mean it."

"*Bella,*" her sister breathed as though she'd felt the knife, too, in the back.

"I have to learn, Gili. I *have* to. I'm going to hang up and I'll call you later—"

"Wait! Let me speak to the Prince. He needs to understand."

Since there was no way Trella could explain it herself, she pushed the phone toward him.

"It's a panic attack," Gili said. "She doesn't need drugs or a hospital or strangers making her relive why this is happening. She needs to feel safe. Is there a hotel where you can secure a room? I don't mean book one. I mean *secure* it."

"We'll be at the palace in ten minutes."

"Good. Get her into a quiet bedroom, keep the lights low, blinds down, guards at the door. She needs to let it run its course without fearing people are going to see her. Keep her warm and whatever she says, remind her she's safe. If you can't stay with her, I'll come."

"I'll stay with her." His voice was grim. He handed back the phone.

She ended the call, mortified by how needy her sister had made her sound. Appalled because it was true. She hadn't tried to weather a spell on her own since they had first started. It had been a disaster.

Nevertheless, she screwed up her courage, pressed the phone between her breasts, and spoke some of the hardest words that had ever passed her lips. "You don't have to babysit me."

She held her breath, dreading the prospect of going it alone.

"I'm not letting you out of my sight until that baby is born."

The harsh words jarred, taking her brief flash of gratitude and coating it in foreboding.

CHAPTER SIX

XAVIER HAD THE car drive to the postern gate, where delivery trucks and other utility vehicles came in. They took a lane through the back garden to the private apartments. It was a longer, slower, but much more discreet entrance into the palace built by a king three hundred years ago.

Did coming in this way also allow him to avoid Mario and any mention of his grandmother's expectation that he present himself? A man did what he had to for the mother of his unborn child.

Xavier didn't *do* emotion. Fits and tempers were signs of poor breeding. He'd been taught that from an early age. When women became histrionic, he offered space.

Not possible today. And as much as he wanted to hold himself apart from the way Trella was behaving, he couldn't. She was shaking, hair damp at her temples, eyes darting. When he helped her from the car, she clung to his sleeve and looked to every shadow.

It was unnerving. Even stranger, her sense of threat put him on guard.

He kept reminding himself this was a panic attack, something he knew very little about except that it was a false response. Nevertheless, her fear provoked a very real primal need in him to offer protection. His heart pounded with readiness and he scanned about as they moved, fingers twitching for a weapon. He'd never experienced such an atavistic, bloodthirsty reaction. He was not so far removed from his medieval ancestors as he had imagined. He was completely prepared to shed his cloak of civility and slay if necessary.

Staff leapt to their feet as they walked through the kitchen. He said nothing, only pulled her into the service elevator.

Gunter came with them, frowning as he saw how distraught she looked. "Are you in pain?" He tried to take her pulse.

Trella shrank into Xavier.

"Leave her alone." He closed his arms around her. Her firm bump nudged low on his abdomen, reminding him that her panic attack was only the tip of the iceberg where this confounding day was concerned.

His valet, Vincente, met them as they entered his apartment. Xavier had moved into his father's half of the rooms when he'd finished university and never even glanced toward the adjoined feminine side, but it was kept dusted for the ghosts of past queens.

He pressed Trella toward the canopied bed of gold and red then started to close the doors, telling Vincente, "I'm locking us in. Leave sandwiches in my lounge. If I need anything else, I'll text. No one comes in here. *No one.*"

"Of course, sir." He read Vincente's apprehension. "But I believe the Queen—"

"Inform her I'll be along when I can, but it will be some time."

Xavier did as he'd promised, moving to lock each door and close all the drapes, turning on one bedside lamp as he went. Then he shook out a soft blanket from a chest and brought it to where Trella sat on the edge of the bed.

She clutched the blanket around her, back hunched, still trembling.

All he could see was a nine-year-old girl. Was this what that experience had left her with? He had a thousand questions, but heeded her sister's advice and only said, "You're safe, *bella*. This is my world. Nothing can harm you here."

Tears tracked her cheeks and she swiped the back of her hand along her jaw, skimming away the drips.

"I didn't want you to see me like this." Her voice was thin as a silk thread. "I wanted you to think I was Gili. She cries at proper things, like weddings and stubbed toes. She's afraid of real things, not stuff she makes up in her head."

Was it made-up? He used the satin on the corner of the blanket to dry her cheeks, not sure where the urge to comfort came from. It wasn't taught or ingrained. Manners and platitudes got him through displays like this, not affection.

But he felt responsible for her and her attack. "I only wanted to talk to you. I didn't expect things to go off the rails like this."

"Don't blame yourself. I take everything further than it needs to go." She drew in a shaken sigh. Her eyes filled again.

"Is this what you were hiding, staying out of the spotlight all those years?"

She nodded jerkily. "It started after Papa died. We were fifteen. I was starting to feel like I might be able to go back to school and have a normal life. But we were seen as sex objects, I guess, because the most disgusting men found us online. I'd already been through an eating disorder and trolls mocking me for it. Then all these men started sending photos and telling me what they wanted to do to me. It hit a switch."

A streak of impotent fury lodged in his chest. His entire life, he had struggled against this particular irony. He was a future monarch, charged with great power and responsibility, godlike in some eyes, but he couldn't control how people treated each other. He couldn't prevent the kind of harm that had Trella drawing up her knees so she was a ball of misery. His inability to help her struck at the deepest part of him.

"I'm a woman of extremes. You might as well know that about me. Give me that pillow."

He dragged it closer and she fell onto her side and buried her face in it. She sobbed so deeply, was in the throes of an anguish so terrible, he was stricken witnessing it. How did she withstand it?

Let it run its course, her sister had said. That seemed cruel.

He settled on the bed behind her, rubbed her arm and soothed her shaking back. It took several minutes for her crying to subside. She lifted her head and breathed as though she'd been running for miles.

"I keep worrying I'll have an attack while I'm in labor. My doctor says this won't hurt the baby, but I'm so scared all this adrenaline is causing damage. What if we go through all of this and our child isn't fit to reign? What if that's my fault because I can't control this?"

"Is there nothing you can take? Something safe during pregnancy?"

"No. I mean, maybe, but I can't. *Won't*." She threw her arm over her eyes. "I tried drugs years ago. They made me depressed and dependent. I was close to taking a whole bottle just to end this."

She dropped her arm and twisted to stare at him from between matted lashes.

"I shouldn't have told you that. You'll declare me unfit and take our baby away. Oh, God…"

She rolled around the pillow again, dragging the blanket with her and pulling it over her head.

"Trella." He was no mental health expert, but he knew a tailspin when he heard one. He settled on the mattress behind her, propped on an elbow, letting his body heat penetrate the blanket as he gave rubs of reassurance against her shoulder and arm. He wanted to fold right around her, absorb whatever had such a terrible grip on her.

"Let's take this one thing at a time. Hmm? The baby is well. Your doctor said so, yes? Do you know the sex?"

It took a minute, but her breathing settled to something more natural.

"I've been afraid to ask, thinking it would make me more attached. I'm so scared I'm going to lose it." She shifted, pushing away the blanket to reveal her face, then peeled the blanket all the way back, piling it on him as she exposed her bump. She smoothed her shirt over the roundness. "It's moving. Do you want to feel?"

He stalled, reality hitting him like a train. He let her draw his hand across the tense swell of her midsection. He had thought it would feel like an inflated beach ball, but she was warm and there was give within the firmness. A shape. Something that felt no bigger than his knuckle pressed outward, moving across the palm of his hand.

He almost jerked back, yet he was too fascinated and kept his hand in place, waiting to feel it again. "Does that hurt?"

"It reassures me. *Hola, bebé. Cómo estás?*"

Another tiny kick struck his hand, prompting a soft noise of amusement deep in her throat. She turned her head to look at him. Her eyelids were red and swollen, but her smile was so filled with joy and wonder, she took his breath away.

The moment snaked out like a rope to encircle and draw them together, binding them, inexorable and eternal.

He sucked in a breath, drawing back as he tried to pull himself free of what threatened to carry him into deep waters like a deadly riptide.

"How are we even here? How—Why me, *bella*?"

"Why did I sleep with you? I didn't plan to sleep with anyone." She curled around her pillow, rubbing her face against it, drying tears. "I only wanted to practice being in public. I was so proud for having the courage to talk to a man, then to be alone with one. You made me feel normal. Safe. I needed that. I was using you. I admit that. But sleeping with you?" She craned her neck to look at him, her expression helpless. Anxious. "I couldn't help myself. You said we were volatile. That…"

He knew what he had said. It had been true. He'd never experienced anything like what he'd felt with her that night. Despite his best efforts, the memory haunted him. He wasn't a dependent person, but he was disturbingly gratified to be this close to her again. The animal inside him had finally stopped pacing with restless frustration.

He was loath to admit any of that, though. Her power to still affect him unnerved him. "It was my last night before I got engaged. We were both attributing significance for our own reasons."

The light in her eyes dimmed with hurt. She withdrew, turning away again.

He closed his fist in the tangle of blanket across their hips, lungs turning to lead.

"Either way, it gave me hope that I could *be* normal. Maybe fall in love and get married, someday. That's all I've ever wanted. To be normal. Now I never will be, because I'm carrying a royal baby and I was so happy to be pregnant, but I knew this was a disaster. You have your life and I've never had any life at all. I deserve a chance to be single and free. Free of *this*!"

Her tension returned in a contraction of her muscles that drew her in like a shrinking bloom, fists coming up to her clenched eyes.

"I told Gili I would run Maison des Jumeaux. When we were little, she was able to count on me. I want to be that person people can rely on, but I'm always going to be this pathetic—"

"Trella. You *have* to stop escalating."

"Do you think I can control it?" Her hands went into her hair, clenching handfuls. "I try. I really try, but the fear *grips* me. Now we have to get married and you don't want some crazy burden of a wife. You'll hate me. I'm *so scared* of what will happen."

"Stop." He couldn't stand it. He pressed his body heat around her, held her in sheltering arms and willed her back to calm. "Hatred is a wasted emotion. It closes all pathways to resolving a conflict. Our situation is difficult, but hating each other won't make it easier."

Her trembling continued, but he felt the moment his words penetrated. Her hands loosened in her hair.

"That sounds very wise," she said on a sniff. "Do they teach you that in monarchy school?"

"Divorce class. My mother was a great believer in practical demonstrations."

She unfolded a few increments more. "When we were in Paris, you said your mother was sent away by your grandmother because she wanted a divorce?"

He eased his embrace, regretting his loose lips. He had learned out of necessity to be comfortable with his own thoughts, never needing confidantes, but keeping her mind engaged seemed to forestall her emotional downtrends, so he answered.

"She made a commitment then didn't accept her lot. Unhappy wives move into the dowager wing. They don't reject royal life altogether. My mother tried separation, but my father and grandmother pressured her to have another baby. Since their marriage was over, she refused. She was granted a divorce on the grounds that she left Elazar. She had family in Germany so she moved there."

"Exiled, you said. But you still saw her? How old were you?" She tried to twist enough to see him.

He used the weight of his arm to keep them spooned. Her hair tickled his lips while the scent of her went straight to the back of his brain, finding where she had imprinted herself in Paris and settling like a puzzle piece matched to its empty space.

He shook off the notion. "I was eight. At boarding school. My life wasn't affected much. We exchanged a few letters, but what was there to say?"

"You didn't see her *at all*?" She tried harder to twist, rolling onto her back and forcing him to meet her gaze. "Do you see her now?"

"We send Christmas cards." He shrugged off the jabs of rejection that still came alive when he revisited the memory. "Chosen by our personal assistants. We're not sentimental people."

Her expression grew appalled. "What about your father? You said you were young when he abdicated?"

"Renounced," he corrected, regretting this. It was becoming too intimate. Too uncomfortable.

"Do you see him?"

"It was best we didn't communicate." *This* communication ended here, he conveyed by drawing back.

"But—" She groaned and rolled to face him fully. He could see a fresh wave of emotion taking its grip on her. Her hand closed on the front of his shirt, catching at a few chest hairs, making him wince. "Now I'm worried you'll drop out of our child's life like that. Swear to me you won't."

He covered her hand, loosening her fist and holding her slender fingers. He had to consciously overcome an urge to draw her hand to his mouth and kiss her bruised knuckles, even as he acknowledged she was far more likely to disappear than he was. Royal life was not easy, especially when shoved to the fringes as his mother had been. He didn't blame his mother for extricating herself, and wouldn't censure Trella when she did it, especially if the stress of life in the public eye put her in paroxysms like this.

"Duty may have skipped a generation, but it is firmly drilled into me. I will never forsake my obligation to our child."

"Obligation." Her brow furrowed. "What about love?"

He dried her cheek with his thumb. "Love is a problem not a solution."

"Who told you *that*?"

"It's an observation. My mother loved my father, which is why she couldn't bear his cheating. My father loved the woman who cost him his kingdom. Duty is more reliable."

She shook her head.

"I don't have to argue with you, *bella*. Time reveals all. Now, let's stop talking about things that upset you. What did your sister say about counting oranges? Tell me why she said that."

Xavier hadn't had his backside handed to him on one of the palace's sixteenth-century gold platters since his teen years. He refused to allow it today.

He had had plenty of time in the night, lying awake making decisions between comforting Trella through crying spells and nightmares, until she fell deeply asleep in the early hours.

He rose to put his plans into action and by the time the Queen summoned him, he was able to preempt a shred-

ding of his character by proving what he had told Trella—
he adhered to duty above all else.

"She has agreed to that?"

"She will."

"And you?"

"Of course. Why wouldn't I?"

The Queen cocked a skeptical brow. "You spent last
night with her. That implies...preoccupation."

"You think we were having sex? No." Despite having
few secrets from his grandmother, her intrusive remark
grated. "She was upset."

"Gunter said she's fragile." Her mouth pursed with disdain. Ruling required strength of every kind, especially
emotional.

He frowned, annoyed that Gunter's report had preceded
his own, especially because it was off the mark. Trella was
besieged. It was different.

"She held off telling me because her pregnancy is high-
risk."

"So, it would seem, is she."

An urge to defend her stayed lodged in his throat. She
was a threat—one he was mitigating to the best of his
ability.

"When would you like to meet her?" he asked instead.

"Perhaps after the baby is born?"

He hadn't slept. That's why the snub struck him as un-
conscionably rude.

Before he could react, Mario entered. "Deepest apologies, your Majesty, but Ms. Sauveterre's brother insists on
seeing her. We've stalled him as long as possible."

"He's *here*?" Xavier's heart lurched with protectiveness
and a jolt of alarm. Trella was catching up on much-needed
sleep. More importantly, "We both spoke to him yesterday.
She told him she was staying for the foreseeable future."

She couldn't leave.

"I believe it's the race-car driver. She has agreed to receive him. I thought you would wish to—"

"I would." Xavier strode from the room. When he heard raised voices as he approached the apartment they now shared, his aggression increased. With a snap of his fingers, security personnel fell into step behind him. He pushed into what had once been his mother's parlor.

Trella was red-faced as she confronted a man who looked like Henri but emanated a hot-tempered demeanor that was in complete contrast to his brother's air of aloof control. "No, *you* shut up—" Ramon was saying to his sister.

"Leave quietly or I'll have you removed." Xavier would do it himself. He was in that kind of mood.

Ramon snorted as he gave Xavier a measuring once-over, hands on his hips, looking willing for the fight Xavier promised.

"Don't." Trella threw herself against her brother's side, looping her arms tight around his waist. "I was saying things he didn't want to hear."

Despite the animosity that had been flaring between them seconds before, Ramon curled a shielding arm around his sister, even as he frowned at her, concern evident beneath his glare of impatience.

Trella looked as rough as the night she'd had. When Xavier had left her, she'd been subdued and exhausted, falling back asleep within seconds after he'd woken her to tell her he was leaving. She still had dark circles under red eyes and hadn't changed out of the silk pajamas he'd given her to wear to bed. In fact, she'd raided his closet for a thick cardigan to belt over them.

Xavier snapped out of searching her expression to realize she was bickering with her brother, refusing to go with him.

"All those times you showed up when I called makes

it possible for me to work through this. I know you *will* come if I ask. That means everything. But until I ask, you *have* to *butt out*."

With a resigned scowl, Ramon dropped his arm from around her. "*Bueno*."

"And be nicer to Iz—"

"No. Butting out goes both ways. And you *will* introduce me to your host."

"Did you call me a *virgin*?" Xavier asked Trella in an ominous tone as they entered his suite hours later. "You switched between French and Spanish so often, I might have heard wrong."

She tried not to snicker. "I told you it was a bad habit. Ramon and I are the worst because we get heated and grab the first word that comes in any language."

Ramon had joined them for a meal that might have been pleasant if so many questions hadn't been hanging over her like a guillotine blade. If he'd caught her alone again, he would have skewered her with all of them, she was sure, but he'd behaved. They had played verbal tennis as they always did, sticking to neutral topics like films and current events.

Sparring with her brother always helped restore her confidence. Where Gili was her security blanket and Henri was her rock, Ramon was her worthy adversary, keeping her sharp and forcing her to hold her own. She was tired and stifling yawns, but her lingering melancholy had lightened. As she looked into the cloudy crystal ball that was her future, she was thinking, *I can do this.*

Especially because, like her, Xavier seemed to be experiencing the same threads of attraction they'd felt when they had made this baby. A selection from her closet in Paris had arrived earlier and she now wore a dark blue skirt and a white maternity top. It draped her breasts in such a flattering way, she'd caught Xavier eyeing her chest more than once while they ate, making her tingle and giving her hope.

She turned her back on him and lifted her hair, silently requesting he release the tiny clasp at the top of her spine, realizing she hadn't properly answered his question. "And yes, I did. Ramon asked me how you did with looking after me through my attack. I said pretty well, for a virgin."

"Lovely. I hope the dining staff enjoyed that." His breath warmed the back of her neck along with the light brush of his fingertips, making her shiver.

"I said worse. I called Ramon a—"

"I heard that one. Very clearly," he cut in dryly, motioning her to lead the way to her side of the apartment. "Because of his engagement to 'Izzy.'"

"Isidora, yes. She's a dear friend. Her father handled our media for years. Aside from Gili, she was my *only* friend for a long time."

Her heart dipped and rolled when he turned, locking them into her bedroom. Despite her rough night, sleeping with him had been more than comforting. She had liked the brushes of contact and the inherent intimacy, the way his strong arms had made her feel so safe. It had given her that bonding feeling she had felt in Paris, one that was incredibly bolstering.

His efforts to comfort also gave her hope for their marriage. All her flaws had been laid bare, yet he had stayed with her. She was deeply gratified. Touched.

Now all she had to explain was that, as much as she might like to, she couldn't make love. Practically blushing at the mere thought, because she was so deeply tempted, she moved to take up her brush and began working it through her hair, trying to act casual as nerves accosted her.

He moved to lean on the footboard of the bed, appearing in the mirror behind her. The way he watched as she stroked her hair made her feel as though she was enticing him. The crackle of tension on the air was exciting, giving her that sense of power in her sexuality he'd instilled the first time. Oh, she wished their timing wasn't so far off.

His expression tightened before he jerked his gaze away, clearing his throat. "If she's such a good friend, why don't you approve of her?"

"Who? Oh. Um." She blushed at having her mind fixated on intimate acts while he was clearly not. "I approve of Isidora completely, but Ramon is sleeping with her."

"Stickler for waiting until after the wedding, are you?" He dropped a pointed gaze to her middle.

"Ha-ha." She tapped the brush against her thigh then set it aside. "No, their engagement is a publicity stunt. Earlier this year, Isidora took over her father's position at Sauveterre International." Trella took off her earrings and bracelet. "You'll notice Ramon's very public proposal coincides with the first photos of my pregnancy showing up online. He does that all the time, takes the spotlight off the rest of us. Izzy is so loyal she went along with it, but she had a terrific crush on Ramon when we were young. He never returned it and shouldn't sleep with her if he has no intention of marrying her. She's going to get hurt. That makes me mad."

"I see. Well, kindly convey that we would prefer fewer stunts in future. My team will handle—" he indicated her middle again "—this."

She blinked, not expecting him to be worried for Izzy, not really, but his cool attention to his own interests sent a premonition down her spine like a drip of icy water.

It occurred to her that he had closed the door not because he wanted to nurture the growing trust between them. He wanted to have a conversation that was best held within the gilded cage he'd assigned her.

Logically she knew she had imprinted on her first lover like a baby duckling emerging from its protective shell. She'd spent weeks reliving Paris and imagining this reunion, dreaming up scenarios where he was as happy about her pregnancy as she was.

It was delusional. She had known that, but apparently she was still building castles in the sky because a minute ago, she had been okay with his knowing all her worst secrets. Now a grossly naked sensation accosted her, like he had leverage on her.

She tried to disguise her apprehension with a tough smile. "It's time to discuss *this*. Isn't it?"

The barest flicker of emotion reflected in his blink. He folded his arms and tilted his head in assent. "Gunter informs me your doctor has accepted my offer of a residency at Hospital del Re, with a mandate to ensure our obstetrics wing is the best in the world. She'll be here tomorrow and has requested a private room be prepared for you."

"Bed rest." Trella had known it was coming, but still made a face of dismay.

"You'll fight it?"

"No." She wasn't able to keep the dread from her voice, though. "It's for the best."

"It is."

Something in his tone, in the subtle shift of his expression, pricked up her ears. Relief? His approval of her going into the hospital had nothing to do with the health of their unborn child. He was protecting his own interests again!

An ache of hurt spread through her until all her sweet imaginings had been pushed out and she was left with the ugly reality. She really had been deceiving herself all these months.

"Keeps me out of sight, does it? Is that the Queen's

preference? Or yours?" Behind the stir of their child, her abdomen tightened.

His expression grew even more shuttered. "It's expedient for all. You said you don't want the attention our association brings."

"Don't pretend you're doing me a favor. Are we not marrying, then?" Clearly not, if he was hiding her away.

Her arms pulled into a defensive fold across her front. Her shoulders grew rock hard while she ignored the creep of anguish that began working in tendrils through her core. What did she care? She didn't want a husband anyway!

Right?

"Of course we'll marry." He mirrored her posture, arms folded, seeming relaxed in the way he leaned on the footboard, but there was a stillness to him, an implacability in his tone. "Elazar had a bastard monarch in the 1700s. It was a bloody fight to keep the reign. We've been sticklers for legitimacy ever since."

She understood she was speaking to a future king now, not the charming prince who had lulled her with something that had resembled caring. Twice.

"Our marriage will be a private ceremony. Announced, but without fanfare. No formal photos. We'll keep it brief."

"The ceremony? Or the marriage?"

"Both."

The tendons in her neck flexed as she fought a choke, doing her best to hide how deeply he was striking against her hard-won self-worth. "How brief?"

"We'll divorce by the end of the year."

Her teeth closed on the inside of her lip, biting down harder and harder until she had to consciously remind herself not to break the skin.

What had she expected after showing him her true colors? A declaration of love? A desire to live out his life with *that*? Well, she knew exactly how much *duty* he felt toward her, didn't she? Not even four months' worth.

"That's quite the virgin birth you're orchestrating."

His eyes narrowed at her shaken tone. "Is this conversation going to bring on another attack?"

Oh, she hated above all things to be managed like she was too delicate for honesty.

"I do better when I know what's coming." Her voice only trembled a little, mostly from the effort to hide the burn of disgrace sizzling under her skin. "Is this room a time machine, by the way? I feel we've gone back to your 1700s and I'm something shameful you're sweeping under the rug."

"It isn't about hiding you." He showed the barest hint of discomfort by dropping his hands to the footboard and pushing to stand. "I'm acknowledging you and the heir you're providing me, but it would be helpful if your role was downplayed, so as not to overshadow Patrizia's."

"You're still *engaged*?"

"It's been called off, since I'm marrying you, but—"

"She's still willing to marry you?" The news pushed her into falling back a step. Maybe it was the realization that he still wanted that marriage himself. Why did that hurt? So much?

"Unless a better offer comes along, she is not averse to reviving our plan after you and I divorce." He must have read the incredulity in her expression, because he said, "We're friends. Both ruled by duty. The fact we *don't* have strong feelings for each other and she's *not* hurt by this—" again with the generic wave at her middle "—is the reason we're a good fit."

"But her child won't be first in line! Or is she hoping mine's a girl?"

"Gender isn't an issue in Elazar. First born is first in line, but..." He seemed to debate whether she could handle his next words before he said, without emotion, "Until you deliver a healthy baby, many aspects of this situation remain fluid."

Trella sucked in a gasp so sharp it went down the back of her throat like a spear, sticking in her heart and pinning her motionless. She tried telling herself the shivery clamp around her was anger, but it was anguish. Dark, blood-red betrayal.

"How *dare* you give someone *hope* that I'll lose our baby."

"It's not hope." He strode away from the foot of the bed in a sudden rush, making her jerk back another step and keep him in her line of sight. "It's caution. You said this will be your only pregnancy. There is a reason for an heir and a spare. If my uncle had lived, this conversation wouldn't even be happening. If my mother had done her duty, I would have other choices. I don't. I will accept what comes of this pregnancy, but I have to ensure there are alternatives."

She was so appalled that she wasn't even sure what the cold feeling against her lips was. Her fingers? All of her felt cold and empty and deeply furious.

She barely tracked that his hand flicked the air. Through her own haze of emotion, she had a brief impression of bitterness before he turned his back on her.

Anything close to suffering on his part was imagined, though. Had to be. Everything she had shared with this man was imagination and faulty memory. A wish. Girlish daydreaming. A rescue fantasy.

He was a spoiled prince who had sullied a maiden and was tidying up that mess the most pragmatic way possible.

"This really is medieval times, isn't it? Women have come all this way, yet I'm still just a vessel. A faulty one." She knew she was broken. It shouldn't surprise her that she was being rejected. She had thought she had prepared herself, but she hadn't. She was gutted and had to fight with everything in her not to reveal how devastated she was.

So many times, she'd wished she could go back to that moment as an impetuous girl, when Gili's math tutor had called out to her. She had run to tell him he had the wrong twin, *that's all*. It had been one second of impulse and she was still being punished for it.

Xavier's head tipped back as he aimed his gaze at the portrait of an ancestor surveying them from high on the wall.

"If I don't produce our next ruler, the crown passes to a family living in America for the last two hundred years. Rather than let that happen, our neighbors would squabble to take control of Elazar. Instability would ripple across Europe. The globe. We're a small country, but a pivotal one. I need more than one child to ensure Elazar's future. I need a wife with connections that cement our alliances."

His voice held not one iota of regret or even concern for how his plan would affect *this* child. Or her.

"Spell it out for me." She grappled for her most pragmatic tone. "Exactly how is this to work? Because I am not allowing some strange woman to raise my baby."

"Our child will be raised by nannies, tutors and servants, same as you and I."

"*I* wasn't!"

"You left for boarding school at *seven*. If you hadn't been kidnapped, you would have grown up there. Your brothers did."

"My parents traveled, but they were very involved. We knew they loved us!"

As she stared into his half-lidded eyes and read indifference, it struck her why he was being so dispassionate rather than weighing his decisions through his heart.

"You don't know what that's like, do you?" She felt

cruel saying it, but everything he had told her about his parents came back to her, bringing his brutally logical plan into focus.

His brow went up in arrogant query. "What?"

"Love."

He might have flinched, but it was gone so fast that she wasn't sure. His sigh was pure condescension as he pushed his hands into his pockets. "I told you last night—"

"I'm not talking about romantic love. *Family* love."

"Love of any kind isn't real." His voice slapped her down for being so gullible. "Look around. Is it here? Keeping anyone in my life but my grandmother? Loyalty. Obligation. Duty. Those are real."

She would have argued that her family loved her, but something else struck with brutal force. "Are you saying—"

She had a flash of her mother crying with joy because Trella was pregnant. Elisa Sauveterre was worried sick and had strong opinions on how Trella had avoided telling Xavier, but beneath all of that was pure, over-the-moon love for her unborn grandchild.

"Is your grandmother happy we're having a baby?" Her voice quavered with strain.

His jaw set. "That is not the word I would use, no."

"Wow." A jagged laugh clawed inside her chest. "Just wow." How did one survive such an emotional desert?

The answer was before her. They turned into this—an image of a man with a heart, but one who was actually incapable of deeper feelings. One who scoffed at love.

A fierce gleam—torment?—flashed in his gaze before he steeled himself behind a visage of hammered armor. "But she recognizes we have a responsibility toward it."

"Precious obligation," she said shakily. "Here's some news for you. I will *not* be shut out of my child's life and replaced by nannies and tutors. I'll call in the rescue team right now and barricade us in Sus Brazos for the rest of our lives if that's what you're thinking."

"Dramatics will not be necessary," he said with pithy disdain. "We'll share custody, fifty-fifty. Aside from security and education, how you meet the needs of our child is your business. Visitations to Spain or elsewhere can be worked out as they arise. But our child lives in Elazar." He pointed at the floor. "I will provide you with a home here in Lirona as part of our divorce settlement."

She shouldn't care how quickly he got rid of her. He was being so cold, acting so far removed from the man she had wanted to believe he was, she could hardly endure facing the next minute in his company let alone four months of marriage.

It still took effort to say, "Well, that's a relief." She held his gaze, saying goodbye to those moments when he had held her and touched her as if there had been more between them than obligation. "I can move on then, too."

His eyes narrowed with warning, gaze so hard and devoid of feeling she struggled to hold the contact. "You can."

How foolish of her to try getting under his skin. She looked away, thinking that she couldn't stay this close to him with her defenses annihilated the way they were.

"Where is this dowager wing of which you spoke?"

"You'll sleep where I can keep an eye on you. You were difficult enough to track down as it was."

"Confinement. How apropos. And *familiar.*"

"I won't apologize. We've agreed it's wasted."

"I still won't forgive you."

"Because I'm not upending my life?"

"Because you don't want our baby!"

"I don't want our *situation.*"

You don't want me! She didn't say it. She was appalled she had thought it and turned her face away, boiling in humiliation. Pressure filled her throat and sat livid behind her eyes.

Into the thick silence, he sighed. "What I want has never mattered, *bella*. Duty to the crown takes precedence. I learned that a long time ago."

His voice was surprisingly gentle, which made the lash of the words all the more cutting and intolerable.

"Don't call me that. It's a family nickname and implies we're closer than we are, but it's just something you say when you can't remember the name of the woman you're sleeping with."

Another loaded silence filled the room like an acrid cloud.

"Explain to me how sniping at each other will make this easier."

"It's the *truth*." She swallowed past the ache in her throat, but it only lodged deeper in her chest. "You called me that in Paris and it made me think you saw *me*, not my sister, but all you saw was a willing partner. I need to stop thinking we're friends. Stop acting like we are."

They were still strangers and would remain so. He kept his heart behind thicker walls than she had ever hidden behind.

"If you insist. Trella."

"Thank you." She wasn't grateful. She was shattered. "Can you—" She waved at the door. "I'm tired."

"Will you be all right alone?"

She had thought he couldn't hurt her any further, but that did it. After rejecting her so roundly, did he really think she would want to cling to *him* through another emotional storm? How did he manage to sound like he *cared* if she suffered alone?

"I have to learn to be, don't I? I've known that for a long time. Goodnight."

CHAPTER SEVEN

I NEED TO stop thinking we're friends.

There was no reason he should have lost sleep over that. Perhaps the *bella* endearment *had* always rolled off his tongue very easily around women, but for some reason knowing it held a more intimate connotation for her made it something he wanted the right to use. He doubted he would ever use it again with anyone else. It was hers now, which made it doubly frustrating she refused to hear it from him.

He went into his first meeting of the day, unrested and gritty eyed, only to face the woman still torturing him. They were about to negotiate their prenuptial agreement.

He introduced her to the palace attorney who fell under her spell at the first flash of her smile. She wore a pin-striped sky blue jacket over a white shirt that draped untucked over her matching skirt. It made her look smart and capable, yet sensual. Achingly vulnerable.

"I should have invited your brother to stay for this," he said as he directed her into a comfortable armchair.

"Why?" She cooled when he touched her arm and delicately removed her elbow from his loose touch, adjusting a cushion behind her back as she sat.

"To protect your interests."

"You can email the draft to him," the attorney said with

a magnanimous smile. "If he has concerns, we can address them before you sign."

She sat back and folded her hands on her lap, smiling in a way that could only be called patronizing.

"Gentlemen. Along with our mother, my siblings and I jointly own Sauveterre International. Ramon votes Gili's share and Henri votes Mama's because they don't take an interest. I vote my own, thank you very much. Maison Des Jumeaux is not the only enterprise I've asked SI to underwrite. One hundred percent of my initiatives have turned a profit because I have a brain and use it. So…" She cut a glance toward Xavier. "The Prince may show the draft to his grandmother before *he* signs, to ensure *his* interests are protected, but I'm confident I can look after my own."

The attorney cleared his throat and shuffled papers.

Xavier held her lofty stare.

He should have been affronted. It was a well-executed burn in front of the attorney and his PA, but he was darkly thankful for that scorn in her.

He had watched her all through their meal with her brother yesterday, captivated by her rallying spirit. The glimpse of her family dynamic and the new facets in her personality had only made him want to know her far better than he would be allowed to. It had taken genuine effort on his part to stick to the plan and outline how they would proceed. If he had had a choice—

He didn't. So he had said what needed to be said.

She'd been angry. Injured. She *was* sentimental. And despite his claims to be anything but, he didn't take pleasure in hurting others. If things were different…

Wistfulness was a useless emotion. He steeled himself against futile *if only*s. "Let's get started."

As promised, Trella protected her abundant interests with pointed questions and clear language. The details were hammered out with very little fuss until the attorney asked, "And the dissolution of the marriage? Midnight, December thirty-first?"

"That's fine. But if I lose the baby, the marriage ends immediately."

Her statement was jarring. Xavier swung his head to regard her, disturbed.

"There would be no reason to draw it out," she said stiffly. White tension ringed her mouth.

A strange void opened in him. Why? She was right. What else was there between them besides the baby?

You don't know what that's like, do you?

Her disturbing accusation last night kept ambushing him, but his parents had been disruptive forces in his life, dividing his loyalty, creating nothing but turmoil and disappointment. If that was love, he didn't need it.

His grandmother's levelheaded reason and clear outline of what was expected from a future monarch had been a welcomed relief. Taking responsibility meant taking control.

Like love, Trella was an unpredictable influence. Too much was at stake to indulge any latent desires for either. She was right. Without the baby, they had nothing holding them in their union.

He lifted a finger, indicating the attorney should record that their marriage would end if the pregnancy did. He ignored the grate in the pit of his stomach.

They signed the contract a few days later, once the DNA results had been confirmed. Afterward, Trella hurried to greet her mother, who had arrived for the ceremony that would be held in the palace chapel.

"We agreed on a private ceremony," Xavier said when she informed him her mother would attend.

"She's giving me away." Trella hadn't mentioned her sister had cried over missing the ceremony. "All of my family wanted to be here, but neither of us is getting the wedding we wanted, are we? Well, I guess you are. Later."

His expression had hardened as he looked away.

She wasn't trying to be "combative," just stating fact. She had hoped she and Xavier would have something to build a family upon, but they didn't.

That made her sad, but all her soul-searching had been done in the months of keeping her pregnancy under wraps. Xavier had given her a chance at motherhood that she had believed was out of reach. For that, she would always be grateful.

But he saw her as, at best, one of the many staff who would tend to his offspring so he wouldn't have to. They might marry, but she wouldn't be his wife.

He didn't want *her*.

She had to ignore how spurned that made her feel. She already had people who loved her, after all.

"*Mi niña hermosa*," her mother exclaimed as she finished buttoning the gown and Trella turned to face her. "Truly, this is your *pièce de résistance*."

Trella had been working on the gown in secret, not even showing it to her mother or Gili. It was understated, like her makeup, with a high waist to cover her bump and a simple bodice with cap sleeves. The seed pearls and crystals had been the time-consuming work and she was proud of how it had turned out.

Her hair was in a loose chignon. Her mother placed a bridal comb over her ear in lieu of a veil. The brushed silver flowers with pearls and diamonds was a family heirloom, not ostentatious, just right for a small afternoon wedding.

They followed the ever-efficient Mario to the palace chapel.

Xavier was already there, speaking to the bishop. He wore a bone colored tunic-style jacket with dark gold ep-aulettes and gold leaf embroidery at the cuffs and hem. His royal red sash sat across it, decorated with a number of pins, including a key and a family shield. A sword hung off his hip.

My prince, she thought, and ached inside.

He wasn't, and he never would be.

Xavier turned and splendor kicked him in the stomach.

Her dress was white, which somehow wasn't ironic de-spite being a maternity gown. Perhaps it was the fact her bump was still modest, or the way the gown drew his eye to the beading at her neckline and across her shoulders. The detailing resembled angel wings but also projected strength. Delicate armor.

The rest of her was incandescent. Her skin held the warm glow he had noticed the night they'd met, as if fire-light reflected off a creamy nude. She was both waif and warrior. Goddess and maid. Infinitely fascinating.

She came forward, expression guarded as she intro-duced her mother.

Elisa Sauveterre was a tall, elegant woman of Spanish ancestry with sensual features and a single streak of white in her black hair.

As she held his hand in both her warm ones, shadows in the misty depths of her eyes told him she had feared this day would never come for her daughter. It made him feel churlish for bristling when Trella had informed him her mother was coming.

"It's an honor to have you here." He was embarrassed now that his grandmother wasn't attending, and that they hadn't extended an invitation for Elisa to stay at the palace. His impatience with himself sharpened his tone as he told Trella, "You look beautiful."

Her mouth tightened. "Thank you." But she might have been speaking to Mario who handed her a bouquet.

Mario was Xavier's witness, which suddenly felt like a disregard for the significance of the occasion. Xavier understood ceremony. His entire country was up in arms, wanting to witness this moment. The least he could have done was invite a friend to be his best man. He might not have many friends, but he had some.

Friends would come next year, though, when he married Patrizia in a spectacle he already dreaded.

Today's occasion was far more to his liking, even though the exchange of words seemed to hold extra power when spoken in such an intimate setting, heard only by the three witnesses. Even those few extra pairs of eyes and ears fell away as he spoke directly to Trella, losing himself in the shift of gray and green in her irises.

When she said, "I do," it reverberated within him, so visceral he knew that he would feel bound by this promise his entire life. She was his responsibility now, but he would have to turn away from her to perform the rest of his obligations. The war of dueling duties already hammered a crack into his psyche, causing a schism that would never heal.

"Do you have the ring?" the bishop asked.

"I'll only have to remove it when I go into the hospital." Trella waved off the case.

It was an unexpected swipe of claws at a part of him Xavier hadn't realized he'd exposed. What did he care that she didn't even glance at the ring he'd spent more than an hour dithering over, wanting it to match her sparkling, multi-faceted personality?

Her mother's tiny sniff broke the silence. Mario smoothly

withdrew the ring. The bishop quickly finished the ceremony.

"You may k-kiss the bride..." Everyone had got the memo this was not a conventional marriage.

Her wary gaze grew even more vulnerable.

Should he have forgone this custom? Probably. But he set his hand at her waist and drew her toward him.

She braced her forearm along his and clenched her fist into his jacket sleeve, leaning on him for balance as she offered her mouth.

He brought his hand to the side of her neck, felt the cool tickle of a few strands of hair, and reminded himself not to make a fool of himself. Keep it brief.

He nearly groaned at the onslaught of sensation when his mouth covered hers.

As tenuous as everything else might be, in this second, they were as united as they'd been in Paris. Everything in him wanted to deepen and ravish, requiring all his willpower to keep the kiss short and sweet.

Her mouth moved under his with equal restraint, but he tasted the desire for more in the way her lips clung to his. Paradise hovered like a promise, but he couldn't surrender to whatever this thing was between them. All he could have was this. One kiss.

And it was already over.

"Mario tells me you wish to cancel Australia." The Queen looked up from her breakfast. "Why?"

He *had* cancelled, if Mario had done his job. Xavier filled his plate and gave the butler a nod, sending him from the room so they could speak in private.

"Don't play dumb," he said as the door closed.

"It's an important initiative."

Unlike some of his counterparts, the royals of Elazar

took specific, active roles in government. His entire year had been a series of trade talks in various regions. It wasn't appearance for the sake of it, but business meetings and presentations to push for expansion of existing agreements that would keep his country from going bankrupt.

"She isn't due for weeks," his grandmother continued. "Even when she goes into labor, what help do you think you will be?"

"She's alone in a strange country, stuck in the hospital. I'm not leaving for a month of press interviews where the first question will be, 'Why aren't you with your wife?'"

"Is that why you visit her every day? Because I'm told she keeps herself amused. Drawing. Chatting to family. You wouldn't be missed."

Perhaps not. Even Trella had asked if he was only visiting for appearances' sake.

The press release on their marriage and impending parenthood had been short and vague, playing to concern for a successful pregnancy without going into detail. It had made Xavier sick to hear his team discuss how spinning the pregnancy as a miracle would create a groundswell of support, overcoming judgments about a scandalous, ill-timed affair.

Trella hadn't reacted beyond a remote, "I've played this game a long time. Say whatever you have to."

She had played the isolation game as well and did know how to amuse herself. He wasn't needed and didn't know why he counted down the minutes until he could dodge the paparazzi on the hospital steps and enter the guarded sanctum of her room.

Her prison was as cozy as it could be made. Monitors and equipment feeds were tucked behind panels. The walls were a comfortable mocha, the blankets printed with Elazar's national pasqueflower—the white buttercup that grew wild in their alpine meadows. Trella even wore regular clothes rather than a functional hospital gown.

But she reclined on the bed twenty-four-seven. Rising to use the toilet or shower was all the activity she was allowed.

Because of potential rupture.

Her doctor had scared the hell out of him when Trella had been admitted, explaining the need for such vigilance.

Trella had been stoic. She had checked into Hospital del Re the night they'd married and, despite only having resided in his apartment for a week, he'd felt her absence. Why? She'd been angry with him, cool when she'd been forced to speak to him, but somehow she had infused a sense of liveliness to the palace. The sound of her laugh in another room, or even just the splash of color from an abandoned scarf, made it less of a museum and more of a... Hell, it had always been his *home*. How could it suddenly feel like one?

He shook off the impression.

"You're very well-informed," he said, realizing the silence was stretching. "Yet you've never once asked *me* how she is."

"How is she?" She used her among-the-people tone of fabricated warmth, smile inching toward supercilious.

Anxious, he wanted to say. Trella *was* keeping herself busy, but he read the stress that lingered in the corners of her mouth and the tension between her brows.

"As well as could be expected."

"Then you should be able to leave her."

"I know what you're thinking." He shook his head. "I'm acting like a decent human being, not becoming attached."

Yet he was indulging himself with the visits. She hadn't asked him to come.

I've done this before, she'd said of her seclusion, then

had revealed her best coping strategy. She was an accomplished sketch artist.

Practice, she had dismissed when he went through her book. He'd been taken with each image. Some were graceful gowns, some intricate patterns for beadwork. Some were colored as brightly as a children's book and others were shades of gray.

Then he had found one of their wedding day, copied from a photo her mother had taken. Trella's hint of a smile as she gazed up at him held shy awe. He wouldn't call his expression tender, but there was no hiding that he was absorbed by her doe-eyed stare. The captured moment was uncomfortably revealing, yet honest enough he couldn't be ashamed.

"I meant that for Mama, but I think you should hide it in the palace, to be discovered a hundred years from now. Give the art historians something to get excited about." She tore the page from the book and signed it. Her conspiratorial grin as she rolled it had tugged at him to play along.

It had been the first time she'd warmed up to him since their marriage, eyes sparkling with the vivacity that had first ensnared him in Paris.

He'd accepted the drawing with the strangest tingle of pleasure, liking the idea of her being resurrected generations from now, pulled from the footnotes and celebrated.

For a moment, there'd been nothing between them but this frivolous secret they were planning to keep. Then, as their gazes stayed locked, sexual awareness had crept in. The attraction was still there, ignored and subverted, but in those seconds, he felt the lava churning below the surface, swirling and burning, building with pressure against the cracks.

"Surely you can make arrangements with one of her

family members if the round-the-clock care at the hospital isn't sufficient?"

He snapped back to the breakfast room and his grandmother's facetious tone. The heat in him faded.

"I've discussed that with her." He had suspected Trella was homesick after catching her tearily viewing photos of her infant nieces. "Her brother and his wife are tied up with their new twins. Her mother is on hand to help them. Her sister can't leave her new husband." They were trying to get pregnant, if Xavier was reading the subtext correctly. "And something has gone off the rails with the brother who was engaged. She'd rather not speak to him, so…"

"You're being manipulated."

"By whom?" He held her gaze, turning one of her best weapons—barely disguised derision—against her.

"You have obligations," she began in a very quiet voice that held no hint of a tremble. It was the very lack of emotion, the stamp of inarguable logic, that made her words so powerful.

The splinter he had experienced on his wedding day rent deeper, ringing with agony as he felt himself stretched on the rack of conflicting duties. Wife. Crown. Temporary commitment. Eternal service.

A sharp rap on the door had them turning their attention to Mario as he stepped in without waiting for an invitation.

"Apologies, Your Majesty, but the Prince is requested to go the hospital. Immediately."

"They're prepping her for surgery," he was told when he called from the back of his car. He broke into a sweat and urged his driver to hurry.

He was shown to a lower floor when he arrived. She was in pre-op, flat on her back in a hospital gown, hair covered in a blue cap, lips white, tubes taped to her arm.

"You made it." She held out her free hand.

He grasped her fingers, disturbed to find her grip clammy and weak. "What happened?"

"Pain. Tearing. They scanned and said it has to be now." Her mouth trembled.

Thirty-four weeks. So early.

"Shh." He leaned to shelter her, trying to smooth her tense brow with his thumb, but feeling the trembles coursing through her. "Are you having an attack?"

"No," she choked. "This is real fear, Xavier."

"It will be okay," he insisted, undone because she had every right to be scared and there wasn't a damned thing he could do. *He* was scared. "I'll come in with you."

What help do you think you will be?

"You can't. I asked."

How did that reach inside him and squeeze his lungs dry? Her wanting him with her spun and wrapped and pierced his heart like a barbed hook, deeply uncomfortable, but inexorable, tethering them together. "I'll come in anyway."

"You *can't*, but listen. I asked them to wait until you were here so I could ask… I've texted my family. Tell them how it goes as soon as you can. If I don't make it—"

"Of course you'll make it." He closed his ears against any other outcome.

"*Listen*. If I don't, swear to me you'll give the baby fair time with them. They'll need it." Her eyes filled. "Our baby deserves to know what love is."

Her words punched a hole clear through him, leaving an expanse of emptiness that was replaced with agony. The gentle rebuke in her eyes was another blow, searing and brutal, too painful to withstand, too impactful to avoid.

"You're going to come through this," he managed. What if she didn't? He couldn't even.

"Promise me on everything you hold sacred. Your crown. Everything." Her nails dug into the back of his hand.

"If you need to hear it, yes. I'll take the baby to your family myself." He would promise anything to ease that terror in her eyes. To ease his own sense of failure. Of being so lacking she had no faith in him to give their child what it needed. Their baby *did* deserve to know what love was. If she wasn't here to offer it...

"Sir, we have to take her now."

"Kiss me goodbye," Trella whispered.

He swooped without hesitation, felt the tremble in her pouted lips, thought he ought to be gentle, but he took. Ravaged. He invaded her mouth with his tongue and drowned in all she was, trying to slake a hunger he feared would last all of eternity. Her lips opened, surrendering, even as she responded, flavoring the kiss with sweetness amid the shared desperation.

He kissed her as though it was the last one they would ever share. He couldn't bear the thought that it might be.

"Sir—"

He straightened abruptly, feeling the loss like he was torn away by a tornado, hating that he was forever doing what *must* be done.

Trella covered her mouth with her wired hand, eyes blinking above her white fingers. She kept her grip on his fingers until she was forced to let go.

"Sir, there's an observation room for students. Let me show you."

A nurse showed him to a small room with a window. Beyond, he saw Trella nod at the anesthesiologist before her face was covered with a mask. Her doctor motioned gloved hands to the team then everyone moved into place so all he saw were backs clad in scrubs.

"It shouldn't take long," the nurse said. "If you feel lightheaded, there's a chair."

He ignored her, all his attention on the surgery.

"They're waiting for confirmation she's out," the nurse said. "There they go."

They began to move in a controlled, efficient way and the nurse was right. In a very short time, the doctor was handing a tiny, naked infant to the nurse standing by with a towel. The nurse angled the baby to the window, showing him it was a boy.

The anguish in the small face at being separated from his mother pierced Xavier unexpectedly. He felt ridiculously helpless, wishing he could comfort the boy.

"We've been preparing for a premature birth. He's small, but that attempt to cry is a good sign. That's the pediatrician who's taking him. He'll run tests and place the Prince in an incubator then come speak to you. You'll probably be able to hold him. Your son, I mean," she said with a wry attempt at humor. "Not the pediatrician."

Son. Xavier nodded and texted Trella's family, including his grandmother.

A boy.

It seemed such an inadequate few letters for the magnitude of what was happening to him. He had a child. A son.

His phone buzzed with returned texts from Trella's siblings, congratulating him and asking after her.

He glanced up and something had changed. The team around Trella had snapped into frantic action. The anesthesiologist was clearly alarmed and the surgeon's movements became agitated. Through the glass, he heard raised voices issue sharp commands.

"What happened?" Xavier slapped his hand to the window, even as his gaze looked for the door to enter the room.

"Sir, I—" The nurse made as if to close the curtain.

"Find out what's happening."

"Of course." She hurried away.

He pressed his forehead to the cold glass, terror snaking to squeeze his heart. He strangled on the one word he managed to whisper.

"Bella."

CHAPTER EIGHT

TRELLA CAME TO in a blurred awareness of voices and stark white. Even Xavier looked carved from pale marble, his blue eyes translucent as antique glass. Bottle blue, she wanted to call it. She should use that shade in next season's collection.

Why was he leaning over her like that? So close and grim?

"Baby?" She tried to say, but there was no sound. Her voice had evaporated.

"Fine. Really well, considering how small he is." He backed off as a nurse picked up her wrist, but his eyes stayed locked on her.

He. "A boy?" That came out in a raspy whisper.

"Yes."

She blinked heavy eyelids and tried to smile. "Sadiq."

"What?"

"He saved me." She was becoming aware that she was stoned. Recreational drugs weren't her thing, but she'd been prescribed so many pharmaceuticals to quell her panic attacks that she knew what this foggy haze was. She hated it and fought to think through it. "I wouldn't be here without him."

"Dr. Lagundo saved you," he snapped.

"Why are you mad?" She frowned, startled to find the

nurse was still beside her, fussing with her arm. Whatever she did hurt, but distantly. "Can I see him?"

"Soon." The nurse seemed familiar. Her smile was nice, but Trella couldn't recall her name.

She hated drugs. Hated being dopey and disassociated. She ought to be upset as Xavier's remark belatedly penetrated. "I almost died?"

"There were some tense moments," the nurse said. "Your doctor will tell you more. I'll let her know you're awake."

She left and Xavier came back to her side, mouth pinched.

"Are you angry that I pulled through?"

"What? No! Why would you think that?"

She tried to think through a brain made of cotton balls. "You don't like me. You're mad about the baby."

"None of that is true." He loomed over her again, very intimidating. If she wasn't so spaced-out, she would think he sounded tortured. "You scared the hell out of me."

Was he holding her hand? Something cupped her fingers in warmth. It was nice. She liked the gentle stroke across the back of her hand.

"But it would have been easier for you." She was briefly thankful for the drugs because despair didn't overtake her. "I make things harder. I don't mean to. My family forgives me because... I don't know. They love me, I guess. But you don't, so it's okay if you wish I had died."

"Stop saying that. What would Tyrol do without you?"

"Who's Tyrol?"

"Our son."

She frowned. "I expected a girl."

"I texted you the name a couple days ago." He sounded disgruntled. Maybe self-conscious. "You said you liked it."

"When? I hate drugs. They make me so stupid. Is it Tuesday or Wednesday?"

"Wednesday. I texted on Monday and asked what you thought of Tyrol or Trentino." He seemed to be petting her arm, combing his fingers into the gaps between hers. "They're family names. You said you liked Tyrol. We're *not* naming him Sadiq."

"But picture your grandmother's face if we did."

He choked out a laugh, turning his face away, shoulders shaking. "You're funny when you're high, I'll say that much."

"You should laugh more."

He looked back at her with an expression she couldn't decipher. Regret maybe, but something like appreciation?

She closed her eyes against his sorcery.

"Did you know, *bella*? Is that why you said those things before you went in?"

"I don't get into trouble on purpose," she grumbled, ignoring the number of times Ramon had accused her of doing exactly that. "And I don't apologize when I do. It makes people feel good when they help me. My whole medical team is feeling super heroic right now."

He let out another incredulous laugh. "That is some seriously backward logic. Exactly how ripped are you?"

"Admit it. This morning you were ambivalent about having a son. Now you're grateful. You're welcome for the clarity."

Stunned comprehension seemed to blank his face, but she didn't gloat.

"I want to see him." She weakly squeezed the hand that gripped hers. "Is he beautiful? Does he look like you?"

"He looks mad." His voice wasn't quite steady. More emotion shifted across his profile, things she couldn't interpret. Concern? "He wants you."

It's the drugs, she warned herself, even as her heart turned over with sweetness that he might feel something on their son's behalf. *Don't start seeing things that aren't there.*

She didn't doubt he'd been worried on some level when he thought she would *die.* He wasn't a monster, but he had made it abundantly clear that his heart was beyond reach. He was capable of kindness, but that was the limit.

His phone buzzed. "That's your family. I'll let them know you're awake. Smile." He held up his phone to take her photo.

She stuck out her tongue and crossed her eyes. "Tell them we named him Sadiq."

"That's the friend whose wedding you attended earlier this year, isn't it? His wife would object, wouldn't she?" He tapped the screen.

"She would stab me in the eye. That's why it's funny."

"I'll tell them his name is Tyrol." He leaned down to press a kiss between her brows. "I like your eyes the way they are."

"Xavier?" She touched the side of his head, keeping him from straightening. "It's really confusing when you're nice to me."

His thumb traced near the corner of her mouth. "I never said I didn't like you, *bella.* You do make things hard. All of this is hard. But I am grateful for our son."

And me?

His eyes were an endless blue that only grew more intense the further she fell into them, but even in her muddy-minded state, she knew better than to ask.

And he didn't say.

CHAPTER NINE

XAVIER LEFT FOR Australia ten days later.

Trella and Tyrol were released from the hospital and went directly to her family's compound in southern Spain. Her brother was in residence with his four-month-old twin girls. Her mother was there, along with a team of nannies and servants and guards. Xavier could not have arranged better, safer care for either of them.

Trella had bounced back from near-death with startling cheer, pouring such tenderness and joy over their son Xavier almost thought it was fake; it was so far removed from anything he had ever experienced himself. Her words from pre-op kept echoing in his head. *Our child needs to know what love is.*

Did he? Because the limited feelings Xavier had allowed himself to feel toward her had amplified his fear when her surgery had gone sideways. This level of concern for someone wasn't comfortable. Was he a bad parent for setting up his son to love and possibly to lose?

He needed distance as a buffer against becoming more deeply invested in both of them so he went to Australia as scheduled. He hated every single one of the thirty days he was gone, which only underscored why the separation was necessary, he supposed.

It didn't help that things went exactly as he had warned

his grandmother they would. He answered the same question so many times he muddled his lines at one point.

"The plan was tripped last year."

The blond newscaster tittered.

"The trip was planned," he corrected, yanking his mind back from Spain to Adelaide and the trade talks he'd been in. "The early birth made it possible for me to travel as scheduled. I was on the brink of canceling, which would have been a shame."

Several handshake deals were already moving toward more formal agreements. His adherence to duty was producing much-needed results.

"But you must miss him!"

"Technology is a wonderful thing. We check in often. He's thriving and Trella is recovering. That's the most important thing." He flicked a glance at one of his handlers, silently conveying that if they didn't swerve back to topic, this interview was over.

The newscaster took the hint. "We wish them well. About your meeting with the state representative today..."

Did he miss his son, Xavier wondered later? If such an emotion had never been acknowledged, internally or externally, did it register with anyone if it somehow manifested today?

How *could* he miss the boy? Tyrol was an infant who wanted to suckle and sleep. Trella was adept at keeping Xavier apprised of their son's progress, such as it was. She texted often, telling him about a gain of an ounce or other small milestones. She sent him photos—probably half a dozen a day. A more pragmatic man would say one was plenty, but Xavier found himself studying each one, fascinated by tiny eyelashes and miniature fingernails. The boy's eyes looked like his own, but his mouth was definitely Trella's.

One grim night, Xavier let himself recall that for a few moments, this boy's resemblance to his mother had been all that might have been left of her. The despondency that had engulfed him at the thought had had him placing a video call to her.

She had been surprised since she usually initiated the calls if she happened to be nursing and the time was right on his end. She had asked him about his day, which he didn't care to talk about, and he had listened to whatever she volunteered, silently mocking himself for being riveted by small talk about her family and a few shower gifts.

There shouldn't have been any holes of curiosity or unmet sense of obligation within him. His wife and child were well. He was getting on with his life exactly as he should.

So why did he nearly go through the roof when he woke to a fresh message from her?

Ramon and Izzy are getting married! The wedding is at the end of the month, in Madrid. We decamp to the family mansion the day before I'm due to return to Elazar. I'll extend our stay until after the ceremony since it's only an extra weekend.

On the surface, it was a perfectly reasonable assumption. Moving her and Tyrol with the rest of the staff to Elazar for a few days so she could turn around and go back was a needless expense. Royal detractors would have a field day. She was nursing, so she couldn't leave Tyrol in Elazar while she attended the wedding. Xavier had no reasonable basis to refuse her request.

Nevertheless, the only word that came to mind was, *No*. He didn't analyze it, he only knew he would not go back to the palace and wait for her.

* * *

As the youngest, Trella sometimes thought she had received all the leftover DNA after her siblings had taken the best of it. Henri had their father's sense and logic. He was stubborn, yes, but *she* was outright obstinate. Ramon had their mother's passion and determination, but Trella was an opinionated hothead. Gili scooped up all the sensitivity and generosity while Trella selfishly stole all the attention with her nervous breakdowns.

None of them were small-minded or jealous, but Trella—the baby who was spoiled and deferred to all the time—was drowning in envy of all of them.

Why couldn't she have a partner in parenting like Henri had with Cinnia? Why couldn't she have a big wedding that had everyone buzzing with excitement, like Ramon was planning with Isidora? Why couldn't she have a husband who not only couldn't keep his hands off her, like Kasim with Gili, but refused to have any other woman by his side as he took the throne of his country?

Why did she have so much negative self-talk eating away at her self-esteem? *They* didn't. They were all better and smarter than that.

She was the broken one.

With her arms braced on the side of the pool, she gave desultory kicks behind her while watching Cinnia hand off a freshly fed Rosalina to Henri.

"I'll put her down and work through siesta. You'll finish your lunch then rest before we travel?"

"I will," Cinnia promised, smirking at Henri's overprotectiveness before he erased it with a tender kiss. "Thank you, darling." She gave her wrap dress a final straighten and turned back to the salad she'd been picking at while nursing.

Henri glanced at Tyrol, asleep in the cot in the shade.

"Do you want me to take him up? You should sleep before we leave, too."

The flight was an hour and Trella was five weeks postpartum, but her scare during delivery had set them all back to watching her like she was made of spun glass.

"I'll take him when Cinnia goes up. The weather won't be as warm in Elazar. I want to enjoy the pool while I can."

"I'm going to miss you when you go back to Elazar," Cinnia said as Henri left.

"I know. This has been really nice."

Quite by accident, Cinnia had been the first to know Trella was pregnant, when she had been hiding her own pregnancy from Henri. They had become very close in those early months and sharing these weeks of new motherhood had deepened their sister-like bond.

"Is it going to be okay living there, do you think?" The simple question was the reason Trella loved Cinnia. Her sister-in-law invited confidence but didn't intrude.

Trella sighed, daunted enough by the future to admit, "I have no idea. I feel good. Physically, I mean. And stable, mentally. But I'm *here*. That always helps."

"At least I knew Henri when I was in your shoes." Cinnia had been Henri's mistress for years before her pregnancy tore them apart and drew them back together. "It must be hard, having a baby and still being at the getting-to-know-you stage. You two haven't had a proper chance, have you?"

"No." Two nights and daily hospital visits that she'd said she didn't need.

She had, though. She'd soaked up his duty visits like sunshine, trying not to read into the kiss they'd shared when they wed. He'd seemed to be pretending it hadn't happened, sticking to chatting very generally about whatever meeting he'd been in or whatever political scandal was trending.

When he'd gone through her sketchbook, she'd felt very vulnerable, especially when he found the one she'd done of them. Why had she thought it was a good idea to give it to him? He'd probably thrown it out, but she had longed so badly for him to feel *something* about their wedding day.

He'd looked...touched? Whatever the softening in his face had been, it had caused her to moon so obviously, he'd flinched and looked away.

She was such an idiot. He was probably feeling put-upon. When they did connect over the tablet, he had seemed remote. He wasn't impatient, but she had the sense his prevailing mood was resignation.

She was trying to resign herself as well. Years of therapy had taught her to focus on one small piece of the future at a time. When he had crushed her soul with his news that their marriage would be temporary, she hadn't tried to imagine what her life would look like after their divorce. She had focused on making it to term with her pregnancy.

Once Tyrol had arrived, she'd come here, where she'd been able to focus on Tyrol and her recovery. Returning to Elazar and her looming divorce wasn't something she was ready to contemplate. She didn't even know how to handle the two and a half months left in their brief marriage!

Making a concerted effort to include Xavier in Tyrol's progress had seemed like the right thing to do. She told herself it was her way of encouraging a bond between father and son, but she knew there was a part of her that liked having an excuse to reach out to him. She was still trying to push for something that was futile.

But just when his reticence had her convinced he felt nothing, he would surprise her by phoning to ask how things were going. He would linger on a video call after she'd run out of things to say, seeming content to stare at a sleeping baby over a screen.

Such a confounding man.

She glanced to where Tyrol slept; the one thing in all of this that made her unspeakably proud. If everything she'd been through in her life, all the pain and traumas and anguish had had to happen in order to bring her son into this world, so be it. She accepted all of it.

"Has your doctor really forbidden you to have another?"

"We talked it over several times through the pregnancy. It was my idea that she would tie my tubes during delivery, so I wouldn't need another surgery in the future. She did. I'm not sorry, or even very sad. I resigned myself a long time ago to not being able to get pregnant. He's truly a miracle. The delivery was such a near miss, though. I wouldn't want to push my luck, especially now he's here and needs me."

Cinnia nodded. "What about a surrogate? I'm sorry. Maybe that's not something you'd consider?"

"Gili told me years ago she would be my surrogate, but that was before Kasim." She tucked her chin. "Can you imagine his reaction?"

"He gives her anything she asks for." Cinnia closed her grin on her fork. "His head would literally explode trying to decide whether to be possessive or indulgent."

"Right?" They both chuckled, then Trella sobered. "They would want to secure his heirs before even thinking of it, anyway. I don't see Xavier wanting to wait." *There is a reason for a spare.* "Maybe I'll find a surrogate someday, but I don't think that would change Xavier's mind about us. It's not just about another baby. We're not you and Henri." Or Gili and Kasim. Or Ramon and Isidora. "He has other considerations."

He doesn't want me.

She *had* to accept that.

It made her chest grow tight, though. Her throat ached.

She ducked under the water to hide how she was tearing up. She stayed there, diving deep and crawling along the bottom until her lungs were about to burst, only coming to the surface when she reached the stairs.

"Pah!" She stood and wiped the water from her eyes.

Cinnia had come to her feet and was saying hello to someone.

Henri had returned with a striking blond man in tailored dark gray pants and a collared T-shirt that hugged the fit muscles of his shoulders and revealed his tanned gorgeous biceps.

The newcomer glared at her from his familiar, laser blue eyes. "Should you be *swimming*?"

Suddenly dizzy, Trella panted, "*Hola, cariño.* I missed you, too."

Xavier was distantly aware of Henri retreating with his wife, but if the woman had a name, he had already forgotten it. His entire focus was eaten up by the way Trella rose from the water like Venus herself.

Water sluiced down her body, washing away the grinding aggravation that had propelled him here. He had needed to see her without understanding why. He might have labeled it homesickness if that wasn't such a juvenile emotion and he was in Elazar, not a part of Spain he'd never seen before.

But he'd come here with single-minded determination and when he'd finally clapped eyes on her, she'd been on the *bottom of the pool*, trying to give him a heart attack all over again.

All his concern, pining and every other thought in his head drained away, however, as she walked toward him.

Coming here was a mistake. He saw that as clearly as he saw she wore a red bikini, the triangles of fabric tied off at her hips and between her breasts. She had been quite comely with the weight of a baby distending her middle, always turning herself out stylishly, even when she'd been in the hospital.

Keeping his mind off sex while she'd been in a delicate condition had been, if not easy, at least quickly forestalled by worst-case scenarios. He had told himself any attraction he still felt was a byproduct of his not having had sex since they'd made the baby sleeping in the cot to his left. Maybe the two kisses they'd shared had ambushed his memory when it was least convenient. Definitely, he relived their night in Paris far too often.

It all added up to an obsession he should have put behind him by now.

He hadn't.

Her approach coiled him tight. He hadn't seen her naked since Paris and her hourglass figure was as spectacular as his libido recalled. Better. Glittering droplets sparkled on her golden skin and her breasts were positively voluptuous, swaying as she padded toward him, bare feet slapping the tile.

His mouth watered. A distinctly male pulse tugged behind the fly of his pants. He had to resist a telltale swallow and consciously regulated his breathing. The animal, that restless beast that had been scratching and digging inside him, howled as she drew near, wanting to leap on her. Reunite.

"What are you—?" She was squeezing water from her hair, but as she met his gaze, her eyes widened in reaction, pupils exploding like fireworks. Her breath caught, expanding her chest and drawing his attention to her nipples, already sharp from the chill, but poking even harder under his gaze.

"Wh-what are you doing here?" Her hand went to a nearby chair back as if she needed to steady herself.

He was acting directly against his responsibilities, despite the rationalizations he'd concocted. Angry with himself for the hunger clawing through him, he searched his brain for the reasons that underpinned his arrival.

"I'm taking you to Madrid. You'll stay with me there."

Her shoulders fell. "You don't trust me?"

That wasn't it, but he didn't want to admit—even to himself—that he hadn't been able to wait three more nights to see them. Not just his son. Her.

He found his gaze straying to the curve of her hips and the dip of her navel and forced his attention to drag across to the infant in a pale green onesie. The strangest yank in his chest had him stooping to pick up the boy.

The sleeping baby gave a small start of surprise, fingers splaying, then relaxed into a warm ball against the hollow of Xavier's shoulder. He felt heavier. Sturdier.

"He's growing."

"He is." She wrapped a towel around her middle, hands shaking. "Xavier, I swear I wasn't trying to avoid coming back. The wedding is a rushed thing. Izzy's father has been ill. It's a big deal for him to be able to walk her down the aisle so they're indulging him. It's also the only chance for the bunch of us to be together for the foreseeable future. That's why I need to be there."

"I'm not saying you shouldn't go. But it's your first public appearance since we married. We should be seen together."

"Well, of course you were invited. I just didn't think…" She was taken aback, which was justified, he supposed. "Doesn't it send the wrong message?"

Because of the way their press release had been worded.

*Given Ms Sauveterre's preference for avoiding the
spotlight, the marriage is a formality to ensure the
legitimacy of Prince Xavier's heir and won't be continued in the new year.*

"I've spent a month having my devotion to my family
questioned. I'd like to change the optics." There. That was
the excuse he had given his grandmother and he stood by
it. Their countrymen were going mad over the three photos
he'd released of the young prince, but they were questioning why he wasn't spending more time with him.

Trella understood how the PR game was played. She
wouldn't fault this move.

The warmth that had pinkened her cheeks drained away,
though. Her expression stiffened. "Of course. And we both
know how unimpeachable your sense of obligation is. Most
of my packing is done. I only have to shower and change.
Shall I send a nanny to take him? After you've had time
to post some selfies, of course."

He had set himself up for that, but it still landed on tar-
get. "I'll keep him," he said in a tone that let her know she
was walking a fine line.

She flipped her wet hair and walked away.

Trella fell asleep on the flight so they were in Madrid before she was alone with Xavier again. Physically she was
recovered, but Tyrol was so little he needed to feed often,
even if that meant waking him. She was up several times
a night so tended to nod off midday. But rather than dozing, she would have preferred to spend the time working
through Xavier's surprise appearance.

Optics? Really? It was incredibly insulting. Her entire
family had been used a million times over to sell magazines and promote products, all without their consent. She

was tempted to tell him what she thought of him, but part of her disbelieved him.

For a minute, as they'd stood by the pool, she'd thought—But, no. His carnal look had been gone once he'd picked up Tyrol. She had imagined it. What kind of wanton did it make her that she had responded to blatant lust, anyway?

She *had* responded, though. She had run to the shower to cool off, slowing the race of her pulse and willing away the thrumming awareness in her loins.

Fat lot of good it did. Flutters of intrigue were still playing like butterflies in her middle, gaze straying to the cut of his pants over his butt and the sculpted muscles beneath his shirt as he paced in front of her. She had missed him!

Tyrol finished nursing and was fast asleep so she unlatched him and handed him off to a nanny, then she struggled to put herself together behind the screen of a receiving blanket that didn't want to stay in place.

Yes, I'm half-naked under here. *Stop staring.*

A flush of heat went through her. It was a lusty reaction that had simmered at merely sensual while she'd been feeling squat, scared and vulnerable in a hospital. Or when he'd been on the other side of the planet.

Now she was more confident on so many levels, but still unsure of herself with her husband. This was as bad as his ambush in Innsbruck when he'd left her with nowhere to hide.

"Ready?" he said, tucking away the phone he'd been tapping while she'd nursed.

"For?"

"I've been waiting to look around. I haven't seen the house, either."

"Oh. Um, sure." The mansion was on a small estate in La Moraleja, farther out of the city from the historical home in the Salamanca neighborhood that had been in her mother's family for generations. This house was built with old-world touches like columns and wrought iron rails, but it was very modern, perhaps only a few years old.

"Did you lease it? Or...?" Surely he hadn't purchased something for a long weekend?

"It belongs to a friend. We studied architecture together. He showed me the plans a few years ago. I'm interested to see how it all came together."

He waved for her to lead him from the lounge to a small dining area that was likely used for intimate lunches. The gallery that overlooked the main door was above them. A row of tall windows afforded a view of the landscaped grounds.

"I didn't know you were interested in architecture." She watched him take in the elevator, set in a convenient location, but made unobtrusive by disguising it with the rise of the stairs. Why did a bit of small talk make her so nervous?

"I'm an architect."

"Really! What have you designed?"

"My chalet." He bypassed the entrance to the kitchen and opened a door to the patio, inviting her to exit ahead of him.

"You did well. I liked it." A wind had come up beneath the overcast skies, making her hug her arms and try to tuck her wayward hair behind her ears as they walked past flower pots that lined the covered pool.

He was looking sideways at her.

"I wasn't trying to escape because I didn't like the floor plan."

He rolled his eyes, which made her smile, but self-consciousness stuck like a burr, prickly and sharp. It was strange to be with him again, in person, alone, without nurses or valets hovering. With sexual awareness sizzling within her.

"I'm serious," she said, trying to hide her nervousness. "I know you don't need my approval, but I thought it felt cozy despite the open plan. You obviously placed the windows very carefully. Each view was a well-framed photograph of the natural world—what?" she demanded as his look grew penetrating. "I'm an artist. I notice when care has been taken for a particular effect. Don't you? Look at these stairs."

She waved at the way they curved down from the upper terrace.

"Most people see convenience, but the placement balances the turret on the other side, which is probably the master bedroom, situated to overlook—" She turned to look across the expanse of grounds, charmed as she noticed the brook and the wooden bridge. "Oh, that's lovely, isn't it?"

"He wanted to put the master bedroom on this end," Xavier said. "At the top of the stairs, closer to the pool. I suggested the turret and told him to curve the stairs."

She pivoted to face him, watching his gaze track the upper terrace, profile dark with critique, but also…envy?

"What else have you designed?"

"Nothing. My attention is needed elsewhere." He said it without emotion, but she felt the pang that he refused to betray.

"You're frustrated."

His lids came down so the heat of his gaze glowed fiercely behind the veil of his spiky lashes. "We're talking about that, are we?" His attention dropped to her mouth.

Suddenly they were poolside again. Such a hard streak of sexual heat shot through her, it physically stung from the base of her throat, behind her breastbone, sank like a hot coal in the pit of her belly and radiated warmth into the juncture of her thighs. Her heart took off at a gallop while birds took flight in her midsection.

"I meant as an artist!" She blushed, embarrassed at how quickly and blatantly she reacted to a simple look.

His mouth deepened at the corners. He pushed his hands into his pockets. "There are many ways to apply form and function to the role I occupy. I don't have to design something."

"It's not the same." She was still flustered, stewing in heat and being confused by it. "I told you about the time I was depressed? It was because the medication made it impossible for me to create. The need was there, but when I sat down to draw or sew, it was like sending a bucket into an empty well. I wasn't having panic attacks, but I didn't see any point in being alive if I couldn't…" She held up her hands.

"I'm not depressed."

"But you're denied."

"So what?"

"It's something you need."

"It's something I *want*. Desire can be ignored in favor of more important things."

"We're not talking about architecture, are we?" She let her hands fall and blinked, eyes watery from the wind. Or so she hoped he believed.

A long silence followed where only a distant wind chime rang.

"Are you really here because of optics?" It made her lungs feel heavy and raw.

He hissed out a long breath. "I came because I wanted to." He set his teeth after he said it, as though absorbing some inner thought that displeased him, then said in a voice rife with subdued turmoil, "But we don't get everything we want, *bella*. You know that as well as I do."

He wasn't mocking her. He was saying it with deep understanding of the things she would never have—a carefree childhood, another pregnancy. She choked up, wanting to ask if he had come because he'd wanted to be with her, but she was too scared of the answer.

So she only said, "Have you forgotten my name? You're calling me *bella*."

"It's not an endearment. It's who you are. It's what you are." The last bit sounded as though it came out against his will.

She wanted to believe him, but her misshapen heart was so very conscious of her flaws. Of the fact he had rebuffed her.

"I've never felt beautiful." She toed a pebble. "I was the messy one, always grass-stained and needing my hair combed. After my kidnapping, the press called me 'the fat one,' because I comfort-ate. I starved myself in retaliation and cut my own hair and looked like a Goth for years, dark circles under my eyes, makeup smudged and face pale from not sleeping properly. It took ages after I got my panic attacks under control to look as healthy and happy as my sister."

She squinted as she looked up, startled to find she had his full attention. That wasn't pity in his expression, though. He was engrossed, which made a squiggling sensation tremble in the pit of her stomach.

"You asked me that night in Paris, remember? You asked if I was as beautiful as my sister. I thought it was funny to say yes because I was impersonating her. The only time I feel beautiful is when I look like her." She knew better intellectually, but deep down, she still had a lot of demons.

"You were stunning when you were pregnant. You're beautiful now. When I saw your sister in Berlin, I thought she was beautiful because she looked like you."

She shook her head. "You didn't even know—"

"I *knew*. I could tell the second I saw her. I just didn't believe it. I thought—"

"What?" She held her breath, brimming with dread and hope, not sure what she wanted to hear.

He grimaced. "I thought I'd been a fool. That the way we'd reacted to each other had been a one-off thing."

She swallowed. "It wasn't?"

His gaze slammed into hers, pupils expanding the way a cat's dilated before it pounced. Lines of tension pulled the rest of his face into the harsh countenance of a barely restrained barbarian. "Clearly."

She stood on a tipping point, vibrating under the strain, drawn, drawn, drawn. The pull in her chest was nearly irresistible. A prickling wash of sensations made her hyper aware of everything around her, the pale heat of the sun, the scent of the grass, the dampness in the air and, most especially, the way he was looking at her mouth. At the way such a tiny expression of interest from this man could send wildfire through her whole body.

She tore her gaze from his, seeing only a blur of green and blue.

"Please be careful, Xavier." She scraped at the hair tickling her cheek, shaken. "My self-esteem is full of holes. Don't give me hope if there is none."

"For what? You don't want to be married to me. You said so."

"I don't want to be married to a man who doesn't want me." She had to press her lips tight so they wouldn't tremble. Meeting his gaze was hard. She couldn't hide the struggle, the longing, that was eating her up. "If you do…"

"I don't *want* to want you," he ground out.

She jerked back as though he'd struck her. He winced. "I mean I can't *afford* to want you. My father followed where sexual interest led. It was a disaster. I didn't expect this," he grated. "I wouldn't have come."

She breathed through each of the blows, eventually able to ask, "That's all you feel?" The question was too revealing. She regretted it, even before he answered.

He took a long time, then, "Don't hope, *bella*. You know my views on love."

His gentle reply broke her chest open, leaving her heart pulsing like an open wound. *This* was what she had been avoiding accepting. This was why she couldn't bear to look into her future. He was never going to love her.

Engulfed in agony right to the backs of her teeth, she nodded dumbly. "Will you listen for Tyrol when you go in? I want to see the bridge."

She didn't notice the hand he reached out as she walked away.

CHAPTER TEN

HE HAD HURT HER. He hadn't wanted to. Cruel to be kind, he had thought, and he had regretted it immediately. What could he do, though? Admit that what he felt was not purely sexual. Even if he was capable of love, which he wasn't, they had no future. He couldn't lead her on.

He hated that he'd returned her to that stiff wariness, though. The woman who had texted without hesitation for the weeks they'd been apart suddenly had a full schedule and little to say. By the time they were at a dinner hosted by the bride's parents the next evening, the tension between them was palpable. Her family smiled around it.

Angelique hadn't arrived yet, Henri was there with his wife and twins along with her mother, and Trella spent most of the evening needling Ramon.

Xavier tried to intervene at one point. Ramon wasn't above getting personal in retaliation and neither was Trella. It was escalating, but the bride, Isidora, tugged him aside. She was a stunning woman with auburn hair and a smile that put anyone at ease.

"It's a rookie move to get involved. Better to ignore them. Trust me."

He waited until they had left to ask Trella, "Why were you being so contentious with Ramon?"

"I wasn't. That's how we communicate." The passing streetlights flicked over her stoic expression.

"I thought you might bring on an attack."

"No." She sounded petulant. "We fight like that all the time. It's fine."

"It wasn't because you're angry with me?"

Silence, then, "I'm not angry. I'm hurt."

He should have left it there, but said, "Either way, you should take it out on me, not him." *Punish me.* He couldn't stand the guilt he was carrying.

"I'd rather fight with Ramon." Her hands twisted in her lap. "I know he won't let me win. Any points I score, I've earned. It builds my confidence. And no matter what I say, he'll still love me. I don't have that kind of trust with you."

Be careful what you wish for, Xavier thought, flayed to the bone. He didn't speak of it again.

Trella was a dam filled to the brim, gates stuck. When Xavier bowed out of joining Ramon and his racing friends at a sports bar the next evening, the pressure inside her climbed a notch higher.

"The bar isn't Kasim's thing, either. I invited him to come over with Gili for the evening after they see Mama. Cinnia wants to give the girls a quiet night so she's staying in." Trella desperately needed time with her sister. "Do you mind?"

"You're not going clubbing with the bridal party? I'll stay with Tyrol."

"Isidora will have enough paparazzi as it is. If Gili and I went? We're doing her a favor staying away."

"I see. Of course. Invite them. That's fine." They were being exceedingly agreeable and polite since she'd admitted to her hurt feelings last night. It was horrible. She kept wondering how she would endure two more months of this. A lifetime, really. Would it be worse or better when they divorced and lived apart?

She was so caught up in her own turmoil, she completely forgot that Xavier had met Gili before. *Gili* hadn't, the darling. She rushed him when she arrived, taking both his hands to say beseechingly, "I'm so glad we have this chance to clear the air. I can't imagine what you thought of me in Berlin. You must have been so shocked. But I hope we can be friends because I already adore your son."

Her sister's warmth could melt glaciers and Xavier's expression eased in a blink. "It's already forgotten," he assured with his patented charm.

Trella felt a stab of jealousy. Why couldn't she win him over as easily?

Gili turned to her then, concern in her eyes, because of course she had picked up on Trella's distress. At the same time, something glowed from her like a beacon, a happiness so bright, it blinded.

Oh, Gili. Anytime Trella thought she couldn't survive whatever anguish was gripping her, her twin found a way to lift her out of it. Smiling tearily, she hugged her pregnant sister tight.

Xavier was glad to have an evening with the King of Zhamair. Asking Kasim about a complex situation in one of his neighboring countries was a welcome distraction from his struggle between duty and desire. Between wanting to mend fences with Trella and letting her bruised feelings keep her at a distance.

Thirty minutes in, he realized the women hadn't come back from fetching Tyrol. "Did we bore them? I'll find—"

"Please let them be," Kasim said. "She needs time with her sister."

"Which one?" Xavier asked dryly, hoping Trella wasn't shedding tears over him.

"A fair question." Kasim took up his drink. "Their interdependence takes getting used to, doesn't it? But this…" He chucked his chin toward the ceiling, where the women were likely in Trella's room. "She was bursting at the seams."

"Pregnant?" A surprise rush went through Xavier. He was astonished to realize he was pleased for the couple. Why? It had nothing to do with him.

Except that he knew how good it felt to have a child. It struck him then how important Tyrol had become to him. Not because he secured Elazar's future, but because Tyrol was... Tyrol. Not an insurance policy for the future, a relation.

Disconcerted, he had to clear sudden emotion from his throat as he rose to shake Kasim's hand. "Congratulations."

"Thank you." Kasim darkened with a flush of pride and hitched his pants to sit again. "It's very early days, only confirmed the day before we left Zhamair. Not something we're making public."

Xavier fetched his own drink and offered to tap glasses, experiencing envy as he thought of Kasim sharing the moment of discovery and every single day of the pregnancy, along with the birth. Feeling robbed was not a new sensation for him. He got over it quickly, but he wondered if Kasim realized how lucky he was, able to go through this process as many times as his wife was up for.

He could, too, he supposed, with Patrizia.

His brandy tasted like snake venom. He abandoned it.

"I'd like you to consider something," Kasim said, sounding like someone unused to requesting favors. "Closer to the birth, I'd like Trella to come to Zhamair."

A strange void opened in Xavier. "We won't be married any longer." It took enormous effort to state that with equanimity. "Trella may go where she pleases." The knowledge knotted his gut.

Kasim's smile tightened. "I expect she'll want to bring Tyrol. I know Angelique will want to see him by then."

Which would require Xavier's permission. He instantly rejected the idea. He had sent Trella to Spain while he'd traveled Australia before he'd realized how unbearable it would be. The King of Zhamair was not plotting to steal his son, he was sure, but at least if Tyrol stayed in Elazar, he knew Trella would come back.

He looked away, disturbed by the dependence that train of thought suggested.

"It was very hard on Angelique to be apart from Trella when Tyrol was born." Kasim took a healthy sip of brandy, like he needed it, and hissed out his breath. "She fainted when Trella flatlined. Then your text came through and I realized why. She was hysterical until Trella was revived."

So was I, Xavier could have said, but they were already sharing far past his usual level. He loathed thinking about those long terrifying minutes. It put him in a cold sweat.

"I'll see what I can do," he said woodenly, mostly to end the discussion. Doing a favor for one of the most powerful men in the Middle East was a smart move, he reasoned, but was repelled by the idea of using his son for political gain.

Duty. It wasn't a double-edged sword. It was two branding irons pressing him front and back, pinning him in place, allowing no escape and only sinking deeper into his flesh when he tried.

Much later, when the couple had left, he was still thinking about where the line was drawn. Would his grandmother say Tyrol was doing *his* duty by going to Zhamair, cultivating warm relations with a foreign entity?

The poor boy didn't even know what he was in for. He lay unswaddled in Trella's lap, gaze wandering the ceiling, arms flailing and fingers catching in the curtains of her loose hair as she looked over him.

"Who gets another cousin?" she asked the boy with soft excitement.

Xavier sat with his feet propped on the ottoman. Her top afforded him a lovely view down her cleavage and her gentle laughter was as erotic as her tickling hair might feel, sweeping across his skin. It was sheer torture to sit here, wanting without having, but far too soon he wouldn't even have this much so he savored the pain.

"Did you know she was pregnant? Before she told you? Kasim made it sound like you have a supernatural link." He was skeptical, but Angelique had called her that time in the car, seeming to know Trella's panic attack was upon her.

"Was he worried I spied on them while they were making that baby?" She lifted her head, so stunning, with amusement curving her lips, that his heart lurched. "No, it's nothing like that. More an emotional thing." Her smile faded. "I should have realized how happy she was, but I've been distracted."

Pensive because of him. Upset. At least she was talking to him again.

"Do you feel it with your brothers?"

"They're too pigheaded, especially Ramon. Isn't he?" she said to Tyrol. "*Tío* Ramon is a *toro*." A bull.

"But you still love them." Xavier was beginning to see how love wasn't just a romantic notion, or even a desire, for her. It was as vital to her as oxygen. It drove the very blood in her veins.

"I love them very much," she agreed, sober and ultra-gentle as she kissed Tyrol's bare feet. "They got me through my darkest times. I hung on because of them. Pushed through *for* them. Now I have Tyrol." She dipped to nuzzle his tummy, making his little arms jerk.

You have me, Xavier thought, but thorns had invaded his windpipe. He was starkly aware he couldn't pledge anything more than the pittance he'd already offered.

"You never wished for brothers or sisters?" Her head came up. "Your mother didn't have more children?"

"My father has a daughter. Maybe three or four years old by now? My mother has two boys. Teenagers, I think."

"You've never met them?"

"There's no place for them in my life." That's what he'd always thought, but he heard how cold it sounded, especially as she looked so askance.

"You could have made one."

"What would I have in common with them?"

"*Parents*?"

"They didn't act like parents." He shook the cubes of ice in his glass, wondering if he could judge when he'd barely grasped the ropes himself. "Neither were a great example of the importance of sibling relationships, either. I was young, but I picked up on jealousy and resentment between my mother and her sister. Because of her marriage into royalty, I suppose. And my father lost his brother."

"It wasn't his fault, was it?" She gathered Tyrol to her shoulder, tucking his blanket around him. "How old was he?"

"He was sixteen, his brother was eighteen. It was just a bad wind that came up while he was sailing. My father didn't talk about him often, but when he did…" Xavier swallowed, still affected by the memory of his father growing teary. "He missed him. Made me think I was better off without that kind of risk."

"But you'll give Tyrol a sibling."

"I have to." It was the stark truth, but again he heard how indifferent it made him sound when really his emotions on the matter were so tangled he couldn't even begin to name them.

Her brows pulled together and her mouth pouted. "I'll do it because I *want* to."

Without his need for biological children, many options were open to her, adoption among them. He suppressed a flinch, surprised how much it hurt to think of her starting a family with another man.

"You should," he made himself say. "You're a natural at motherhood. Family is clearly your source of strength."

She stared at him like he was a dog that had been hit on the highway.

"Are you going up?" he asked, trying to change the subject. "Leave him with me. I'll put him down when he falls asleep."

Her mouth twitched, but if she was surprised at his desire to hold his son, it was quickly blinked away. He let out a breath as she placed the boy's warm weight in his hands, relaxing as he embraced one of the few responsibilities he was pleased to have.

Trella hovered, watching Tyrol rub his fist against his cheek, chasing it with his mouth. They shared a chuckle at his efforts, but Xavier's was bittersweet.

"My family was not yours, *bella*. The way you are with them is a foreign culture to me. I can't emulate something I never had. But I do want Tyrol to be happy. Happier than I was."

Her hand settled on his shoulder. It was unnerving not only because they hadn't touched since she'd been in the hospital, but because she gathered the torment rippling through him into a hot ball in the corner of his chest, so it pulsed under the feathery weight of her fingers. He held very still, as if her hand was a shy bird and he didn't want to startle her into flitting away.

"I know." Her thumb moved in a brief caress. "And I know you're starting to love him. I'm glad."

His heart swerved as her hand lifted and he watched her retreat.

* * *

Trella was trying hard to resign herself to Xavier's limitations. Gili had hugged her and wiped her tears and said, "Give it time." Things had been rough between her and Kasim before they'd married. *She* wasn't ready to give up on Trella finding happiness with Xavier, but that was Gili. She wanted to believe the best of everyone and everything.

Trella wasn't so sure, but she took heart from the way Tyrol had begun prying himself through Xavier's defenses. Xavier took every opportunity to hold his son. Not for optics. No one was seeing him walk down the hall in the middle of the night. He *wanted* to hold him. He expressed concern about a little spit-up, then worried the damp patch would make Tyrol uncomfortable and changed him. He talked to his son about architecture, for heaven's sake, then broke off when he realized Trella was listening.

Still, when she had accused him of starting to love his son, she suspected he had been more surprised by his capacity to do so than she was.

And therein lay the problem. She had told him she didn't want to be married to a man who didn't want her. She had meant a man who didn't *love* her. If there was a chance he might develop feelings for her, surely she owed it to Tyrol to give their marriage a chance?

Or was that a foolish rationalization because she was smitten?

Either way, she had to keep the struggle off her face and smile for the wedding photos. Ramon and Isidora's marriage should be perfect, even if hers wasn't.

The ceremony was held in a five-hundred-year-old cathedral, conducted by an archbishop, witnessed by royalty, aristocrats, heads of state and celebrities from film, stage and the athletic arena. The route to the hotel, where the reception was held, had been blocked off and was lined ten-people deep with bystanders, photographers and even television cameras. Drones buzzed between the cars and a helicopter pattered overhead.

They hurried from the cavalcade up the red carpet, past the deafening cheer of the throng behind the velvet ropes, through the security checkpoint and into the relative peace of the ballroom where they finally caught their breath.

Mirrored tabletops reflected the lush floral arrangements of orchids and roses. Wisteria dripped from the ceiling along with crystals that glinted like snowflakes. A harpist's delicate notes welcomed them along with uniformed staff carrying trays of gold-rimmed glasses of champagne.

"That was insane," Xavier said, not dropping his protective hold across her back.

"Small wonder I've never been on a date before, isn't it? We're a nightmare to take anywhere."

Surprise loosened his clean-shaven jaw. "You never dated? *At all*?"

"Well, there was this one stranger I met in Paris." She gave him a cheeky wink and made a tiny adjustment to his boutonniere. It was a delicate creation of spotted feather and red-throated orchid with a lacy fern frond behind it. She deliberately avoided looking at the red sash that scored his chest, announcing his station—the role that was more important than she could ever hope to be.

"Seriously? I'm the only one?"

She shrugged. "One of Ramon's friends recovered from a crash at Sus Brazos two years ago. I ate dinner with him by the pool a few times. We kissed once, but it was…"

"What?" His fingers dug into her hip, something flashing in his eyes as his expression grew unreadable. She wouldn't let herself believe it was possessiveness.

"Nothing. Over before it started. Like you and me." Affair, pregnancy, marriage. They were all slipping like sand through her fingers, refusing to be slowed. "But thank you for coming with me tonight. I should have said that before. I was dreading coming alone and having to dodge awkward questions about our marriage."

She made herself smile and meet his eyes as she started to step out of his embrace. His arm hardened.

"The things I'm still learning about you," he muttered. The fingers of his free hand looped around her wrist. He looked across the room, expression tight then came back, fierce and hot. "I hate this, *bella*. We had one damned night that was perfect. The only regret I had was that I didn't have more time to get to know you better and now we have time and we're wasting it."

Edginess came off him in waves, rattling whatever defenses she still managed to hold up against him. Her bottom lip grew wobbly and she had to tuck it between her teeth. "I thought you were just putting the time in, waiting for us to be over."

"No." He shook his head, voice deepening. "No, I'm… I'm trying to protect you."

"Oh, Xavier." She sighed. "I'm *tired* of being protected. That's why I slept with you. I wanted to feel what other people feel. The ones who aren't sitting in a vault waiting for their lives to start. I wanted to flirt. Feel pretty. Dance."

"Go on a date?"

"Yes."

His thumb stroked the thin skin inside her wrist. "This is a date."

Not a real one, she thought. People who went on dates were hopeful of a future. But beggars couldn't be choosers. She forced herself to make a face of forbearance as she said, "It's not dinner and a movie, but I suppose it will do."

His expression relaxed, lips twitching. "Too cliché. I've

brought you star gazing." He deliberately let his attention scan the growing crowd of celebrities.

Relief as much as amusement sent laughter bursting out of her. She slid her arm around him, hugging herself into him as lightness filled her. "If you promise to have me home by curfew, then yes, I would love to be your date."

Over before we started.

These last few days had given Xavier an unprecedented glimpse into Trella's world. She was right. All too soon they would be strangers again. He couldn't countenance it. Like his last night of freedom in Paris, he was compelled to grasp this chance with her.

Unlike Paris, he couldn't steal her away and it was delicious torture standing beside her, setting a subtly possessive touch upon her, but unable to do more. All the while, he fell under her spell, as did everyone she spoke to.

It was humbling, in a good way, to be with a woman whose attention was as valuable as his own. Rather than having to consciously include her in a conversation, they operated as a unit. One minute she introduced him to a family friend with a pedigree that matched his own, the next he was catching up with a diplomat he'd dealt with in the past whose wife was a client at Maison des Jumeaux.

Then they were interrupted and she threw herself into a man's arms. "Sadiq!"

The man's wife, who happened to be Kasim's sister, Xavier learned, was clearly a close friend, too. They spoke with the couple for a long time, until Xavier couldn't wait to dance with Trella again.

"Explain to me exactly how he saved you?" He prompted when they were on the floor.

"Hacking." She glanced around as she said it. "We're not supposed to talk about it. He still does some high-level work on the side. He found out where I was being held and alerted the police."

"How old was he?"

"Fifteen. Crazy to think of, isn't it? He didn't know us very well, either, just had some classes with the boys. I think it was the challenge of it. He's stubborn that way. It definitely wasn't a desire to be a hero because you can see how self-effacing he is. But he wanted to help and persevered until he had something. Every time I see him, I'm reminded that he gave me this life and I should be grateful for it. Not waste it."

She met his eyes as she echoed what he had said earlier, but he read the deeper question in the longing look she gave him. They'd been engaging in subtle foreplay all night, not pawing each other, but neither shy about taking the other's hand or pressing close. He'd watched her nipples harden and heard her breath catch and felt the goosebumps that rose on her arms under the brush of his hand.

God knew he was aroused just by her nearness, never mind the scent that had hardwired itself into him or the way watching her quick mouth as she talked and laughed made him want to kiss the hell out of her.

He touched her chin then couldn't resist letting the backs of his fingers slide down the heat of her soft throat. As he let two fingertips rest on her pulse, the one that confirmed she was alive when she might very well have been lost and he never would have known her at all, he wondered how the hell he was ever going to say no to her again.

CHAPTER ELEVEN

TRELLA CHECKED ON Tyrol as soon as they arrived at the mansion. He was sleeping soundly, completely oblivious to the potential shift in his parents' relationship.

As she stood over him, she thought of all the reasons her marriage was impossible. Progeny, publicity, even Xavier's rejection of love over duty. His refusal to open himself *to* love.

She thought of all the ways she was broken, but miracles happened. This tiny boy, for instance. She owed it to him to try with his father, didn't she? Really try to reach his heart?

Was it a rationalization? Perhaps. She couldn't deny that lust was alive and well inside her, but so was something deeper and more nascent. She didn't want to believe it was love. Not yet. Not when she was about to risk rejection. Not when there was every chance she would have to spend her life yearning for a man who might very well be incapable of the emotion.

"How is he?" Xavier asked in a whisper, coming up behind her.

His need to see his son fed her hope that he was more than capable of deeper feelings.

"Perfect," she answered, watching his profile soften as he looked at Tyrol.

"He is," he agreed, turning up the flame of desire inside her.

She led him from the room, heart hammering, and went to his room, not her own.

"Bella," he protested as he followed, but stayed in the open door, backlit by the light from over the stairs.

"Close the door, please."

He sucked in a long breath, like he needed it to face a Herculean task. "I can't. You know I can't."

"I don't want to make a fool of myself in front of the guard in the hall."

He pushed the door shut and leaned on it, breath hissing out. He was a dark shadow in the unlit room. She saw his fist close against the hardwood next to his thigh.

"Can you even make love?"

"As of midnight, yes," she said ruefully.

His head thumped back against the door. He swore. "You know this is impossible. You know—"

"I do." She went to him and picked up that rock hard fist, gently rubbing his fingers, trying to coax the tension from his hand. "But who else am I going to have sex with? Hmm? Who else do I trust with myself?"

"I still don't understand why you ever did."

She kissed his fingers. "Because no one else makes me feel like this." She set his open hand above her breast, where her heart raced. "If it's not the same for you—"

"It is, damn you." He hooked his hand behind her neck and dragged her closer, voice growing hoarse. "No one else has *ever*—"

He covered her mouth with his, cutting off whatever he'd been about to say.

She didn't care. All she cared about was being up against his lean, powerful body, feeling him devour her mouth as though it was the only thing he would ever need.

It was an onslaught, his hand shifting to her hair to drag her head back. His other arm crushed her into him while his lips ravaged and his tongue invaded.

Her heart knocked into her rib cage, sending sweet pulse beats through her arteries, weakening her limbs. She felt helpless, but not to him. To this yearning. Lethargy stole her strength when she longed to cling to him. All she could manage was to crush the edges of his jacket in her fists and moan into his mouth.

He made a jagged noise and dragged his teeth along her generous lower lip, tugging then releasing. "I'm being too rough."

"I need to know you feel the same. I want you so *bad*. You have no idea."

"I do." Another rough noise scraped from his throat. He dragged up the skirt of her gown, so when he picked her up as he pushed off the door, her legs were free to twine around his waist.

"But it's only lust, *bella*. Tell me you understand that."

She was on the verge of laughing, loving his easy strength. Her self-assurance slipped a notch, but she could feel him hard and straining between her legs. It was too beguiling to ignore, making her tighten her arms and legs, trying to increase the pressure there. "Whatever it is, I need it."

He walked her unerringly to the bed and came down to settle his weight on her, mouth sealing to hers again. Writhing under him, she tried to touch all of him with her whole body, tried to drag his clothes out of the way while searching for hot naked skin.

"Slow down." He grabbed her hands and pinned them over her head, then dragged his mouth along her jaw, down her throat and bared her breast for his fierce gaze. "This will *not* end before it starts." He used his teeth on the swell of her breast, making her shudder. "I've fantasized about it too many times to rush now that I have you where I want you."

A surge of moisture hit her loins. "I think about us when I'm in the bath."

He lifted his head and with a hiss said, "You witch." He levered up and rolled her over, swept her hair out of the way then slowly tugged open the ties behind her neck. "Tell me exactly what you do when you're in the bath." He set kisses down her spine. "Be specific."

"I could show you." She lifted into his hardness.

He grasped her hip and met her pressure with thrusts of his own, breaths thick and animalistic as he ground his erection into her soft cheeks. Then he slid a hand under her bunched skirt and across her stomach, fingers delving beneath her silk panties as he settled on her again. "Keep moving," he said, gently sawing two fingertips between her damp lips, mouth planting wet kisses on her nape. "Show me how much you want me."

She did. She rocked herself between his hand and his heavy hips until she was trembling with desire. She stopped, shaking with arousal. "I'm so close. I want to feel you inside me."

"Not yet." He shifted and settled his hand deeper, so his fingers slid inside her, so satisfying yet maddening. "Keep going."

Helpless to her own body, she did, until she was releasing broken cries, fists clenching the blankets, body clasping uncontrollably at his penetration, shivering and completely lost. Utterly his.

"So good," he said, licking between her shoulder blades, still mimicking lovemaking with light thrusts of his hips, drawing out her orgasm as he kept his hand in place. "I want you in a thousand ways. There will never be enough time for how much I want you."

And he called it *only lust*?

She pushed against the mattress, trying to twist beneath him. He withdrew his hand, but hooked his fingers in her panties and pulled them down and off, sitting up on the edge of the bed to throw them away, then he shrugged off his jacket and kicked off his shoes.

She knelt behind him and reached to work down the buttons of his shirt. He turned his head to catch at her mouth with his, easily distracting her. Their tongues met and the heat kept growing, not appeased in the least. She sobbed and he turned to scrape his hands down her shoulders, brushing her gown away so she knelt in a puddle of near-black velvet.

He stood then, chest expanding in deliberate breaths between the edges of his open shirt, as if he strained to keep control of himself. "Don't ever ask me again if you're beautiful. Know it, *bella*. You are the kind of beautiful that could topple a kingdom."

He reached out and wound her hair around his hand then bent to kiss her.

She tried to balance the bitter with sweetness in her own kiss, but her desire was too potent. It was all lust. He pulled back to yank his pants open then stripped, checking for a moment with one hand and reaching toward the night table.

"I can't get pregnant," she reminded.

He snorted and found a condom anyway, tearing it open with his teeth.

It shouldn't have made her want to cry, but it did.

"Bella," he chided as he pressed her flat and used a knee to part her legs, "I'm protecting *you*."

It didn't feel like it. But when he stroked his tip against her, hot and beguiling, he seemed to send electric lines of pleasure radiating through her. She forgot to be outraged or hurt. She set her hands on either side of his head and kissed him. Extravagantly. Invitingly.

And when he sank into her, it was her turn to bite his lip and groan.

"I'm going to make it last," he said into her mouth. "All night."

"Yes, please…"

Mario met them as they entered the palace. He smiled benignly at Tyrol, who was fussy after the travel, and said to Xavier, "The Queen expects you. She'd like to hear about Australia."

Completely attuned to her husband after their night of lovemaking, Trella felt his surreptitious sigh.

"Of course." He glanced at Trella from eyes bruised by their sleepless night. "Eat. Get some rest."

She nodded and followed his retreat with her gaze, feeling as though he took her heart and spun it out like twine behind him.

All of her felt undone and achy. They'd had one conversation in the dawn light, bodies still damp with exertion, while her nerve endings had still been singing with joy.

"You know this doesn't change what has to happen." His voice had been grave, his body steely against hers.

She had shifted her head on his shoulder. "I know. But I'm not sorry. Are you?"

"I'm trying to be."

She had turned her lips in to his throat and they had started all over again.

"Gerta can take the Prince up to the nursery, Ms. Sauveterre," Mario said as they arrived on the second floor.

Signora Deunoro, Trella longed to say, but it had been agreed from the outset that she would not change her name. After Tyrol's christening, she was to receive an honorific title of *Dama*, the lowest of Elazar's ranks. A future monarch could not have a parent who was common.

"I'll keep him. He's having an off day." And she was feeling neglectful after leaving him in Gerta's care during the wedding last night. "You go settle in," she said, since Gerta hadn't actually seen where she would be living in the palace. "I'll bring him when he's ready for a long nap."

With a curtsy, Gerta followed Mario's direction to the nursery level while Trella turned toward the room she'd occupied before she'd gone into the hospital, the ones adjoined to Xavier's.

Mario cleared his throat. "You're in the dowager's wing now, Ms. Sauveterre."

This doesn't change what has to happen.

Speechless, composure fraying, she let Mario escort her across the gallery, through a pair of doors, down a long hall where paintings of Xavier's ancestors watched her progress in silent judgment, and through another set of doors.

The temperature grew cooler as they walked. Tyrol's fussy cries echoed off the high ceiling with the sounds of their footsteps. She didn't try to soothe him, just let him express exactly what she was feeling, and was viciously pleased to see Mario's obsequious expression grow more and more strained.

She understood that the dowager's wing had been deliberately placed to provide as much distance as possible between former queens and new ones. It wasn't a horrible place. It had been prepared for her occupancy with cheerful floral arrangements, a new sofa and her very own lady's maid, Adona, who was eager to prepare her some soup.

Mario offered a quick tour, pointing to a bright, empty room as a potential studio, if she wanted to provide a list of items she would like placed there.

"A crib and a change table," Trella said, growing as fractious as her son. "Tyrol needs a nursery."

Mario tilted his head in a way that was unbearably condescending. "Royalty inhabits the royal wing."

"I see." She sat on the sofa and dug in her shoulder bag for the receiving blanket she carried. She shook it out with a snap then tucked a corner into her collar as she met Mario's gaze with a challenging one of her own. "And do I go on safari to the nursery to feed him? Or does he exercise his lungs through the palace every two hours as he is brought to me?"

Tyrol was showing off the growing strength of his lungs, recognizing the feeling of the soft flannel against his cheek as she draped it over him and growing frantic for her to open her buttons.

"It was understood the Prince was taking a bottle," Mario said, mouth pinched, gaze averting self-consciously while his whole face went red.

Oh, was he uncomfortable with her breastfeeding? What a shame.

"He'll *need* a bottle, won't he? Or he'll starve to death before we get to each other. Am I even allowed into the palace without an escort? He's *six weeks old*. Still a few days shy of his due date. He's not weaned and won't be for a *year*."

"As I see." Mario cleared his throat and turned to the door. "I'll leave you to it."

"Do."

This doesn't change what has to happen. Xavier should have told her *this* was going to happen. How *dare* he use her up last night, thinking this would be okay.

Trella woke thick-headed from a heavy nap to hear Xavier's hushed voice, "Give him a bottle if he needs it." A door closed.

She jackknifed to sit up and shot a look to the travel cot she'd had Gerta bring down from the nursery. It was empty.

Sucking in enough breath for a scream, she leapt from the bed and stumbled into the lounge, wearing only the oversized T-shirt she'd thrown on for sleep. Xavier was there, but no one else. No Gerta, no Adona, no *Tyrol*.

"Oh, *hell* no," she informed and rushed after her son.

"Trella." He caught her arm and reaction kicked in. She used the momentum to round on him, heel of her hand aimed straight for his nose.

He deflected, tried to catch her into a hold, but she expertly twirled out and broke his grip, the movements ingrained in her muscles from years of practice. Knocking a lamp in his direction to force him to leap back, she backed up too, out of his reach, neatly balancing on the balls of her feet, breathing in hisses as she gauged the distance between him and the door and how she would take him out in order to get there.

"I didn't *know*," he growled, holding himself in ready stance. "*Calm down*."

"Bring him back." She reached for a slender vase and flicked its three tall irises at his feet, spattering water on the bottoms of his pant legs, then tested the heft of the blown glass as a weapon.

"You're going back to the room you were in, next to mine. I sent him up because he needs a bath. I stayed to tell you that and keep you from throwing a righteous fit when you woke and saw he was gone. Calm the hell down."

"You should have told me last night this could happen. This, by the way, is how you put up a fight." She shook the vase at him, mocking his lame attempt to turn her away last night.

"This was always going to happen!" He pointed at the door. "If not today, soon enough. In a few weeks, you'll move out of the palace and he'll come and go between us. That is reality, Trella. I have damned well made that clear to you. More than once. *You* came to *my* room, last night, knowing that. Don't pretend this is news."

She threw the vase at the fireplace so it shattered and droplets of water made the dancing flames sputter and crackle. Then she stared at the destruction, chest heaving.

"Is this bringing on an attack?"

"Don't pretend you care if it does."

"I *care*," he bit out. "Why the hell do you think I'm here?" He looked positively tortured as the words escaped him. He wiped his expression away with a stroke of his hand, releasing a heavy sigh.

"I've just been raked over the coals for *one* photo." He held up his finger. "And because a debate has sprung up online. Team Trella or Team Patrizia. My fault." He turned his hand to tattoo his chest with his finger. "I promised to undo all of that, as if it's even possible, and walked back to my room to learn you'd been sent here. Do you know how much furniture *I* wanted to break? Do you understand what I'm doing, taking you back there? It's pure weakness!"

No, it wasn't. That's not what caring was. He wasn't ready to hear or believe it, though, and she was too angry and hurt to explain it.

"Why does she hate me so much? Why—?"

He closed his eyes. "I keep trying to tell you. Emotion has nothing to do with it. It can't. That's the point."

"The crown is all that matters."

"Yes."

"I hate your crown! I hate that our son will be raised with this same hard-hearted attitude."

"Hate away. It changes nothing."

"And you want me to come to your rooms again, anyway."

"Yes."

"Even though it won't change anything, either."

"Yes."

Mouth trembling, she knew that, like him, she didn't have a choice. She would go with him and believe what she believed, that he would change, and one of them was going to lose.

She nodded jerkily, but before she could step forward, he leapt to meet her, not letting her walk through broken glass to get to him. Then he was cupping her cheek, tilting her lips up to the hungry weight of his own. She moaned, knowing what that taste was now. That narcotic that filled her with hope when he kissed her. *Love.* She was madly, deeply, hopelessly in love with him.

CHAPTER TWELVE

"YOU'RE NEGLECTING YOUR DUTIES. The Australian agreements have completely fallen apart." His grandmother had called him on the carpet before he'd even digested his breakfast.

"Both parliaments have risen for the year. The committees adjourned," he said.

"Yet I am informed the deadline is the end of the year. If it's not finalized, we start over in the new year." She held out a missive.

He took it and quickly gathered how certain opportunistic corporations were manipulating the fine print, trying to push Elazar into a stress position and a renegotiation that would be advantageous to their own interests. She was right. He should have caught on when the meetings had begun experiencing delays two weeks ago.

"This is the first I'm hearing of this," he muttered.

"Because you've been distracted. Dating. *Shopping.*"

He gritted his teeth. Trella was preparing to move her design house's head office to Lirona. The fashion industry was waiting with baited breath for her to purchase her property. Real estate and tourism would boom the minute the new fashion district was born. Squiring her to potential locations, ensuring the choice worked as well for

Elazar as it did for her, fell right into Xavier's trade negotiation bailiwick.

His grandmother ought to be thanking Trella, but she only said, "Mario has set up an emergency meeting of the council. You're expected at ten o'clock. We cannot afford to lose this, Xavier."

Duty. It was killing him. Quite literally chipping away at his flesh. His belt had had to go in an extra notch and the scale had him four pounds under his usual weight. He had no appetite. Of course, he was on his wife like a stallion with a mare every chance he got. No wonder he was skin and bones.

Bristling with culpability, he returned to his apartment. He would have to hurry to make the meeting, but he was more aware of the clock ticking down on his marriage.

In a few days it would be Christmas, his one and only with his son's mother. Then their marriage would melt away like snow under rain. Gone, gone, gone.

He nodded at Vincente to leave his jacket on the bed and dismissed him, then he went through to Trella's room, where he slept every night with her naked body resting against his. They tried to keep a low profile but were fooling no one, except possibly themselves. Despite the intensity and excruciating pleasure and profound satisfaction they gave each other, they had to keep rising and moving apart.

Soon that would be permanent.

Not yet. His hand closed in a tense fist. He wasn't ready.

"I have to run to a meeting—" he began as he entered.

She sniffed and turned with surprise. She had showered while he'd been to see the Queen and wore only a slip. She was on the phone.

"*Esta bien, Mama. Te amo,*" she finished and signed off, then swiped her cheek.

His heart lurched. "What's wrong?"

"Nothing." She turned away for a tissue. "Ramon and Isidora arrived safely at Sus Brazos. Gili and Kasim will be there tomorrow."

And this was her first year apart from them. She was homesick. She didn't have to say it. He watched her wither daily, saying nothing because they both left many things unsaid, aware their days with each other were numbered. They didn't want to waste them with animosity and problems they couldn't solve.

Guilt assailed him, though. He was *stealing* time with her. Neglecting his duties while he neglected her needs. He pinched the bridge of his nose. "If you want to spend Christmas with them, you should."

"With Tyrol?" She brightened.

"Bella." He hated saying no to her, but it echoed in his voice. "You're upset. You miss them." She was going to need them more than ever soon.

"I can't leave him! He's still feeding in the night. I would miss *him*." She waved in the direction of the nursery, where a nanny took him for a bath every morning while they ate breakfast and started their day. She softened her tone, her expression so vulnerable she put an ache in his chest. "You could come."

You're neglecting your duties.

"No, I can't." This was it, he realized. The fracture that had begun working its way through him on their wedding day began to cleave open, tearing him apart. *But he had no choice.* "The Deunoros spend Christmas here."

"And I'm not a Deunoro. Why should he spend Christmas with her? She hasn't even looked at him since—"

"Leave it."

She buttoned her lip, but the glare she sent dropped the room temperature lower than it had been on the sleeting day of Tyrol's christening.

He couldn't let her bring it up because he was ashamed of his grandmother's behavior. Rather than the traditional pomp of open-topped carriages and a public stroll with the future monarch back to the palace, they'd all traveled by car. His grandmother had come in her own, arriving last and leaving first. Exactly one photo had been taken of Queen Julia standing with her grandson at her side and her great-grandson in his bassinet. Trella had been left out of the picture.

He closed his eyes, afraid he couldn't do this if he looked at her. His voice was hoarse with strain. "You should go see your family and come back to the new house."

He heard her breath suck in, sharp and mortal. "No, Xavier. Not yet."

"I was hoping we could get through Christmas, but we're only putting off the inevitable."

"What about…" Her voice faded. "What about a surrogate?" He had seen her afraid before, but not like this, with her throat exposed while she offered a knife.

He had to consciously remember to breathe. "It's not about another baby, *bella*."

His own composure threatened to crumble as her chin crinkled and her eyes filled. She caught her mouth into a line to hide its tremble, then that glorious Valkyrie in her came forward, steeling her spine and refusing to be cowed.

"I'm not leaving Tyrol. I'll move into your stupid ugly house if you make me, but I'm taking him with me."

That stung more than it should. He hadn't been able to design a home from greenfield for her, which felt like a breach of duty in itself, but he'd personally overseen all the renovations and security upgrades to the one he'd bought. He'd taken the utmost care with every detail.

"Don't make this ugly. The agreement is three and a half days each." That was not renegotiable.

"You're *busy*. Why should someone else feed him a bottle when he could be with me?" Oh, she was fierce when she wanted to be. Flushed, with her eyes glimmering, she threw the forces of nature at him. "At least I *love* him."

"So do I!" It exploded out of him. Within him. *Nothing* would come between him and his son.

She threw her head back, fury fading into sorrow. "But you don't love me. I can live somewhere else."

He jerked his head to the side, slapped by the torment in her voice.

"Say it," she choked. "Tell me these last weeks of..." She waved at the bed where they had writhed with passion. "I have tried *so hard* to show you we could make this work. Every breath I take is carefully measured to make sure I don't impinge on your role in any way. I should bite my tongue right now. You have a meeting to get to, right? I give and give and you can't offer me a crumb? A maybe? A *chance*?"

"You think I like seeing you holding back, afraid to laugh too loud, keeping to these rooms when you should be able to say and do whatever the hell you please? I hate what I'm doing to you. You never wanted this."

"But if you *loved* me—"

"I *can't* love you! I've upended my world as far as I can. Things are tipping off. *This has to end.*"

She rocked as if buffeted by a hurricane wind. He watched her lips go white with the rest of her. Her fingers twitched at her sides and she swayed again then locked her knees.

"Bella." He reached out, feeling the chasm in him widen to a canyon, pushing her further and further beyond him.

She drew a jagged breath and leveled her shoulders. "You should go. I don't want to be blamed for you missing your meeting."

* * *

Had that really happened?

One minute she had been feeling sorry for herself over her siblings getting together without her, the next her tiny nascent family of three had been torn down to one and a half.

How had she not fought hard enough? Aside from viewing a few buildings for Maison des Jumeaux, she had lived as a shut-in again, not wanting to make headlines. As painful as she'd found it when he disappeared for a few days on palace business, she had never once complained. Even his grandmother's frosty behavior at the christening had gone unremarked until today.

All the while, she'd been aware of the days lifting off the calendar like ravens, one by one, swooping away and forming a black, jeering cloud on the horizon. They'd mocked her for loving him despite his lack of commitment. For waiting so patiently for words of love that were never going to come.

Did she regret trying to make their marriage work? No. But failing despite leaving her heart wide open was liable to kill her.

Shaking, she pressed a fresh tissue to her closed eyes, soaking up the leak through her lashes, taking a slow breath and consciously softening her shoulders.

Uno naranjo, dos naranjos…

It struck her what she was doing. *Oh, no.*

She pressed the tissue harder into her eyes, becoming aware of the sensations pinging to life in her. A roiling stomach, a creep of foreboding down her spine. Cold specters began to float in her periphery, voicing the ugliest of thoughts. *Why would he want you? You're the broken one. You're soiled.*

"No," she whispered, certain that being susceptible to

these attacks *proved* how unworthy she was of love. Was that the ghouls talking? Or the unvarnished truth?

"*Dama*?" Her maid knocked, making her heart leap. Adona entered. "The Private Secretary is here. Her Majesty wishes to see you."

Not now. She couldn't. Not with a spell coming on. All of her went rigid while her blood moved like acid in her arteries.

Why did the Queen even want to see her? Her mind raced, trying to think of an excuse, but what could she say?

"Please give me a moment to dress." *Uno naranjo, dos naranjos...*

She chose the dress she'd worn to the christening, since its red and gold were Elazar's national colors and quietly proclaimed her station as the mother of a future monarch. Adona gave her hair a twist while Trella dabbed on light makeup, even though it didn't matter if she put on clown pants or a G-string with water wings. She was going to the guillotine.

As if that were true, the flutters deep in the pit of her belly grew worse. Mario's dour face made his silent escort that much more ominous. Her feet felt like they didn't belong to her. She couldn't make her throat swallow.

The ghouls chuckled as they stuck to her clammy skin, following her into a stately room of powder blue and white striped wallpaper.

The Queen wore a dark green sweater set and a severe expression. She was seated and Trella was not invited to do so.

Trella ordered her fists to loosen and clasped them in front of her. She took measured breaths, nodded in greeting as the door behind her closed, shutting her in with what she had long suspected was an enemy.

"I'm a woman of well-cultivated patience, but mine

has run out," Queen Julia stated. "It would benefit all if you went to Spain for Christmas and did not come back."

Her nails dug into her palm beneath the cover of her other hand. "Xavier suggested the same thing."

Surprise flickered in the Queen's face before she blinked it away. She nodded. "Good. He's finally showing sense."

"I said I'd go if Tyrol came with me." She wanted that so badly, she would buckle into the carpet if the Queen agreed.

The older woman hardened before Trella's eyes. "*No*. But allow me to lend my voice to my grandson's. You do more damage than good by lingering."

The words hit so hard, Trella had to press into her toes to stay on her feet. Still, her inherent streak of bellicosity reared its head. Another woman would have taken this chance to make a good impression and reason with the woman. She wouldn't pour gasoline over the one bridge open to her and light a match.

"Is that what you said to *his* mother when you exiled her?"

The Queen's eyes were so much like Xavier's, it was sheer agony to look into the contempt they held.

"I was told you have a predilection for dramatics." She was like a cat that knew its prey's weakest spots, but took her time piercing them, preferring to terrorize before putting a creature out of its misery. "Xavier's mother has always had access to him. He chose not to pursue a deeper relationship."

"Because you didn't approve of one. Did you? And he couldn't afford to alienate you. He didn't have anyone left." She showed the Queen how she had won more staring contests than she'd lost.

After a moment, the Queen reached very casually to

polish her glasses, then perched them back on her nose. "*My* relationship with my grandson is not up for discussion. But if he's asked you to leave, yours with him is clearly over."

Breathe. Uno naranjo, dos naranjos...

"Xavier has been conditioned to believe that people who love him leave and don't come back. I plan to show him that's not true." Would it work? She couldn't think about that right now.

"What he *knows* is that a country can't maintain stability when it's ruled by emotion. Scandal and division among its people are poison. How can he be regarded as a man of integrity when he's with a woman who is nothing but racy headlines?"

"I can't control my headlines!"

"No. You can't. That's why removing yourself is the least you can do. If you care anything for him and your son, protect them."

Score one for the Queen. She knew it, too. She didn't move, but her verbal rapier kept whipping the air, cutting into Trella with casual ease as she spoke again.

"You have no idea the strength required to hold this position. Your weaknesses would become theirs, undermining what has taken five hundred years to build."

"Loving is a weakness?" Where had she heard that before?

The Queen narrowed her eyes. "Your background, your extensive need for therapy and your delicate mental state are weaknesses."

It was as if she saw into Trella's soul where the specters were swirling and cackling, dragging icy fingers over her bones. *She sees you. She knows.*

"The toll of the throne would break someone like you. This is a marathon that lasts a lifetime. What are you going to do when it becomes too much? Retire behind closed doors and burden the palace with making explanations? If that's to be the end result, do it now. Fade into the background before you do any more damage."

"Someone like me," she repeated darkly.

They won't come for you. They won't want you after this. It was the oldest, darkest, ugliest voice. The one that made her eyes sting and her heart shrink.

She hadn't come back to her family in pieces because she had passively accepted her situation, though. She had fought with every ounce of will she possessed, from the first moment through all the other struggles to today.

"You know *nothing* about me and what I can endure. Do not confuse my capacity for love as an inability to stand and fight. In fact, love is my *weapon.* You want to go to war with me? Gird your loins. You might rule this country, but I rule the online world. I'm beloved by *billions.* You want to protect what's taken five hundred years to build? I belong to something that's lasted millennia. *Family.* When you die, do you think *duty* will squeeze a single tear from Xavier's eye?"

The Queen went white. "You're becoming hysterical."

"You unleashed this!" She stabbed the air between them. "Love is the only thing that pulls us through hardship. *I know that.* And your tepid love isn't enough to sustain him. Yes, you love him in your stunted way, but you're afraid to show it. Why? Because you might have to deal with grief again? Is that why you don't even look at Tyrol? You're afraid he'll die and you don't want to be attached? Now who's weak?"

Queen Julia gave her bell a resounding shake.

"What's wrong? This is what someone looks like when they're fighting for the people they love. Still think I'm not tough enough for the job?"

"*Get out.*"

"Ms. Sauveterre!" Mario entered. "Please."

She shot him a bitter look on her way past him then ran blindly to her room.

Voices were droning around him, but Xavier wasn't tracking. He was lost in a fog he hadn't experienced since childhood. Twice. The miasma was cold and gray and left him rudderless. His grandmother had been there to lead him along those other two times, but she was the last person he wanted to turn to right now.

Not because he blamed her. No, he blamed himself.

All he could hear was Trella saying, *If you loved me.*

He had said he couldn't love her as if he didn't have the capacity. For a long time, he had believed he didn't. The love he'd once felt for his parents had stagnated under their leaving, stunting him into an inability to feel anything beyond superficial liking.

And yes, Trella had been a distraction lately as they had tried to cram a lifetime into the short marriage they had agreed to, but the fact that their time was finite had put that pressure on them. Hell, he'd called it off and he was still distracted.

I can live somewhere else.

The doom he'd felt at that statement couldn't be measured. He tried to picture Patrizia in the room where he'd held Trella and bile rose to the back of his throat.

No, the real problem was that he was afraid to *admit* he loved her. Otherwise, he might feel like this when their marriage ended. But he did feel like this now, which must mean—

"You agree, Your Highness?"

"Pardon?" He sucked in a deep breath, like he was coming out of a coma. What the hell had he done?

"We were discussing where the tax rate should break."

He shook his head, taking in the dozen people slouched over a boardroom table, surrounded by laptops and scratch pads and coffee cups while snow fell beyond the windows.

"Get the Australians on the phone. We'll request an extension into January. We'd rather be with our families through Christmas and I'm sure their people would, too."

Screw duty. He had to fix things with the woman he loved.

He rose just as his PA slipped into the room and hurried across with a message that Angelique was trying to reach him.

Frowning, Xavier excused himself and turned on his phone. It lit up with missed calls and texts.

What happened?
Where is she?
Are you with her?

His heart lurched. He hit reply on a video call, moving farther down the hall to an alcove where he had some privacy.

Angelique appeared, her pinched expression deeply anxious. "Are you with her? She keeps texting that she's fine, but she's not fine. I can tell."

"I'm not with her—"

"Damn it, Xavier, you can't leave her alone when she's having an attack!"

Her tone made Xavier's scalp prickle. He only half-believed in the twin connection, but her alarm was genuine enough that he looked for his PA to signal for his car.

"Is there someone who could check on her and get back to us?" Kasim asked.

"She's really scared, Xavier." Angelique sounded half-hysterical herself.

"I'll try her right now. But if you two feed off each other's mood, you should try dialing back your worry and send her some calming thoughts." It came off the top of his head out of frustration and sounded too metaphysical.

Her wet face went blank with surprise. "I honestly never thought of that. God, I'm such an idiot. Of course. I'll text her that I love her."

His conscience twisted as he thought of his own refusal to say those words this morning. He ended the call and tried Trella. She declined to answer, but texted a moment later to say she was napping.

"Everything all right, sir?" his PA approached to ask.

Xavier held up a staying hand as he reached Vincente. "Have you seen Trella today?"

A brief hesitation, then, "Adona said she locked herself in her room after her audience with the Queen."

"She spoke with my grandmother? The car," Xavier snapped at his PA. "Now."

CHAPTER THIRTEEN

SHE WAS DOING this for Tyrol, she kept telling herself, as she bit down on one of his teethers and counted her oranges. Some women went through the pains of childbirth. Her lot was to weather waves of terror. The irrational, fearful thoughts would pass. The sweating and sobs of insecurity needed to run their course. She just had to breathe and count her oranges and wait it out.

It was easier when someone she loved and trusted sat with her and told her she was safe. She didn't feel safe right now. She felt very temporary and unwanted. Abandoned. Forsaken.

"Shh," she breathed, pushing those thoughts away.

I am strong. I am loved. I can do this.

She should have brought her phone in here. All the texting had been breaking her concentration. She had left it on the night table, but now she wished she was reading Gili's comforting words. It was almost as good as having her here.

"Trella!"

Oh, God. What was he doing here? She had locked up and told Adona not to let anyone in. Now he would see her like this and know how cracked she really was.

His footsteps crossed into her bathroom. There was a systematic banging noise. He was opening all the cupboards beneath the dual sinks, looking for her.

"You're sure she didn't leave?"

He had someone with him? And someone who saw him searching cupboards for her? She pulled her feet in tighter, driving the curve of her spine into the wall behind her.

The closet light flicked on, blindingly bright even against her clenched eyes. She made a noise of protest and ducked her head.

"Are you here?" he demanded.

She plucked the teether from her bite. "I don't want you to see me like this."

"Get out and lock the doors."

"Yes, sir." It was Adona and a moment later, a distant noise of a door closing sounded.

Xavier came to the back of the closet and swept aside the gowns. He swore when he found her huddled in the corner on the floor. He crouched and wiped her wet cheek with his hand, drying it on his thigh. "Why didn't you call me?"

"I have to do this alone."

"No, you don't," he said grimly and started to gather her.

"Don't." She pressed as hard as she could into the corner, holding him off with one shaking arm.

"What did she say to you?"

She didn't know if her mental state made him sound that lethal, or if he really was murderous.

"Nothing I don't say to myself." She clenched her eyes in anguish. "I am a detriment. A hindrance. You shouldn't be here. What are you going to do? Run out of every high-level meeting because I'm having an episode? This can't happen. You can't be here. I *have* to do this *alone*."

"Look at me," he said gently.

"No, *you* look at *me*. Is this a queen? It's *not*. I pretended for a while that we could find a way and you followed me through the looking glass because duty chafes and the sex is great, but we knew it couldn't last. You were right, Xavier. This was always going to happen. *This*—" she pointed at her position on the floor "—will happen when I can least afford it. I wish I wasn't this person, but I am. And if you stay in here and nurse me through this, you're only proving that I'm a burden. *I have to do this alone.* I'm an adult who will be a single mother. *I* have to know I can do it."

The mention of living alone sent a tumble of unvoiced fears through her head. Intruders. Kidnappers. A million bad, horrible, terrifying things.

"Bella," he said gently. "I want to talk to you about that. Come on. Come out of here."

"No." She slapped at his reaching hands and said very clearly, "There is no way. None. Just—go look after Tyrol. Please? I can't look after him when I'm like this. If you want to help me, go do that. Please?"

He stared at her, jaw clenched. "I'll bring him to you. Will that help?"

"I can't use him as a crutch. It would turn into me using him all the rest of my life. I won't put that on him. But I'll feel better if I know you're looking after him. Please?" She clutched his wrist. "Will you do that for me?"

"Trella—"

"I'm begging you, Xavier. *Please.*"

He left her in the closet like a child hiding from monsters, hating himself for abandoning her, but she'd knocked the wind out of him. Blind shock held him in stasis for long minutes outside her door.

She thought her attack made her unfit to be his wife?

This was his fault. Not just her breakdown, but her belief that she had to be perfect to be his queen. She was already perfect in the way of fierce storms and jagged mountains and a flower blooming on a broken stem. Her perfection was in her resilience. That's what was needed in his partner. He loved her for her strength and her ferocious capacity to love and her ability to move forward despite how many times she'd been knocked down.

With her emotional bravery top of mind, he strode to the nursery where Tyrol had just woken.

"I was about to bring him down for a feed—"

"Warm a bottle. I'll take him." He carried his son through the palace, pushing into his grandmother's parlor where she was meeting with Mario.

"Out," he said to Mario, and gave the door a light kick behind the man.

"Your meeting?" his grandmother prompted.

"My wife was indisposed. Someone upset her. I had to care for our son."

"We pay staff to care for him."

"He shouldn't need his parents because you and I didn't? We'll never know, will we?" He set Tyrol in her arms.

"What—"

"Hold him. Feed him."

"What do you think you're proving?" She lifted her brows and calmly silenced the boy with the nipple.

"What are *you* trying to prove? Look at your great-grandson. Can you honestly say you feel nothing toward him? Because that's certainly how you act."

She looked at the boy. His hand found her thumb and gripped it. A dribble of milk leaked from the corner of his mouth and his eyes were focused on her.

A flinch of anguish crossed her expression before her mouth softened in tenderness. "He looks like your father. Let's hope he doesn't have his temperament. Your father wasn't cut out for the crown. I let him go because I had to, Xavier." Her head came up, blue eyes clouded with sorrow and a pleading for forgiveness. "He wasn't his brother. He wasn't you. He was never going to survive the demands. I let him go and yes, you suffered, but I had already lost both my sons. I couldn't let you go, too."

It was the most sentimental thing he'd ever heard her say. Shaken, he lowered to sit across from her. "I'm a parent now. I do understand," he said at length. "I can't stomach the idea of his being across the city three and a half days a week, let alone not in my life at all."

"You shouldn't have agreed to share him."

"I intend to renege."

Her head came up, surprise in her lined face.

"They're both staying with me. I'm not asking you. I'm telling. If that means you stay on the throne the rest of your natural life, so be it."

"So she's won you over." She sniffed her disdain.

"No, it's up to me to win her."

Her gaze came up again.

"If I can't give the woman I love what she needs, how the hell can I give our country what it needs? She makes me whole. Stronger. I want to be a better man *for her*. That can only make me a better leader. A better king."

Tyrol finished his bottle. She set it aside and brought him to her shoulder to rub his back, exactly as if she'd been mothering infants all these years.

"After the risks she took bringing him into this world, how can you not want to know her? If you knew the things she's been through…" It was killing him, what she was enduring right now, but she seemed to need to prove something to herself and he had to give her that. "She's stronger and more determined than either of us can conceive."

"Her reputation, Xavier. Patrizia is such a good fit."

"I don't love Patrizia. I love Trella." It was conviction. Will. Fate. But he couldn't help pointing out, "So does everyone else, judging by the online polls. She's the more popular choice by a long shot."

"Don't be vulgar," she said crossly. "What about another baby?"

"We'll find a way. I am going to find a way to make it work. I have to. I can't live without her."

She let out a sigh of defeat. "Some monarchs would rather die than watch the next generation struggle to master the art of ruling. I've always thought I could give up the throne to you quite confidently. You rarely make mistakes. I will trust your judgment holds true in this instance."

He didn't need her approval, but he was glad to have it. Now he only had to convince Trella to stay.

Trella woke to bright light beyond the cracks in her blinds. She squinted gritty eyes at her clock. It was late morning. She had pumped milk a few hours ago when her swollen breasts had woken her, so she wasn't too uncomfortable, but she missed Tyrol enough that her chest hurt just thinking about him. She texted the nursery, then glanced at herself in the bathroom mirror, cringing.

She had done it. She splashed her face, brushed her teeth, then texted her sister.

It's over. I'm okay.

She earned a heart emoji in response.

The residual depression of an attack hovered like a cloud, though, along with profound loss as she accepted she and Xavier would never be. It had been a serious trip to hell and back, but she was *back*. That was something, she reassured herself. She had proved to herself she could not only grit her way through an episode, but that it wouldn't actually kill her.

Where was Tyrol? She checked her phone and saw Gerta had replied.

The Prince is with the Prince.

Xavier had had more meetings today. Was Tyrol sick?

She tugged a robe over her nightgown and yanked open her door—to find Xavier slouched in an armchair, clothes rumpled, eyelids heavy. Tyrol was fast asleep on his shoulder. It was such a tender scene, it pushed tears into the backs of her eyes.

"Is he okay?" She gently gathered the sleeping baby into her arms.

"Missing you, but otherwise fine. He just ate. That's purely for show," he added as Tyrol began to stir and fuss at the sound of her voice.

She sat to feed him, but Xavier was right. Tyrol nodded off before he'd taken more than a few gulps and she cuddled him instead. Oh, he smelled good and his skin was so soft. His hair was fine against her lips and his grip on her finger, endearing.

I'll always come back to you, my sweet, sweet boy. She had thought about him a lot last night. She had thought about Xavier and how delusional she had been, ever thinking she could be his queen when she had this awful shortcoming.

Fresh agony washed over her.

When she couldn't avoid it any longer, she looked at where Xavier hadn't moved.

"Was it a rough night?" she asked.

"For him? Not particularly. For me? Yes."

With a lurch in her heart, she noticed the glass on the table beside him. "Are you hungover?"

"No. I poured it, then thought I'd prefer to be sober if you decided you needed me."

"Were you worried? I'm sorry."

He snorted and reached for the glass. "Now, she's sorry." He made a face at his first sip and clunked the glass back onto the table. "Mostly water now. How was your night?"

"Awful."

He nodded in grim agreement.

"Why are you angry? Xavier—"

"I'm not angry." He shot to his feet, though, and paced a few steps only to turn back abruptly. "I am angry. I respected your wishes because fine, I accept that you had to feel you could get through an attack alone. But I have issues, too. *Because* of you. You ignored my texts for months before you admitted you were pregnant. Then you locked me out of a delivery room while you *flatlined*. We've been apart more than we've been together. You damned well need to stay accessible to me. I need to know you're alive, even if you're not at your best."

That was the problem. Sometimes she was at her absolute *worst*.

And she really wasn't up for a scolding over it. Or facing how she was supposed to be accessible from across the city. Much as she had given his grandmother a show of bravado, that's all it had been. She couldn't be his wife. She knew that now and it hurt so badly; she had to escape to hide how anguished she was.

"I want to shower. Can you take him and order breakfast?"

He said nothing as she handed him Tyrol again.

Swallowing, heavy with a melancholy that would never lift, she went back to her room and started the shower, blinking hot eyes as she did. She wasn't ready. If she hadn't had that stupid attack, if they hadn't had that big fight yesterday, they could still play alternate universe a few more days. Why had she shortchanged them like that?

She stepped under the spray and turned to see Xavier had come in behind her.

"Where's Tyrol?"

"Nursery." He peeled off his clothes, dropping them to the floor as the glass walls gathered steam.

"What are you doing?"

"What does it look like?" He opened the door and came in, crowding beneath the head that rained from the ceiling.

They'd showered together before, daily, but that was *before*.

"Xavier, I can't." Her heart was too tender, still pulling at all its old fractured lines and itching from fresh stitches.

"What did I just say about locking me out?" He cupped her wet head and planted a single kiss on her mouth, hot and possessive. Oddly tender.

She moaned and ducked her face as soon as he let her, tucking her forehead into his collarbone. Her vision filled with the golden skin she loved, taut and smooth over hard muscles. He was growing aroused, which always excited her.

"You know we're just putting off the inevitable. You were right all along," she muttered.

"You're staying here. We're staying married."

For a couple of heartbeats, she thought she'd imagined it, then she jerked back her head and looked at his implacable expression. The wetness in her clenched eyes wasn't from the water raining on her face.

"The future king decrees it? We both know I'm not a suitable queen."

"You are."

"You saw me last night!"

"And I see you this morning, having survived it. That's who and what you are, *bella*. You survive. You push through hardship to come out the other side, bruised maybe, but you make it. You don't give up on yourself, you would never give up on Tyrol and I won't let you give up on us."

Her mouth trembled. "If you loved me—"

He made a noise of imprecation. "If? *If*?" His hands cupped her face again. "You put a spell on me the first time we met. You gave me a son and helped me kick-start my heart so I could give him the love he deserves. Of course I love you, you infernal woman. How the hell else are we here?"

"You don't have to yell about it. What about Patrizia?"

"Are you seriously worried about a woman you have never met? You've ruined her life, *bella*. Just as you have ruined mine. But you won't feel bad about it because you've saved us both from a terrible mistake."

"Tyrol did. Lay the blame where it belongs."

"I thought I just did. God, I love you." He kissed her and this time he meant it, fusing his mouth to hers and letting her taste his desperation.

She grasped his wrists and pulled away, gasping, trying to speak from soul to soul. "Do you mean it? Because I don't think you understand how much it means to me that you can accept me, with all my breaks and imperfections. Don't say it unless it's true."

"You are flawed. You're unpredictable and defiant and shameless. You're also brave and creative and you love with everything in you. If you can rise out of your past and risk your heart, what kind of coward would I be if I refused to do the same? I'm privileged to be one of the people you love, Trella. I know what an exclusive club it is."

They kissed again and this time they didn't stop. The water rained down, washing away any ghosts that lingered, leaving only the love they had for each other.

Her body melted against his and she found herself pressed into the wall by his flexing muscles.

"Mine," he growled, kissing and licking at her neck and shoulders, across her breasts then between them. "There is no more locking yourself away. Understand? Not from me." The kisses continued, down her arms, across her hips.

She needed this doting attention. This all-consuming passion from him. It soothed and healed and made her feel cherished. By the time he knelt and hitched her thigh onto his shoulder, she was nearly weeping at the sweetness of him pouring such love all over her.

Her stomach jumped in reaction at the way he claimed her. He pleasured her until she was delirious, crying out with abandon. Then he stood and took her where she was, against the hard tiles, naked and slick as he drove into her, hard and deep. It was lust and bonding and naked unabashed love. When the climax came, they were in it together, trying to meld their slippery bodies into one being so they could never be separated again.

Then they leaned there, panting and wrung out, the water cooling, barely able to find the strength to get to the bed. They fell asleep in each other's arms, waking to make love again without the frantic pace driving them.

"We have time, *bella*. All our lives," he murmured, rocking lazily within her.

She released a shaken sigh, combing her fingers through his hair and was astonished at the lightness in her. The breadth of view. Years and years to come of this.

"I love you. You're the only man who could have given me this."

"You're the only woman I want or need. The only woman I could love so much."

Later that evening, he placed his rings on her finger as they dressed for dinner. The Queen wasn't one for making apologies, either, but she invited them to dine with her and suggested Xavier take his son and wife to Spain the day after Christmas if it was something Trella wanted.

It was, he did and it was wonderful.

EPILOGUE

Press release five years later...

Inconceivable Twins!

The Deunoro Palace surprised the world today by announcing that King Xavier and Queen Trella are celebrating the arrival of their daughter, Vivien.

Queen Trella's sister, Queen Angelique of Zhamair, also celebrates with her husband King Kasim the arrival of their third child, and first daughter, Genevieve.

While it was widely reported that Queen Angelique was carrying twins, it has now been revealed that, with the help of the world-renowned fertility clinic in Lirona, Queen Angelique was implanted with one egg from each set of parents.

Mother and babies are in excellent health.

The Queens' brothers, Henri and Ramon Sauveterre, were on hand with their own growing families to welcome this latest and most unusual pair of Sauveterre twins.

* * * * *

INDIAN PRINCE'S
HIDDEN SON

LYNNE GRAHAM

CHAPTER ONE

It was a dull winter day with laden grey clouds overhead. Fine for a funeral as long as the rain held off, Jai conceded grimly.

In his opinion, English rain differed from Indian rain. The monsoon season in Chandrapur brought relief from the often unbearable heat of summer, washing away the dust and the grime and regenerating the soil so that flowers sprang up everywhere. It was a cool, uplifting time of renewal and rebirth.

His bodyguards fanned out to check the immediate area before he was signalled forward to board his limousine. That further loss of time, slight though it was, irritated him because, much as he knew he needed to take security precautions, he was also uneasily aware that he would be a late arrival at the funeral. Unfortunately, it was only that morning that he had flown in from New York to find the message from Brian Allerton's daughter awaiting him, none of his staff having appreciated that that message should have been treated as urgent.

Brian Allerton had been a Classics teacher and

house master at the exclusive English boarding school that Jai had attended as a boy. For over two hundred years, Jai's Rajput ancestors had been sending their children to England to be educated, but Jai had been horribly homesick from the moment he'd arrived in London. Brian Allerton had been kind and supportive, encouraging the young prince to play sport and focus on his studies. A friendship had been born that had crossed both age barriers and distance and had lasted even after Jai went to university and moved on to become an international businessman.

Brian's witty letters had entertained Jai's father, Rehan as well. A shadow crossed Jai's lean, darkly handsome face, his ice-blue eyes, so extraordinarily noticeable against his olive skin, darkening. Because his own father had died the year before and Jai's life had changed radically as a result, with any hope of escaping the sheer weight of his royal heritage gone.

On his father's death he had become the Maharaja of Chandrapur, and being a hugely successful technology billionaire had had to take a back seat while he took control of one of the biggest charitable foundations in the world to continue his father's sterling work in the same field. Jai often thought that time needed to stretch for his benefit because, even working night and day, he struggled to keep up with all his responsibilities. Suppressing that futile thought, he checked his watch and gritted his teeth because the traffic was heavy and moving slowly.

Brian's only child, Willow, would be hit very hard by the older man's passing, Jai reflected ruefully, for, like Jai, Willow had grown up in a single-parent family, her mother having died when she was young. Jai's mother, however, had walked out on Jai's father when Jai was a baby, angrily, bitterly convinced that her cross-cultural marriage and mixed-race son were adversely affecting her social standing. Jai had only seen her once after that and only for long enough to register that he was pretty much an embarrassing little secret in his mother's life, and not one she wanted to acknowledge in public after remarrying and having another family.

It was ironic that Jai had come perilously close to repeating his father's mistake. At twenty-one he had become engaged to an English socialite. He had been hopelessly in love with Cecilia and had lived to regret his susceptibility when she'd ditched him almost at the altar. In the eight years since then, Jai had toughened up. He was no longer naive or romantic. He didn't do love any more. He didn't do serious relationships. There were countless beautiful women willing to share his bed without any promise of a tomorrow and no woman ever left his bed unsatisfied. Casual, free and essentially *forgettable*, he had learned, met his needs best.

As the limousine drew up outside the cemetery, Jai idly wondered what Willow looked like now. Sadly, it was three years since he had last seen her father, who had turned into a recluse after his terminal illness was diagnosed. She had been away from home studying on his last visit, he recalled with an effort. He had not regretted her absence because as a teenager she had had a huge crush on him and the amount of attention she had given him had made him uncomfortable back then. She had been a tiny little thing though, with that hair of a shade that was neither blond nor red, and the languid green eyes of a cat, startling against her pale skin.

Willow stood at the graveside beside her friend, Shelley, listening to the vicar's booming voice as he addressed the tiny group of mourners at her father's graveside. Brian Allerton had had no relatives and, by the time of his passing, even fewer friends because as his illness had progressed he had refused all social invitations. Only a couple of old drinking mates, one of whom was a neighbour, had continued to call in to ply him with his favourite whiskey and talk endlessly about football.

A slight stir on the road beyond the low cemetery wall momentarily captured Willow's attention and her breath locked in her throat when she realised that a limousine had drawn up. Several men talking into headsets entered the graveyard first, bodyguards spreading out in a classic formation to scan their surroundings before Jai's tall, powerful figure, sheathed in a dark suit, appeared. Her heart clenched hard because she hadn't been expecting him, having assumed that the message she had left at his London home would arrive too late to be of any use.

'Who on earth is *that*?' Shelley stage-whispered in her ear, earning a glance of reproof from the vicar.

But no, contrary to Willow's expectations, Jai, technology billionaire and media darling, had contrived to attend and, even though he had missed the church service, she was impressed, hopelessly impressed, that he had actually made the effort. After all, her father had, during his illness, stopped responding to Jai's letters and had turned down his invitations, proudly spurning every approach.

'Wow…he's absolutely spectacular.' Shelley sighed, impervious to hints.

'Talk about him later,' Willow muttered out of the corner of her mouth, keen to silence her friend. Shelley was wonderfully kind and generous but she wasn't discreet and she always said exactly what she was thinking.

'He's really hot,' Shelley gushed in her ear. 'And he's so tall and *built*, isn't he?'

Jai had been hugely popular at school when Willow was growing up in the little courtyard house that had gone with her father's live-in employment. The last in a long distinguished line of Rajput rulers and warriors, Prince Jai Singh had been an outstanding sportsman and an equally brilliant scholar and Willow had often suspected that Jai had been the son her father would've loved to have had in place of the daughter who had, sadly, failed to live up to his exacting academic standards.

And even though it had been three years since Willow had seen Jai she still only allowed herself a fleeting glance in his direction and swiftly suppressed the shiver of awareness that gripped her with mortifying immediacy. After all, a single glance was all it took to confirm that nothing essential had changed. Jai, the son of an Indian Maharaja and an English duke's daughter, was drop-dead gorgeous from the crown of his luxuriant blue-black hair to the toes of his very probably hand-stitched shoes. Even at a distance she had caught the glimmer of his extraordinarily light eyes against his golden skin. His eyes were the palest wolf-blue in that lean, darkly handsome face of his, a perfect complement to his superb bone structure, classic nose and perfectly sculpted mouth.

Jai, her first crush, her only infatuation, she conceded in exasperation, her flawless skin heating with the never-to-be-forgotten intense embarrassment of her teenaged years as the mourners came, one by one, to greet her and she invited them back to the house for an alcoholic drink as specified by her late parent, who had ruled against her providing traditional tea and sandwiches for the occasion. Even so, she would have to make exceptions for the vicar and for Jai.

As Jai strode towards the small group, his keen gaze widened infinitesimally, and his steps faltered as soon as he recognised Willow, a tiny fragile figure dressed in black, with an eye-catching waterfall of strawberry-blond waves tumbling round her shoulders that highlighted bright green eyes and a lush pink mouth set in a heart-shaped face. The shy, skinny and awkward teenager, he registered in surprise, had turned into a ravishing beauty. His teeth clenched as he moved forward, inwardly censuring that last observation as inappropriate in the circumstances.

A lean hand closed over hers. 'I apologise for my

late arrival. My deepest condolences for your loss,' Jai murmured softly.

'Hi... I'm Shelley,' her friend interrupted with a huge smile.

'Jai...this is my friend, Shelley,' Willow introduced hastily.

Jai grasped Shelley's hand and murmured something polite.

'Come back to the house with us,' Willow urged him stiffly. 'My father would've liked that.'

'I don't wish to intrude,' Jai told her.

'Dad wouldn't see anyone while he was ill... It wasn't personal,' Willow told him chokily. 'He was a very private man.'

'Your dad was right eccentric,' Shelley chimed in.

'His desire for privacy must've made his illness harder for you to deal with,' Jai remarked shrewdly. 'No support. I know you have no family.'

'But Willow does have friends,' Shelley cut in warmly. 'Like me.'

'And I am sure she is very grateful for your support at such a difficult time,' Jai responded smoothly.

That reminder of her isolation hit Willow hard. Losing her father, who had been her only parent since her mother had died when she was six, was already proving even tougher than she had envisaged. Worse still, the reality that they were stony broke, for those last months had broken her father's heart and hastened his end. Evidently fantasising about leaving his daughter much better off than they had been, her father had, as his life had drawn to a close, begun using his pension fund to play with stocks and shares without seeming to grasp the risk that he was taking.

Convinced that he was onto a winning strategy, Brian Allerton had been devastated when he'd lost all his savings. He had spent his last months grieving for the mistake he had made and the truth that he was leaving his daughter virtually penniless. They were fortunate indeed that her father had arranged and settled the expenses of his own funeral as soon as he had appreciated that his condition was incurable. But only their landlord's forbearance had kept a roof over their heads as they had inevitably fallen behind with the rent, and that was a debt that Willow was determined to somehow settle.

'I'll get by,' she parried with a stiff little smile. 'Dad and I were always alone.'

'Let me give you a lift,' Jai urged smoothly.

'No, thank you. Our neighbour, Charlie, is waiting outside for us,' she responded with a rueful smile that threatened to turn into a grimace.

Shelley, proclaiming that *she* would've enjoyed the opportunity to travel in a limousine, hurried after Willow in dismay as she turned on her heel to head out to the ancient car awaiting them beyond the cemetery wall. Willow, not having noticed her friend's disappointment, was all of a silly flutter, and furious with herself, butterflies darting and dancing in her tummy and leaving her breathless as a schoolgirl simply because she had been talking to Jai. Any normal woman would have grown out of such immature behaviour by now, she told herself in mortification. Unfortunately, through living with and caring for her father and lack of opportunity, Willow hadn't yet managed to gain much real-world experience of the opposite sex.

Aside of a couple of summer residential stays, she had always lived at home, having studied garden design both online and through classes at the nearest college. Add in the work experience she had had to complete with a local landscape firm, the need to earn some money simply to eat while they had steadily fallen behind with the rent, the demands of her father's illness and his many medical appointments, and there hadn't been enough hours in the day for Willow to enjoy a social life with her friends as well. Gradually most of her friends had dropped away, but Shelley had been in her life since primary school and had continued to visit, oblivious to Brian Allerton's cool, snobbish attitude to her.

Willow arrived back at the tiny terraced house and she put on the kettle while Shelley set out the drinks and a solitary tray of shortbread. Just as Jai arrived, the vicar anxiously asked Willow where she was planning to move to.

'My sofa!' Shelley revealed with a chuckle. 'I wouldn't leave her stuck.'

'Yes, I'll be fine with Shelley until I can organise something more permanent. I have to move out of here tomorrow. The landlord has been wonderfully understanding but it would be selfish of me to stay here one day longer than necessary,' Willow explained, thinking that, tough though the last weeks had been, she *had* met with kindness in unexpected places.

* * *

A *sofa*? Willow was homeless? Expected to pack up
and move in with a friend the same week that she had
buried her father? Jai was appalled at that news. Honour demanded that he intervene but Willow had been
raised to be proud and independent like her father and
Jai would have to be sensitive in his approach. He was
convinced that out of principle Willow would refuse
his financial assistance.

'Coffee, Jai?' Willow prompted as she handed the
vicar a cup of tea.

'Thank you,' he murmured, following her into the
small kitchen to say, 'Was your father at home at the
end, or had he been moved to a hospice?'

'It was to happen next week,' Willow conceded
tightly, throwing his tall dark figure a rueful appraisal,
her heart giving a sudden thud as she collided involuntarily with ice-blue eyes enhanced by wondrously
dense black lashes. 'But he didn't make it. His heart
gave out.'

In an abrupt movement, she stepped back from him,
disturbingly conscious of his height and the proximity
of more masculinity than she felt able to bear. The very
faint scent of some designer cologne drifted into her
nostrils and she sucked in a sudden steadying breath,
her level of awareness heightening exponentially to add
to her discomfiture. She could feel her face heating,
her knees wobbling as her tension rose even higher.

'What are you planning to do next?' Jai enquired,
shifting his attention hurriedly from her lush pink lips

and the X-rated images bombarding him while he questioned his behaviour.

Yes, she was indisputably beautiful, but he was neither a hormonal schoolboy, nor a sex-starved one, and he was challenged to explain his lack of self-discipline in her radius. She did, however, possess a quality that was exclusively her own, he acknowledged grudgingly, a slow-burning sensual appeal that tugged hard at his senses. It was there in the flicker of her languorous emerald eyes, the slight curve of her generous lower lip, the upward angle of challenge in her chin as she tilted her head back, strawberry-blond hair falling in waves tumbling across her slim shoulders like a swathe of rumpled silk.

'I'll be fine as soon as I find full-time work. These last weeks, I was only able to work part-time hours. Once I've saved up some money, I'll move on and leave Shelley in peace.' She opened the fridge to extract milk and Jai noticed its empty interior.

'You have no food,' he remarked grimly.

'I genuinely haven't had much of an appetite recently,' she confided truthfully. 'And Dad ate next to nothing, so I haven't been cooking.'

She had removed her coat and the simple grey dress she wore hung loose on her slender body. Her cheekbones were sharp, her eyes hollow and his misgivings increased because she looked haunted and frail. Of course, common sense warned him that nursing her father would have sapped her energy and left her at a low ebb. Certainly, she was vulnerable, but she was a young and healthy woman and she would probably be fine. But *probably* wasn't quite good enough to satisfy Jai. He would make his own checks and in the short term he would do what he could to make her future less insecure.

Willow watched Jai leave, a sinking tightening sensation inside her chest as it occurred to her that she would probably never see him again now that her father was gone. Why would she want to see him again anyway? she asked herself irritably. They were only casual acquaintances and calling him a friend would have been pushing that slight bond to the limits.

Shelley departed only under protest.

'Are you sure you're going to be OK alone here tonight?' the brunette pressed, unconvinced. 'I don't feel right leaving you on your own.'

'I'm going to have a bath and go to bed early. I'm exhausted,' Willow told her ruefully. 'But thanks for caring.'

The two women hugged on the doorstep and Shelley went on her way. Willow cleared away the glasses and left the kitchen immaculate before heading upstairs for her bath. First thing in the morning a local dealer was coming to clear the house contents and sell them. There wasn't much left because almost everything that could be sold had been sold off weeks earlier. Even so, her father's beloved books might be worth something, she thought hopefully, her teeth worrying at her lower lip as she anxiously recalled the rent still owing. It would be a weight off her mind if she could clear that debt because their landlord belonged to her church and she suspected that he had felt that he'd had no choice but to allow them to remain as tenants even though the rent was in arrears. The sooner he was reimbursed for his kindness, the happier she would be.

The bell shrilled while she was putting on her pyjamas and she groaned, snatching her robe off the back of the bathroom door to hurry barefoot down the steep stairs and answer the door.

When she saw Jai outside, she froze in disconcertion.

'I brought dinner,' Jai informed her as she hovered, her grip on the robe she was holding closed loosening to reveal the shorts and T-shirt she wore beneath and her long, shapely legs. He drew in a stark little breath as she stepped back and the robe shifted again to expose the tilted peaks of her small breasts. In a split second he was hard as a rock, his body impervious to his belief that he preferred curvier women.

'D-dinner?' she stammered in wonderment as Jai stepped back and two men with a trolley moved out from behind him and, with some difficulty, trundled the unwieldy item through the tiny hall into the cramped living room with its small table and two chairs.

Those wolf-blue eyes of his held her fast, all breathing in suspension.

'My hotel was able to provide us with an evening meal,' he clarified smoothly.

No takeaways for Jai, Willow registered without surprise while she wondered what on earth such an extravagant gesture could have cost him. Of course, he didn't have to count costs, did he? It probably hadn't even occurred to him that requesting a meal for two people that could be transported out of the hotel and served by hotel staff was an extraordinary request. Jai was simply accustomed to asking and always receiving, regardless of expense.

'I'm not dressed,' she said awkwardly, tightening the tie on her robe in an apologetic gesture.

'It doesn't bother me. We should eat now while it's still warm,' Jai responded as the plates were brought to the table, and she settled down opposite him, stiff with unease.

A bottle of wine was uncorked, glasses produced and set by their places.

'I thought you didn't drink,' she commented in surprise as the waiters went back outside again, presumably to wait for them to finish.

'I take wine with my meals,' he explained. 'It's rare for me to drink at any other time.'

His eyes had a ring of stormy grey around the pupils, she noted absently, her throat tightening as her gaze dropped to the fullness of his sensual lower lip and she found herself wondering for the first time ever what Jai would be like in bed. She had been too shy and immature for such thoughts when she was an infatuated teenager and, now that she was an adult, her mental audacity brought a flood of mortified colour to her pale cheeks. Would he be gentle or rough? Fiery or smoothly precise? Her thoughts refused to quit.

'Why did you feel that you had to feed me?' she

asked abruptly in an effort to deflect his attention from her hot cheeks.

'You had no food in the kitchen. You've just lost your father,' Jai parried calmly as he began to eat. 'I didn't like to think of you alone here.'

He had felt sorry for her. She busied herself eating the delicious food, striving not to squirm with mortification that she had impressed him as an object of pity. After all, Jai had been raised by his benevolent father to constantly consider those less fortunate and now ran a huge international charity devoted to good causes. Whether she appreciated the reality or not, looking out for the needs of the vulnerable had to come as naturally to Jai as breathing.

'Why are you moving out of here tomorrow?' he pressed quietly.

Willow snatched in a long steadying breath and then surrendered to the inevitable, reasoning that her father could no longer be humiliated by the truth. She explained about Brian Allerton's unsuccessful stockmarket dealing and the impoverishment that had followed. 'I mean no disrespect,' she completed ruefully, 'but my father was irresponsible with money. He never saved anything—he only had his pension. All his working life he lived in accommodation provided by his employers and most of his meals and bills were also covered and it didn't prepare him very well for retirement living in the normal world.'

'That didn't occur to me, but it should've done,' Jai conceded. 'He was an unworldly man.'

'He was so ashamed of his financial losses,' she

whispered unhappily. 'It made him feel like a failure and that's one of the reasons he wouldn't see people any more.'

'I wish he had found it possible to reach out to me for assistance,' Jai framed heavily, his lean, strong face clenched hard. 'So, you are being forced to sell everything? I will buy his book collection.'

Willow stared across the table at him in shock. *'Seriously?'*

'He was a lifelong book collector, as am I,' Jai pointed out. 'I would purchase his books because I want them and for no other reason. We will agree that tonight and hopefully that will take care of your rent arrears.'

Willow nodded slowly and then frowned. 'Are you sure you want them?'

'I have a library in every one of my homes. Of course, I want them.'

Willow swallowed hard. 'How many homes do you have?' she whispered helplessly.

'More than I want in Chandrapur but it is my duty, as it was my father's, to preserve our heritage properties for future generations,' he countered levelly. 'Now let us move on to other, more important matters. Your father was too proud to ask for my help. I hope you are a little more sensible.'

Reckoning that he was about to embarrass her by offering her further financial help, Willow pushed back her plate and stood up to forestall him. 'I'm going upstairs to get dressed first,' she said tightly.

Jai sipped his wine and signalled the staff to remove the dishes and the trolley. He pictured Willow sliding out of the robe, letting it fall sinuously to her feet before she took off the top and removed the shorts. His imagination went wild while he did so, his body surging with fierce hunger, and he gritted his teeth angrily, struggling to get his thoughts back in his control.

Upstairs, Willow stood immobile, reckoning that Jai taking her father's books could well settle the rent arrears. Did he really want those books? Or was that just a ploy to give her money? And when someone was as poor as she was, could she really afford to worry about what might lie behind his generosity?

Her attention fell on a sapphire ring that lay on the tray on the dressing table. It was her grandmother's engagement ring and it would have to be sold too, even though it was unlikely to be worth very much. Her father had refused to let her sell it while he was still alive, but it had to go now, along with everything else. She could not live with Shelley without paying her way. She would not take advantage of her friend's kindness like that.

She spread a glance round the room, her eyes lingering on the precious childhood items that would also have to be disposed of, things like her worn teddy bear and the silver frame housing a photo of the mother she barely remembered. She couldn't lug boxes of stuff with her to clutter up Shelley's small studio apartment. Be practical, Willow, she scolded herself even as a sob of pain convulsed her throat.

She felt as though her whole life had tumbled into

broken pieces at her feet. Her father was gone. Everything familiar was fading. And at the heart of her grief
lay the inescapable truth that she had *always* been a
serious disappointment to the father she loved. No matter how hard she had tried, no matter how many tutors
her father had engaged to coach her, she had continually failed to reach the academic heights he'd craved
for his only child. She wasn't stupid, she was merely
average, and to a man as clever as her father had been,
a man with a string of Oxford degrees in excellence,
that had been a cruel punishment…

Downstairs, enjoying a second glass of wine, Jai heard
her choked sob. He squared his shoulders and breathed
in deep, deeming it only natural that at some point on
such a day Willow's control would weaken and she
would break down. There had been no visible tears at
the funeral, no emotional conversations afterwards that
he had heard. Throughout, Willow had been polite and
pleasant and more considerate of other people's feelings
than her own. She had attempted to bring an upbeat
note to a depressing situation, had behaved as though
she had already completely accepted the changes that
her father's death would inflict on her.

When the sounds of her distress became more than
he could withstand, Jai abandoned his careful scrutiny
of her father's books—several first editions, he noted
with satisfaction, worthy of the fine price he would
pay for them. He drained his glass and forced himself
to mount the stairs to offer what comfort he could. All
too well did he remember that he himself had had little

support after his father's sudden death from a massive stroke. Thousands had been devastated by the passing of so well-loved a figure and hundreds of concerned relatives had converged on Jai to share his sorrow, but Jai hadn't been close enough to any of those individuals to find solace in their memories. In reality only *he* had known his father on a very personal, private level and only *he* could know the extent of the loss he had sustained.

Willow was lying sobbing on the bed and Jai didn't hesitate. He sat down beside her and lifted her into his arms, reckoning that she weighed barely more than a child and instinctively treating her as such as he patted her slender spine soothingly and struggled to think of what it was best to say. 'Remember the good times with your father,' he urged softly.

'There really *weren't* any…' Willow muttered chokily into his shoulder, startled to find herself in his arms but revelling in that sudden comforting closeness of another human being and no longer feeling alone and adrift. 'I was always a serious disappointment to him.'

With a frown of disbelief, Jai held her back from him to look down into her tear-stained face. The tip of her nose was red, which was surprisingly cute. Her wide green eyes were still welling with tears and oddly defiant, as if daring him to disagree. 'How could that possibly be true?' he challenged.

'I didn't do well enough at school, didn't get into the *right* schools either,' Willow confided shakily, looking into his lean, strong face and those commanding ice-blue eyes that had once haunted her dreams. 'Once I

heard him lying to make excuses for me. He told one
of his colleagues that I'd been ill when I sat my exams
and it *was* a lie… Dad wanted a child he could brag
about, an intellectual child, who passed every exam
with flying colours. I had tutors in every subject and I
still couldn't do well enough to please him!'

Jai was sharply disconcerted by that emotional admission, which revealed a far less agreeable side to
a man he had both liked and respected. 'I'm sure he
didn't mean to make you feel that way,' he began tentatively.

Willow's fingers clenched for support into a broad
shoulder that felt reassuringly solid and strong and she
sucked in a shuddering breath. It was a kind lie, she
conceded, liking him all the more for his compassion.
Even so, she was still keen to say what she had never
had the nerve to say before, because only then, in getting it off her chest, might she start to heal from the low
self-esteem she had long suffered from. 'Yes, Dad did
mean it. He honestly believed that the harder he pushed
me, the more chance he had of getting me to excel! He
didn't even care about which subject it might be in, he
just wanted me to be especially talented at *something*!'

'I'm sorry,' Jai breathed, mesmerised by the glisten-
ing depth of her green eyes and the sheer passion with
which she spoke, not to mention the unexpected pleasure of the slight trusting weight of her lying across
his thighs and the evocative coconut scent of her hair.
The untimely throb of arousal at his groin infuriated
him and he fought it to the last ditch.

'Dad wasn't remotely impressed by my studying

garden history and landscaping. And that's why I'm crying, because I'm sorry too that it's too late to change anything for the better. I had my chance with him, and I blew it!' Willow muttered guiltily, marvelling that she was confiding in Jai, of all people. Jai, who was the cleverest of the clever. It didn't feel real; it felt much more like something she would imagine to comfort herself and, as such, reassuringly unreal and harmless. 'I never once managed to do anything that made Dad proud of me. My small successes were never enough to please him.'

And the sheer honesty of that confession struck Jai on a much deeper level because he wasn't used to a woman who told it as it was and didn't wrap up the ugly truth in a flattering guise. Yet Willow looked back at him, fearless and frank and so, *so* sad, and his hands slid from her back up to her face to cup her cheek-bones, framing those dreamy green eyes that had so much depth and eloquence in her heart-shaped face. She looked impossibly beautiful.

He didn't know what to say to that. He did not want to criticise her father, he did not want to hurt her more, and so he kissed her…didn't even know he was going to do it, didn't even have to think about it because it seemed the utterly, absolutely natural next step in their new understanding.

CHAPTER TWO

THE TASTE OF JAI, of fine wine and a faint minty after-flavour, threw Willow even deeper into the realms of fantasy.

Because fantasy was what it felt like, totally un-threatening fantasy in which Prince Jai Hari Singh, Maharaja of Chandrapur, kissed *her*, Willow Aller-ton, currently unemployed and soon to be homeless into the bargain. Being in his arms didn't feel real but, goodness, it felt *good*, the delve of his tongue into the moist aperture of her mouth sending a shower of fire-works flying through her tummy, awakening a heat that surged enthusiastically into all the cold places in-side her, both comforting and exhilarating all at once.

It was everything she had dreamt she might find in a man's arms and it felt right as well as good, glo-riously right as if she had been waiting her whole life for that moment and was being richly rewarded for her patience. In the dim light from the bedside lamp, Jai's eyes glittered with the pale ice of polar stars, but the ice that powered him burned through her like a rejuve-nating drug, banishing the grief and the guilt and the sadness that had filled her to overflowing. Her fingers drifted up to curve to his strong jawline.

'I like this,' she whispered helplessly.

'I like it too much,' Jai conceded in a driven undertone, lifting her off his lap to lay her down on the bed where her strawberry-blond hair shone in the lamplight, leaning over her to cover her lush mouth with his again.

'How...*too much*?' she pressed.

'I was trying to comfort you, not—'

Featherlight fingers brushed his lips before he could complete that speech. 'Kiss me again,' she urged feverishly. 'It drives everything else out of my head.'

She wanted forgetfulness, not the down-to-earth reminder that such intimacy was untimely. Jai's stern cautious side warred with his libido, his body teeming with pent-up desire. They were alone and free-to-consent adults, not irresponsible teenagers. He gazed down at her and then wrenched at the constriction of his tie with an impatient hand, suddenly giving way to the passionate nature that he usually controlled to what he deemed an acceptable level. The allure of her pink ripe lips was more than he could withstand.

That next explosive kiss sealed Willow's fate, for she could no more have denied the hunger coursing through her than she could have denied her own name. There was also a strong element of wonder in discovering Jai's desire for her. That was thrillingly unexpected and wonderfully heartening, that she could have it within her to mysteriously attract a man well known for his preference for gorgeous models and Bollywood actresses, a gorgeous, incredibly sexy man, who could have had virtually any woman he wanted. It changed her view of herself as the girl next door, low on sex appeal.

'I want you,' Jai ground out against her reddened mouth as he shed his jacket with a lithe twist of his broad shoulders.

Only for a split second did she marvel at that and then all her insecurities surged to the fore because she was skinny and lacked the curves that were so often seen as essential to make a woman appealing to a man. But an internal voice reminded her that Jai wanted her, and she opened her mouth beneath the onslaught of his, let her tongue dart and tangle with his, feeling free, feeling daring for the first time ever.

There was intoxication in the demanding pressure of his mouth on hers and the long fingers sliding below her top to cup a small pouting breast while he toyed with the tender peak. Her body arched without her volition as that sensual caress grew more intense, tiny little arrows of heat darting down into her pelvis to make her extraordinarily aware of that area. Her hips shifted as he pulled her top off, exposing the bare swell of her breasts, bending over her to use his mouth on the plump pink nipples commanding his attention. She tingled all over, goose bumps rising on her arms as he suckled on the distended buds. Between her thighs she felt hot and damp and surprisingly impatient for what came next.

And she knew what came next, of course she did, but her friends' bluntness on the topic had warned her not to expect triumphant bursts of classical music and glimpses of heaven in the final stages. It would be her first time and she was aware that her lack of experience would not affect his enjoyment but that it might well detract from hers. All a matter of luck, a friend had told her sagely.

Dainty fingers spearing through Jai's silky black hair, Willow was revelling in the intimacy of being able to touch him while still marvelling over how fast things could change between two people. Yet she had no doubts and was convinced she would have no regrets either because she had already reached the conclusion that she would rather have Jai as her first lover than anyone else.

Jai dragged off his shirt, returned to kiss her again, his wide, powerful torso hard and muscular against hers. She made a little sound of appreciation deep in her throat even as her hands skated up the hot, smooth skin of his ribcage to discover the muscles that flexed with his every movement. She couldn't think any more beyond that moment because the craving he had unleashed grew stronger with every demanding kiss and utterly controlled her, dulling her brain with an adrenalin boost that was wholly physical.

She writhed under his weight as he traced the hot, swollen centre of her, touching her where she desperately needed to be touched so that her body arched up to him, her heartbeat thundering, her entire being quivering with feverish need. A finger penetrated her slick depths and she gasped, all arousal and captive energy, wanting, *wanting*...

'Is it safe?' Jai husked, wrenching at his trousers to get them out of his path and so overexcited he barely recognised himself in his eagerness but her response, the passage of her tiny hands smoothing over his overheated body, had pushed him to the biting edge of a hunger greater than anything he had ever known before.

Safe? *Safe?* What was he talking about? She wasn't expecting any more visitors; they were alone. Of course, they were safe from interruption or the potential embarrassment of discovery.

'Of course, it is,' Willow muttered.

Jai came down to her with a wolfish smile of relief. 'How very fortunate... I don't think I could stop unless you ordered me to.'

'Not going to,' Willow mumbled, entranced by the fierce black-fringed eyes above hers into absolute stillness.

Jai tipped her legs back and slid sinuously between them, shifting forward in a forceful surge to plunge into her. Eyes closing, Willow felt the burn of his invasion as her untried body stretched to accommodate him and then a sharp stab of pain that jolted her even as he groaned with satisfaction.

'You're so tight,' he breathed appreciatively.

The pain faded and, as it had been less than she had feared, her stress level dropped, and her body relaxed to rise up against his as he withdrew and forged back into her again. Little tendrils of warming sensation gathered in her pelvis and the excitement flooded back, kicking up her heartrate simultaneously so that even breathing became a challenge. She moved against him, hot, damp with perspiration, losing control because the insidious tightening at her core stoked her hunger for him. His fluid insistent rhythm increased, and she felt frantic, pitched to an edge of need that felt unbearable. She lifted to meet his every thrust, need driving her to hasten to the finish line and then, with a swoosh of drowning sensation, the tightness transformed into an explosion of sheer pleasure unlike any she had ever envisaged and she fell back against the pillows, winded and drained, utterly incapable of even twitching a limb.

'That was incredible,' Jai purred like a well-fed jungle cat in her ear, long fingers tracing the relaxed pout of her mouth and trailing down to her shoulder to smooth the skin before he pressed his mouth hungrily to the slope of her neck. 'All I really want now is to do it all over again.'

The tension of discomfiture, of not knowing how to behave, beginning to rise in Willow ebbed. He was happy, *she* was happy, there was nothing to fret about. *Again*, though? She had assumed that men were once-only creatures in need of recovery time, but Jai was already shifting sensually against her again, his renewed arousal brushing her stomach. That he could still want her that much gratified her and she smiled up at him.

That smile full of sunshine disconcerted Jai. His conscience twinged and it took him a moment to recognise the unfamiliar prompting because it was rare for him to do anything that awakened such a reaction. 'You do realise that this...*us*, isn't likely to go anywhere?' he murmured.

'How could it? I'm not an idiot,' Willow parried in

surprise and embarrassment that he felt the need to tell her that they had no future as a couple.

'I didn't want you to get the wrong impression,' Jai told her levelly. 'I only do casual with women and I never raise expectations I have no plans to fulfil.'

'Neither do I,' Willow assured him cheerfully, secure in her conviction that he had not guessed that she was inexperienced and relieved because pride demanded that he believe that he was no big deal in her life. 'I wouldn't want you getting the wrong idea about me either.'

Faint colour edged Jai's high sculpted cheekbones because no woman had ever dared to tell *him* that he was just a casual encounter. 'Of course not.'

'Then we're both content,' Willow concluded, refusing to recognise the little pang of hurt buried deep within her...hurt that she wasn't a little different from other women in his eyes, more special than they were, somehow less of a casual event in his life. He was telling it as it was and she should be grateful for that. This way she knew exactly where she stood and she wouldn't be weaving fantasies around phone calls that would never come or surprise visits. After all, he didn't have her phone number and even she didn't know where she'd eventually be living. She and Jai really *were* ships that passed in the night.

'I want to kiss you again,' Jai breathed with a raw edge to his dark deep voice.

He had only one night with her, and he wanted to make the very most of the best sex he had ever had. He would move on; she would move on. That was the way of the world, yet a stray shard of guilt and regret still pierced him because she was so open with him, so impervious to his wealth and status. He would check that she was all right from a safe distance, stay uninvolved, he promised himself. He supposed there *were* ties between them that he was refusing to acknowledge lest they make him uncomfortable. He had vague memories of her as a child, could remember her shouting his name in excitement at sports events and could recall the way her eyes had once clung to him as though magnetised. But she had grown out of all that. Of course, she had.

'I'm cold,' Willow admitted, snaking back from him to tug the edge of the duvet up and scramble under it with a convulsive shiver.

Jai peeled off his trousers, shaken that in his haste to possess her he had not even fully undressed. Nothing cool or sophisticated about that approach, he told himself ruefully, wondering what it was about her that had made him so downright desperate to have her. For the first time with a woman sexual hunger had overwhelmed him and crowded every other consideration out. It was something more than looks, maybe that unspoiled natural quality of hers, not to mention her disconcerting honesty in assuring him that he was just a one-night stand and that she had no desire to attach strings to him. Jai didn't think he had ever been with a woman who *didn't* want those strings, no matter how coolly she was trying to play the game. He was too rich and too powerful not to inspire women with ambitious hopes and plans.

'Let me warm you,' Jai urged, hauling her into contact with his hot, muscular length, driving out the shivers that had been assailing her.

And it all began again and this time she was wholly free of tension and insecurity and the excitement rose even faster for her. The pleasure stole her mind from her body and left her exhausted. She dropped into sleep, still melded to Jai and still amazed by what had happened between them. At some stage of the night he kissed her awake and made love to her again, slow and sure this time, and achingly sexy. It occurred to her that Jai had made her initiation into sex wondrously sensual but, even then, she knew she ached in bone and muscle and would be wrecked the next morning.

In the dull light of dawn, she was surprised when Jai shook her awake. Dressed in his dark suit and unshaven, he stood over her, studying her with wolf pale blue eyes that burned. He yanked back the duvet, rudely exposing her, and said roughly, 'There's blood all over the sheet! Did I hurt you?'

Willow wanted to die of humiliation where she sat and she snatched at the duvet in desperation and covered up the offending stain, her face burning as hot as a furnace. 'Of course, you didn't. I didn't realise I would bleed the first time,' she whispered shakily. 'I know some women do but somehow I assumed I wouldn't...'

Slow, painful comprehension gripped Jai and rocked him to the depths of his being. He stared down at her in dawning disbelief. 'Are you saying that you were a virgin?'

'Well, it's not something I can lie about now, is it?'

Willow muttered in embarrassment, her chin coming up at a defiant tilt. 'But I don't know why you would think that you have a right to make a production out of something that is my business and nothing to do with you.'

'I would not have chosen to sleep with you had I known I would be your first,' Jai framed fiercely.

'Well, if that was a personal concern of yours, you should've asked in advance,' Willow countered mutinously. 'It's not as if I dragged you into bed!'

'How the hell could I have guessed that you were still a virgin at your age?' Jai demanded.

'I'm only twenty-one. Twenty-two in a few months,' she added stiffly. 'I'm sure I'm not that unusual.'

Jai was not appeased. She was years younger than the women he usually took as lovers, but he hadn't registered that fact the night before, had been too turned on and in too much of a hurry to register anything important, he conceded, angry at his own recklessness.

'Perhaps not, but I assumed you were experienced,' he admitted flatly.

'Well, now you know different. Can we drop this discussion? I want to get washed and dressed,' Willow told him without any expression at all, her small, slight body rigid with wounded pride and resentment in the bed as she continued to hug the duvet to her. 'You know last night was lovely…but now you've ruined it.'

'I'll see you downstairs,' Jai countered grimly.

Willow scrambled out of bed as soon as the door closed behind him and then winced, her body letting her know that such sudden energetic movements would be punished. Just at that moment she did not want that reminder of the intimacy they had shared when Jai, so obviously, regretted it. She pulled out fresh clothing and trekked across to the small shower room. A damp towel lay on the floor and she bent to scoop it up and lift it to her nose. It smelled ever so faintly of Jai while her body smelled even more strongly of him. Shame engulfed her in a drowning flood of regret. Evidently in sleeping with him she had made the wrong decision, but surely it had been *her* decision to make?

Of course, there had been men who'd shown an interest in her in recent years, but none had attracted her enough for her to take matters any further. She had never been much of a fan of crowded clubs or parties and her father's demand that she come home at a reasonable hour had proved to be a restriction that had turned her into a deadbeat companion for a night out. She had taken the easy way out when faced with her father's domineering personality and she had spent her free evenings at home watching television and catching up with Shelley, none of which had given her any experience of how to handle Jai in a temper. But never again would she lie down to be walked over by an angry male, she told herself urgently. From now on she would stand her ground and hold her head high, even if she did have misgivings about her own behaviour.

Jai paced the small living room, feeling the claustrophobic proportions of its confines in growing frustration. Willow was twenty-one years old. Far too young for an experienced man of twenty-nine. Why hadn't he remembered how young she was? What had he been thinking of? The answer was that he *hadn't* been thinking, hadn't stopped to think *once*. Everything that had happened with Willow had happened so fast and had seemed so deceptively natural that he had questioned nothing and now it was too late to change anything.

'Last night was lovely...but now you've ruined it.'

That complaint, towering in its naivety, echoed in his ears and made him flinch. As a rule, he avoided starry-eyed girls and she was one he should definitely have avoided getting more deeply involved with. A woman who'd had a massive crush on him as a teenager? How much had that influenced her willingness to give him her body? He emitted a harsh groan of guilt and self-loathing.

A decent man didn't take advantage of a vulnerable woman! And what had he done?

Within hours of her father's funeral, when she was grieving and distressed, he had pounced like some sort of self-serving seducer. She had deserved more care and consideration than he had given her. Yet he had started out simply trying to offer both care and consideration and could not for the life of him explain how trying to comfort her had ended up with them having sex. She hadn't flirted with him. She hadn't encouraged him but she hadn't said no either. Was that what he was blaming her for? No, he was blaming her for not telling him that she was a virgin, for not giving him that choice...

'I'll have to nip out to get something for breakfast,' Willow told him from the doorway.

Jai swung round, his eyes a pale glittering brilliance in his lean, darkly handsome face. 'I'll eat back at the hotel,' he told her drily. 'Why didn't you tell me that I would be the first? I wouldn't have continued if I'd known. I feel as though I took advantage of your inexperience.'

'It didn't occur to me that I should tell you. I wasn't really thinking. I don't think either of us were. Everything happened so fast,' Willow murmured defensively, wishing he would have given her the time to provide breakfast and sort matters out in a more civilised manner. But Jai, she was beginning to recognise, was much more volatile in nature than she had ever appreciated. Without skipping a beat, he had taken the dialogue they had abandoned in the bedroom straight back up again, which suggested that while she'd showered and dressed, he had merely continued to silently brood and seethe.

'There's nothing we can do about it now,' she pointed out thinly.

Jai looked back at her, scanning her small, slight figure in jeans and a top. Even with the shadows etched below her eyes, she was still lovely, eminently touchable, he reflected as he tensed. Daylight and cold reason had not made her any less appealing. 'No, but it was *wrong*.'

'You don't get the unilateral right to say that to me,' Willow snapped back at him. 'It was *not* wrong for me!'

'You had a crush on me for years,' Jai countered levelly. 'Is that why it wasn't wrong for you?'

Willow's soft mouth opened and closed again as she

gazed back at him in horror, hot, painful colour slowly washing up her cheeks. 'I can't believe you are throwing that in my face.'

'It's relevant to this situation,' Jai breathed sardonically.

'The only person making a situation out of this is you!' Willow condemned, fighting her mortification with all her might. 'Yes, I may have had a crush on you when I was a schoolgirl, but I grew out of that nonsense years ago!'

'I'm not sure I can believe that some sentimental memory didn't influence you.'

'It didn't. Whether you believe that or not is up to you,' Willow replied curtly. 'I'm all grown up now. I don't have any romantic notions about you...and if I had, you'd have killed them stone dead.'

Her continuing refusal to be influenced by his attitude surprised Jai. He was accustomed to those he dealt with coming round to his view and supporting his opinion, but Willow was stubborn enough and independent enough not to budge an inch. Meanwhile those bright green eyes, reminiscent of fresh ferns in the shade, damned him to hell and back.

'Then let's get down to business,' Jai suggested, disconcerting her when she was bracing herself for another round of the same conversation. 'I want to buy your father's books.'

Willow regrouped and contrived to nod. 'I'm content with that.'

'Is the dealer you mentioned last night a book dealer?'

'Nothing so fancy…why?'

'At least two of the books are quite valuable first editions and you could do better auctioning them,' Jai warned.

'I haven't time for that. I didn't know any of them would be worth anything,' she completed stiffly.

'I will buy them at a fair price but you may wish to take further advice.'

Willow groaned out loud. 'Oh, Jai… I don't think you're likely to cheat me!'

'Very well. The books will be packed for you and collected later this morning and I will pay you in cash as that may be more convenient for you right now,' Jai murmured levelly. 'Will you allow me to pay for you to stay in a hotel until you get on your feet again?'

'Would you be offering me that option if you hadn't slept with me last night?' Willow asked suspiciously.

His eyes clashed with her sceptical appraisal. 'Yes.'

'No. Thanks, but no,' Willow told him without hesitation. 'I don't mind staying with Shelley for a while.'

'Will you accept any further assistance from me?' Jai enquired.

'I'd prefer not to,' Willow responded truthfully.

'Life isn't always that straightforward,' Jai replied wryly as he settled his business card on the table. 'If at any time you need help, you can depend on me to deliver it, no strings attached. Phone me if you are in need.'

'And why would you make me an offer like that?' Willow demanded shortly.

'I wish you well,' Jai admitted levelly.

Willow spun around in a rather ungainly circle and went to open the front door. 'I'll get by fine without you,' she told him with a defiantly bright smile. 'But thanks for caring.'

And on that hollow note, Jai departed. As soon as he was gone, Willow felt empty, exhausted and horribly hurt. She would never see him again except in newspapers or magazines at some glamorous or important event, but that was for the best because Jai had rejected her on every level. He had switched back to treating her like a distant acquaintance, whom he was willing to help in times of trouble, smoothly distancing himself from their brief intimacy.

He not only regretted sleeping with her, but also suspected that she had slept with him because she had once been infatuated with him. He had made mincemeat out of her pride and humiliated her.

Goodbye, Jai, she thought numbly. *Goodbye and good riddance!*

CHAPTER THREE

WILLOW SAT ON the side of the bath and waited for the wand to give her a result while Shelley sidled round the door, too impatient to wait outside. 'Well?' she pressed excitedly.

'Another thirty seconds,' Willow muttered wearily.

'I love babies.' Shelley sighed dreamily.

'So do I… I just thought it would be years before I had one. And maybe it will be,' Willow contended, trying not to be too pessimistic.

After all, skipping a period wasn't always a sign of pregnancy even in a woman with a regular cycle. But then there was also the soreness of her breasts, the occasional light-headed sensation and her sudden sensitivity to smells and tastes that had never bothered her before. Yet Willow still couldn't credit that an unplanned pregnancy could happen to her. Surely Jai had used condoms? She hadn't thought to check or ask him, had simply not even considered the danger of conception, which had been exceedingly foolish when it was she who would fall pregnant if anything went amiss. Maybe a condom had failed, maybe during the night he had forgotten to use one, maybe she was just one of the unfortunate few who conceived regardless of the contraception used.

'Congratulations!' Shelley carolled irrepressibly and grabbed her into an enthusiastic hug. 'You're pregnant.'

Willow paled. 'Are you sure?' she gasped, peering down at the wand for herself, and there it was: the line for a positive result.

'You'll have to go to the doctor ASAP,' Shelley warned her. 'I mean…you must be at least eight weeks along now and you should be taking vitamins and stuff.'

In no hurry to approach a doctor for confirmation, Willow wandered back out to the very comfortable sofa she slept on and sank heavily down. *Pregnant!* Just when her life was slowly beginning to settle again into a new routine, fate had thrown her onto a roller coaster of a ride that would destroy all her self-improvement plans. Of course, there were options other than keeping the baby to raise, she reminded herself doggedly, even while she knew that neither termination nor adoption had any appeal for her.

But how on earth would she manage? Currently she was waitressing in the bar that Shelley managed. The tips were good, particularly at weekends, and in another couple of months she would have saved up enough for a deposit for a little place of her own. After making that move, she had planned to polish up her CV and start trying to find work in the landscaping field that would pay enough for her to live on. She had her qualification now and even the most junior position would be a good start to a decent career and perhaps, ultimately, her own business. Throw a baby into the midst of those plans, however, and it blew them all to smithereens!

And yet the prospect of having Jai's baby was already beginning to warm her at some deep level, although she felt guilty about feeling that way. He mightn't have wanted her, but he couldn't prevent her from having his child and she did love babies, and the thought of one of her own pleased and frightened her in equal parts. She didn't have a single relative left alive, but her baby could be the foundation of a new family, she reflected lovingly.

She had lain awake on the sofa many nights reliving that night with Jai, wishing she didn't feel like such an immature idiot for having slept with him in the first place and wishing that she didn't miss him now that he was gone again. She wasn't kidding herself that she was in love with him or anything like that, but she could not deny that Jai, the Maharaja of Chandrapur, had always fascinated her and that he had attracted her more powerfully than anyone else ever had. Those were the facts and she tried not to dress them up. She felt that she should've called a halt to their intimacy, but she hadn't and the coolness of his departure had been her punishment. He had hurt her, but she tried not to dwell on those wounded feelings because what would be the point in indulging herself in such sad thoughts?

'I'll help you every step of the way,' Shelley told her, sitting down beside her to grip her hand comfortingly. 'We'll get through it together…and at least you won't have to worry about money, not with the father being rich.'

'I'm *not* going to tell Jai!' Willow exclaimed in dismay. 'He didn't want me so he's even less likely to want a baby with me!'

'It takes two to tango.'

'And one to have common sense, and neither of us had any that night.' Willow sighed and then groaned out loud. 'Why should I make him suffer too? It would be so humiliating as well. I can't face that on top of everything else.'

Shelley's freckled face and bright blue eyes were troubled below her mop of brown curls. 'Well, then, what are you planning to do?'

'I don't want to tell Jai… To be frank, I don't want anything more to do with him,' Willow admitted unhappily. 'I'll work this out without bothering him for help. Somehow I'll work it out even if it means living on welfare benefits to survive.'

Two weeks later, while Willow was at work, Shelley had to deal with the surprise of Jai himself turning up on the doorstep asking after Willow because he hadn't heard from her. Aware that her friend wanted no further contact with him, Shelley lied and said that Willow had moved out and hadn't yet sent her a forwarding address. Jai left his mobile number with her.

Thirteen months later, the private investigation agency Jai had hired to find Willow finally tracked her down and, in the midst of his working day in his London office, Jai immediately settled down with a sense of urgency to flick open the ominously slim file.

The first fact he learned was that the investigation team had only contrived to find Willow by covertly watching and following her friend, Shelley. Jai was disconcerted to learn that Willow's friend had lied to him when he had only had Willow's best interests in mind. He would have been satisfied with the assurance that she was safe and well. He assumed that Willow had confided in her friend and it was conceivable that that night he had spent with her had muddied the water in her friend's eyes and made his motivations seem more questionable, he conceded grudgingly.

After all, what could Willow possibly have to hide from him? Why would she get lost and neglect to get in touch with him when he had been so specific on that point? Had he offended her to such an extent?

He knew he had not been tactful. He had been too outspoken. He had embarrassed her, hurt her, he recalled unhappily. But he had been very shocked to realise that he had taken advantage of her innocence and his self-loathing on that score had still to fade, as had his recollections of that night. It seemed even worse to him that the memories of her still remained so fresh. Averse as he now was to any kind of casual encounter, he had not been with a woman since then. He had broken his own code of honour unforgettably with Willow and had buried himself in work while struggling to come to terms with that depressing truth.

Her disappearance and continuing silence had seriously worried him and had only made him even more determined to locate her.

The bald facts of what came next in the file shook Jai to his essentially conservative core and he was instantly grateful that he had refused to give up on his search for her because she was in trouble. Willow had had a child and was now living in a hostel for the homeless, waiting for the local council to find her more suitable accommodation. A *child*? How was that possible in so short a time frame? Had she turned to some other man for comfort after he had left her? He focussed back on the printed page and his blood ran cold in his veins when he saw the birthdate of the child and then, startlingly, his own middle *name*... Hari.

Far across London, Willow knelt on the floorboards while Hari sat on his little blanket and mouthed the plastic ball he was playing with. Everything went into his mouth and she had to watch him like a hawk. He was almost seven months old and, although he couldn't yet crawl, he had discovered that he could get around very nicely just by rolling over and over so that he could get his little chubby hands on anything that attracted his attention. And *everything* attracted Hari's attention, which meant that she needed eyes in the back of her head to keep him safe.

She had not known that it was possible to love anyone as much as she loved Hari. Her love for the father she had continually failed to please paled in comparison. From the moment Hari had arrived he had become her world and she was painfully conscious that as a mother she had nothing to offer in material terms. Sadly, moving into the hostel had been a necessity to get on the housing list. Shelley hadn't wanted them to move out of her apartment but staying any longer hadn't been an option in the chaos that she and Hari had brought to her friend's life. So she might be, for the moment, a less than stellar mother to her son, but in time she would get better and provide him with a decent home where their life would improve.

The knock that sounded on the door made her jump and she peered through the peephole to identify another resident, the woman from the room next to hers, before she undid the lock.

'Reception asked me to tell you that you have a visitor waiting down in the basement,' the woman told her.

Willow suppressed a sigh and bundled Hari, his blanket and a couple of toys up into her arms. Visitors weren't allowed to enter the rooms in the hostel, but the basement was available for necessary meetings with housing officials, social workers and counsellors. Willow hadn't been expecting anyone, but the number of people now involved in checking up on her and Hari and asking her to fill in forms seemed never-ending.

My goodness, maybe somewhere had finally been found for her and Hari to live, she thought optimistically as she walked down the steps to the basement to enter a large grey-painted room furnished mainly with small tables and chairs, few of which were occupied. She hovered in the doorway and then froze when she saw Jai standing by the barred window that overlooked a dark alleyway.

Jai looked so incredibly out of place against such a backdrop that she could not quite believe her eyes and she blinked rapidly. Clad in a black pinstriped suit teamed with a white shirt and gold tie, he looked incredibly intimidating. But he also looked impossibly exclusive and gorgeous with that suit sharply tailored to a perfect fit over his tall, powerful frame. The stark lighting above, which flattered no one, somehow still contrived to flatter Jai, enhancing the golden glow of his skin and the blue-black luxuriance of his hair and accentuating the proud sculpted lines and hollows of his superb bone structure. He was stunning as he stood there, absolutely stunning, his light eyes glittering in his lean, strong face, and she swallowed convulsively, wondering how he had found her, what he wanted with her and how on earth she could possibly hide Hari from him when she was holding him in her arms.

Jai noticed Willow at almost the same moment, lodged across the room, a tiny frail figure dressed in jeans and an oversized sweater, against which she held a child. And he stared at the child in her arms with helpless intensity and, even at that distance, he recognised his son in the baby's olive-toned skin and black hair. His *son*... Jai could not work out how that was possible unless Willow had lied to him about it being safe for them to make love without him taking additional precautions. But just at that moment the *how* seemed less significant than the overpowering and breathtaking sense of recognition that gripped him when he glimpsed his infant son for the first time.

Willow walked towards him and he strode forward to greet her, noticing that she was struggling to carry the child along with the other things she held. Without hesitation, Jai extended his hands and lifted the baby right out of her arms.

Hari chortled and smiled up at him. Evidently, he was a happy baby, who delighted in new faces. Jai looked into eyes as pale a blue as his own, his sole inheritance from his British mother, and knew then without a shadow of doubt that, hard as he found it to credit, this child *had* to be *his* son, *his* child, *his* responsibility. He moved away again, and Willow hovered, feeling entirely surplus to requirements, until one of the four bodyguards seated at a nearby table surged forward to pull out chairs at another table and Jai took a seat with Hari carefully cradled in his arms.

Willow dropped into the seat beside Jai's and Hari grinned at her while he tugged at Jai's tie. 'How did you find me?' she whispered.

'A private detective agency. They've been trying to trace you for months,' Jai imparted, his wide, sensual mouth compressing at that unfortunate fact. 'I only wish I'd found you sooner.'

'I can't imagine why you've been trying to find me,' she confided.

'But isn't it fortunate that I did?' Jai traded smoothly as he stroked a gentle finger through the spill of Hari's black hair. 'You must realise that you cannot stay in such a place with my son.'

Paper pale at that quiet declaration, Willow gazed

back at him. '*Your*...son?' she almost whispered, shaken by the certainty with which he made that claim.

'He is my image. Who else's son could he be?' Jai parried very drily as if daring her to disagree or throw doubt on the question of his child's parentage. 'And as this is not somewhere that we can talk freely, I would like you to go back to your room right now and pack up all your belongings to leave.'

'I can't do that. I'm here waiting to get a place on a council housing list and if I leave, I'll lose my place in the queue,' she protested in a low intent voice.

Jai settled Hari more securely on his lap. 'Either you do as I ask...*or* I will seek an emergency court order to take immediate custody of Hari as he is at risk in such an environment. That is unacceptable. Be warned that I hold diplomatic status in the UK and the authorities will act quickly on my behalf if I lodge a complaint on behalf of my heir. The usual laws do not apply to diplomats.'

In sheer shock at that menacing information, Willow went rigid, her blood chilling in her veins. 'You're threatening me with...legal action?' she gasped in astonishment, barely able to believe her ears. *'Already?'*

Jai sent her an inhumanly cool and calm appraisal, the dark strength of his resolve palpable. 'I will do what I must to put right what you have got wrong...'

Stabbed to the heart by that spontaneously offered opinion, Willow bent her head. *No judgement here*, she thought sarcastically, but she was so deep in shock that Jai would actually threaten her with losing custody of her child that she didn't even know what to say back to him. She didn't want to take the risk of being too frank, didn't want to row in public, didn't want to make a bad situation worse by speaking without careful forethought. She sensed that the Jai she had thought she knew to some degree was not the Jai she was currently dealing with. This was Jai being ruthless and calculating and brutally confrontational, which, logic warned her, had to be qualities he had acquired to rise so high and so fast in the business world. Unluckily for her, it was not a side of him she had seen before or had had to deal with.

'We will not argue here in a public place,' Jai informed her in the same very polite tone. 'We will both ensure that the needs of our child remain our first consideration.'

'Of course, but—'

'No, there will be no qualification of that statement,' Jai interposed levelly. 'Now, please pack so that we can leave this place behind us.'

Willow leapt upright and reached down for Hari.

'I will look after him while you pack,' Jai spelt out as he too stood up, towering over her in her flat heels with Hari still clasped in his arms.

'You could walk away with him while I'm upstairs,' Willow pointed out shakily, not an ounce of colour in her taut face as she looked up at him fearfully.

'I give you my word of honour that I will not do that. You are his mother and my son needs his mother,' Jai murmured soft and low, the hardness of his expression softening a little. 'Although I grew up without mine, it would never be my choice to put my son in the same position.'

Willow backed off a step, still uncertain of what she should do. 'If I pack, where are you taking us to? A hotel?'

'Of course not. To my home here in London,' Jai proffered as Hari tugged cheerfully at his hair. 'I have already had rooms prepared for your arrival.'

'You took a lot for granted,' Willow remarked helplessly.

'In this situation, I can afford to do so,' Jai told her without remorse.

And with that ringing indictment of her ability to raise their child alone, Willow headed upstairs. There wasn't much for her to pack. She gathered up Hari's bottles and solid food and put them into the baby bag Shelley had bought her. She settled the bin bags filled with their clothing and Hari's toys into the battered stroller, donned her duffle coat and wheeled the stroller to the top of the stairs before stooping to lift it and battle to carry it downstairs. Halfway down the second flight one of Jai's bodyguards met her and lifted it out of her arms.

'Is that the lot?' Jai asked, turning from the reception desk, Hari tucked comfortably under one arm.

'Yes. I left stuff with Shelley.'

'There's a form for you to fill in. I put in the forwarding address,' Jai advanced.

Willow was surprised that there was only one form because before she had even moved into the hostel, she'd had to fill out a thirty-page document. She signed

her name at the foot, briefly scanning the address Jai
had filled in, raising a brow at the exclusivity of the
area. Mayfair, no less. Five minutes later, she was
climbing into a limousine for the first time in her life,
breathless at the unknown ahead of her.

Jai strapped Hari into the car seat awaiting him.

'When did you learn to be so comfortable around
babies?' Willow asked tautly.

'There are many children in my extended family.
High days and holidays, they visit,' Jai told her. 'I was
a lonely only child. Hari will never suffer from a lack
of company.'

On her smoothly upholstered leather seat, Willow
tensed, registering that Jai was already talking about
her son visiting India. She supposed that was natural,
and an expectation he would obviously have. Even so
the prospect of her baby boy being so far away from
her totally unnerved her, and she couldn't help feeling
overwhelmed, most especially when Jai had already
threatened her with legal action.

'Now for the question that taxes my patience the
most,' Jai breathed, his nostrils flaring with annoyance, his light eyes throwing a laser-bright challenge.
'Why would you move into a homeless shelter rather
than ask me for help?'

Willow froze. 'There's nothing wrong with living
in a homeless shelter. They're there for when people
are desperate.'

'But you weren't desperate, not really. You could've
turned to me at any time. And don't try to misinter-
pret my question. I probably know a great deal more

than you about the individuals who use such shelters. Some are those who have fallen on hard times through no fault of their own, others have mental health issues or are drug addicts or ex-cons. None of those elements make a homeless shelter safe or acceptable for a child,' Jai completed harshly.

'Nonetheless there are quite a few children living in them!' Willow shot back at him stubbornly.

'Why didn't you contact me?' Jai demanded, out of all patience with her reluctance to answer his original question. He had been denied all knowledge of his son for more than six months and that enraged him, but he was grimly aware that this was not the right time to reveal his deep anger, particularly not if he wanted her to tell him the truth.

Willow swallowed convulsively. 'I didn't think you'd want to know. It was my problem. He's my child.' She hesitated. 'When I was pregnant, I was afraid that you would want me to have a termination and I didn't want to be put in that position. I didn't want to feel guilty for wanting to have my own child. It was easier to get on with it on my own and I managed fine while I was pregnant and still able to work.'

'I would never have asked you to have a termination. Hari is my child too,' Jai retorted crisply. 'I would have ensured that you had somewhere decent to live and I would have supported you.'

Willow sighed. 'Well, it's too late now to be arguing about it.'

Jai's eyes flashed at that assurance and he struggled to repress his anger, because her misplaced pride and lack of faith in him had ensured that his son had endured living conditions that were far less than his due.

'So, how *did* you manage to conceive when you told me it would be safe for us to have sex?' he asked next, battening down his volatile responses to concentrate on the basic facts.

Willow could feel her whole face heating up and she glanced across at Jai with noticeable reluctance. *Safe* to have sex? That was what he had meant that night? She shook her head slowly as clarity spilled through her brain and she squirmed in retrospect over her own stupidity. 'I misunderstood. When you asked if it was safe, I assumed that you were asking if we would be interrupted…if I was expecting anyone,' she admitted stiffly, her cheeks only burning more fierily at the look of incredulity that flared in his ice-blue eyes. 'I'm sorry. I wasn't thinking about contraception. That danger honestly didn't cross my mind.'

And the whole mystery of how she had become pregnant was clarified there and then, Jai conceded in a kind of wonderment. She had misunderstood him, and he had been too hot for her to reflect on the risk that he had never taken with any other woman. They had had unprotected sex several times because the young woman he had slept with had still had the mentality of a guilty, self-conscious teenager, determined to hide her sex life from the critical grown-ups. He supposed then that he had got exactly what he deserved for not considering questioning the level of her sexual experience.

Or was he being very naive in accepting that explanation? Was it, indeed, possible that Willow had *wanted* to become pregnant by a rich man? A rich man and a baby by him could secure a woman's comfort for a comfortable twenty years. In one calculating move, such a pregnancy would have solved all Willow's financial problems. And not contacting him and keeping him out of the picture until the child was safely born could well have been part of the same gold-digging scheme to set him up and profit from her fertility in the future.

Jai frowned, ice-blue eyes, enhanced by velvety black lashes, turning glacier cool as he surveyed her. She looked tired and tense and hadn't made any effort to do herself up for his benefit, but then, why would she bother when she was now the mother of his son and already in an unassailable position in his life?

At the same time, he had made the first move that night after the funeral, at least, he *thought* he had. In truth, all he recalled was the heady taste of her lips, not *how* he had arrived at that point. The pulse at his groin kicked up a storm at that recollection, reminding him that he was still hungry for her. His jaw clenched. He would soon find out if she was mercenary and, really, it didn't matter a damn, did it? After all, whatever she was, whoever she turned out to be, he *had* to marry her for his son's sake…

CHAPTER FOUR

WILLOW WALKED INTO the Mayfair town house and was plunged straight into palatial contemporary décor that was breathtakingly large and impressive.

'Come this way,' Jai instructed, heading straight for the elegant staircase with Hari still clasped to his powerful chest. 'My former *ayah*, Shanaya, arrived this morning. She has a full complement of staff with her and they will look after Hari while we talk.'

'Ayah?' Willow questioned with frowning eyes.

'She was my nursemaid…nanny—whatever you want to call it,' Jai explained. 'She is a kind and gentle woman. You need have no fear for our son's welfare while he is with her.'

Willow didn't want to hand over care of Hari to anyone, no matter who they were, particularly when she could not imagine that she and Jai had much to discuss. He had threatened her to make her vacate the homeless shelter and he doubtless planned to press his advantage by making her accept his financial support. Using the threat of legal action straight away had warned her that he would not listen to her protests. His bottom line, his closing argument would always zero in on what was best for Hari. And how could she argue with that sterling rule when she wanted the same thing?

Therefore, bearing in mind that she did not expect to be spending very long in Jai's luxurious town house, she pinned a pleasant smile to her face to greet the grey-haired older woman awaiting her in a room already furnished as a nursery. She had three smiling younger women by her side, all of them dressed in brightly coloured saris, and they welcomed Hari with a sort of awed reverence that disconcerted Willow. Hari, however, did love to be admired and he beamed at all of them.

'His Royal Highness is very confident,' Shanaya remarked approvingly in hesitant English.

'His Royal Highness?' Willow hissed in disbelief as Jai whisked her back out of the room again.

'Hari is my official heir, known as the Yuvaraja in our language. He is a very important child to my family and to our staff,' Jai explained, ushering her downstairs and into a very traditional library lined with books and pictures and what looked like a wall of official awards. 'This was my father's room and, although I have certainly not kept it like a shrine, I did not have it updated after his death like the rest of the house. I still like to remember him seated here at his desk or drowsing by the fireside with his nose in a book.'

Willow had faded memories of the older man on his visits to the boarding school, which he had once attended himself. She also recalled him taking tea once in their small home with her father, the correctness of his spoken English, the warmth of his smile and the tiny brocade box filled with sweets that he had dug out of his pocket for her.

'It means a great deal to me that you named our son after me,' Jai admitted.

Willow went pink. 'I wanted to acknowledge his background.'

'Hari has been a family name for generations. My father would have rejoiced in our son's existence.'

'In these circumstances?' Willow said uncomfortably. 'I hardly think so.'

'I assume you are referring to Hari's illegitimate birth,' Jai breathed in a raw undertone. 'That problem will vanish as soon as we marry.'

Willow's knees shook under her and she had to straighten her back to stay upright. Her incredulous gaze locked to his lean, dark features and the flaring brilliance of his pale gaze. 'I beg your pardon?' she murmured with a frown. 'As soon as we...*marry*?'

'Hari's birth will be legitimised by our marriage. He cannot take his place as my heir *without* us getting married,' Jai countered levelly. 'I want us to get married as quickly as it can be arranged.'

Willow gave up the battle with her wobbly knees and dropped heavily into a comfortable armchair beside the Georgian fireplace. Slowly she shook her head. 'Jai...men and women don't get married any more simply because a child has been born.'

'Perhaps not, but Hari can only claim his legal right to follow me if we are man and wife. It may seem old-fashioned to you, but it is the law and it is unlikely to be changed. My inheritance, which will one day become his, is safeguarded by strict rules. My business interests I can leave to anyone I want, but my heritage, the properties and land involved and the charitable foundation started up by my grandfather can only be bestowed on the firstborn child, whose parents must be married for him to inherit,' Jai outlined grimly.

Disconcerted by that information, Willow snatched in a deep jagged breath. 'But you can't *want* to marry me?'

'I don't want to marry anyone right now,' Jai admitted wryly.

Willow stiffened, reckoning that she had just received her answer about how best to treat his proposition. His suggestion that they should marry was sheer madness, she reasoned in astonishment. Her entire attention was now welded to him. A blue-black shadow of stubble was beginning to accentuate his wide mobile mouth and a tiny little shiver ran through her, her breasts tightening and peaking below her sweater, those little sensations arrowing down into her pelvis to awaken a hot, tense, damp feeling between her thighs. She thrust her spine rigidly into the embrace of the chair back, furious with herself but breathless and unable to drag her attention from the wild dark beauty of Jai as he paced over to the desk, his stunning eyes glittering over her with an intensity she could *feel* and which mesmerised her.

'Obviously you don't *want* to marry me,' she remarked in a brittle undertone.

'Aside of my little flirtation with the idea of marriage when I was twenty-one, I have always hoped to retain my freedom for as long as possible,' Jai confessed with a twist of his shapely mouth as he studied her, appreciating the elegant delicacy of her tiny figure in the overly large chair, but not appreciating the way his attention instinctively lingered on the swell of her breasts below the sweater and the slender stretch of her denim-clad thighs. 'I planned to marry in my forties, while my father was even older when he took the plunge. Hari's birth, however, has changed everything. I cannot deny Hari his right to enjoy the same history and privileges that I had.'

'I understand that, *but*—' she began emotively.

'No matter what you say, it will still come down to the same conclusion. Our son *needs* his parents to be married,' Jai delivered with biting finality. 'Only imagine his angry bitterness if some day he has to watch another man inherit what should have been his…because *if* you refuse to marry me, I will inevitably marry another woman and have children with her. It is my duty to carry on our family name and a second son born from that marriage will become my heir instead.'

The content of that last little speech shook Willow rigid because she realised that she didn't want to imagine *any* of those events taking place…*not* Jai marrying someone else and fathering children by her and certainly *not* her son hurt by being nudged out of what could have been his rightful place. It was a distressing picture, but Jai was being realistic when he forced her to look at it. Sooner or later, it seemed, he had to

marry and have a child and why shouldn't his firstborn
son benefit from their marriage?

'You're ready to bite the bullet because Hari and
I would be the practical option?' Willow suggested
tightly.

'Those are not the words I would have used,' Jai
chided. 'This may not be what I once innocently
planned, but Hari is here now and, as his parents,
shouldn't we do what we can to make amends for his
current status?'

Willow stared stonily at the rug on the floor, because it was an unanswerable question. Of course, Hari
should be put first, not left to reap the disadvantages
his careless parents had left him facing. Would her son
even want to follow in his father's footsteps to eventually become the Maharaja of Chandrapur? She reckoned that, as an adult, her son would want that choice
and wouldn't wish to be denied it over something as
arbitrary as the accident of his birth. She swallowed
hard. 'Right, so if I agree to marry you, what sort of
marriage would it be?'

'A normal one,' Jai murmured, soft and low, a little of
his tension dissipating as he grasped that she was willing to proceed. 'Of course, if we are unhappy together
we can separate and divorce but we will both make a
big effort for Hari's sake because two parents raising
him together must surely be better than only one.'

Of course, neither of them knew what it would be
like to grow up with two parents, Willow conceded.
But she had seen that dynamic in the homes of her
friends, parents pulling and working together to look

after their families. She had also visited the homes of single-parent families and had only noted there that the parent carried a much heavier burden in doing it all alone. Would she and Jai be able to provide Hari with a secure and happy home? Jai didn't love her, while she was still insanely attracted to him, she acknowledged uneasily, lifting her head to collide with the frosty glitter of his eyes, feeling the almost painful clench of internal muscles deep down inside.

'Do you think we could do it?' she whispered.

'I think we *must* for his benefit,' Jai countered levelly. 'And as soon as possible. Are we agreed?'

Almost mesmerised by the blaze of his full attention, Willow nodded very slowly. 'Yes.'

She was going to marry Jai and the concept was surreal: Jai the playboy with his polo ponies and trophies, his heritage palaces, his long backstory of glamorous and impossibly beautiful former lovers. Yet she was so ordinary, so unexciting in comparison, she thought in dismay. Even worse, he didn't want to marry *her* and he had admitted it.

But that honesty of his was good, she told herself fiercely. Should she be ashamed of the reality that the very idea of being freed from all her financial worries was a relief? Did that mean that she was greedy? Or simply that she was tired of feeling like an inadequate mother? Without Jai, she had found it impossible to give Hari the comfort and security he deserved. With Jai, everything would be different. In addition, she would have far more rights over her own son if she married Jai. In terms of custody they would be equal partners then, she reasoned, and no matter what happened between her and Jai she would have very little reason to fear losing access to her little boy.

What would it be like, though, being married to a man who didn't love or really want her? Jai hadn't even wanted her enough to ask to *see* her again, she reminded herself doggedly, reeling from the toxic bite of that fact. Yes, sure, he had tried to check up on her a couple of months afterwards, she conceded grudgingly, but by that stage only an ingrained sense of responsibility towards Brian Allerton's daughter had been driving him, nothing more personal.

Of course, she didn't love him either, she reminded herself doggedly. All the same, she couldn't take her eyes off Jai when he was in the same room and her heart hammered and her mouth ran dry every time he looked at her. If she was honest with herself, she was sort of fascinated by Jai, always hungry to know more about him and work out what made him tick. He had accepted Hari without question and moved them straight into his home.

Yes, he had threatened her with legal action but only on Hari's behalf, not to take her son away from her, indeed only, it seemed, to pressure her into leaving the hostel and agreeing to marry him. With shocking shrewdness, he had accomplished that objective within hours, she registered in belated dismay. Yet he had done it even though at heart he didn't *want* to marry her! But that was the mystery that was Jai. He was volatile and emotional and very hot-blooded, yet he was still apparently willing to settle for a practical marriage...

* * *

Jai watched Willow walk away from him to return to their son. Evidently, he was about to acquire a wife. He gritted his teeth, for being forced to marry to bring Hari officially into the family was even less attractive than increasing age prompting him to the challenge. Marriage was difficult, as his parents' failure to surmount their differences proved. But he knew in his heart that he *owed* Willow a wedding ring. It *was* that simple, because what he had done with her broke every principle he had been raised to respect: he had greedily and irresponsibly taken an innocent woman and slept with her when she was vulnerable, and even in the act he had not protected her as he should've done.

He found it hard, though, to forgive her for hiding Hari from him and denying him precious moments of his son's babyhood that would never be repeated. But he had to set that anger aside, he reminded himself fiercely, shelve the pointless regrets that he could have been such an idiot and concentrate instead on the present. He should be relieved that she still attracted him, even if he resented the constant disturbing pull of her understated sensuality. He didn't know how she still had that effect on him, and he wasn't planning to explore it again, not until they were safely, decently married.

'You look a treat,' Shelley said, patting Willow's hand as they travelled in a limousine to the civil ceremony at the register office.

Willow shivered, scolding herself for having picked

a wedding dress unsuited to autumn, but then she had been living on a dizzy merry-go-round of change and struggling to adapt throughout the past week in Jai's London home. Agreeing to marry Jai had been like jumping on an express train that hurtled along at breakneck speed. He had pointed out that getting married in Chandrapur would entail a solid week of festivities while getting married *discreetly* in London would only require an hour and a couple of witnesses.

She had spent most of the week with Hari because Jai had been busy working. She had, however, seen Jai at mealtimes and had tripped over him in the nursery more than once. Surrounded by a bevy of admiring nursemaids, Jai was attempting to get to know his son and Hari was thriving on the amount of attention he was receiving. Willow could already see that the biggest problem of her son's new lifestyle would be ensuring that Hari did not grow up into an over-indulged young man, unacquainted with the word 'no.'

Her wedding gown left her arms and throat bare. With cap sleeves, a crystal-beaded corset top and a sparkly tulle skirt, it was a fairy-tale dress and very bridal. In retrospect, Willow was embarrassed about the choice she had made and worried that it was too excessive for the occasion. But who knew if she would ever get married again? And when she was faced with choosing her one and possibly *only* wedding dress, she had gone with her heart.

Luckily, she had had Shelley's support when a stylist had arrived at the house and informed her that she had been instructed to provide Willow with a whole

new wardrobe. A huge wardrobe of clothes tailored
to fit Willow had been delivered within forty-eight
hours, outfits chosen to shine at any possible occasion and many of the options decidedly grand. Hari
now also rejoiced in many changes of exclusive baby
clothing. Jai, Willow reckoned ruefully, was rewriting
their history and redesigning his bride into a far more
fashionable and exclusive version of herself. Did he
appreciate that that determination to improve her appearance only revealed that he had previously found
her unpolished and gauche?

She walked into the anteroom with Shelley by her
side. Jai approached her with his best friend, Sher,
and performed an introduction. Sher was the Nizam
of Tharistan and he and Jai had been childhood play-
mates. Sher was tall, black-haired and as sleekly handsome as a Bollywood movie star. Beside her, she felt
Shelley breathe in deep and slow as though she was
bracing herself and she almost laughed at her friend's
susceptibility to a good-looking man until it occurred
to her that she was even more susceptible to Jai.

'You chose a beautiful dress,' Jai murmured. 'It will
look most appropriate in the photographs.'

'What photographs?' she asked with a frown.

'I have organised a photographer to record the occasion. Brides and grooms always want to capture such
precious memories on film, I believe,' he advanced
calmly. 'A photo will be released to the local media
in Chandrapur and some day Hari may wish to look
at them.'

Willow grasped that he had wanted her to look suitably bridal in the photographs and understood that there was nothing personal in the compliment. He was simply keen for her to visibly fit the bridal role so that the haste that had prompted their marriage was less obvious.

They entered the room where the ceremony was to take place. Willow focussed on a rather tired-looking display of flowers in a cheap vase and tensed as Jai threaded the wedding ring onto her finger. She turned in the circle of his arms, thinking numbly, *I am married to Jai now*, but it didn't feel remotely real. It felt like a fevered dream, much as that night in his arms had felt.

It felt a little more real when she shivered on the steps outside and posed for the photographer that awaited them. Jai smiled down at her, that killer smile of his that made her stupid heart flutter like a trapped bird inside her chest, and she remembered him smiling down at her that night in the aftermath of satisfaction. And, of course, Jai was pleased, she told herself ruefully—he had accomplished exactly what he wanted for Hari.

They returned to the house for a light lunch. Hari was brought down to meet Sher and then Sher offered to give Shelley a lift home.

'Does he have a limousine?' Willow asked with amusement in her clear eyes after she had hugged her scatty friend and promised to invite her out to Chandrapur for her annual holiday.

'I should think so. Sher made his fortune in the film

world before he went into business,' Jai told her. 'And
we need to make tracks now for the airport.'

'I'll get changed.' But, still immobile, Willow hovered in the hall as Jai closed the distance between them
and reached for her, his eyes as bright as a silvery blue
polar flame.

'It is a shame that you have to take off that dress
without me to do the honours,' Jai husked soft and low,
his fiery attention locking so intently to the luscious
pout of her pink lips that a convulsive shiver rippled
through her slender frame. 'But if I joined you now, if
I even dared to *touch* you, we would never make the
flight this side of tomorrow.'

Her breath feathered dangerously in her throat, her
entire body quickening and pulsing in response to that
heated appraisal and the smooth eroticism of those
words while he kept his lean, powerful frame carefully separate from hers. Her five senses were scream-
ing with a hunger that hurt, the achingly familiar scent
of him, which only made her want to be closer to taste
him, the tingling in her fingertips at the prospect of
touching him, the rasp of his dark deep voice in her
ears throwing up the recollection of his ecstatic groan
in the darkness of the night. It was an overwhelmingly
potent combination.

'Go upstairs, *soniyaa*,' Jai urged thickly.

On trembling legs, Willow spun away, only to get
a few steps and halt again to turn back to him. 'What
does that mean?'

'In Hindi? Beautiful one,' he translated.

Shaken, Willow climbed the stairs, breathless from

the spell he had cast over her, the sheer shocking effect of that high-voltage sexuality focussed on her again. And yet he had not touched her once since she had moved into his house, had left her alone in her bed, maintaining a polite and pleasant attitude without a hint of intimacy when they met at occasional meal-times. Why was that? Why had he kept his distance even after she had agreed to marry him?

It had made Willow feel that his former attraction to her had been a short-lived thing, a flash in the pan, one of those weird, almost inexplicable incidents that struck only in a moment of temptation. Now it seemed that Jai was much more drawn to her than he had been willing to reveal but, while he had maintained his reserve, he had damaged her self-esteem because the awareness that she still craved him when he did not seem to return that compliment or share that weakness had felt humiliating.

After checking on Hari, who was enjoying a comfortable nap after his midday feed, Willow changed into one of her new outfits, an elegant fitted sheath dress and slender high heels teamed with a jacket for the cooler temperatures of London.

She had never travelled in a private jet before and Jai's was spectacularly well-appointed in terms of comfort and space. She sat down beside Hari's crib in the sleeping compartment and fell deeply, dreamlessly asleep. Jai glanced in at the two of them and when he saw her curled up on the bed next to his son's crib, his chest tightened, and he breathed in deep and slow. They were his wife and child, his family now, and, in spite of what he had expected, he didn't feel trapped. No, so intense was his hunger for her that he couldn't think further than the night ahead when that raw hunger would finally be sated.

Willow's strawberry-blond waves tumbled across the pristine pillow, her soft mouth tranquil, her heart-shaped face relaxed in slumber. She was a beauty and his tribe of relatives would greet her like manna from heaven for they had long awaited his marriage. Hari would simply be the cherry on the top of an award-winning cake.

Willow wakened to the news that they were landing at Chandrapur in half an hour and with the time difference it was almost lunchtime. Hari occupied the first fifteen minutes until Shanaya took over and the remainder of the time Willow hurtled around showering and changing.

Jai's bodyguards moved round them as their party emerged from the VIP channel and a roar of sound met her ears. Dozens of photographers were leaning over the barriers with cameras and shouting questions. The flashes blinded her. Until that unsettling moment she had forgotten how famous Jai was in his birth country. Single as well as very good-looking and immensely successful, he was highly photogenic and a media dream. His sports exploits on the polo field, his business achievements and the gloss of his playboy lifestyle provided plenty of useful gossip-column fodder.

'Sorry about that. I should've timed the announcement of our marriage better,' Jai breathed above her head as he steered her down a quiet corridor and back out to the sunlit tarmac. The heat of midday was more than she had expected as she scanned the clear blue sky above them and she was relieved to climb into the waiting vehicle that, Jai assured her, would quickly whisk them to journey's end.

'Where's Hari?' she gasped worriedly.

'In the car behind us. I often make this transfer by helicopter but Shanaya doesn't trust a helicopter with a child as precious as Hari.' Jai chuckled.

Precious, Willow savoured, enjoying that word being linked to her son. A crush of noisy traffic surrounded them, and she peered out of the windows. There were a lot of trucks and cars, colourful tuk-tuks painted with bright advertisements and many motorbikes with women in bright saris riding side-saddle behind the driver in what looked like a very precarious position. Horns blared, vehicles moved off and then ground to a sudden halt again to allow a herd of sacred bulls to wander placidly through the traffic. Bursts of loud music filtered into the car as they drove along beside a lake. By the side of the dusty road she saw dancers gyrating.

'It's a festival day and the streets are crammed. Luckily our palace isn't far,' Jai remarked.

Our palace.

Willow almost smiled at the designation, for she had never dreamt that those two words used together would ever feature in her future. 'So, you're taking me to where your family's story began—'

'No. My family's story began at the fortress in the

fourteenth century. Look out of the window,' Jai urged. 'See the fort on the crags above the city...'

Willow looked up in wonder at the vast red sandstone fortress sprawling across the cliffs above the city. 'My ancestor first invaded Chandrapur in the thirteenth century. It took his family a hundred and forty years of assaults and sieges but eventually they conquered the fort. We will visit it next week,' he promised. 'At present it's full of tourists...we would have no privacy.'

'Then, where are we going now?'

'The Lake Palace,' Jai told her lazily. 'It's surrounded by water and a private wildlife reserve and immensely private. It is where I make my home.'

'So you like...have a *choice* of palaces to use?' Willow was gobsmacked by the concept of having a selection.

'The third one is half palace, half hotel, built by my great-grandfather in high deco style in the twenties. We will visit there too,' Jai assured her calmly.

'*Three?* And that's it...here?' Willow checked.

'There is also the Monsoon Palace. A very much loved and spoilt wife in the sixteenth century accounts for that one,' Jai proffered almost apologetically. 'I leave it to the tourists.'

'You own an awful lot of property,' Willow remarked numbly.

'And now you own it too...as Sher reminded me, I didn't ask you to sign a pre-nuptial agreement,' Jai parried, shocking and startling her with that comment.

'We did get married in a hurry,' Willow conceded ruefully.

'Let us hope that neither of us live to regret that omission,' Jai murmured without expression.

'I'm not greedy. If we ever split up,' Willow told him in a rush, rising above the sinking sensation in her stomach at that concept, 'I won't *ever* try to take what's not mine. I'm very conscious that I entered this marriage with nothing and all I would ask for is enough to keep Hari and I somewhere secure and comfortable.'

'My biggest fear would be losing daily access to my son,' Jai confided with a harsh edge to his dark, deep voice.

Willow suppressed a shiver. 'Let's not even talk about it,' she muttered, turning to look at a quartet of women, their beautiful veils floating in the breeze as they carried giant metal water containers on their heads.

On both sides of the road stretched the desert, where only groves of acacia bushes, milk thistle and spiky grass grew in the sand. It was a hard, unforgiving land where water was of vital importance and only a couple of miles further on, where irrigation had been made possible, lay an oasis of small fields of crops and greenery, which utterly transformed the landscape.

His hand covered her tense fingers. 'We won't let anything split us up,' Jai told her. 'Hari's happiness depends on us staying together.'

'Did you miss your mother so much?' Willow heard herself ask without even thinking.

'I was a baby when she deserted my father and I have no memory of her,' Jai admitted flatly as he removed his hand from hers. 'I met her only once as an adult. I don't talk about my mother...*ever.*'

Willow swallowed painfully hard as her cheeks burned in receipt of that snub and she knew that she wouldn't be raising that thorny topic again.

CHAPTER FIVE

THEY DROVE ALONG a heavily wooded and fenced road
and over a very decorative bridge on which a cluster
of pale grey monkeys was perched. A tall archway
ushered the car into a large central courtyard, ringed
by a vast two-storey white building, picturesquely ornamented with domed roofs and a pillared frontage.
Only then did Willow appreciate that they had arrived
at the Lake Palace.

As she climbed out of the car, she was surprised to
see a group of colourfully clad musicians drumming
and playing with enthusiasm to greet their arrival. A
trio of maids hurried down the steps fronting the long
pillared façade of the building, bearing cool drinks, hot
cloths for freshening up and garlands of marigolds. Behind them, from every corner of the complex poured
more staff.

'It's traditional,' Jai dismissed when she gaped and
commented.

'But why on earth do you employ so many people?'

Jai frowned. 'My father raised me to believe that our
role in society is to provide employment wherever we

can. Yes, I appreciate that we don't *need* the five-star triumphal welcome that my ancestors all enjoyed, but you must also appreciate that those who serve us rely on their employment here. One person may be responsible for keeping an entire tribe of relatives. Never seek to cut household costs unless you see evidence of dishonesty,' he warned her.

'I wasn't criticising,' Willow backtracked uncomfortably, self-consciously skimming her gaze across the lush garden fronting the palace instead. Glorious shrubs were in full bloom all around them. She couldn't immediately identify even one of the shrubs and was immediately keen to explore a new world of tropical plants. She turned as the other cars drew up behind them and immediately moved forward to reclaim Hari from Shanaya, her heart lifting as her son greeted her with a huge smile.

'I keep up the traditions as my father did,' Jai murmured softly by her side, lifting his son from her as the baby stretched out a hand to touch him and screwed up his face at his failure to make contact with his father. 'I employ as many people as possible. When I was younger, I was less far-seeing. When a household custom seemed outdated, I banned it, but it wasn't always possible for those involved to find another position on my staff. Modernising is to be welcomed but not if it means I'm putting people on the breadline to achieve it.'

'I understand,' Willow murmured, aware of the stares from the assembled staff, whom Jai invited closer to see their son. The level of their appreciation for the little boy in Jai's arms warmed her from inside out.

One of the gardeners approached her with a beautiful pink and yellow flower and extended it to her before bowing very low.

'He is proud to be the first to welcome the new Maharani to her home and he swears that even the frangipani blossom is not your equal,' Jai translated with an amused grin.

They walked into a huge circular hall fashioned entirely of marble and supported on carved pillars while Jai directed her towards the curving staircase and up to the landing. He walked down an imposing corridor lined with portraits of the former Maharajas of Chandrapur and showed her into a room already set up as a nursery for Hari.

Willow reclaimed her son and sat down with him.

'When you're free I'll join you for a late lunch. I have some work matters to take care of,' Jai told her before leaving again.

Hari needed to be changed and fed and there were innumerable staff hovering, eager to take care of his needs for her, but Willow didn't want to lose her position of being first and foremost in her baby's life, nor did she want him exposed to too many new faces and different childcare practices at once. Overpowered by the grandeur of Jai's home, she also needed a moment or two of doing ordinary things to feel comfortable again. Thanking everyone cheerfully for the help she wouldn't accept, she saw to Hari herself before finally laying him down for his nap.

When she emerged from the nursery again, a moustachioed man in a bright red turban and traditional attire spread open an inlaid brass door on the other side of the landing and bowed his head in a deferential invitation. Willow passed by him into the most breathtaking interior and her steps slowed as she paused to admire the intricate glass mosaic tiles set into the walls to make superb pictures of a bygone age. Depicted on the walls were hunting scenes with elephants and tigers and grand and very vivid ceremonial processions. Talking on his phone, Jai was striding across the shaded terrace beyond the room that overlooked the lake. In that airy space a table and chairs were arranged.

Willow watched him move, absorbing the elegant grace of his lean, powerful figure as he moved and talked, spreading expressive fingers, shifting his hands this way and that in fluid stress or dismissal of a point. A thrill of desire pierced her soft and deep, making her breath catch in her throat. He was so extremely good-looking and she was married to him now, which still didn't seem real to her. His head turned as he noticed her hovering for the first time and the heat of his stare sent the blood drumming up beneath her skin.

Willow sank down into a dining chair. A napkin was laid over her lap with a flourish by a bearded middle-aged man.

'This is Ranjit,' Jai explained, dropping his phone down on the tabletop and settling down opposite her. 'He speaks excellent English and oversees our household. Anything you need, you ask him, and he will provide it. After we've eaten, I'll show you around.'

'It's a fascinating building and the surroundings only make it more exotic,' she commented, watching a crocodile slide off a mudflat into the lake, his two beady eyes creepy bumps above the surface as he swam. 'But I shouldn't like to meet that gator on a dark night.'

'For safety we only ever leave this building in vehicles. I'll take you on a mini safari some afternoon, although it's amazing how many of the animals you can view from up here. Sooner or later, they all visit the water. He's not a gator, by the way, he's a marsh crocodile.'

'I don't know much about wild animals,' she confided. 'Only what I've learned from watching documentaries. Tell me, why so many palaces?'

'Every generation wanted to be current. Centuries ago this palace and the land around it was for the royal family to hunt.' Jai grimaced. 'And now it's a wildlife reserve. The original fortress above the city is magnificent but could not possibly be adapted to modern life and my grandfather's deco palace is more of a showpiece than a home. Approximately two thirds of that building is now an award-winning hotel and the remaining wing remains ours. We will entertain my relatives and friends there at a party to be held in a few weeks to celebrate our marriage. Is there anyone you wish to invite on your own behalf?'

'No relatives left alive,' she reminded him. 'And no friends who could afford to fly out to India just for a party.'

'I would cover the expense for any of your guests. Shelley?'

Willow winced and coloured. 'She has no holiday leave left. She had to take time off to help me with Hari after he was born.'

His ebony brows furrowed. 'Why? Was he very challenging?'

'No, I was the problem,' Willow confessed. 'I had to have an emergency Caesarean and it was a couple of weeks before I was fit enough to look after him on my own. They don't keep you in hospital after surgery for long these days.'

Jai compressed his lips. 'And yet you *still* didn't think of contacting me for help?'

'We got through it,' Willow muttered with a troubled shrug.

'Why…an emergency?' he pressed. 'What happened?'

'I'd been in labour for hours and it wasn't progressing as it should've done. Hari was a big baby and they had to operate for his sake.' Willow relaxed a little as the food arrived and relaxed even more when she registered that it was entirely a British chicken meal without even a hint of spice.

Jai's high cheekbones were prominent beneath his bronzed skin. He could have lost his son without ever knowing he existed. He could have lost Willow as well. The acknowledgement shook him and her lack of guilt on that score annoyed him, no matter how hard he worked at suppressing such negative reactions. Jai was accustomed to being in charge, used to women who were eager to please him, certainly not a woman who shunned his support and thrust her independence unapologetically in his face. Or perhaps it was the fact that she *still* refused to admit that she had made a mistake in not telling him that she was pregnant. Had behaved as though he could have no possible importance as a father in his son's life.

Or, more probably, had she thought of her own father's cruel indifference to her feelings when she'd failed to meet his exacting academic standards? Possibly she had decided that a father figure was not so necessary. Jai, however, had enjoyed a father who was caring and supportive and it was a role he took very seriously. Suddenly impatient, he thrust his plate away and stood up.

'Let me show you the palace,' he urged, watching as she rose to her feet, her jewelled eyes bright in her heart-shaped face, her lush mouth pink and succulent. Even as he dragged his attention from her mouth, he was hard and full and throbbing. The result of more than a year's celibacy, he told himself in exasperation. In those circumstances, it was natural, even normal, for him to be almost embarrassingly wound up. He had not gone that long without sex since he became an adult. There was no reason whatsoever for him to get worked up about the prospect of having sex with his wife when it was a purely practical element of a marriage undertaken simply to confirm his son's status.

He escorted her downstairs to the two-storey library that had been his father's pride and joy. Sheltered beneath one of the domes, it rejoiced in a twisting narrow marble staircase to the upper floor.

Willow stopped dead to look around herself in amazement at the towering columns of bookcases. In several places there were alcoves backed by stained-glass window embrasures and upholstered with comfortable cushions, little reading nooks, she registered in fascination, never having entered so inviting a library space. 'It's absolutely gorgeous,' she murmured appreciatively. 'I may not be academic but I love to read, so it's ironic that all the books here will mostly be in another language.'

'No. There are many English books in this library.' Jai watched her sink down into one of the reading nooks. A tiny delicate figure in a pale blue dress that somehow brought out the peach glints in her hair and the perfect clarity of her porcelain skin, against which her green eyes gleamed like emeralds.

Willow inched back on her elbows until she was fully reclined, her head resting back against a soft cushion, and grinned. 'I can tell you now... I'll be spending time in here.'

Jai studied her with helpless intensity. She was entirely unaware of her own appeal, entirely divorced from the reality that her hem had ridden up and a deeply erotic view of the space between her slender thighs was open to him. Without even being aware of it, prompted more by his senses than by anything else, Jai moved closer. 'You're the most beautiful thing in here,' he said in a driven undertone.

'Less of the sauce, Jai...as Shelley would say,' Willow teased, coming up on her elbows again and preparing to get up. 'I'm not and have never been a beauty. You don't need to say that sort of stuff to me just because we're married. I don't expect it.'

Jai moved so fast she was startled when he came down over her, caging her in the nook with his lean, powerful body. 'I very rarely say anything I don't mean,' he rasped, coming down to her to claim her mouth with a hungry brevity that only made her crave him more. 'It is for me to tell you that you are beautiful, not for you to disagree, because what would *you* know about it?'

Willow blinked, disconcerted by that sudden kiss. 'Well...er...'

'Because you haven't got a clue!' Jai growled in reproof, pushing down on her with his lean hips and shifting with sinuous grace against her pelvis to acquaint her with his arousal.

It was the most primal thing he had ever done to her and it set Willow on fire, inside and out. It was as though he'd lit a pulse in the most sensitive area of her body, a part of herself she had more or less forgotten existed after the discovery that she was pregnant. There had been no more lying awake restless in the night hours, shifting in frustration while she wantonly recalled the heated expertise of his body on hers. No, she had shut that sensual side down, recognising that that was what had got her into trouble in the first instance and that, with a child on the way, she had more important stuff to focus on. But in that moment, there was *nothing* more important than the powerful allure of Jai's hot-blooded invitation and the wanting took her by storm. Her arms reached up of their own seeming volition and snaked round his neck to pull him down to her.

'No, *not* here...perhaps some other day but not on

what is virtually our wedding night,' Jai specified authoritatively.

Willow pushed him back from her, the taste of humiliation burning in her cheeks and souring in her mouth, which had so readily, so eagerly opened for his. She came upright, smoothing down her rucked-up frock like a bristling kitten. He was always so much in control that it infuriated her at that moment. One minute he was luring her in, the next pushing her away! It bore too many reminders of how much he had craved her that first night in contrast with his cold withdrawal the next morning.

'One of the servants is sweeping rugs on the upper level,' Jai added in an undertone. 'I could order him to leave but it seems unnecessary when we have a bedroom.'

'I suppose by the time you get to your age you get settled in your ways!' Willow snapped back at him tartly, because she was mortified and not really listening, had been so far gone to common sense indeed for several seconds as she reached for him that she wouldn't have noticed if a trumpet band had marched past her. 'I'm more of an al fresco kind of girl!' she added, even though she wasn't quite sure that those two words matched what she had intended to convey: an image of her being more sexually brave and adventurous than he was, which was of course ridiculous when he was the only man she had ever been with and his experience was presumably much greater than hers.

'No. I know that my bride deserves a level of care and esteem from me that she did not receive on the last occasion we were together,' Jai countered flatly, wondering what other sexual expectations she had of him, coming to grips with that apparent challenge with a shot of adrenalin charging through his veins.

In reality, Jai had never been challenged or questioned in the bedroom. Women invariably reacted as though everything he did there was incredible and told him so repeatedly. For the first time he wondered if it was a fact that he *was* too conservative, raised as he had been by a rather elderly parent from a different generation from those of his peers, a father with a distinctly Victorian take on the opposite sex.

Willow rolled her eyes at him, eyes that turned a darker catlike green in temper, he noted, marvelling that he had gone twenty-nine years on Planet Earth without ever before meeting a woman prepared to disagree with him. On the surface she seemed so mild in temperament and shy, although she was a wild woman in bed, Jai acknowledged, reaching for her hand, finding she snatched her fingers back, smiling because he was genuinely amused.

And that sunlit smile of Jai's steamrollered the temper out of Willow as though he had thrown a bucket of water over her because, deep down inside, she *knew* she was being childish, bitter and insecure and that he hadn't earned that response. She looked up at him and those eyes of his were bright between lush black curling lashes and her heart literally went ka-boom inside her and clenched. She slid her hand back into his and in silence they left the library.

'I'll show you the rest of the place some other time,'

Jai told her, walking her along the corridor to the double doors at the other end of the landing. A servant somehow contrived to snake at phenomenal speed round from the other side of the landing and throw the doors open for them and quietly shut them again in their wake.

The main bedroom was another awe-inspiring room, all of a glitter, with flowers and foliage hand-painted in shades of cream and gold with tiny inset mirrors everywhere on the walls, reflecting light into an interior that could otherwise have seemed dark because there were no windows. Instead there were densely carved stone screens open to the elements to filter in fresh air.

'It was remodelled a century ago. It used to be part of the *zenana* where the royal women lived in *purdah*, only allowed to be seen by male family members. My father could still remember elderly relatives who grew up in that lifestyle, men and women living separately,' Jai told her softly as she fingered the screen to look out through the tiny holes to the courtyard below, trying to imagine what it would have been like to only have a view of a life one was not allowed to actively share.

'It must've been horrible,' she whispered, her tiny nose wrinkling up expressively.

'Perhaps not if it was all a woman knew. Going back only a handful of generations, we are talking mainly about women who couldn't read or write or really do anything without a host of servants. Of course, there were exceptions, the educated daughters of more enlightened men, who were able to establish more equal relationships with their husbands. Women prepared to shout back…like you.'

Willow whirled round. 'Like *me*?' she gasped. 'Jai, I'm one of the most easy-going women you'll ever meet!'

Ice-blue eyes gleamed, sentencing her to stillness. 'Not in my experience…and I like it,' he completed almost as an afterthought.

Was your mother like that and was that why your parents divorced? she suddenly wanted to ask, and her teeth worried at her lower lip before she could make that mistake. 'You…do?'

'If I have expectations of you, naturally you must have expectations of me,' Jai traded, settling his hands to her slender hips in the smouldering silence that seemed to be filtering through the room.

Her heart was banging so hard inside her chest that even catching her breath was a challenge. She gazed up into those extraordinary pale blue eyes welded to her and her heart hammered even faster while a clenching sensation assailed her between her thighs. Sometimes he struck her as so beautiful, he left her breathless. No points for that inane thought, she tried to scold herself, but her body wasn't listening when right at that moment she craved Jai's mouth more than she had ever craved anything. And he gave it to her, hot and hard, exactly what she wanted and needed, the urgency of his lips on hers, the tangling of their tongues, the sudden tightening of his strong arms around her quivering form. She was only dimly aware of her feet leaving the floor and being brought down on the wide low bed.

With an effort, Jai restrained himself from tearing off her clothes like a barbarian because he was burning up for her. It would be different between them this time, the way it *should* have been the night of Hari's conception, he assured himself, snatching in a sustaining breath as he raised her up from the pillows to run down the zip on her dress with the finesse he had somehow forgotten that first time. Stray half-formed thoughts were running through his brain, his father confiding that love in combination with unalloyed lust was a trap of the cruellest order, a trap that had almost destroyed the older man. Jai had always known that he didn't have to worry about such a weakness because he was controlled, cautious, far less naive and trusting than his unfortunate parent had been when he had fallen like a ton of bricks for Jai's mother. Cecilia, the apparent love of his life when he had been twenty-one, Jai conceded cynically, had done that much for him, at least.

Jai lifted the dress over her head and the instant he glimpsed the pouting perfection of her tiny breasts cupped in something white and intrinsically feminine, the blood ran roaring through his veins. He gritted his teeth, briefly marvelling at the fierce possessiveness shock-waving through him. Willow was his wife, the mother of his son, and it was perfectly natural for him to experience such responses, but it was something new, which had to be why alarm bells were shrieking inside his head.

'What's wrong?' Willow asked abruptly.

'Nothing whatsoever, *soniyaa*,' Jai declared, crushing her mouth under his in a surge of denial at those alarm bells.

Willow's hands crept up to his shoulders, her anxious gaze pinned to his lean, darkly handsome face. 'Take your shirt off,' she almost whispered.

Jai laughed at her sudden boldness, watching the colour build in her cheeks as he leant back and loosed the buttons before peeling it off, enjoying the way in which her eyes stayed glued to him, recognising with satisfaction that his bride wanted him as much as he wanted her. He slid off the bed and began to strip, deliberately taking his time, reacting to the synergy between them.

Willow rested back against the pillows, entranced by the display because she hadn't seen Jai naked on the night of the funeral, had only caught little glimpses of him in the dim light filtering into her bedroom from the landing. And the more he took off clothes-wise, the harder it got for her to breathe through her constricted lungs, because he was a masculine work of art, dark-hair-dusted, lean muscles flexing with his every movement, that long, powerful body of his making her fingers tingle and her breasts swell and tighten inside her bra. She had not known that it was even possible for such a response to assail her and it shook her and then he was coming back to her on the bed, a symphony of lean bronzed masculinity, boldly aroused, and she acknowledged the surge of dampness at the heart of her with burning cheeks.

'What are you blushing about?' Jai husked, sliding a hand to her slender spine to release her bra.

'I liked watching you undress,' she said, as if that was some kind of revelation.

'Let me tell you a secret,' Jai rasped, long fingers curling round a straining nipple. 'I would like watching you undress just as much. I want you as much as you want me...'

'Honestly?' Willow exclaimed as she quivered all over, not quite believing that statement of his.

Jai watched her soft pink mouth open and suddenly he knew he was done with talking, the raw hunger he was struggling to keep within acceptable boundaries overpowering him. He pressed her back against the pillows with the force of his mouth on hers, all the keyed-up ferocious urgency of his need released in that kiss.

Willow squirmed beneath his weight, her hands lifting to clutch at the smooth skin of his strong shoulders, the sheer heat of him an education, a memory, another burning coal to add to the bonfire in her pelvis and the hot, sweet ache stirring there. 'Oh, Jai...' she muttered, pulling her lips free to get some oxygen back into her starved body. 'I don't know what it is that you do to me but it's almost scary.'

That admission so exactly matched Jai's thought about her effect on him that it spooked him, and he buried it fast, too full of need to concentrate on anything else...

CHAPTER SIX

WILLOW QUIVERED AND shook as Jai worked his sensual path down over her squirming body.

She was back in that sensual world where her heart hammered and her body burned with hunger. Her nipples were stiff little points begging for his attention and he dallied there a long time, driving her insane with frustration as her hips rocked on the mattress because she wanted more, *needed* more. 'Jai, *please...*' she gasped, the burning ache throbbing between her thighs more than she could bear.

'This time, we're going to do this *right*,' he ground out, his bright gaze glittering with resolve.

'But there is no right or wrong here...only what we want,' Willow protested, running an exploring hand down over a long, lean expanse of his torso and delving lower, finding him, stroking him, revelling in the satin-smooth hardness of his thrusting manhood, which every cell in her body craved.

Above her, Jai groaned, pushed her hand away, determined not to be deflected by his hunger. But her fingers slid up into his hair to drag him down to her so that she could have his mouth, the deep delve of his tongue, the awesome nip of his teeth along her sensitive lower lip until she was panting for breath and straining up to him, slender thighs wrapping round his narrow hips to hold him there.

Anticipation was licking through Willow in a raging storm of electrifying impulses as she tangled with his tongue, arched her back so that the hard wall of his chest abraded the straining tips of her breasts and ran her hands down his long, lean flanks. Her hunger was racing out of control, the way it always seemed to be with Jai, and she knew she would be mortified later, but just then she couldn't prevent herself from urging him on by every means within her power.

And with a raw expletive, Jai suddenly surrendered without warning. He reached for a condom, dealing with it fast before pushing her back and plunging into her so hard and deep that her neck extended, and her head fell back. Her hair tumbled like rumpled silk across the pillows as she cried out at the raw sweet force of that invasion. He rode her like a runaway horse and she angled up to him in feverish yearning, the wild excitement he fired in her shock-waving through her in a storm of response. It was everything she remembered from that first night, the naked, burning, demanding heat of the violent passion that had brought her alive. There was nothing cool about it, nothing scheduled or controlled. It took over, wiped everything else from her brain and it was, she dimly registered, incredibly addictive.

All the lean power that was Jai drove her to an explosive orgasm that went splintering through her and lit up every nerve ending in her trembling body. In the aftermath of what had felt like a hurricane striking and devastating every sense, she was weak.

'Epic,' Jai breathed with driven honesty, yet still furious with himself for having failed to meet his own standards yet again and for having fallen on her like an animal. Once again he questioned what it was about her that made everything go wrong when it should have been going right *this* time around, and that only put him in mind of something else he was keen to discuss. No time like the present, he decided, tugging her into the shelter of his arms and dropping a kiss on her smooth brow.

'I wish I'd been around when you were carrying Hari,' he admitted.

Surprise winged through Willow and she was so taken aback she sat up to look down at him while simultaneously thinking how very beautiful he was in the sunlight filtering in through the screen. A five o'clock shadow accentuating his superb bone structure, his extraordinarily light black-fringed eyes intent on her. She swallowed hard. 'Yes, well, it's not something we can do much about now.'

'No?' Jai pressed. 'But surely you regret the decisions you made back then.'

Willow stiffened. 'I'm not sure that I do. I did the best I could at the time, and I believed I was doing what was best for both of us.'

Jai sat up with a jerk, his lean, powerful bronzed body tense. 'But you were wrong and *I* missed out on you being pregnant and on Hari's arrival, not to mention every little change in him during the first seven months of his life!' he shot back at her with unexpected ire.

Willow breathed in deep. 'Well, I'm sorry about that,' she muttered uncomfortably, wondering why on earth he was in such a dark mood.

Jai sprang out of bed. 'I don't think you're one bit sorry for having denied me knowledge of my own child!' he fired back at her accusingly.

'Obviously I'm sorry that it upset you but be fair,' Willow urged, disconcerted by that sudden anger of his. 'I honestly didn't realise how much Hari would mean to you or that you would feel so committed to our child once you found out about him.'

'Had it been left to you I would *never* have found out about him!' Jai intoned grimly. 'And I still don't understand what I did or said to deserve that treatment.'

Hugging the sheet round her, Willow had turned very pale, registering that she was finally catching a glimpse of the kind of feelings that Jai had, for whatever reason, concealed from her. He was still furious that she had not told him that she was pregnant. 'It was the way you treated me the morning after that night we spent together,' she told him honestly, for that was the truth of how she had felt at the time.

'Nothing I said justifies your silence when you were carrying my child and in need of my support!' Jai launched back at her without hesitation.

'I managed perfectly well without your support,'

Willow snapped back defensively. 'But that morning you condemned me for not telling you that I was a virgin, insisting that you would never have touched me had you known.'

'That was the truth!' Jai sliced in ruthlessly.

'You also said that what we had done was *wrong*,' she reminded him stubbornly. 'And you accused me of still having a teenaged crush on you. I don't know many women who would've wanted to contact a bloke who said stuff like that afterwards.'

'It was your duty to contact me!' Jai interposed icily.

But Willow was only warming up, a keen memory of her feelings back then awakened by his censure. In a sudden movement she bodily yanked the sheet from the bed and left it, but only after wrapping it securely round her, and her colour was high. 'Oh, forget your stupid duty, Jai…it was how you made me *feel* that ruled how I behaved!' she slammed back at him. 'You made it sound like sleeping with me was the biggest *mistake* you had ever made.'

Jai flung his proud dark head back, his sensual mouth flattening into a thin hard line. 'It *was*…'

'Well then, don't be surprised that I didn't get in touch because if that night was such a mistake for you, I was in no mood to tell you that, to add to that mistake, I had also conceived a child that you obviously would not want.'

'Those are two separate issues,' Jai objected. 'My night with you was ill-advised but my child could *never* be a mistake.'

'You see how you're simply changing your wording to make yourself sound better?' Willow condemned angrily and, although she was always slow to anger, she was very, very angry just at that moment because, once again, Jai was making her feel bad. 'Why is it so hard for you to accept that you are not the only one of us to have pride? And you humiliated me that morning and made me feel *awful*. You spent more time talking about my father's books than you did on what had happened between us!'

'That is untrue.'

'No, it is true!' Willow hissed back at him, green eyes blazing. 'I disagreed with what you said about that night and, because I dared to disagree, that was the end of the discussion. You didn't *care* about how you were making me feel.'

Jai registered that a huge argument had blossomed and decided to walk away rather than continue it, continuing it being beneath his dignity in his own mind. He flung open the concealed door in the panelling to the en suite bathroom and closed it firmly behind him, shaken by the fire in his bride and forced to consider her explanation by the essential streak of fairness that he had been raised to respect.

He had *not* humiliated her, he told himself fiercely as he stepped into his luxury rainforest shower, and then he recalled an image of her standing, small and pale and stiff, that morning. Well, *if* he had humiliated her, he had certainly not intended to do so. All he had done was express his feelings concerning their sexual encounter. But he had done so to a former virgin, who

could understandably have felt very rejected by such a
negative attitude, his conscience slung in with unwelcome timing. He had consciously been trying to distance himself from a chain of events that shamed him,
he acknowledged grimly. And she had vehemently disagreed with him and he hadn't known how to handle
that, he conceded in grudging addition.

The door of the en suite bathroom opened, Willow
finally having realised that the panelling effectively
concealed doors into dressing rooms and other facili-
ties only obvious to someone who actually saw a door
being used.

'And now you're doing it to me again!' Willow
declared angrily from the doorway, incensed by his
departure. 'Walking away because I disagree with
you!'

In the spacious shower cubicle Jai grimaced. 'I'll
join you in a few minutes and we'll talk.'

'Oh, don't bother on my account!' his bride said
sharply. 'It's probably jet lag but I'm exhausted and
I'm going back to bed for a nap!'

Tears lashing her hurt eyes and angrily blinked
back, Willow clambered back into the comfortable bed
and curled up into a brooding ball of resentment. Some
people didn't like conflict and maybe he was one of
them. Obviously, she needed to brush up on her communication skills and stop her temper jumping in first
because she was willing to admit that nobody had *ever*
made her as angry as Jai could. He was the very first
person she had ever shouted at and in retrospect she
was full of chagrin and regret because even she knew

that that was not the way to persuade anyone round to a new point of view.

But she just felt so wounded by his outlook because those months pregnant and alone but for Shelley had been very tough. And she truly hadn't appreciated that Jai was still so bone-deep outraged at her failure to tell him that she had conceived. No, he had managed to hide that reaction very effectively until he'd got her to the altar, she reflected bitterly, and only now was she seeing that, for all his appearance of frankness, Jai was much more complex below that surface façade of cool than he seemed and quite capable of nourishing reactions that she'd not even begun to detect.

But then, shouldn't she have expected a few surprises when they were only really getting to know each other now? When it was only a practical marriage rather than one based on love and caring? Well, he definitely had all the caring genes when it came to their son, Willow conceded reluctantly, he just didn't have them for *her*. She felt hollow inside, as if she had been gutted, and a quiver of self-loathing ran through her that she could still be so sensitive to Jai's opinions.

He thought she had let Hari *and* him down by not informing him that she was pregnant. He would hold it against her to the grave, she thought morosely, suspecting that Jai was as proverbially unforgiving and hard as that vast sandstone fortress above Chandrapur. He expected, he wanted perfection and she had a whole pile of flaws. Jai had flaws too but, unlike her, seemed supremely unaware of them. Of course, she rather suspected that his father had been of a very different nature from hers, not the type to linger on his child's every failing. On that deflating note, Willow fell asleep.

A smiling, dark-skinned face above hers wakened her with a gentle touch on her shoulder.

'I am your maid, Alisha,' the young woman informed her, bobbing her head. 'His Royal Highness the Maharaja will be dining in an hour.'

Dimly, Willow registered that daylight had gone and wondered in dismay how long she had slept, before glancing at her watch and discovering that she had slept for far longer than she had planned.

'I have run a bath for you...but there is a shower... it is your choice,' Alisha added with yet another huge good-natured smile. 'I have also laid out clothes for you.'

Willow was bemused by being awarded that amount of personal attention until it occurred to her that she was receiving it purely as a mark of respect towards Jai's wife, a sort of reflected glory she felt ill-prepared to handle. But she would have to *learn* to handle it, she told herself urgently, because she was living in a formal household crammed with servants and she was always going to be the Maharani of Chandrapur within these walls even if she didn't feel as though she had any true right to such high status and esteem.

'A bath would be great,' she agreed, since it had already been run for her, and she sat up to slide her arms into the silky robe being extended for her use, thinking that Shelley would adore hearing about such luxuries because that kind of personal attention was non-existent in the world in which she and her friend had grown up in. Not so much a world, she ruminated wryly, as the school of hard knocks, which had formed them both from childhood.

Her bathroom was separate from Jai's, Willow re-alised with a guilty grimace as she sat in her bath surrounded by floating rose petals and some sort of scented oil. No wonder he had seemed startled by her following him in there to confront him yet again, she conceded, heat flushing her cheeks in sudden morti-fication. No, arguments when she was overtired and cross were not to be recommended, she conceded rue-fully, although she had said nothing that even now, calmer and cooler, she would have been willing to re-tract.

Her maid had laid out a long dress for her and Wil-low winced, getting a hint of what her life was expected to be like in the Lake Palace. She was supposed to dress up simply to dine with her bridegroom. Had she been a more conventional new bride, she would've been doing that automatically though, she reflected ironi-cally, an arrow of remorse piercing her that that was not the case between her and Jai. On the surface their marriage might seem normal but underneath it was a sham, bereft of the understanding, love and knowledge that what he had termed 'a normal marriage' would need to thrive.

Alisha directed her downstairs, where Ranjit guided her across the echoing main hallway into yet another splendid room furnished with a formal dining table and chairs. Coloured glass panels portraying a fanciful for-

est full of fantasy animals decorated the walls and it
was wonderfully cool and air-conditioned.

'So, some of this place is air-conditioned,' Willow
remarked as Jai strode in, and in stark comparison to
her moreover, barefoot and clad with almost laughable
informality in an open-necked red shirt and well-fit-
ted designer jeans that outlined his lean hips and long,
powerful thighs. As always, he looked amazing and her
breath shortened in her throat as involuntarily she relived the feel of his hot skin below her stroking fingers,
the springy softness of his black hair and, ultimately,
the crashing intoxicating surge of his mouth on hers.

Burning up with chagrin inside her own skin, Willow dropped hastily into a chair.

'Yes, those rooms where it was possible without seriously damaging the décor. If you find our bedroom
too warm, just tell me. I will make it possible there too,
but I do not expect us to spend much time here during
the hottest months of the year,' he imparted smoothly,
his dark low-pitched voice, richer than velvet, brushing against skin suddenly pebbling with goose bumps.
'The summer heat can be unbearable.'

Willow nodded as a wide selection of little bites was
brought in to serve as a first course and Ranjit carefully
indicated the spicy items lest they not be to her taste,
while Jai talked about the local sights he intended to
show her. She tried a sample of flavours while wondering if Jai intended merely to act as though that argument had not taken place, but, once the staff had
melted away with delivery of their main course, Jai
fell suddenly silent and she glanced up from her plate

anxiously to find those wolfish ice-blue eyes locked hard to her.

'There is something I must say,' he began, uncharacteristically hesitant in tone. 'There are times when we will perceive events in a dissimilar light because of the different cultures in which we grew up...'

'Obviously,' Willow breathed tightly.

'The morning after we spent that first night together is one of those events. For me, it *was* inexcusably wrong to take a woman's virginity when I was not in a serious relationship with her. I could not treat that as though it was something of no consequence, but I was equally guilty of having made the assumption that you would *not* be so innocent, living in your more liberal society,' he completed levelly.

'Jai, I—' Willow began awkwardly, not having foreseen quite how much of an issue that had genuinely been for him.

'Let me finish,' he urged, topping up her wine glass with a lithe and elegant hand. 'I felt very guilty that day. I was deeply ashamed of my behaviour. I took advantage of you when you were grieving and alone and in need of support.'

'It didn't feel that way to me,' Willow protested, breaking in.

'We are talking about how it felt to be *me* that morning,' Jai reminded her drily. 'I felt like a total bastard, who had seduced an innocent young woman, and clearly how I felt fed into making you feel rejected and insulted...but that result was *not* intentional. I remained sincerely concerned for your well-being, which is why

I attempted to see you again a couple of months later, by which time you must've known you were pregnant.'

At the reminder, Willow flushed a discomfited brick red. 'And Shelley lied for me and said she didn't know where I was because she *knew* I didn't want to see you again,' she filled in for him uneasily. 'I'm sorry but that was just how I felt back then. I was a bit naive. I was feeling well and I thought I would manage fine without you. Before I forget, can I ask you something off-topic?'

His winged ebony brows drew together in a frown at that query. 'You can ask me anything although I cannot always guarantee an answer.'

'Why did I have to get all dressed up in a long fancy gown when you're wearing jeans and no shoes?'

And the tension still thick round the table just evaporated then and there as Jai flung his handsome dark head back and laughed with disconcerting appreciation of that simple question. Raking a long-fingered brown hand through his silky black hair, he surveyed her with amusement still glittering like stardust in his bright black-lashed eyes. 'I can only assume that it was my mother's practice or my grandmother's practice to get "all dressed up" for dinner because that is how long it has been since this palace had a mistress. Your maid will have been given advice on what you would want to wear for such an occasion and, since you are English, it may well date back to the years of the British Raj,' he warned her with a wide smile. 'And be generations out of date. You don't need to dress up for dinner for my benefit. You can wear whatever you like, *soniyaa.*'

That smile of his and the endearment on top of the explanation he had carefully outlined melted that hard little knot that had formed in Willow's chest earlier that day. Jai was trying and she recognised that, respected him for it, *liked* him for it. But at the other end of the scale she was wondering what other misunderstandings would crop up when there were such basic differences between their outlooks on life. Even so, stifling that anxious thought, she smiled back at him, shaken to discover how fast she wanted him again, as if that afternoon of passion had only been a dream.

'This evening I will show you around what remains of your new home and tomorrow we will go out and explore,' Jai promised her lazily.

And the week that followed was full of enjoyment, occasional challenges and surprises and the beginning of a fascination with her surroundings that rooted deep. There was the ancient old gardener who brought her flowers every day, and the cook who had a burning desire to know what her favourite foods were, and the sharing of playtimes with Hari and his father, so that a lifestyle that at first had seemed strange became her new normal. Hari was always surrounded by loving carers and it was not unusual to hear his chuckles as he was rocked in a solid-silver nursery swing that had rocked his ancestors for generations and which really should have been in a museum.

Willow visited the Hindu temple and the white marble park of elaborate ancestral tombs that overlooked the holy lake. She accepted garlands and blessings and small gifts for Hari as well as her share of the awe that

Jai's mere presence inspired amongst the locals. She posed for photos for the local journalists, who were much more respectful than those they had encountered at the airport.

She learned that English was widely spoken and became less intimidated by strangers, her confidence growing at the warm welcome she received everywhere. She explored the massive old fortress on the cliffs above the city, bowled over by its magnificent décor and huge rooms, with Jai by her side sharing funny stories about his heritage, which no guide could ever have equalled. And she saw a tiger in the wild for the first time, ironically not on the mini safari in an open-topped SUV that Jai had taken her on, but from the shaded dining terrace she watched the animal slink in his glorious orange and black striped coat out of the jungle to pad down at his leisure to drink at the edge of the lake.

By day they explored the sights but by night, mostly, they explored each other, she reflected with a wanton and slightly self-conscious little wriggle of recollection. She couldn't keep her hands off Jai, and it seemed to be a case of a mutual chemical reaction. Jai electrified her every time he touched her, but when he had pressed her down in one of those reading nooks in the library that day, and possessed her with uninhibited passion in one of their most exciting encounters to date, she had realised afterwards, by his faint but perceptible discomfiture, that Jai wasn't in control either.

Jai was pondering that problem for himself in his office. He had been spending too much time with his

wife and not enough time working, he censured himself, well aware that he was sidestepping the real issue
nagging at him. He had married her for his son's sake,
he reminded himself impatiently. He had planned on a
perfectly civilised but essentially detached and sophisticated partnership in marriage, in which both of them
nourished their own interests and friendships. He had
never planned on hot, sweaty, wildly exciting naked
encounters in every secluded corner of his home. He
had never planned to keep her awake half the night
in the marital bed to the extent that she regularly fell
asleep in the afternoon heat, exhausted by his demands.
Nobody needed to warn Jai that he was already in the
grip of the overpowering lust that he had been warned
against many times.

And that acknowledgement disturbed Jai on every
level. He didn't do love; he flatly refused to do love.
He was a great believer in moderation in all things.
He had, after all, grown up with the tragic evidence of
what love could do to a man, not to mention his own
disillusionment at the hands of his former fiancée, Cecilia. Love, however, had totally broken his father, a
strong man, a good man, an intelligent man, yet none of
those strengths had saved him from the consequences
of losing the wife he had adored. His father's depres-
sions, loneliness, bitterness, his inability to replace that
lost wife with even a female friend, had taught Jai how
dangerously harmful those softer emotions could be
for a man when it came to a woman.

He didn't want the stress of that complication with
Willow: he was determined not to *need* her, to look

for her when she wasn't there or to allow her to sink
so deeply into the fabric of his everyday life that she
became more important than she should be. Liking,
kindness and respect were absolutely all that were required from him as a husband and anything beyond that
would be madness…a madness that he wouldn't touch.

CHAPTER SEVEN

A WEEK AFTER Jai reached that decision, and unhappily warding off her low spirits as a result of that decision, Willow was dealing with the post her social secretary had gathered for her to peruse.

Yes, she was tickled pink by the idea that she could possibly require a social secretary. Only after she had seen the pile of invitations, congratulatory letters and wedding gifts in Samaira's small office had she realised that she had been ridiculously naive not to appreciate that Jai's position with an international charity foundation, his local role as a former ruler and his recent marriage would not also make demands on *her*.

'And there was *this*,' the tiny, beautiful Samaira finally declared, sliding a sheet of paper across the desk and rising at the same time to leave the library. 'It's an email that arrived on the Maharaja's historical website and I was given it by his PA, Mitul. He took the liberty of printing it out, which I hope was correct,' she added hopefully. 'We felt that the enquiry was for you and best given to you.'

Surprised by that seemingly unnecessarily detailed explanation, Willow frowned and glanced down at the paper, looking first at the signature. Milly St John, a name that meant nothing whatsoever to her. She studied the couple of lines in the message before comprehension gripped her with sudden dismay.

As you have recently married my son and are the mother of my grandson, I would be very grateful if you would agree to meet with me alone and in private at my hotel in Chandrapur on the seventeenth.'

Willow paled, because it was an extraordinary request from a woman that Jai would not even discuss. It was also a hot potato that had passed quickly from hand to hand, the staff probably striving to work out the best way to deal with it since Jai's aversion to anything relating to his mother was clearly well known. And Samaira was right, it *was* an invitation for Willow but undoubtedly not one of which Jai would approve.

'Thank you,' Willow said quietly, keen not to embellish the staff grapevine by commenting on an email that had very probably already caused a wave of gossip and speculation.

And while she was pondering that problem and what to do about it, she too left the library and wandered down to the far end of the palace in the direction of the suite of offices that had been neatly tailored from what had once been staff quarters. There she hesitated, uncertain that she even wanted to raise such a prickly topic, for in recent days Jai had become progressively more elusive. Yes, she had accepted that he would have to return to work, but she had not appreciated quite how much business would occupy his time. He usually joined her for dinner but rarely for breakfast or lunch, invariably rising before her and retiring after she had. She was relieved, however, that in spite of that relentless schedule he had still made time for their son, even if any notion of making time for *her* seemed to have died a total death after that first glorious week together.

Willow understood, however, that he was very busy, and she wasn't the clingy type. She didn't need him to fill the daylight hours when she had Hari to occupy her, a beautiful garden and an entire library of books, but she couldn't help thinking that Jai was treating her rather like a new and shiny novelty whose initial lustre had quickly worn off and ended up boring him instead. On that note, she turned her steps in another direction and decided to ask him what she felt she needed to ask him over dinner instead.

Later, Jai strolled out to the big domed terrace that was shaded throughout the day and cool. Willow sipped her wine and savoured his long-legged grace and sheer bronzed beauty with his black-lashed arctic-blue eyes glittering. A little quiver ran through her slender length, her breasts peaking almost painfully below the bodice of the sundress she wore, a clenching sensation tightening deep in her pelvis so that colour flared up in her cheeks. 'Hello, stranger,' she heard herself say even though she had not intended to make any comment on his recent inaccessibility.

Jai lifted a black brow in query, as if that greeting had totally taken him aback.

'I haven't seen you since I woke to see you walking out of our bedroom yesterday morning,' Willow pointed out, watching the faint rise of colour that scored his exotic cheekbones with curiosity. 'Hey, I'm not complaining. I'm just pointing it out.'

Disconcerted by that statement, Jai breathed. 'Has it really been that long? I'm sorry but I had to attend a board meeting for the foundation last night. It ran late and I didn't want to disturb you, so I used another room.'

'I think you need to learn to delegate more,' Willow responded with determined lightness. 'It's not healthy for anyone to be working twenty-four-seven.'

Jai gritted his teeth, belatedly recognising in that moment that he had gone to quite absurd lengths to avoid his wife for the sin of attracting him too strongly. He dimly wondered if there was a streak of insanity somewhere in his family genes. What had seemed like such a good idea a week earlier had now blurred and become questionable. In the midst of scanning her tiny slender figure in a sunflower-yellow dress, which accentuated the strawberry-blond waves curling round her piquant face and framed her catlike green eyes, he reckoned that no normal man would have behaved as he had done: resisting his beautiful wife's allure as though she were both toxic and dangerous.

He could only assume that the literal act of getting married had afflicted him with some very weird and deferred form of cold feet. All to prove some kind of point to himself? That he was in control? And able to *wreck* his marriage before it even got off the ground? He breathed in deeply, recognising in bewilderment that his usual rational outlook inexplicably seemed to always send him in the wrong direction with Willow.

'Even with the party scheduled, next week won't be half as frantic for me,' Jai assured her hurriedly as Ranjit poured the wine and retreated.

'Good,' Willow replied with a smile that lit up her face like sunshine. 'But the party event has also given me some questions I feel I *have* to ask you about your background.'

Jai tensed. 'My…background?'

'I feel awkward about asking but I feel I should know the basic facts, because I will be mixing with your relatives, who presumably already know those facts, and I don't want to trip up in my ignorance and say anything that sounds stupid,' Willow outlined, trotting out the excuse she had prepared and reddening hotly because simply telling him the truth would have come much more naturally to her.

Yet in her heart of hearts she had already guessed that Jai would absolutely forbid her to have anything to do with his mother, but Lady Milly was *her* mother-in-law and Hari's grandmother and, although she was a stranger, Willow still felt that she surely ought to have the right to form her own opinion.

'Facts about what?' Jai prompted.

'About why your parents broke up, about why your mother left you behind,' she murmured tightly, guilt still jolting through her in waves.

'My mother is the daughter of an English duke, which is still virtually all I know about her. The marriage didn't last long and ended in divorce...' Jai compressed his sensual mouth into a flat bitter line '... *because* apparently she believed that her alliance with an Indian and the birth of a mixed-race child were adversely affecting her social status.'

'That's weird... I mean, if she believed that why would she have married your father in the first place?' Willow pressed with a furrowed brow.

'I have never had a conversation with her, consequently I don't know,' Jai admitted flatly.

'You've never even *met* her?' Willow exclaimed in disbelief.

'I don't think you could call it a meeting... I did run into her once quite unexpectedly at a public event and she pretty much cut me dead. Her second husband and children were with her,' Jai explained, and his strong bone structure might have been formed with steel beneath his olive skin, his forbidding cast of features as revealing of his feelings on that occasion as the ice in his gaze.

'That was unforgivable,' Willow conceded, shocked and unhappy on his behalf.

Jai frowned. 'Of course, she did attempt to come back from that very low point. Shortly afterwards, she came to my London home in an attempt to see me, but I had her turned away. In fact, there were several attempts, but I have no desire to either see or speak to her. She sent letters as well, which I returned unopened.

At this stage in my life and with my father dead, I see no reason to waste time on her.'

Willow, however, saw with great clarity that Jai had been cruelly hurt by his mother's twin rejections and that, no matter what he said in that measured and cool voice of his, he was still scarred by the damage his mother's abandonment had inflicted. And so stubborn too, so set in his views that he had completely rejected the olive branch and the explanations that the woman had tried to offer. Of course, in such circumstances that was his right, she accepted ruefully, resolving in that moment not to interfere on behalf of a woman who, it seemed, was a most undeserving cause. She herself would sooner have cut off her arm than walk away from Hari.

'I'm sorry I asked,' she told him truthfully. 'I can't blame you for feeling the way you do about her.'

And she decided not to mention the personal approach that had been made to her by his mother, which would undoubtedly only annoy Jai and where was the point in that? It would be yet another wounding reminder of the wretched woman that he didn't need. No, she would stay safely uninvolved in a matter that was none of her business and ignore that email.

Jai strolled round the courtyard garden with her after dinner, but Willow was quiet and withdrawn in receipt of that unexpected attention. After all, she really didn't know where she stood with Jai any more. Her first week with him had been magical and then he had virtually vanished, and with that vanishing act all her insecurities had been revived. Why would he

want to spend time with her when he had never really
wanted to marry her in the first place? How could she
feel neglected when she had known beforehand that
she was entering a marriage without love? How could
she even complain?

'I screwed up this week,' Jai declared, in a driven
undertone.

In silence, Willow shrugged a stiff shoulder and
hovered below the ancient banyan tree in the centre of
the garden, which sheltered a sacred shrine much re-
vered by the staff. '*I* didn't complain about anything,'
she reminded him with pride, studying him with clear
green eyes.

Her problem, though, was that Jai was gorgeous,
in whatever light and in whatever clothing. Nothing
detracted from his sheer magnificence: the luxuriant
black hair, the chiselled cheekbones and flawless skin,
the stunning ice-blue eyes and the dramatic lashes that
surrounded them, and he had an equally beautiful body,
she allowed, her face warming at that unarguable acknowledgement. Unfortunately for her, on every physical plane, Jai drew her like a magnet. One certain look,
one smile and she was all over him like a stupid rash
and that both infuriated her and made her feel weak
and foolish. After the week she had endured of being
ignored in *and* out of bed, she knew that in reality she
meant very little to Jai and it felt degrading to still be
attracted to a man who could simply switch off and
forget her very existence.

The real source of Willow's frustration, however,
was, undeniably, that she had no idea what was going

on inside his head. She was beginning to wonder if it was possible that, aside of sex, Jai hadn't a clue how to behave in the sort of relationship that a marriage required. The first week with him had been heavenly and she had been so happy with him that she had practically floated, but the past week of being ignored had been a sobering wake-up call that hurt her self-esteem. One minute she had seemed as necessary to him as the air he needed to breathe, the next she had become the invisible woman.

'I will spend more time with you from now on,' Jai intoned with deadly seriousness.

Willow paled and walked on down the path. 'Don't push yourself,' she heard herself say curtly, the colour of embarrassment stinging her cheeks.

'It's not like that,' Jai assured her levelly, lifting a long-fingered brown hand to rest on her shoulder with an intimacy she resented because it reminded her too much of those carnal, expert hands sliding over her body.

'Well, going by the past week, it *is* like that,' Willow replied, squaring her slight shoulders and stepping away to break that physical connection. 'You don't know what you want from me…apart from the obvious…*sex*,' she condemned between gritted teeth. 'And this past week, not even that. You married me and I don't think you know what to do with me now that you've got what you *said* you wanted!'

Evidently stunned by that disconcerting burst of frankness, Jai briefly froze, his darkly handsome features taut.

'Goodnight, Jai,' Willow murmured quietly and walked back indoors, for once proud of herself for not succumbing to the sexual infatuation that had entrapped her into something that felt disturbingly like an obsession.

Why was she feeling like that? Even not seeing Jai hurt, never mind not being touched by him or talking to him. Somehow, he had sparked off a hunger inside her that tugged at her through every hour of the day and she resented him for reducing her to that needy level. He should've started their marriage on cooler, more detached terms if that was how he intended it to be. Instead he had given her deceptive false messages and had shaken her up from the inside out.

Well, she was not some pushover for him to lift and literally *lay* whenever he fancied, she was strong, independent and nobody's fool, she reminded herself doggedly. She might not have been her father or Jai's intellectual equal, but had always been shrewd when it came to people and the often confusing difference between what they said and what they actually did. She knew how to look after herself even if she had once been foolish enough to succumb to a one-night stand with Jai.

Tense from that encounter in the garden, she went upstairs to look in on Hari as he slept, safe and smiling in the baby equivalent of the Land of Nod, probably dreaming of being rocked in a silver swing by devoted handmaidens while being fed ambrosia. If only life were so simple for her, she thought wryly. Lifting her head high, she scolded herself for that downbeat thought. She had Hari and life was very good for him. She had health and security too. There *was* no excuse for feeling that her life lacked anything. In that mood, she scooped up silk pyjamas from her cavernous collection of lingerie and went for a bath.

She was lying back on her padded bath pillow engaged in aggressively counting the many blessings she had to be grateful for when, with a slight knock and only a momentary hesitation, the door opened to frame Jai on the threshold, tall and lean, dark and hazardous, pale eyes glittering like stars framed by black velvet. Willow jerked up in surprise and hugged her knees with defensive hands, feeling invaded. 'I didn't ask you to come in.'

Jai tilted his dark head back, a dangerous glint in his bright gaze. 'What makes you think I need permission to speak to my wife?'

Willow lifted a pale brow. 'Courtesy?'

Jai closed the door and sank down on the edge of the bath, deliberately entering her safe space. 'Courtesy won't get us anywhere we want to travel right now.'

Willow lifted her chin. 'Then get out of here…*now*!' she challenged.

Disturbingly, Jai laughed and trailed a forefinger through the rose petals swirling round her knees. 'I don't think so. I am where I *want* to be. If you can be direct, so can I. I want you.'

At the sound of that declaration the blood drummed up through Willow's body like an adrenalin boost. 'Since…*when*?' she mocked.

'I can't switch it off. With you, it's a primal and

very basic urge and it hurts to deny it.' Jai's fingertip glided up out of the water to slowly stroke the soft underside of her full lower lip and her heart hammered at an insane rate.

'So, why did you?' she whispered unevenly.

'I thought I should. I don't know why. I don't like feeling out of control,' Jai admitted thickly, his mesmeric gaze holding hers with sheer force of will. 'And you often make me feel out of control...'

And a huge wave of heat that had nothing to do with the temperature of the water shot up through Willow. Her brain was blurring as though it had been enveloped in fog. She could feel her own heart thrumming inside her chest, the tautness of her pointed nipples, the pool of liquefying warmth at her core, but she couldn't think straight and when he angled his mouth down to hers, her mouth opened, only anticipation guiding her. His mouth on hers was like paraffin thrown on a bonfire, shooting multicoloured sparks of heat through every fibre, and only a slight gasp escaped her throat when he lifted her, dripping, out of the water and melded his lips to hers again with all the urgency she had dreamt of.

'I'm soaking wet! This wasn't supposed to happ—' she began, common sense struggling to get a look-in as he laid her down on the bed and arranged her like some ancient sacrifice on an altar.

'Shush, *soniyaa*,' Jai breathed hungrily against her mouth and she was vaguely aware of him peeling off his clothes in the midst of kissing her, but she was too connected to the sheer power surge of his urgency to make even the smallest complaint.

He ran his palms slowly down over her smooth body as if reacquainting himself with her slender contours and she shivered, every skin cell primed for more, her breath trapped in her throat as if breathing might prevent the excitement already licking through her. He slid down the length of her, all lithe bronzed grace and tenacity, his skin hot where it brushed hers, his bold arousal brushing her stomach, filling her with heat and the kind of wanting that burned. He tipped her thighs back, settled his lips to the most sensitive part of her quivering body and slowly, surely, with his mouth and his wickedly knowing fingers, proceeded to drive her out of her mind with throbbing waves of pleasure. She squirmed and then she writhed, unable to stay in control and flying involuntarily into an intense climax, with his name breaking from her tongue and then the taste of herself on her lips as he kissed her with ferocious demand and settled over her.

From that shattering point on, it was as it always was between them: wild. He plunged into her with a growl of satisfaction and she gasped in delight from the first thrust, the delicious stretching of her tingling body, the sleek hardness of his body driving over and in hers and the raw sexual connection that destroyed her every inhibition. He flipped her over onto her hands and knees, pressing her down, entering her powerfully and deeply again, making every sense sing in high-voltage response. Sobs of excitement were wrenched from her convulsing throat as another climax seized hold of her and shock-waved through her with an intensity that wiped her out. She flopped flat on the bed like a puppet who'd had her strings cut, smiling dizzily into the silk bed cover at his shout of completion, knowing that never in her life before had she dreamt of that much excitement and that much drowning pleasure.

'No more starting work at dawn, no more late nights,' Jai breathed with ragged resolution as he turned her limp length over and back into contact with the hot, damp heat of his body, sealing her there with both arms, his hands smoothing her slender back in a soothing motion.

'You're going to delegate?' she whispered with effort because it was a challenge to kick her brain into gear again.

'With the foundation, yes. My life has changed now that I have you and Hari and I need to adapt,' he murmured, setting the edge of his teeth into the exact spot on the slope of her neck that drove her crazy and making her jerk against him. 'In many ways.'

And Willow was satisfied by those assurances. He was making a major effort. He hadn't approached her simply for sex. No, he had recognised that change would be required from both of them if their marriage was to survive and that was good, wasn't it? She shouldn't *still* want more, should she? She couldn't understand the lingering hollow sensation in her chest, particularly when her body was already warming up again to the stimulation of his.

Of course, he wasn't going to start talking about emotions—that was a female thing, wasn't it? Concentrate on the positives, she told herself sternly. Both of them were finding their way in a new and very different situation as parents and partners. Of course, there would be misunderstandings and clashes along the way. All that should really matter was that Jai cared enough to put in the work to keep their relationship ticking over.

Obviously, he was unlikely to ever give her the kind of rapturous reception he gave Hari every time he lifted his son into his arms. She had seen that look, that intense emotion he hid around her and, if she was honest, had envied her son, who had inspired love in his father practically at first sight. But she was only human and it was normal to make comparisons, even if they were unwise comparisons, because love and devotion had featured nowhere in their agreement. Even worse, logic warned her that Jai, a tough businessman to his fingertips, would stick exactly to the deal he had made with her.

She didn't have what it took to inspire Jai with romantic feelings. That had been made clear to her the morning after their first night together. Yes, he had visited to check on her a couple of months later but that had only been a knee-jerk sense of responsibility she owed to his friendship with her late father. It had not related to her *personally*. Her main attraction for Jai was self-evidently the passion that virtually set fire to their bedsheets and she was beginning to recognise that she ought not to be turning her nose up at that rather lowering truth when it might well prove to be the glue that kept their marriage afloat in the future.

Or would familiarity breed contempt? She shivered,

wondering why her thoughts continually took a negative direction around Jai. What was the matter with
her? Why couldn't she simply be content with what
they had? Why was she always seeking...*more*?

CHAPTER EIGHT

JAI LOOKED MAGNIFICENT.

Indeed, Willow was flooded by distinctly sensual and, admittedly, superficial impressions of Jai garbed in traditional Maharaja dress in readiness for the party that would introduce her as his wife to his family and friends. In the black and silver frogged silk tunic and pants, he took her breath away. In fact, virtually everything about the pomp and ceremony of the occasion and their surroundings was having the same effect on her. His grandfather's art deco palace was a sumptuous building with soaring marble columns and ceilings, glittering Venetian glass chandeliers and intricately designed marble floors and even the furniture and the grounds around the building matched that splendid classic elegance, but Jai had been quite correct: it was too grand a place for mere comfort.

As soon as they had arrived in their finery and in advance of the party, official photographs had been taken in the Greek-style marble temple in the centre of the lawns. They had leant against pillars, posed on the layers of steps, looked pensively into each other's eyes until she'd succumbed to an uncontrollable bout of giggles and then she had twirled in her gown for the photographer to show off the full skirt of her gorgeous dress.

She had felt remarkably like a Bollywood movie actress and Jai had told her that all photos taken for special occasions had a dash of that spirit in India. When she had asked Jai if she should don a sari to blend in better at the party, Jai had only laughed before informing her that many of their guests would be European and that some of his countrywomen would dress traditionally while others would wear the latest Western fashion, that, in actuality, however she chose to dress would be acceptable.

Willow had picked a spectacular ball gown out of her crammed wardrobe, a brilliant cerise-pink shade much favoured by Rajasthani women. The finest lace covered her shoulders and upper arms, the style closely tailored to her slender figure down to the hip and then flaring out in volume into the beaded silk skirt. It was one of those ridiculously beautiful fairy-tale dresses that made a woman feel like a million dollars and to complement it she had worn very high heels. In addition, Jai had brought her a glorious emerald and diamond necklace and earrings, which had belonged to his grandmother, as well as having gifted her a diamond bracelet and a gold and diamond watch that very same week. It was little wonder that she kept on wanting to pinch herself to see if she was still living in the real world because, only weeks earlier, she could never have dreamt that such incredible luxury would ever feature in her life.

In the echoing marble hall, there was a huge display of wedding gifts and they wandered around examining them. Willow was disconcerted by the large amount of jewellery she had been given, gleaming gold necklaces and armbands and earrings, and there were even some pieces for Jai, which he assured her with a groan that he would never wear. She strolled up to him when he was holding something in his hand and signalling his hovering PA, Mitul, to ask him a question.

With an exclamation in his own language he set the ornate little box down again in haste, his sensual mouth compressing. Curious, Willow scooped it up. 'What is it?' she asked.

'An eighteenth-century *inro*—an ornamental box in which Japanese men used to carry seals or medicine. I collect them,' he told her in a curt undertone.

'A very good friend must've given it,' Willow assumed, because everything on the tables struck her as valuable. 'But why are you annoyed? Was it an unsuitable gift from the friend concerned?'

'In my opinion, yes,' Jai conceded crisply. 'The giver is my ex-fiancée, Cecilia.'

'The one that ditched you?' Willow gasped in surprise.

All of a sudden, Jai grinned, the tension in his lean, handsome features evaporating again. 'You're no diplomat, are you, *jaani*?'

Willow reddened because she knew that she hadn't

been tactful. 'I know nothing about her…but what upsets you about the present?'

'That I have only just learned that she and her husband have been invited to the party. Odds are that she won't come. But if she does, it's entirely *my* fault that she received an invite,' he acknowledged in exasperation. 'I told Mitul to use the same guest list for my friends that was used ten years ago at a party I held here. But he didn't work for me back then and he wouldn't have recognised the significance of her name. Of course, I should've checked the list myself.'

'It's a very big party,' she reminded him. 'Will it really matter if she turns up?'

Jai shrugged, a brooding expression etched to his flawless features, his wolf eyes veiled by his lashes. 'Her presence would be inappropriate at a reception being staged for my bride's introduction.'

'Well, if she turns up, *I'm* not bothered,' Willow confided, reckoning that she only had curiosity to be satisfied in such a scenario. 'It must be almost ten years since you were with her. I have the vaguest memory of Dad mentioning your wedding being cancelled and I was so young back then that it feels like a very, *very* long time ago.'

'You have a wonderfully welcome ability to ignore developments or mistakes that would enrage and distress other women I have known,' Jai remarked, his pale glittering gaze fully focussed on her as he smiled down at her appreciatively.

Her heartbeat sped up so much she almost clamped her hand to her chest, and she swallowed back the dryness in her throat. 'But that doesn't mean that I'm not nosy,' she told him playfully, fighting her susceptibility to that smile with all her might, for he might have the power of command over her every sense but she didn't want him influencing her brain into the bargain. 'Tell me about her...'

'Some other time,' Jai parried, closing down that informational avenue without hesitation, the hand he had braced lightly against her spine urging her forward to greet the couple who had entered. 'Our first arrivals... congratulations, Jivika! How did you get your husband out the door this early?' he asked with a grin, clearly on warm, relaxed terms with the older couple.

'I thought your bride might enjoy some support at a family event like this and, like most men, I doubt it even occurred to you that this *is* a rather intimidating event for a newcomer,' the older woman said drily to Jai as she walked towards Willow and extended her hand. 'I'm Jai's aunt, Jivika, his father's sister. I'll give you the lowdown on the family members to avoid and those you can afford to encourage,' she promised with a surprisingly warm smile lighting up her rather stern features.

'Jivika!' her husband scolded.

Jai just laughed. 'I could put my wife in no safer hands. Willow, be warned... Jivika was a leading barrister in London and retirement is challenging for her.'

'Only during Indian winters,' his aunt corrected. 'The rest of the year we live in London.'

Willow was grateful for the older woman's assistance as a slow steady flood of guests flowed through the giant doors and drinks were served in the vast drawing room. 'Grandad was *so* pretentious,' Jivika said of her surroundings.

And her commentaries on various relatives were equally entertaining. Willow got used to asking Jai's aunt to identify guests and when she saw her husband deeply engaged in conversation with a tall, shapely blonde, beautiful enough to pass as a supermodel, she couldn't resist asking who she was.

'Cecilia Montmorency. What's she doing here?' Jivika asked bluntly in turn.

Jolted by that name, Willow explained the mistake on the guest list while becoming disconcerted that Cecilia was constantly touching Jai's arm and laughing up into his face in a very intimate manner. She registered that she was not quite as safe from jealous possessiveness as she had cheerfully assumed. But then how could she be? Jai must have *loved* Cecilia to want to marry at the age of twenty-one, and love was a binding emotion that people didn't tend to forget, not to mention a deeper layer of commitment that Willow had lacked in her marriage from the outset.

'You're seeing a not-so-merry divorcee on the prowl for her next meal ticket,' Jivika commented. 'It must be galling to know that she once dumped one of the richest men in the world.'

It was Willow's turn to stare and exclaim, *'Jai's...?'*

His aunt smiled. 'I like that you didn't know but you can bet your favourite shoes that Cecilia knows what he's worth down to the last decimal point.'

Willow guiltily cherished the older woman's take on

Jai's ex as a gold-digger and, relaxing more and more
in her company, she became more daring and asked
about Jai's mother, asking what sort of woman she had
been that she could walk away from her child.

'Been listening to Jai's version of reality, I assume?'
Jivika shot her a wry glance. 'Jai was indoctrinated by
my brother from an early age. Milly *didn't* walk away
from her son by choice. My brother, Rehan, fought her
through the courts for years and succeeded in denying
her access to her son, even in the UK while Jai was at
school there. In the end she gave up—the woman really didn't have much choice after the legal system in
both countries had repeatedly failed her.'

Stunned by that very different version of events,
Willow studied the other woman in disbelief. 'Why
didn't you tell Jai?'

Jivika spread her hands and sighed, 'At first, loyalty
to my much-loved but misguided brother and, since
his death, no desire to raise sleeping dogs and upset
Jai. He's astute. He's capable of making his own decisions. It's not my place to interfere and he could hate
me for it.'

Willow swallowed hard, thinking of the judgements
she had made about Jai's mother simply by listening to
his opinion of his mother's behaviour. That he might
not know the truth had not once occurred to her. Now
she was barely able to imagine what it would be like for
him to learn that the father he had loved and respected
had lied to him for years on the same subject and she
fully understood his aunt's unwillingness to intervene.

Jai deserved to know the truth and yet who would want to be the one to *tell* him? she thought ruefully.

Sher joined them and was about to move on when a question from Jivika revealed that Willow had trained as a garden designer. His handsome features sparked with sudden interest and he turned back to say, 'I'll call over in a few days and put a project in front of you...*if* you're interested? I have a garden to restore.'

'I'd be happy to offer advice but I haven't had a huge amount of working experience,' Willow admitted ruefully, because Hari's impending birth and her need to earn money had forced her to put her potential career on a back burner.

'Good enough for me,' Sher told her reassuringly. 'What counts is not the number of projects you have completed but whether or not you have the eye and the skill and can interpret my preferences.'

'I'll let you decide that,' Willow said, colouring a little with relief, encountering Jai's bright shrewd gaze as he joined them and swept her onto the dance floor with the quite unnecessary explanation that it was expected of them.

'You seem to have managed beautifully without me by your side,' Jai observed.

Willow looked up at him, wondering why she couldn't decide whether that statement was supposed to be a positive or negative comment. Her nose wrinkled and she smiled. 'Having your aunt by my side was like having an entire army backing me,' she confided with helpless honesty.

Jai laughed out loud. 'I'm very fond of Jivika,' he admitted. 'She was particularly stellar when I was home-sick in London as a child. Of course, she and my father were very close.'

Not quite as close as they could've been, Willow reflected, thinking of that exchange relating to Jai's mother, before conceding that the Singh family dynamic was vastly different from anything she had ever seen before, because even his family treated Jai with the reverence his status as Maharaja commanded, a bred-in-the-bone awe that his father must have enjoyed as well. Such men might not have the right to rule any longer in a republic, but the people still viewed them as being very special and unquestionably royal. Every month Jai held an audience at which any of his father's former subjects could approach him for advice or assistance of any kind and he still saw it as his duty to give that attention to those in need.

'So, my family and friends haven't been as intimidating for you as Jivika feared?' Ice-blue eyes inspected her face with unmistakeable concern.

Touched by that consideration, Willow shifted a little closer to him and his arms tightened round her before his hands smoothed down to the gentle curve of her hips. 'No, everyone's been wonderfully welcoming. How was Cecilia?' she dared.

The faintest colour fired the exotic slant of Jai's hard cheekbones. 'Unchanged. She has one of those amazingly bubbly personalities that always charms, even though she's been through what sounds like a pretty brutal divorce. I was surprised that her arrival and her approach didn't annoy me more...but then we broke up a long time ago and, looking back, I'm prepared to admit that at that age I was more of a boy than a man. It's time to forgive and forget.'

Willow hadn't been prepared to detect quite that much enthusiasm on the topic of the ex who had jilted him. Dimly, she supposed it was healthier that Jai wasn't bitter and had clearly long since moved on from that period of his life.

'She'll probably visit us. She's gasping to meet Hari,' Jai added lightly.

'Why on earth would *she* want to meet Hari?' Willow demanded with an astonishment she wasn't quick enough to hide.

'Because he's my son and possibly because she can't have children of her own,' Jai proffered, his intonation cool and on the edge of critical, his far too clever ice-blue eyes locking to her flushed face, his lean, strong length stiffening a little against her as he moved her expertly around the floor. 'That's why her husband divorced her. Apparently, he's desperate for a son and heir.'

Willow's brain kicked into gear again. 'How very sad,' she remarked, literally stooping to the level of *forcing* fake sympathy into her voice. 'But I thought she had come only for the wedding.'

'No, seems she's doing a tour of Rajasthan while she's here,' Jai interposed, the tension in his lean, powerful frame dissipating again. 'I said I'd draw up a list of sites she shouldn't miss…'

As if there weren't at least a thousand tour guides for hire in Chandrapur alone, Willow thought sourly, because tourism was a huge source of income in the Golden Triangle, as the area was often described.

'I'm sure she would find that very helpful,' Willow commented blithely, annoyance with him, even greater annoyance with Cecilia and a tumble of confusing emotions raining down on her from all sides. Jai was teaching her to lie like a trooper, as the saying went, she conceded guiltily, but nowhere in their relationship was there any given right for her to make a fuss on such a score as a too-friendly ex-girlfriend. They had a marriage of convenience, not a love match, such as he had once almost achieved with Cecilia.

There was no avoiding the obvious: she was jealous and possessive of the man she had married. Disquiet gripped her. When had that happened? How had she failed to notice such responses creeping up on her? In the midst of her turmoil, Jai kissed her, one hand on her shoulder, one framing her face, and she fell into that kiss like a drowning swimmer plunged fathoms deep without warning. Her body lit up like a firework display, nipples tightening, pelvis clenching as if he had done something much more intimate than press his sensual mouth to hers. But then Jai had a way with a kiss that could burn through her like a flame. Like honey being heated, she was warming, melting, pressing closer to the allure of his hard, muscular physique, no detail of him concealed by the fine silk he wore. An arrow of satisfaction pierced Willow then, for Jai might have talked fondly about his ex but it was still *his wife* who turned him on.

'We'll have to stay on the floor,' Jai growled in her ear. 'I'm not presentable right now.'

Willow chuckled, her cheeks colouring, for over the past week she had learned that she and Jai always seemed to scorch each other when they touched. She wanted to reach up and kiss him again, more deeply and for longer, but she resisted the urge, reminding herself that they were surrounded by people.

Later, Jivika and her husband were leaving when the older woman signalled her, and Willow walked over to her with a wide smile. 'It occurs to me that a wife who is loved could tackle that difficult subject we discussed earlier,' she murmured sibilantly. 'If you break the ice, I will be happy to share all that I know with my nephew.'

Willow maintained her smile with difficulty, but she could feel the blood draining from her face because she was *not* a loved wife, not even close to it, she acknowledged painfully, utterly convinced that her strongest bond with Jai was sexual rather than emotional. And that awareness stabbed through her in an almost physical pain, she registered then in dismay. Of course, she had kind of known from the start that she wanted more than sex from Jai, but somehow it hadn't crossed her mind that she was *already* much more deeply involved in their relationship than he was.

There was no denying it: she had fallen hopelessly in love with the man who had married her only to legitimise his son's birth. It had started way back that first night when she had fallen into bed with him and Hari had been conceived in the flare-up of passion between them…and if she was honest with herself, even though she didn't feel she could be *that* honest with Jai, it was an attraction that Jai had *always* held for her.

That long-ago adolescent crush had only been the first indication that she was intensely susceptible to Jai and exposed to him as an adult, the remnants of that crush had simply morphed that first week they were married into something much more powerful. She loved him. That was why she was constantly insecure and prickly and, now, possessive of him. If she hadn't been in love with him, she would have been much less anxious and hurt when he'd chosen to step back from her during the second week they had been together.

And nothing was likely to change, she reflected, deciding to tuck away all her anxiety and bury it, because there was nothing she could do to change either Jai's feelings or her own. It was what it was, and she had to live with it. Certainly, interfering on his mother's behalf, as even his aunt had feared to do, was out of the question.

Even so, she *did* feel that she should meet Lady Milly discreetly and discover the facts for some future date when hopefully she and Jai would have been married long enough for her to trust that they had a stable relationship. After all, it seemed wrong that she, as Jai's wife, should also stand back and do nothing while the poor woman suffered for sins she hadn't committed. It might not be her business in many ways, but Willow had a strong sense of justice. It would do no harm for her to at least listen to the woman while simultaneously introducing her to her grandson, she told herself squarely.

Furthermore, Jai still had the time to mend his relationship with his mother, who clearly loved him. His mother had to love him, for why else would she have fought for years to see him again? Her persistence was self-explanatory. What was more, Milly was family and surely everyone was willing to go that extra mile for a family member? Jai now had a chance that Willow had never had with her own father. She had failed to win her father's love time and time again because really the only thing he had appreciated in a child was the ability to achieve top academic results. But Jai's mother was offering love even after multiple rejections. Unfortunately past hurt and pride would prevent Jai from giving his mother the chance to redeem herself, but what if Willow could take that chance for him and use it?

Cecilia arrived at the Lake Palace for a visit the following afternoon and caught Willow unprepared. She was down on her knees playing with Hari in the nursery with tumbled hair and not a scrap of make-up on when Jai strolled in with Cecilia in tow and not the smallest warning. In that moment, Willow genuinely wanted to kill Jai. She sat up with a feverishly flushed face and struggled to smile politely as Cecilia dropped gracefully down beside her and exclaimed over the resemblance between Hari and Jai.

'He's got your eyes, Jai!' Cecilia crooned in delight, smoothing a hand over Hari's curls. 'He is adorable.'

'Yes, he is,' Willow conceded fondly, stifling her irritation with difficulty.

'Do you remember your father taking us on a tour of the desert that first summer?' Cecilia asked Jai.

And that was the start of the 'do you remember?' game that stretched throughout coffee downstairs as Cecilia encouraged Jai to reminisce about friends from their university days and brought him up to speed on the activities of those he had lost touch with. Willow might as well have been a painting on the wall for all the share she got of the conversation, while Cecilia became more and more animated at the attention she was receiving. It was a total surprise to Willow when Jai smoothly mentioned that they were going out to lunch, an arrangement that was news to her, and moments later Cecilia began making visibly reluctant departure moves.

'So, when was this lunch with Sher arranged?' Willow enquired curiously on the steps of the palace as the blonde was driven off by her driver in an SUV.

'Oh, that's tomorrow,' Jai admitted with a tiny smile of superiority as he absorbed her surprise. 'It was time for Cecilia to leave.'

Disconcerted, Willow turned back to him. 'You mean—?'

'I lied? *Yes*,' Jai interposed with dancing eyes of amusement at her astonishment. 'I will always be polite to Cecilia but I have no wish to socialise with her. Yesterday I was curious, today I was bored with her.'

Relief sank through Willow in a blinding wave. 'But I thought—'

'That I am still naive enough to be duped by a woman who chose to welcome a richer man into her bed?' Jai said, sliding an arm round her slender spine. 'No, I'm not.'

'A richer man?' Willow queried, recalling his aunt's opinion of the beautiful blonde.

'Within a month of breaking off our engagement, Cecilia was married to the owner of a private bank. Her affair with him began while she was *still* with me,' Jai breathed with sardonic bite. 'Shortly before her change of heart, she had learned that my sole wealth at that point was based on my share of the family trust, and at the time my business was only in its infancy. She went for a more promising option—a much older man with a pile of capital.'

Still frowning, Willow glanced up at him. 'But when it happened you must have been devastated.'

'Not so devastated that I didn't eventually recognise that I'd had a narrow escape,' Jai quipped with raw-edged amusement. 'Her marriage to a man old enough to be her father was the first evidence of her true nature. My mother made the same move,' he extended in a rare casual reference to his parents' marriage. 'Money must've been her main objective too. I can't believe she ever loved my father.'

Willow set her teeth together and said nothing, thinking that his father really had done a number on him, leaving him not one shred of faith in the woman who had brought him into the world and, by achieving that, had ensured that Jai never became curious enough to meet the woman and decide for himself.

Jai came to bed late that night because he had been working. He was a tall sliver of lean, supple beauty in the moonlight, sliding in beside her and reaching for her in almost the same movement.

'You can't,' she told him, feeling awkward because it was that time of the month.

'You mean—?'

'Yes,' she confirmed drowsily.

'Doesn't mean I can't hold you, doesn't mean I can't kiss you,' Jai teased, folding her into his arms regardless. 'This is the very first time I've met with that restriction since my engagement.'

Thinking of all the years he had been free and single, Willow said, 'How can it be?'

'After Cecilia the longest I stayed with a woman was a weekend. It was a practical choice for me, selfish too, I'll admit, but I didn't want anything deeper or more lasting.'

'Oh, dear, and here I am planning to last and last and *last*,' she whispered playfully. 'Maybe you'll eventually love me too because you're stuck with me.'

His lean, strong physique tensed. 'No, the love trail isn't for me. That would be excess, and we don't need it to be happy or raise Hari together. Be practical, *soniyaa*. What we've got is much more realistic.'

A hollow sensation spread inside Willow's chest along with a very strong urge to kick the love of her life out of bed. It was early days, though, she reminded herself, and she was being greedy and impatient. In a year's time she might have grown on him to such an extent that he did love her. Or was that simply a fantasy? If he hadn't been bowled over by her from the outset, she was unlikely ever to become the sole and most important focus of his wants, logic warned her. Unfortunately for her, her heart didn't jump at the words, 'practical' or 'realistic.'

CHAPTER NINE

THEY LUNCHED WITH Sher the following day at his family home, which his late father had allowed to fall into rack and ruin.

Only a small part of the ancient Nizam of Tharistan's palace had so far been made liveable, and they dined in that wing on a shaded terrace overlooking a vast stretch of uncultivated land, which Sher admitted had once been the gardens. At Willow's request he had gathered old records, paintings and photographs from Victorian times in an effort to provide some evidence of what the gardens had once looked like, for what remained was simply undergrowth with the occasional hint of the shape of a path or flowerbed.

'It'll be a massive project,' she warned him. 'And hugely expensive.'

'Not a problem for Sher.' Jai laughed.

'Would it be possible for me to take these records and old photos home with me?' Willow pressed the other man. 'What you really need is an archaeological garden survey done.'

'No, I'll be content with something in the spirit of

the original gardens, rather than requiring an exact replica,' Sher admitted. 'I'll bring the old maps over to you tomorrow. I keep them in a climate-controlled environment but as long as you wear gloves handling them, they'll be fine.'

'I can't wait to see them,' Willow confided, excitement brimming in her sparkling green eyes, all her attention on Sher. 'Of course, I'll wear gloves.'

Lunch with two highly creative people was not to be recommended, Jai decided at that point, unless you were of a similar ilk. And Jai *wasn't*. A garden was only a green space to him that complemented a building. Books, technology and business alone held his interest.

When they had climbed back into the limo, Jai thought he should warn his wife of the possible pitfalls of what she was planning. 'As you said, it will be a huge project,' he reminded her smoothly. 'Do you really know what you're taking on?'

Willow straightened her shoulders and turned to him with an eager smile. 'I can't wait!'

'But it will demand a lot of your time.'

'What else do I have to focus on?' Willow prompted.

Myself and my son, Jai reckoned. But he was too clever to say it out loud, admitting that it sounded like something his elderly father would have said and inwardly wincing at the comparison. 'I had been hoping that you would take on some duties with the foundation when you have the time to decide which of our charitable groups would most interest you,' he commented, and it wasn't a lie, he reasoned, even if that possibility had only just occurred to him. 'It would get you out and about more and give you a role of your own.'

'That's a wonderful suggestion,' Willow said warmly. 'But maybe best saved for when I've fully found my feet here.'

'I thought you already had…found your feet,' he admitted.

'Different country, different culture, different languages, different *everything*,' she enumerated with quiet emphasis. 'I love my life here but right now I'm still acclimatising to the changes. I don't think I'm quite ready yet to step out in a social setting as your Maharani, particularly when everyone will be expecting someone like you, experienced at making speeches and knowledgeable about community work.'

That explanation silenced Jai because he immediately grasped that he had not even considered the changes that her move to India on his behalf had made to her life. Rare discomfiture afflicted him. Had he always been so self-absorbed that he only saw in terms of what best suited him? That disposed to be selfish and arrogant? He gritted his teeth at the suspicion and said no more, quite forgetting the irritation that his best friend had inexplicably evoked in him.

The next morning, Sher brought the maps over and, together, he and Willow pored over the old parchments in the library, Jai soon taking his leave. Searching for evidence of former paths, banks, sunken areas and even small garden buildings, they discovered a wealth of useful facts. Thoroughly enjoying herself, Willow did sketches and made copious notes while Sher talked at length about what he liked to see in a garden. When Jai walked in again, they were trading jokes about what they suspected was the marking for an ancient surprise fountain that had been designed to startle the ladies as they walked past by drenching them.

For a split second, Jai froze on the threshold. Willow and Sher were on a rug on the floor laughing uproariously, one of his friend's hands on her slim shoulder to steady her as she almost overbalanced in her mirth into the welter of papers that surrounded them.

'Lunch,' Jai announced coolly.

'Oh, my goodness, is it *that* time already?' Willow carolled in astonishment, almost as if she hadn't been camping out in the library for a solid four hours with his best friend, Jai thought in disbelief. Evidently when in Sher's company time had wings for his wife.

Sher's entire attention was pinned to Willow's face. His friend was attracted to her. Jai had already guessed that, for Willow was a classic beauty, but then Sher was attracted to a lot of women and, as a former Bollywood star, he flirted with *all* of them, be they grandmothers or teenagers, because he was accustomed to playing to admiring crowds. Even so, Jai trusted Sher with his wife, *totally* trusted him. He was fully aware that his friend would never *ever* cross a line with a married woman because that same scenario had destroyed Sher's parents' marriage.

No, Jai didn't blame Sher for the intimate scene he had interrupted, he blamed Willow for getting too friendly, for curling up on the floor and making herself recklessly, dangerously approachable, *his* Maharani, acting like a giggly, frisky schoolgirl, he thought furiously. A man less sophisticated than Sher might have read her signals wrong and taken advantage, might have *made a move* on her, the concept of which sent such a current of lancing rage shooting through Jai that he clenched his lean hands into angry fists of restraint by his sides.

He wouldn't lose his temper when he spoke to Willow later, but he would give her useful advice on how to keep other men at a safe distance, advice she certainly needed if what he was seeing was likely to be typical of her behaviour in male company.

'You've been very quiet,' Willow commented over dinner, hours after Sher had departed, leaving her free to spend a contented afternoon pondering the old photos while trying to visualise the lush and colourful garden that Sher would most enjoy.

That was the moment that Jai became aware that what he had *planned* to say to his wife didn't sound quite the same as when he had first thought the matter over. He breathed in deep and decided that tact was all very well, but it might not get across the exact message he wanted to impart and that message was too important to hold back.

'You flirt with Sher and I dislike it,' Jai delivered bluntly, pushing back his chair and rising from his seat with his wine glass elegantly cupped in one lean brown hand.

For the count of ten seconds, Willow simply gaped at him in disbelief. *He did not just say that, he could not have accused me of* that, she was thinking, and then she looked at him, really looked at his lean, darkly handsome face, and realised by the glitter of his ice-blue eyes and the taut line of his sensual mouth that, no, sadly, he hadn't been joking. She was stunned, incredulous that he could have misunderstood her banter with Sher to that extent, and then just as quickly angry at the speed with which he had misjudged her. In turn, she too rose from her chair and left the table.

'For goodness' sake, I don't flirt with Sher,' she said defensively. 'It's only a friendly thing, nothing the slightest bit suspect about it. I don't know how you could possibly think otherwise.'

Jai's cool appraisal didn't waver. 'But I do. You need to learn how to keep a certain distance in your manner with other men.'

'And you need to learn how not to be irrationally jealous!' Willow slammed back at him without warning, her patience tested beyond its limits and flaming into throbbing resentment.

Those two words, 'irrational' and 'jealous,' struck Jai like bricks. He didn't do either emotion. Unfortunately, those same words also hooked into a phrase his aunt had, many years earlier, once used to describe his father. Later, when challenged by Jai, Jivika had withdrawn the comment and, unfortunately, Willow's use of those offensive words sent a wave of antipathy travelling through him. 'I'm not jealous, Willow. I'm merely asking you to monitor your behaviour in male company.'

'But you'd really prefer me *not* to have male friends?' Willow darted back at him.

Disconcerted by that surprising question, Jai frowned. 'Well, yes, that may be the wisest approach.'

'So, quite obviously, you *are* the jealous, possessive, irrational type you think you aren't…or possibly a throwback to the dinosaurs when men and women didn't make friends with the opposite sex?' Willow shot back at him wrathfully. 'Obviously you have about as much self-awareness as a stone in the wall! Sher's like the brother I never had!'

'You don't have a brother!' Jai fired back at her.

'Didn't I just say that?' Willow exclaimed furiously. 'There was no flirting between us, nothing anyone could criticise. I like him and that's *it*! I certainly don't fancy him.'

Marginally mollified by that admission and aware that Ranjit was loitering in the dining room beyond the doors opening out onto the terrace, Jai murmured in an effort to lower the volume of their dispute, 'I'm not even saying that you knew that you were flirting. It may have been quite unconscious on your part.'

'Well, it must have been unconscious because I don't think I even know *how* to flirt, with my lack of experience in that field!' Willow slung back at him even louder. 'Whatever you think you *saw* between Sher and me, you got it wrong, Jai.'

The doors eased shut with diplomatic quietness and colour edged Jai's spectacular cheekbones. She was being unreasonable, and he didn't know how what he had said had escalated into a full-blown acrimonious scene. He was not the jealous type and he was never, ever irrational and, had he been possessive, he would have stopped Sher from offering her the project in the first instance. And now, he wished he *had* done that, he conceded grimly.

'I didn't get it wrong,' he insisted, refusing to yield an inch.

Willow lifted her chin, outraged green eyes locking to his. 'You got it wrong in every way possible,' she told him succinctly. 'There was no flirting but if you can't even admit that you're jealous, how is anyone to persuade you that you're wrong? All right, I'll even make it easier for you. I'll admit that initially I was jealous of Cecilia.'

'Why on earth would you be jealous of *her*?' Jai demanded in astonishment.

'Because she was all over you like a rash at the party and at no time did I see *you* pushing her away and respecting the sort of boundaries you're accusing me of breaking with Sher!' Willow accused.

'That was a different situation,' Jai argued. 'She was a friend long before I became more deeply involved with her.'

'Oh, have it your own way!' Willow snapped back in frustration, wishing she could get inside his head to rearrange his brain into a pattern she could recognise. 'I'm done here. I've got nothing more to say to you until you admit that you're a jealous, possessive toad, and then I *might* forgive you for insulting me!'

Beneath Jai's speechless gaze, Willow rammed open the door and vanished back into the palace without another word. He refilled his wine glass and stood looking out over the lake, watching a sloth bear slurp a noisy drink at the edge of the lake while the chitter chatter of monkeys at dusk filled the air. Slowly he breathed in deeply, telling himself he had been foolish to assume that marriage would be an easy ride.

And yet it generally *was* with Willow, he conceded grudgingly. She had slotted into his life as though she had always been there, and he shared more with her than he had ever shared with a woman. At the outset, he had assumed that their marriage would be all about Hari, only it wasn't. Their son was a point of connection, but it was Willow's unspoilt, gentle nature, her lack of feminine guile and her interest in learning about everything that was new to her that continued to intrigue Jai. The flirting, most probably, had been unconscious, he decided, and possibly he should have kept his reservations about the degree of friendliness between his wife and his best friend to himself.

After all, he fully trusted Sher, so why hadn't he had the same amount of faith in Willow? Hadn't he once even cherished the insane suspicion that Willow might have been a fortune hunter? Was he so truly a prisoner of his father's unhappy past and Cecilia's mercenary betrayal that he could not trust a woman? That idea shook him and put him into a brooding mood before he went back to his office to work, as was his wont, to escape his uneasy thoughts.

Several hours later, he entered their bedroom quietly and discovered the ultimate bed-blocker blinking up at him in the moonlight: his son, snuggled up next to his mother. Hari closed his eyes again and Jai went off to find another bed.

Willow woke early the next morning with Hari tugging at her hair, and looked down at her son in surprise because she hadn't intended him to spend the night with her, had simply fallen asleep while cuddling him for comfort. It's not safe to sleep with him, her conscience reproached her, and she freshened up and returned Hari to the nursery staff, who greeted him as though he had been absent a week. She breakfasted alone, assuming Jai was already in his office because he was fond of dawn starts. Her annoyance with him was still intense, but she was troubled by the stand-off she had initiated the night before because Jai could be as stubborn and unyielding as the rock she had compared him to.

Willow sighed. She had had to confront him. He had not given her a choice and how could she compromise? The answer was that on such a dangerous point of contention, she *couldn't* compromise, not if she wanted their relationship to have a future. That truth acknowledged, she frowned as she realised that this was also the morning Jai's mother had invited her to meet her. She hadn't had time to dwell on that thorny issue in recent days but now it was first and foremost in her mind.

Did she ignore that invitation as Jai would unquestionably expect her to do, or did she meet Lady Milly because she now knew, thanks to Jivika, that Jai's mother had been cruelly misjudged?

Surely she had a right to discover the facts of the situation for herself? Or, even as Jai's wife, was that background none of her business? Sadly, Jai was too loyal to his father's memory to take advantage of the same opportunity, she reflected, and that was tragic. Maybe she could be a peacemaker, a go-between, she thought optimistically. If the meeting went the right way, it could bring Jai a great deal of happiness, she reasoned, her heart lifting at that optimistic prospect. Even Jai's aunt, however, had been unwilling to run the risk of getting involved and yet Jivika was neither a weak nor timid personality. Willow's teeth worried anxiously at her lower lip as she weighed the odds and then a rueful smile slowly crept across her lips because when it got down to basics, it was a simple decision.

Jai had been badly damaged and hurt by his conviction that his mother had abandoned him as a baby. Willow loved him, even when she was angry with him. If there was anything she could do to ease that pain that Jai fought to hide from the world, she *would* do it. And if he rediscovered a lost mother from the exercise, it would be well worth the risk she took and far more than she had ever managed to achieve with her own father, she conceded sadly.

A couple of hours later, Willow walked into the Royal Chandrapur, an exclusive boutique establishment on the other side of the city. From reception, she wheeled Hari's buggy into the tiny lift and breathed in deep.

The first surprise was that the small blond woman who opened the door to her appeared to be much younger than she had expected. Well-preserved, she assumed, meeting eyes of the same startling pale blue as her husband's and taking in the huge smile on the other woman's face.

'I didn't think you'd come,' she said frankly.

Willow winced. 'I almost didn't. Jai doesn't know I'm here,' she admitted guiltily.

'And this is…little Hari?'

As the door closed behind them, Jai's mother knelt down by the side of the buggy and studied Willow's son in fascination. 'He is spookily like Jai was at the same age,' she whispered appreciatively. 'Just a little older than Jai was when I left India.'

Willow breathed in deep and settled into the seat the other woman indicated with a casual hand. 'What I don't understand is, if you wanted contact with Jai why did you virtually cut him dead when you did finally meet him as an adult?'

'Let me start at the beginning and then perhaps you'll understand better. If you don't, that's fine too. I'm grateful you came here. First of all, I am Milly… and you are… Willow, I gather?'

Willow harnessed the very rude impatience tugging at her and nodded with a smile.

'Would you like tea?'

'No, thanks. Being here with you makes me a little nervous. Let's talk about whatever we have to talk about,' Willow urged.

'A little background first, then,' Milly decided, seemingly magnetised by the tiny fingers Hari was stretching out to her. 'May I lift him?' she asked hopefully.

Leaning down, Willow detached the harness and

watched her son being scooped gently into his grand-mother's arms.

'Where do I start?' Milly sighed then. 'I was twenty and Jai's father was fifty when we married. My family were against it from the start because of the age gap but I was madly in love and I thought I knew it all.'

'I didn't know that there was such a big age gap between you,' Willow admitted.

'The marriage didn't work from the start. Rehan wanted a quiet little wife, who stayed at home, and I was very independent. He was insanely jealous and controlling but the assaults didn't begin until after Jai was born,' Milly murmured flatly.

Willow's clear gaze widened in dismay. 'He *hit* you?' she exclaimed.

Milly nodded. 'We had terrible rows and he couldn't control his temper. But I'm talking about slaps and kicks, not severe beatings.'

'Abuse is abuse,' Willow opined.

'When my mother was dying, I had to return to England to be with her and, before I left, I made the mistake of telling Rehan that I believed we should separate. My biggest mistake, though, was agreeing to leave Jai behind until I came back. I was only away for two weeks,' Milly proffered. 'Rehan attended my mother's funeral and brought what he said were divorce papers for me to sign but they were all in Hindi. I was so relieved that he was willing to let me go without a fuss that I signed... I hadn't the smallest suspicion that I was surrendering my right to have custody of my son or access to him and by the time I realised that it was too late.'

'Jai's father tricked you?' Willow was appalled.

Milly lifted a thick file on the small table between them and extended it. 'If you can do nothing else, give this to Jai. It's the proof of all the years I fought through the courts to try and regain access to him. I failed.'

'But why, if you *wanted* to see him, did you deny him or whatever it was you did when you *did* see him?' Willow demanded bluntly.

'My husband and stepchildren didn't know Jai existed at that stage,' Milly volunteered shamefacedly. 'Steven, my second husband, knew about my marriage to Rehan but I didn't tell him that I'd had a child. My battle to see Jai consumed a decade and a half of my life and I got nowhere in all that time. I needed to move on to retain my sanity and make a fresh start. But I *will* admit that I was fearful of telling Steven that I had been deprived of my right to see my own child because, with three kids of his own, it might have made him doubt the wisdom of marrying me.'

The picture Willow was forming became a little clearer in receipt of that frank admission. 'Steven had three children? They're not yours?' she prompted.

'He was a widower with a young family when we met. I did hope to have another child, but I was almost forty by the time we married and it didn't happen. It was only a few months afterwards that I ran into Jai in the flesh,' his mother confided with tears in her eyes. 'Someone actually introduced me to him… I was floored—there he was in front of me with his face stiffening as he realised who I was and I had been too scared to tell Steven about him! I walked away because I didn't know what else to do with other people all around us. I wasn't prepared.'

'And then you tried to see Jai afterwards to explain,' Willow filled in with a grimace. 'And it was too late. The damage was done.'

Milly's regret was palpable as she rocked Hari, who was curled up in her arms, perfectly content. 'If only people stayed this innocent.' She sighed. 'I left a baby behind and now he's a man and they're much more complicated.'

Tell me about it, Willow ruminated uneasily, wondering whether she should go straight back to the Lake Palace and tell Jai who she had been with, or whether to go shopping instead in an effort to make her cover-up lie the truth, which would give her time to choose the optimum moment for such a revelation. But would there ever be a right moment to tackle so very personal and controversial a subject?

Deepening the deception she was already engaged in, however, felt even more wrong to her. Indeed, even being with Milly without her son's knowledge felt wrong to Willow at that moment. But good intentions had to count for something, didn't they? She argued with herself as she lifted the file and told Milly that she needed to get home but hoped to see her again. The older woman's answering smile was sad, as if she seriously doubted the likelihood of them ever having a second meeting, and she thanked Willow heartily again for being willing to see her and giving her the chance to meet her grandson. When Willow mentioned Jivika's input, Milly simply rolled her eyes, unimpressed.

'Jivika is sincere,' Willow insisted defensively.

'But nothing's changed. My ex-husband and, by the sound of it, now Jai as well have too much influence, too much status to be treated like ordinary people.' Milly studied her with embittered eyes. 'They may not rule any more but they're still royal in the eyes of thousands. That's why I never had a hope of fighting Rehan and winning. It was never an equal playing field. There were witnesses, who could've supported me but who were unwilling to expose their Maharaja for the man he really was.'

'I'm truly sorry,' Willow muttered uncomfortably. 'I can't promise anything, but I will *try* to talk to Jai some time soon.'

Even if it cost her *her* marriage? she asked herself worriedly as the limo drove back to the palace with Hari dozing contentedly in his child seat. Or was that an exaggerated fear? Who could tell how badly Jai would react? No, it wasn't her place to act as a persuader, she reasoned uneasily. She would admit to meeting up with his mother and give him the file and leave it at that. She had interfered enough. He would make up his own mind about what, if anything, he wanted to do with what he learned.

When Jai went in search of Willow mid-morning he assumed she had gone to see Sher until he recalled that his friend had mentioned a trip to Mumbai that day, and he phoned her driver instead to discover where she had gone. A hotel? A moment later he rang the hotel and without hesitation requested a list of the British guests staying there. Only a few minutes beyond that he knew the only possible reason for his wife's visit to the Royal Chandrapur and he could not credit that, after what he had told her, she could have gone to meet his mother. It outraged him and it didn't make sense to him. Even so, by the time acceptance of that unwelcome fact had set in, his outrage had settled into a far more dangerous sense of betrayal.

When Willow climbed out of the limo carrying her sleeping son, eager hands were extended to take him back to the nursery and his lunch. Straightening, she headed up the shallow marble steps and saw Jai poised in the empty hall. One glance at the narrowed chilling glitter of his eyes and the forbidding coolness of his lean, strong features and her stomach dropped as though the ground beneath her feet had suddenly vanished. Her mouth ran dry and she swallowed painfully.

CHAPTER TEN

'YOU KNOW WHERE I've been,' Willow guessed, her fingers biting into the heavy file she clasped in one hand. 'Let me explain.'

'Let me make it clear from the start—there *is* no acceptable explanation,' Jai asserted, his shadowed, well-defined jaw line clenching hard as he strode into the library.

He leant back against the desk in the centre of the room, tall and lean and bronzed and beautiful, and her heart clenched because there was a look in his eyes that she had never seen before and it frightened her. He looked detached, wholly in control and calm but utterly distant, as if she were a stranger.

'How did my mother contact you?' Jai shot the question at her.

'By email. One of your staff gave it to me.' Willow shrugged awkwardly. 'I suppose they didn't want to give it to you. I wasn't even going to mention it to you after what you'd told me about her, but then I had a conversation with...er...someone at the party that made me realise that there are two sides to every story.'

Jai elevated an eloquent black brow. *'Someone?'*

Stiff as a board, Willow angled an uneasy hand in dismissal. 'I'm not going to name names. I don't want you dragging anyone else into this mess. I don't want you to be angry with anyone but me.'

'I'm not angry. I am stunned by your intrusion into a matter that is confidential. But I am repelled by what can only be your insatiable curiosity and your complete lack of sensitivity!' Jai enumerated in a voice that shook slightly, belying his contention that he was not angry.

Willow's tummy turned over sickly and her natural colour ebbed. 'I intended to tell you.'

'But you still went to see her,' Jai condemned harshly. 'You knew how I would feel about that and yet *still* you went to see her—to do *what*? To discuss long-past events that are none of your business? To listen to her lies?'

'It's not rational for you to place a complete block on her side of the story or to assume that she's lying without hearing the facts,' Willow dared, but then fear of the trouble she had already caused between them punctured her bravado. 'But I *am* very sorry that I've upset you.'

Jai raked long brown fingers through his luxuriant black hair. 'You let me down. You deceived me.'

'I didn't deceive you!' she gasped in dismay.

'Not telling me that you were planning to meet her was a deception, an unforgivable deception!' Jai ground out in a raw undertone. 'You quite deliberately went behind my back to do something which you knew went against my principles.'

'But I had good intentions,' Willow muttered frantically, her chest tightening at the bite of that threatening word, 'unforgivable,' being attached to anything she had done. 'Feelings always win out over principles with me.'

'I trusted you.'

'No, you've never trusted me. You don't even trust me with your best friend,' Willow reminded him helplessly.

A tinge of dark colour edged Jai's high cheekbones and he studied her grimly. 'I got over that. I worked it out for myself. I *was* jealous of the bond you seem to have forged with Sher and it unsettled me,' he admitted flatly. 'I wasn't thinking logically when I spoke to you yesterday and the issue would've been cleared up last night had you not taken Hari to bed with you. I didn't want to disturb you.'

'You mean…you came to see me later on?' Willow prompted in surprise.

Jai jerked his arrogant dark head in confirmation.

'Thank you for that,' Willow acknowledged tautly, conceding that at least that issue now seemed to have been laid to rest, but not comforted by that knowledge when a bigger abyss seemed to have opened up between them. A gulf she was wholly responsible for creating, she conceded wretchedly.

And she wasn't surprised by that, not now, when she could see the very real damage that she had done with her foolish attempt at undercover sleuthing on his behalf. Jai still emanated tension and the raw glitter of his pale eyes and the compression of his lips remained unchanged. He was convinced that she had betrayed his trust. She had hurt him, and she hadn't meant to, but that wasn't much consolation for her at that moment. Hurting Jai when she had intended only to help him was a real slap in the face.

But then what had she thought she could possibly accomplish when the subject of his estranged mother was still so raw with him that he didn't even like to discuss it? Trying to play God usually got people into trouble, she reflected unhappily. Her handling of the issue had been downright clumsy and poorly thought through. Her hand ached with the tight grip she still had on the file in her hand and she settled it down heavily on the desk.

'Your mother gave this to me.'

'I don't want it…whatever it is,' Jai bit out.

'It's a record of all the legal action she took while you were still a child when she was fighting to gain access to you. Solicitor's letters, family court decisions. It's all there in black and white. I can explain why she couldn't face speaking to you in public as well.'

'I'm not interested.'

'Well, that's your decision,' Willow agreed tightly. 'But if you want my opinion—'

'I *don't*,' Jai sliced in curtly as he swept up the file in one powerful hand. 'I will ensure that this is returned to her.'

'All right.' Willow raised her hands in a semi-soothing gesture as she stepped back from the desk.

'I won't say any more. I may have blundered in where angels fear to tread but I didn't mean to cause this much trouble or harm anyone.'

Jai stared at her with unnerving intensity. 'Why *did* you do it?'

Willow could feel the blood in her face draining away with the stress of that simple acerbic question. 'I thought I could help. I suppose that was pretty naive of me.'

'*Who* did you wish to help?' Jai demanded in a savage undertone of condemnation. 'I'm a grown man, Willow. My father is dead, and I grew up without a mother. I didn't miss my mother because I never knew her. I am more concerned by the damage you have done to us.'

'Us?' she repeated uncertainly.

His lean, darkly handsome features hardened, his eyes chilling to polar ice. 'How do you think that we—our marriage—can possibly come back from this betrayal?' he slung at her rawly.

Willow stared back at him in shock at that stinging question. Was he saying that he truly could not forgive her for what she had done? Perspiration broke out on her brow. Suddenly she felt sick, shaky with fear.

Jai paced angrily away from her as though he could not bear to be too close to her. 'You keep secrets from me,' he condemned harshly, his distaste unhidden. 'You kept your pregnancy and the birth of my son a secret. You kept my mother's email a secret and you intended to keep your visit to her a secret as well for who knows how long!'

'Only because I wanted to meet her and give her a chance!' Willow argued in desperation.

'You said I lacked trust and understanding but have you considered your own flaws?' Jai asked with cruel clarity. 'What do I care about a woman who walked away from me thirty years ago? You and Hari are supposed to be my family now *and* the only family I need. But when I look at the deceit and disloyalty you are capable of, I feel like a fool and I cannot see a future for us!'

Frozen to the beautiful Persian rug, Willow watched Jai walk back out of the library again while her heart plummeted to basement level. Shattered, she just stood there. If he couldn't see a future for them, where did that leave her? Did that mean he was thinking about a divorce? *Truly?* Was their marriage over now because she had angered and disappointed him? But Jai believed that she had betrayed him and that went *deep*.

When she walked through the hall, Ranjit reminded her that lunch was ready. Although she had absolutely no appetite, she struggled to behave normally, to behave as though her life hadn't just fallen apart in front of her, and she headed out to the coolness of the terrace with a heavy heart, praying that Jai would join her and give her the chance to reason with him.

There, however, she sat in solitary splendour, striving to act as though nothing had happened while pushing food round her plate. She had messed up. Correction, she had messed up spectacularly. Jai had moved on from his dysfunctional beginnings. He might still be sensitive about his mother's apparent desertion, but he had learned to live with it, and he hadn't needed her stirring up those muddy waters again.

More tellingly, Jai was much more disturbed by the truth that she had kept secrets from him and acted without his knowledge. Her heart sank because she *was* guilty of making those mistakes and had little defence to offer on that score.

She hadn't known Jai when she'd conceived a child with him. She hadn't known how straight and blunt and honest he was or how much he valued those traits. Loving him, however, she had blundered in, convinced she could act as a peacemaker between him and his estranged mother. How on earth had she been so stupid that she had gone digging into his past, believing that she could somehow heal old wounds and make him happy? Nothing was ever that simple and adults were much more multifaceted than children. As he had reminded her, he was an adult now with a different outlook and values and he was infinitely more disturbed by the reality that the wife he had just begun to trust had let him down than by old history.

Jai had looked at her and found her wanting, Willow registered sickly. Her own father had always looked at her in that light, as his disappointing daughter, who had failed to live up to his fond hopes for her. Being a disappointment was nothing new to Willow but, when the judge was Jai, her failure to reach his standards cut through every layer of skin and hurt as fiercely as an acid burn. Distressed, she left the table to go and find Jai again and attempt to explain the motivation behind her interference.

He wasn't in his office and she wandered through the beautiful rooms until she found him in the relatively small room that his father had used as a study. Above the desk hung a handsome portrait of his late father, Rehan, in a traditional Rajput warrior pose. Jai was in an armchair, his lean, lithe body sleek and taut in an innately graceful sprawl. He had a whiskey glass in his hand and a reckless glitter lit up his bright gaze. Willow's eyes zoomed straight to the file that lay open on the desktop.

'I need to explain things,' she murmured tautly. 'You have to understand why I did what I did…'

'What's to explain?' Jai asked flatly, his wide sensual mouth settling into a grim line. 'There is no arguing with what's contained in that file. Obviously, the father I idolised lied to me all my life and behind those lies there *must* be even worse revelations. People with nothing to hide don't lie.'

'Jai… I—'

'The someone who tipped you off could only have been my aunt, Jivika,' Jai guessed, rising abruptly from his seat. 'Jivika will know everything and that's who I need to speak to now and finish this.'

Willow froze on the threshold of the room, recognising the pain darkening his eyes and shrinking from it in the knowledge that she had inflicted it on him by forcing him to deal with painful truths. 'Let the dust settle first. Mull it over. And don't forget,' she muttered ruefully, 'we all have a good side and a bad side. No matter what you find out one fact doesn't change—you still had a wonderful father who loved you.'

'Who told me that my mother was the love of his life…and yet, according to those documents, he abused her,' Jai breathed with a shudder of revulsion, his shame at such a revelation palpable. 'He lied on so many different levels that are unpardonable. Jivika, however, will know everything and she's family. It will be confidential. I have to know it *all* now.'

For the first time, Willow understood why Jai's aunt had resisted the temptation to interfere, because the ugly truth about his parents' marriage had devastated Jai, rolling a wrecking ball through his every conviction and fond memory. 'I was so naive about this situation,' she confided with heartfelt regret. 'I thought I could fix things but all I've done is cause more damage.'

'No,' Jai contradicted squarely, springing upright and towering over her. 'Even the toughest truths shouldn't be concealed from those concerned.'

'Even when you consider what it's done to our relationship?' she pressed unhappily.

'You were trying to right an injustice. I can respect that,' Jai told her tightly. 'But I don't know if I can accept it and still live with you.'

His savage honesty crushed her. It contained none of the emotion she had longed to see coming in her direction. As Jai left the palace to visit his aunt, her tummy gave a nauseous flip and she turned away again, reckoning that whatever he learned would only cause him more distress. Ultimately, Jai *could* forgive her because she had exposed a truth that should never have been hidden from him, but it didn't mean he would like her for it or that he would want to continue their marriage with a woman he didn't feel he could trust. Nor was he likely to love her for shining a bright light over his father's deceit and his mother's victimhood. And love was what she was always seeking from Jai and least likely to receive, because love had much more humble beginnings.

Sometimes she thought that she had fallen in love with Jai the first time he smiled at her. Or had it happened when he wrapped an arm round her and offered her comfort, showing her a level of tenderness and understanding that she had never experienced before? Yet, it had been his raw, uninhibited passion that had exploded her out of the almost dreamlike state in which she had then lived her life, humbly accepting her limitations while doggedly following her own path and striving to rise above her father's dissatisfaction with her. In matters of the heart, however, she had been naive until Jai came back into her life. Back then she had kept safe within narrow guidelines, never taking a risk, never allowing herself to want anything that seemed as if it might be out of reach. Jai, however, had been a huge risk, and marrying a man so far removed from her in terms of looks, status and wealth had been a challenge because right from the start she had felt out of her depth.

And now she was drowning in a deep sense of loss because she knew that Jai would never look at her in the same way again. Whatever she had achieved, whatever wrong she had tried to put right, she had been disloyal to him and once again she had acted behind his back, employing the secrecy that he abhorred. A prey to her tumultuous emotions, Willow found it impossible to settle to any task while Jai was still out.

Mid-afternoon, she heard the musicians strike up and watched Ranjit make a beeline for the entrance before forcing herself to walk upstairs and take refuge in their bedroom. If he wanted to discuss anything with her, he could come and find her. In the short-term it would be tactless of her to intrude when he probably still needed time and space to absorb what he had learned. Fed up with the warring thoughts assailing her and the almost overwhelming desire to run to his side and offer comfort, she kicked off her shoes and lay down on the bed, fighting her own inclinations to leave him alone rather than crowd him. After all, if she crowded him, she might only encourage him to dwell on the negative feelings he had been having about their marriage before his departure.

When Jai strode through the bedroom door and gave her a brilliant shimmering smile, it utterly disconcerted her. In consternation, Willow sat up and stared at him.

'After what I said to you in my state of shock, I'm surprised that you're still here,' Jai admitted tautly, 'and not on the first flight back to London.'

'Some of what you said was fair. I *did* keep secrets, but only because I didn't want to upset you. I honestly believed that telling you I was pregnant would be the worst news you'd ever heard,' Willow confided ruefully. 'And I couldn't face it.'

'After you, Hari's the best thing that ever happened

to me,' Jai murmured in confident rebuttal. 'I didn't appreciate that when I first found out about him. But he gave us the chance to be together in a way that I could cope with.'

Her smooth brow furrowed because she didn't understand. She had expected Jai to return angry or despondent, but he was demonstrating neither reaction. 'Cope with?' she queried.

'I've never been into relationships. I've avoided normal relationships as if they were toxic,' he reminded her uncomfortably. 'My father never recovered from losing my mother and I was always very aware of that. It made me very reluctant to get in too deep with a woman and, when I did break that rule, I ended up with Cecilia and that was a hard lesson too. I didn't have another relationship until I met you and that's why it's been rocky between us and I've been...' his shrug was uneasy '...all over the place with you.'

'All over the place?' she repeated uncertainly.

'When I married you I assumed we would have a detached marriage where after a while we each operated separately, but it didn't turn out like that and I found the closeness that seemed so natural between us...well, for me it was primarily unnerving. I hadn't bargained on feeling that way and I backed off fast,' he extended ruefully.

Recalling the second week of their marriage, Willow released a sigh. 'That hurt me.'

A wry smile slashed the tension from Jai's beautifully modelled mouth. 'And you called me on it, which was typical of you. I wasn't used to that either. Women have always treated me as though everything I do is right and amazing…and then *you* came along.'

Willow winced. 'Yes, and then I came along,' she echoed unhappily.

'And you challenged me every step of the way. You insisted that I treated you with respect. You had your opinions and your own way of looking at things and, while you were happy to listen to my viewpoint, you were independent, and I've never met with that before in a woman. You disagree with me. You were different and I liked that,' he admitted tautly. 'It's a remarkably attractive talent, frustrating too, but I've discovered that I find it much more stimulating than having my ego stroked.'

Willow breathed in deep, wondering where the conversation was heading. 'Really? Well, that's fortunate because I think you have a very healthy ego as it is. You'd become unbearable if I agreed with everything you said.'

Jai laughed softly. 'Probably, but not while you're around,' he acknowledged. 'I haven't been a mega success at being a husband, have I?' He shifted an expressive brown hand and groaned. 'You get to me on levels I never expected to visit with a woman. It throws me off balance and then I get all worked up and I overreact like I did last night when I accused you of flirting with Sher…and as I did today.'

Willow nodded slowly. 'I hope you now realise that's there's nothing—'

'I was jealous,' Jai framed with grim finality. 'Jealous for the first time ever, so *that* meant the fault had to be yours, not mine. I didn't want to *talk* about it last night. I wanted to slide into bed with you and whisper, "I'm a jealous toad," and drown my hurt pride in sex, but you had Hari with you and I didn't want to disturb the two of you. I bet Hari would have started crying if you tried to return him to his lonely cot.'

Her natural smile drove what remained of her tension from her heart-shaped face. 'Oh, dear…' she whispered, and she extended a forgiving hand to him. 'You should've woken me. I wouldn't have minded. I didn't mean to fall asleep with Hari. I was sort of using him like a teddy bear for comfort.'

'I'd much rather you used me for comfort,' Jai confided, closing his hand over hers and using that connection to tug her off the side of the bed and into his arms. He covered her mouth slowly and urgently with his and kissed her breathless. She leant against him for support, letting the remainder of her tension drain away.

'I went to see your mother because—' she began awkwardly.

'No, not now,' Jai interrupted, pressing a fingertip against her parted lips. 'Let tonight be for us. Anyway, I'm reasonably intelligent. I've already worked out *why* you did it.'

'Have you really?' she asked.

'Yes,' Jai assured her with satisfaction. 'I'm getting better at understanding how your mind works. Jivika dropped you in it. Her knowledge has been burning a hole in her brain for years and she jumped at the chance to share. And, you being you, you couldn't resist the urge to try and create a happy ending for everyone involved.'

'Principally you,' Willow whispered. 'It was arrogant of me to think I knew best.'

'And even more arrogant of me to start ranting about disloyalty and deception because the woman I know and love isn't capable of that kind of betrayal,' he concluded.

Willow froze. 'Know…and *love*?'

'Passionately love,' Jai qualified levelly. 'I love you in a way I have never loved any woman and I didn't even realise it was love. I told myself all sorts of face-saving lies when I stopped having sex with other women after that night I spent with you.'

Her gaze flew up to his in shock. 'Are you saying that you weren't with anyone else after me…all those months?' she prompted in disbelief.

'Yes. I persuaded myself that my celibacy was down to guilt at having taken advantage of you. I even assumed that I'd somehow gone off sex. When I tried repeatedly to check up on you afterwards, I told myself it was because I felt responsible for your well-being. In fact, what I was feeling was really quite simple, I just wanted to *see* you again, but I wasn't ready to admit that to myself.'

Willow, however, was still in shock and concentrating on only one startling fact at a time. 'You mean all that time while I was pregnant and raising Hari you didn't—'

'I haven't been with anyone else since our first night,' Jai confirmed. 'I didn't *want* anyone else. What

I found with you was so good that every other experience paled in comparison. So, yes, I was in love with you from way back then and, no, I didn't understand that.'

Willow's eyes rounded in wonder and she looked up into those gorgeous arctic-blue eyes and suddenly she was smiling. 'I love you too,' she told him quietly and without fanfare.

'I was hoping so,' Jai admitted, smiling down at her with love and tenderness gleaming in his intent gaze. 'I mean, you had the bravery to confront me with something everyone else ran scared from, and I very much hoped that love gave you the strength to go against my wishes in the belief that what you found out might make me happier.'

'You understand,' she breathed in relief.

'Of course I do. In the equivalent position I would have done the same thing for you. I very much regret that I wasn't around when your father was doing a number on your self-confidence,' he confessed. 'It also made me appreciate that he had a side to his character that I never saw, a less presentable side.'

'I'm sorry about what you've had to hear about your father.'

'Later, not now,' he insisted again, brushing her hair back from her cheeks and reaching behind her to run the zip down on her dress. 'Tonight is all about us and I'm determined that nothing will come between us.'

'Literally!' She gasped as her dress pooled round her feet and he dispensed with her bra even faster.

Jai skimmed off her panties and lifted her back onto

the bed, standing back from her to strip off his clothes with near indecent haste. 'I'm burning for you,' he groaned.

He came down to her, his skin on hers feverishly hot and his sensual mouth hungry and urgent, both hands holding hers to the mattress until they fought free to sink into his luxuriant hair. In the space of minutes her life had been transformed by the simple truth that the man she loved not only understood her, but also loved her back with all the fierce emotion she had long craved. Happiness flooded her like a rejuvenating force, every insecurity forced out and forgotten because what she had most wanted in the world had suddenly become hers.

'I'm crazy about you,' Jai husked in the aftermath of their unashamed passion. 'I couldn't wait to get back here to be with you because I so much regretted what I'd said to you and nothing else mattered. The past is the past and I don't want to revisit it, now that the truth is out.'

'Meaning?' she prompted.

'There will be no recriminations. Not on my part. We all get a clean sheet. My father's behaviour almost destroyed my mother and the guilt of knowing that and remaining silent tormented Jivika for years. We'll leave all that behind us now and my mother will be part of our lives,' he outlined.

'You've *seen* your mother? You've spoken to her?'

'Yes, but only very briefly,' Jai told her with a rueful smile as he looked down at her, his lean, darkly handsome face pensive. 'Unfortunately, she's flying back to London tomorrow and it's her stepdaughter's wedding in a couple of days, so she couldn't delay her flight. But she's planning to come back for a visit in a few weeks and spend time with us.'

'She must've been shocked when you showed up at the hotel,' Willow remarked.

'Shocked, delighted, tearful. We have a lot to catch up on, but we'll take our time,' Jai murmured, curving an arm round Willow to press her closer. 'And if it wasn't for you I wouldn't even have had the opportunity to meet her and give her that chance. For that I owe you a debt I can never repay.'

'Oh, I'll take it out of your hide somehow,' Willow teased, running an appreciative hand down over a long, lean, hair-dusted thigh. 'Don't you worry about that. You'll be paying it off for a very long time and, I promise you now, it's likely to use up every ounce of your surplus energy.'

Jai burst out laughing and crushed her lips under his. 'I love you so much, *balmaa*.'

Willow succumbed to a shameless little wriggle of encouragement and pressed her mouth tenderly to a bare brown shoulder. 'I love you too and I'm going to have to learn Hindi to know what you're calling me.'

'Beloved,' Jai translated, a little breathless as her wandering hands stroked across the taut expanse of his flat stomach.

'I like that,' she told him happily. 'I like that very much indeed.'

EPILOGUE

IN AN ELEGANT shift dress the shade of polished copper, Willow studied her reflection in the mirror. The dress was very flattering, the ultimate in maternity wear, and very nearly concealed the bump of her second pregnancy.

A pair of lean bronzed hands settled gently on her hips from behind and she grinned as Jai's hands slowly slid round to caress her swollen stomach. She adored the fact that he was so ridiculously excited about the daughter she carried. They hadn't shared the gender news with anyone else, but Willow could hardly wait to make use of the pretty clothes she had begun to collect.

Even as a toddler, Hari was very much a little boy, stomping through mud and puddles and shouting with excitement as he climbed and jumped and toppled. Of course, their daughter might well be a little tomboy, just as energetic, but Willow knew that she would at least be able to enjoy dressing her daughter in pretty clothes until she became more mobile.

'Happy Birthday, *balmaa*,' Jai husked in her ear, breathing in the rich coconut scent of her tumbling strawberry-blond hair as he pressed a kiss to her shoulder and folded her back against his tall, powerful body.

A split second later, he stepped back to slowly slide a necklace round her slender throat, tipping her head forward to clasp it at her nape. Her fingers lifted to touch the sparkling diamond heart and she whirled with a smile in the circle of his arms to stretch up and find his mouth for herself. Excitement buzzed through her, an ache stirring in her pelvis as he crushed her against him, his urgency only matching her own, because Jai had been away on a business trip for a week and she had missed him.

'I was scared you wouldn't make it back in time,' she confided breathlessly against his shoulder.

'I would never miss your birthday,' Jai censured, watching her finger the delicate heart at her throat. 'That's my heart you hold and it *always* brings me home again.'

Willow giggled. 'You're getting almost romantic,' she teased. 'We should go downstairs and see our guests.'

'My mother was holding the fort when I arrived.'

'Milly is a terrific social asset,' Willow agreed, thinking of the mother-in-law she had never expected to have and her warm relationship with her and Jai's stepfather, Steven, a quiet, retiring older man with a delightful sense of humour.

Over the past two years, their family circle had expanded exponentially, but it was a comfortable and caring expansion, which both of them valued. Jai had dealt with his disillusionment over the father he had once idolised and moved on to develop a strong, deep bond with the mother he had been denied in childhood. He had also become acquainted with his maternal grandfather, the current Duke, who was almost ninety years old. Jai did think, though, that it was sad that his mother had never had another child and that he had no siblings, only stepbrothers and a stepsister, whom they only saw at occasional family events.

Even so, his aunt, Jivika, and her husband were regular visitors, along with various other, more distant relatives. Indeed, Jai and Willow had so many invitations out that they had to pick and choose which they could attend and sometimes it was a relief to return to the tranquillity of the Lake Palace, where life was a little less hectic and they could spend more time together as a couple.

Willow had become broody once Hari outgrew the nursery and turned into a leaping, bounding bundle of energy, no longer content to be cuddled for longer than ten seconds, unless of course he was ill or overtired. She had conceived quickly, and her second pregnancy was proving much easier than the first. She thought that was very probably because she was much less stressed this time and was able to rest whenever she liked.

'You're spoilt rotten!' Shelley had teased her on her last visit to Chandrapur. She was able to see her best friend regularly now because Shelley had more holiday leave in her new job managing a small boutique hotel, which belonged to Jai's cousins. In any case, Willow and Jai spent every spring and summer in London in addition to returning there every year to enjoy a special Christmas at the town house. And when Hari started school, they would be in London even more because Jai did not want his son to board as he had done until he was old enough to make that choice for himself.

And Shelley had spoken the truth, Willow acknowledged with quiet satisfaction, because Jai *did* spoil her and he did make her very, very happy. He also built up her confidence where her father had continually taken her down. Only weeks ago, she had made her first public speech on behalf of the homeless charity she had chosen as closest to her heart from the many supported by the Singh Foundation. Jai's words of praise had made her heart sing and nobody would ever have guessed by his demeanour that he had listened to her rehearse that same speech ten times over.

Now, meeting the arctic-blue intensity of his loving gaze, Willow had everything she'd ever wanted and much that she had not even dared to dream of having, because Jai loved her and their son as much as he loved being part of a family.

'I am crazy about you,' he husked as they descended the stairs to the noisy hubbub of their chattering guests. 'I counted the days until I could come home, and home is always where *you* are, *soniyaa*.'

'I love you too,' she whispered dreamily as his hand engulfed hers, and she whipped round where she stood to claim his sensual mouth for herself again. 'And on *your* birthday promise we'll have a private party for *two*.'

'We're having a very private party for two when everyone's gone home tonight,' Jai assured her, soft and low, running a slow, caressing hand down over her taut spine, making her quiver...

* * * * *

LET'S TALK
Romance

For exclusive extracts, competitions
and special offers, find us online: